A Heron Books Collection

SIR WALTER SCOTT
NOVELS

ROB ROY

VOLUME II

HERON BOOKS LONDON

LIST OF ILLUSTRATIONS

ROB ROY

CHAPTER XVIII

> *And hurry, hurry, off they rode,*
> *As fast as fast might be;*
> *Hurra, hurra, the dead can ride,*
> *Dost fear to ride with me?*
>   BURGER.

THERE is one advantage in an accumulation of evils,
differing in cause and character, that the distraction
which they afford by their contradictory operation
prevents the patient from being overwhelmed under
either.   I was deeply grieved at my separation
from Miss Vernon, yet not so much so as I should
have been, had not my father's apprehended distresses forced themselves on my attention; and
I was distressed by the news of Mr. Tresham,
yet less so than if they had fully occupied my
mind.   I was neither a false lover nor an unfeel-
ing son; but man can give but a certain portion
of distressful emotions to the causes which demand
them, and if two operate at once, our sympathy,
like the funds of a compounding bankrupt, can only
be divided between them.   Such were my reflections when I gained my apartment—it seems, from
the illustration, they already began to have a twang
of commerce in them.

3

I set myself seriously to consider your father's letter. It was not very distinct, and referred for several particulars to Owen, whom I was entreated to meet with as soon as possible at a Scotch town, called Glasgow; being informed, moreover, that my old friend was to be heard of at Messrs. Macvittie, MacFin, and Company, merchants in the Gallowgate of the said town. It likewise alluded to several letters, which, as it appeared to me, must have miscarried or have been intercepted, and complained of my obdurate silence in terms which would have been highly unjust, had my letters reached their purposed destination. I was amazed as I read. That the spirit of Rashleigh walked around me, and conjured up these doubts and difficulties by which I was surrounded, I could not doubt for one instant; yet it was frightful to conceive the extent of combined villainy and power which he must have employed in the perpetration of his designs. Let me do myself justice in one respect; the evil of parting from Miss Vernon, however distressing it might in other respects and at another time have appeared to me, sunk into a subordinate consideration when I thought of the dangers impending over my father. I did not myself set a high estimation on wealth, and had the affectation of most young men of lively imagination, who suppose that they can better dispense with the possession of money, than resign their time and faculties to the labour necessary to acquire it. But in my father's case, I knew that bankruptcy would be considered as an utter and irretrievable disgrace, to which life would afford no comfort, and death the speediest and sole relief.

My mind, therefore, was bent on averting this catastrophe, with an intensity which the interest could not have produced had it referred to my own fortunes; and the result of my deliberation was a firm resolution to depart from Osbaldistone Hall the next day, and wend my way without loss of time to meet Owen at Glasgow. I did not hold it expedient to intimate my departure to my uncle, otherwise than by leaving a letter of thanks for his hospitality, assuring him that sudden and important business prevented my offering them in person. I knew the blunt old knight would readily excuse ceremony, and I had such a belief in the extent and decided character of Rashleigh's machinations, that I had some apprehension of his having provided means to intercept a journey which was undertaken with a view to disconcert them, if my departure were publicly announced at Osbaldistone Hall.

I therefore determined to set off on my journey with daylight in the ensuing morning, and to gain the neighbouring kingdom of Scotland before any idea of my departure was entertained at the Hall; but one impediment of consequence was likely to prevent that speed which was the soul of my expedition. I did not know the shortest, nor indeed any road to Glasgow; and as, in the circumstances in which I stood, dispatch was of the greatest con-

sequence, I determined to consult Andrew Fairservice on the subject, as the nearest and most
authentic authority within my reach. Late as it
was, I set off with the intention of ascertaining
this important point, and after a few minutes' walk
reached the dwelling of the gardener.

Andrew's dwelling was situated at no great
distance from the exterior wall of the garden, a
snug comfortable Northumbrian cottage, built of
stones roughly dressed with the hammer, and
having the windows and doors decorated with huge
heavy architraves, or lintels, as they are called,
of hewn stone, and its roof covered with broad
grey flags, instead of slates, thatch, or tiles. A
jargonelle pear-tree at one end of the cottage, a
rivulet and flower-plot of a rood in extent, in
front, and a kitchen-garden behind; a paddock
for a cow, and a small field, cultivated with several
crops of grain, rather for the benefit of the
cottager than for sale, announced the warm and
cordial comforts which Old England, even at her
most northern extremity, extends to her meanest
inhabitants.

As I approached the mansion of the sapient
Andrew, I heard a noise, which, being of a nature
peculiarly solemn, nasal, and prolonged, led me
to think that Andrew, according to the decent
and meritorious custom of his countrymen, had
assembled some of his neighbours to join in family
exercise, as he called evening devotion. Andrew
had indeed neither wife, child, nor female inmate
in his family. 'The first of his trade,' he said,

'had had eneugh o' thae cattle.' But, notwithstanding, he sometimes contrived to form an
audience for himself out of the neighbouring
Papists and Church-of-England-men, brands, as
he expressed it, snatched out of the burning, on
whom he used to exercise his spiritual gifts, in
defiance alike of Father Vaughan, Father Docharty,
Rashleigh, and all the world of Catholics around
him, who deemed his interference on such occasions an act of heretical interloping. I conceived
it likely, therefore, that the well-disposed neighbours might have assembled to hold some chapel
of ease of this nature. The noise, however, when
I listened to it more accurately, seemed to proceed entirely from the lungs of the said Andrew;
and when I interrupted it by entering the house,
I found Fairservice alone, combating, as he best
could, with long words and hard names, and
reading aloud, for the purpose of his own edifica-
cation, a volume of controversial divinity. 'I
was just taking a spell,' said he, laying aside the
huge folio volume as I entered, 'of the worthy
Doctor Lightfoot.'

'Lightfoot!' I replied, looking at the ponderous
volume with some surprise; 'surely your author
was unhappily named.'

'Lightfoot was his name, sir; a divine he was,
and another kind of a divine than they hae now-a-
days. Always, I crave your pardon for keeping ye
standing at the door, but having been mistrysted
(gude preserve us!) with ae bogle the night
already, I was dubious o' opening the yett till I

7

had gaen through the e'ening worship; and I had just finished the fifth chapter of Nehemiah—if that winna gar them keep their distance, I wotna what will.'

'Trysted with a bogle!' said I; 'what do you mean by that, Andrew?'

'I said mistrysted,' replied Andrew; 'that is as muckle as to say, fley'd wi' a ghaist—gude preserve us, I say again!'

'Flay'd by a ghost, Andrew! how am I to understand that?'

'I did not say flay'd,' replied Andrew, 'but *fley'd*, that is, I got a fleg, and was ready to jump out o' my skin, though naebody offered to whirl it aff my body as a man wad bark a tree.'

'I beg a truce to your terrors in the present case, Andrew, and I wish to know whether you can direct me the nearest way to a town in your country of Scotland, called Glasgow?'

'A town ca'd Glasgow!' echoed Andrew Fairservice. 'Glasgow's a ceety, man.—And is't the way to Glasgow ye were speering if I kend?—What suld ail me to ken it?—it's no that dooms far frae my ain parish of Dreepdaily, that lies a bittock farther to the west. But what may your honour be gaun to Glasgow for?'

'Particular business,' replied I.

'That's as muckle as to say, speer nae questions, and I'll tell ye nae lees—To Glasgow?'—he made a short pause—'I am thinking ye wad be the better o' some ane to show you the road.'

'Certainly, if I could meet with any person going that way.'

'And your honour, doubtless, wad consider the time and trouble?'

'Unquestionably—my business is pressing, and if you can find any guide to accompany me, I'll pay him handsomely.'

'This is no a day to speak o' carnal matters,' said Andrew, casting his eyes upwards; 'but if it werena Sabbath at e'en, I wad speer what ye wad be content to gie to ane that wad bear ye pleasant company on the road, and tell ye the names of the gentlemen's and noblemen's seats and castles, and count their kin to ye?'

'I tell you, all I want to know is the road I must travel; I will pay the fellow to his satisfaction—I will give him any thing in reason.'

'Ony thing,' replied Andrew, 'is naething; and this lad that I am speaking o' kens a' the short cuts and queer by-paths through the hills, and——'

'I have no time to talk about it, Andrew; do you make the bargain for me your own way.'

'Aha! that's speaking to the purpose,' answered Andrew.—'I am thinking, since sae be that sae it is, I'll be the lad that will guide you mysell.'

'You, Andrew? how will you get away from your employment?'

'I tell'd your honour a while syne, that it was lang that I hae been thinking o' flitting, maybe as lang as frae the first year I came to Osbaldistone Hall; and now I am o' the mind to gang in gude

earnest—better soon as syne—better a finger aff as
aye wagging.'

'You leave your service then?—but will you not
lose your wages?'

'Nae doubt there will be a certain loss; but then
I hae siller o' the laird's in my hands that I took for
the apples in the auld orchyard—and a sair bargain
the folk had that bought them—a wheen green trash
—and yet Sir Hildebrand's as keen to hae the siller
(that is, the steward is as pressing about it) as if
they had been a' gowden pippins—and then there's
the siller for the seeds — I'm thinking the wage
will be in a manner decently made up.—But doubtless your honour will consider my risk of loss when
we win to Glasgow—and ye'll be for setting out
forthwith?'

'By day-break in the morning,' I answered.

'That's something o' the suddenest—whare am
I to find a naig?—Stay—I ken just the beast that
will answer me.'

'At five in the morning, then, Andrew, you will
meet me at the head of the avenue.'

'Deil a fear o' me (that I suld say sae) missing
my tryste,' replied Andrew very briskly; 'and, if
I might advise, we wad be aff twa hours earlier. I
ken the way, dark or light, as weel as blind Ralph
Ronaldson, that's travelled ower every moor in the
country-side, and disna ken the colour of a heather-
cowe when a's dune.'

I highly approved of Andrew's amendment on
my original proposal, and we agreed to meet at the
place appointed at three in the morning. At once,

however, a reflection came across the mind of my intended travelling companion.

'The bogle! the bogle! what if it should come out upon us?—I downa forgather wi' thae things twice in the four-and-twenty hours.'

'Pooh! pooh!' I exclaimed, breaking away from him, 'fear nothing from the next world— the earth contains living fiends, who can act for themselves without assistance, were the whole host that fell with Lucifer to return to aid and abet them.'

With these words, the import of which was suggested by my own situation, I left Andrew's habitation, and returned to the Hall.

I made the few preparations which were necessary for my proposed journey, examined and loaded my pistols, and then threw myself on my bed, to obtain, if possible, a brief sleep before the fatigue of a long and anxious journey. Nature, exhausted by the tumultuous agitations of the day, was kinder to me than I expected, and I sunk into a deep and profound slumber, from which, however, I started as the old clock struck two from a turret adjoining to my bedchamber. I instantly arose, struck a light, wrote the letter I proposed to leave for my uncle, and leaving behind me such articles of dress as were cumbrous in carriage, I deposited the rest of my wardrobe in my valise, glided down stairs, and gained the stable without impediment. Without being quite such a groom as any of my cousins, I had learned at Osbaldistone Hall to dress and saddle my own horse, and in a few minutes I was mounted and ready for my sally.

As I paced up the old avenue, on which the waning moon threw its light with a pale and whitish tinge, I looked back with a deep and boding sigh towards the walls which contained Diana Vernon, under the despondent impression that we had probably parted to meet no more. It was impossible, among the long and irregular lines of Gothic casements, which now looked ghastly white in the moonlight, to distinguish that of the apartment which she inhabited. She is lost to me already, thought I, as my eye wandered over the dim and indistinguishable intricacies of architecture offered by the moonlight view of Osbaldistone Hall—She is lost to me already, ere I have left the place which she inhabits! What hope is there of my maintaining any correspondence with her when leagues shall lie between ?

While I paused in a reverie of no very pleasing nature, the 'iron tongue of time told three upon the drowsy ear of night,' and reminded me of the necessity of keeping my appointment with a person of a less interesting description and appearance— Andrew Fairservice.

At the gate of the avenue I found a horseman stationed in the shadow of the wall, but it was not until I had coughed twice, and then called 'Andrew,' that the horticulturist replied, ' I 'se warrant it's Andrew.'

'Lead the way, then,' said I, 'and be silent if you can till we are past the hamlet in the valley.'

Andrew led the way accordingly, and at a much brisker pace than I would have recommended; and so well did he obey my injunctions of keeping silence, that he would return no answer to my repeated inquiries into the cause of such unnecessary haste. Extricating ourselves by short cuts, known to Andrew, from the numerous stony lanes and by-paths which intersected each other in the vicinity of the Hall, we reached the open heath; and riding swiftly across it, took our course among the barren hills which divide England from Scotland on what are called the Middle Marches. The way, or rather the broken track which we occupied, was a happy interchange of bog and shingles; nevertheless, Andrew relented nothing of his speed, but trotted manfully forward at the rate of eight or ten miles an hour. I was surprised and provoked at the fellow's obstinate persistence, for we made abrupt ascents and descents over ground of a very break-neck character, and traversed the edge of precipices, where a slip of the horse's feet would have consigned the rider to certain death. The moon, at best, afforded a dubious and imperfect light; but in some places we were so much under the shade of the mountain as to be in total darkness, and then I could only trace Andrew by the clatter of his horse's feet, and the fire which they struck from the flints. At first, this rapid motion, and the attention which, for the sake of personal safety, I was compelled to give to the conduct of my horse, was of service, by forcibly diverting my thoughts from the various painful reflections which must otherwise have pressed on my mind. But at length, after hallooing repeatedly to Andrew to ride slower, I became seriously incensed at his impudent perseverance in refusing either to obey or to reply to me. My anger was, however, quite impotent. I attempted once or twice to get up alongside of my self-willed guide, with the purpose of knocking him off his horse with the but-end of my whip; but Andrew was better mounted than I, and either the spirit of the animal which he bestrode, or more probably some presentiment of my kind intentions towards him, induced him to quicken his pace whenever I attempted to make up to him. On the other hand, I was compelled to exert my spurs to keep him in sight, for without his guidance I was too well aware that I should never find my way through the howling wilderness which we now traversed at such an unwonted pace. I was so angry at length, that I threatened to have recourse to my pistols, and send a bullet after the Hotspur Andrew, which should stop his fiery-footed career, if he did not abate it of his own accord. Apparently this threat made some impression on the tympanum of his ear, however deaf to all my milder entreaties; for he relaxed his pace upon hearing it, and suffering me to close up to him, observed, 'There wasna muckle sense in riding at sic a daft-like gate.'

'And what did you mean by doing so at all, you self-willed scoundrel?' replied I; for I was in a towering passion, to which, by the way,

nothing contributes more than the having recently
undergone a spice of personal fear, which, like a
few drops of water flung on a glowing fire, is
sure to inflame the ardour which it is insufficient
to quench.

'What's your honour's wull?' replied Andrew,
with impenetrable gravity.

'My will, you rascal?—I have been roaring to
you this hour to ride slower, and you have never
so much as answered me—Are you drunk or mad
to behave so?'

'An it like your honour, I am something dull
o' hearing; and I'll no deny but I might have
maybe taen a stirrup-cup at parting frae the auld
bigging whare I hae dwalt sae lang; and having
naebody to pledge, nae doubt I was obliged to do
mysell reason, or else leave the end o' the brandy
stoup to thae papists,—and that wad be a waste,
as your honour kens.'

This might be all very true, and my circumstances
required that I should be on good terms with my
guide; I therefore satisfied myself with requiring
of him to take his directions from me in future
concerning the rate of travelling.

Andrew, emboldened by the mildness of my
tone, elevated his own into the pedantic, conceited octave, which was familiar to him on most
occasions.

'Your honour winna persuade me, and naebody
shall persuade me, that it's either halesome or
prudent to tak the night air on thae moors without
a cordial o' clow-gilliflower water, or a tass of brandy

or aquavitæ, or sic-like creature-comfort. I hae taen the bent ower the Otterscope-rigg a hundred times, day and night, and never could find the way unless I had taen my morning; mair by token that I had whiles twa bits o' ankers o' brandy on ilk side o' me.'—

'In other words, Andrew,' said I, 'you were a smuggler—how does a man of your strict principles reconcile yourself to cheat the revenue?'

'It's a mere spoiling o' the Egyptians,' replied Andrew; 'puir auld Scotland suffers eneugh by thae blackguard loons o' excisemen and gaugers, that hae come down on her like locusts since the sad and sorrowfu' Union; it's the part of a kind son to bring her a soup o' something that will keep up her auld heart, and that will they nill they, the ill-fa'rd thieves.'

Upon more particular inquiry, I found Andrew had frequently travelled these mountain-paths as a smuggler, both before and after his establishment at Osbaldistone Hall; a circumstance which was so far of importance to me, as it proved his capacity as a guide, notwithstanding the escapade of which he had been guilty at his outset. Even now, though travelling at a more moderate pace, the stirrup-cup, or whatever else had such an effect in stimulating Andrew's motions, seemed not totally to have lost its influence. He often cast a nervous and startled look behind him; and whenever the road seemed at all practicable, showed symptoms of a desire to accelerate his pace, as if he feared some pursuit from the rear. These appearances of alarm gradually diminished as we reached the top of a high bleak ridge, which ran nearly east and west for about a mile, with a very steep descent on either side. The pale beams of the morning were now enlightening the horizon, when Andrew cast a look behind him, and not seeing the appearance of a living being on the moors which he had travelled, his hard features gradually unbent, as he first whistled, then sung, with much glee and little melody, the end of one of his native songs:

> 'Jenny, lass! I think I hae her
> Ower the moor amang the heather;
> All their clan shall never get her.'

He patted at the same time the neck of the horse which had carried him so gallantly; and my attention being directed by that action to the animal, I instantly recognised a favourite mare of Thorncliff Osbaldistone. 'How is this, sir?' said I sternly; 'that is Mr. Thorncliff's mare!'

'I'll no say but she may aiblins hae been his honour's Squire Thorncliff's in her day—but she's mine now.'

'You have stolen her, you rascal.'

'Na, na, sir, nae man can wyte me wi' theft—The thing stands this gate, ye see—Squire Thorncliff borrowed ten punds o' me to gang to York Races—deil a boddle wad he pay me back again, and spake o' raddling my banes, as he ca'd it, when I asked him but for my ain back again—now I

think it will riddle him or he gets his horse ower
the Border again—unless he pays me plack and
bawbee, he sall never see a hair o' her tail. I ken
a canny chield at Loughmaben, a bit writer lad,
that will put me in the way to sort him—Steal the
mear! na, na, far be the sin o' theft frae Andrew
Fairservice—I have just arrested her *jurisdictiones
fandandy causey*. Thae are bonny writer words—
amaist like the language o' huz gardeners and other
learned men—it 's a pity they 're sae dear—thae
three words were a' that Andrew got for a lang
law-plea, and four ankers o' as gude brandy as
was e'er coupit ower craig—Hech, sirs! but law 's
a dear thing.'

' You are likely to find it much dearer than you
suppose, Andrew, if you proceed in this mode of
paying yourself, without legal authority.'

' Hout tout, we 're in Scotland now (be praised
for 't,) and I can find baith friends and lawyers,
and judges too, as weel as ony Osbaldistone o'
them a'. My mither's mither's third cousin was
cousin to the Provost o' Dumfries, and he winna
see a drap o' her blude wranged. Hout awa, the
laws are indifferently administered here to a' men
alike; it 's no like on yon side, when a chield
may be whuppit awa' wi' ane o' Clerk Jobson's
warrants, afore he kens where he is. But they
will hae little eneugh law amang them by and by,
and that is ae grand reason that I hae gi'en them
gude day.'

I was highly provoked at the achievement of
Andrew, and considered it as a hard fate, which a

second time threw me into collision with a person
of such irregular practices. I determined, however, to buy the mare of him, when we should
reach the end of our journey, and send her back
to my cousin at Osbaldistone Hall; and with
this purpose of reparation I resolved to make my
uncle acquainted from the next post-town. It
was needless, I thought, to quarrel with Andrew
in the meantime, who had, after all, acted not
very unnaturally for a person in his circumstances.
I therefore smothered my resentment and asked
him what he meant by his last expressions, that
there would be little law in Northumberland by
and by?

'Law!' said Andrew, 'hout, ay—there will be
club-law eneugh. The priests and the Irish officers,
and thae papist cattle that hae been sodgering
abroad, because they durstna bide at hame, are a'
fleeing thick in Northumberland e'enow—and thae
corbies dinna gather without they smell carrion.
As sure as ye live, his honour Sir Hildebrand is
gaun to stick his horn in the bog—there's naething
but gun and pistol, sword and dagger, amang them
—and they'll be laying on, I'se warrant; for they're
fearless fules the young Osbaldistone squires, aye
craving your honour's pardon.'

This speech recalled to my memory some suspicions that I myself had entertained, that the
jacobites were on the eve of some desperate enterprise. But, conscious it did not become me to be
a spy on my uncle's words and actions, I had rather
avoided than availed myself of any opportunity

which occurred of remarking upon the signs of the times. Andrew Fairservice felt no such restraint, and doubtless spoke very truly in stating his conviction, that some desperate plots were in agitation, as a reason which determined his resolution to leave the Hall.

'The servants,' he stated, 'with the tenantry and others, had been all regularly enrolled and mustered, and they wanted me to take arms also. But I 'll ride in nae siccan troop—they little kend Andrew that asked him. I 'll fight when I like mysell, but it sall neither be for the hure o' Babylon, nor ony hure in England.'

CHAPTER XIX

Where longs to fall yon rifted spire,
As weary of the insulting air,—
The poet's thoughts, the warrior's fire,
The lover's sighs, are sleeping there.

LANGHORNE.

At the first Scotch town which we reached, my
guide sought out his friend and counsellor, to consult upon the proper and legal means of converting
into his own lawful property the 'bonny creature,'
which was at present his own only by one of those
sleight-of-hand arrangements, which still sometimes
took place in that once lawless district. I was somewhat diverted with the dejection of his looks on his
return. He had, it seems, been rather too communicative to his confidential friend, the attorney;
and learned with great dismay, in return for his
unsuspecting frankness, that Mr. Touthope had,
during his absence, been appointed clerk to the
peace of the county, and was bound to communicate
to justice all such achievements as that of his friend,
Mr. Andrew Fairservice. There was a necessity,
this alert member of the police stated, for arresting
the horse, and placing him in Bailie Trumbull's
stable, therein to remain at livery, at the rate of
twelve shillings (Scotch) per diem, until the question
of property was duly tried and debated. He even

21

talked as if, in strict and rigorous execution of his duty, he ought to detain honest Andrew himself; but on my guide's most piteously entreating his forbearance, he not only desisted from this proposal, but made a present to Andrew of a broken-winded and spavined pony, in order to enable him to pursue his journey. It is true, he qualified this act of generosity by exacting from poor Andrew an absolute cession of his right and interest in the gallant palfrey of Thorncliff Osbaldistone; a transference which Mr. Touthope represented as of very little consequence, since his unfortunate friend, as he facetiously observed, was likely to get nothing of the mare excepting the halter.

Andrew seemed woful and disconcerted, as I screwed out of him these particulars; for his northern pride was cruelly pinched by being compelled to admit that attorneys were attorneys on both sides of the Tweed; and that Mr. Clerk Touthope was not a farthing more sterling coin than Mr. Clerk Jobson.

' It wadna hae vexed him half sae muckle to hae been cheated out o' what might amaist be said to be won with the peril o' his craig, had it happened amang the Inglishers; but it was an unco thing to see hawks pike out hawks' een, or ae kindly Scot cheat anither. But nae doubt things were strangely changed in his country sin' the sad and sorrowfu' Union '; an event to which Andrew referred every symptom of depravity or degeneracy which he remarked among his countrymen, more especially the inflammation of reckonings, the diminished size of pint-stoups, and other grievances, which he pointed out to me during our journey.

For my own part, I held myself, as things had turned out, acquitted of all charge of the mare, and wrote to my uncle the circumstances under which she was carried into Scotland, concluding with informing him that she was in the hands of justice, and her worthy representatives, Bailie Trumbull and Mr. Clerk Touthope, to whom I referred him for farther particulars. Whether the property returned to the Northumbrian fox-hunter, or continued to bear the person of the Scottish attorney, it is unnecessary for me at present to say.

We now pursued our journey to the northwestward, at a rate much slower than that at which we had achieved our nocturnal retreat from England. One chain of barren and uninteresting hills succeeded another, until the more fertile vale of Clyde opened upon us; and with such dispatch as we might we gained the town, or, as my guide pertinaciously termed it, the city, of Glasgow. Of late years, I understand, it has fully deserved the name, which, by a sort of political second-sight, my guide assigned to it. An extensive and increasing trade with the West Indies and American colonies, has, if I am rightly informed, laid the foundation of wealth and prosperity, which, if carefully strengthened and built upon, may one day support an immense fabric of commercial prosperity; but, in the earlier time of which I speak, the dawn of this splendour had not arisen. The Union had, indeed, opened to Scotland the trade of the English colonies;

but, betwixt want of capital, and the national
jealousy of the English, the merchants of Scotland
were as yet excluded, in a great measure, from the
exercise of the privileges which that memorable
treaty conferred on them. Glasgow lay on the
wrong side of the island for participating in the
east country or continental trade, by which the
trifling commerce as yet possessed by Scotland
chiefly supported itself. Yet, though she then gave
small promise of the commercial eminence to which,
I am informed, she seems now likely one day to
attain, Glasgow, as the principal central town of
the western district of Scotland, was a place of
considerable rank and importance. The broad and
brimming Clyde, which flows so near its walls, gave
the means of an inland navigation of some importance. Not only the fertile plains in its immediate
neighbourhood, but the districts of Ayr and
Dumfries, regarded Glasgow as their capital, to
which they transmitted their produce, and received
in return such necessaries and luxuries as their
consumption required.

The dusky mountains of the Western Highlands
often sent forth wilder tribes to frequent the marts
of St. Mungo's favourite city. Hordes of wild,
shaggy, dwarfish cattle and ponies, conducted by
Highlanders, as wild, as shaggy, and sometimes as
dwarfish, as the animals they had in charge, often
traversed the streets of Glasgow. Strangers gazed
with surprise on the antique and fantastic dress,
and listened to the unknown and dissonant sounds
of their language, while the mountaineers, armed

even while engaged in this peaceful occupation with musket and pistol, sword, dagger, and target, stared with astonishment on the articles of luxury of which they knew not the use, and with an avidity which seemed somewhat alarming on the articles which they knew and valued. It is always with unwillingness that the Highlander quits his deserts, and at this early period it was like tearing a pine from its rock, to plant him elsewhere. Yet even then the mountain glens were over-peopled, although thinned occasionally by famine or by the sword, and many of their inhabitants strayed down to Glasgow—there formed settlements—there sought and found employment, although different, indeed, from that of their native hills. This supply of a hardy and useful population was of consequence to the prosperity of the place, furnished the means of carrying on the few manufactures which the town already boasted, and laid the foundation of its future prosperity.

The exterior of the city corresponded with these promising circumstances. The principal street was broad and important, decorated with public buildings, of an architecture rather striking than correct in point of taste, and running between rows of tall houses, built of stone, the fronts of which were occasionally richly ornamented with mason-work; a circumstance which gave the street an imposing air of dignity and grandeur, of which most English towns are in some measure deprived, by the slight, unsubstantial, and perishable quality and appearance of the bricks with which they are constructed.

In the western metropolis of Scotland, my guide and I arrived on a Saturday evening, too late to entertain thoughts of business of any kind. We alighted at the door of a jolly hostler-wife, as Andrew called her, the Ostelere of old father Chaucer, by whom we were civilly received.

On the following morning the bells pealed from every steeple, announcing the sanctity of the day. Notwithstanding, however, what I had heard of the severity with which the Sabbath is observed in Scotland, my first impulse, not unnaturally, was to seek out Owen; but on inquiry I found that my attempt would be in vain, 'until kirk-time was ower.' Not only did my landlady and guide jointly assure me that 'there wadna be a living soul either in the counting-house or dwelling-house of Messrs. MacVittie, MacFin, and Company,' to which Owen's letter referred me, but, moreover, 'far less would I find any of the partners there. They were serious men, and wad be where a' gude Christians ought to be at sic a time, and that was in the Barony Laigh Kirk.'

Andrew Fairservice, whose disgust at the law of his country had fortunately not extended itself to the other learned professions of his native land, now sung forth the praises of the preacher who was to perform the duty, to which my hostess replied with many loud amens. The result was, that I determined to go to this popular place of worship, as much with the purpose of learning, if possible, whether Owen had arrived in Glasgow, as with any great expectation of edification. My hopes were

exalted by the assurance, that, if Mr. Ephraim
MacVittie (worthy man) were in the land of life,
he would surely honour the Barony Kirk that day
with his presence; and if he chanced to have a
stranger within his gates, doubtless he would bring
him to the duty along with him. This probability
determined my motions, and, under the escort of my
faithful Andrew, I set forth for the Barony Kirk.

On this occasion, however, I had little need of
his guidance; for the crowd, which forced its way
up a steep and rough-paved street, to hear the most
popular preacher in the west of Scotland, would of
itself have swept me along with it. On attaining
the summit of the hill, we turned to the left, and
a large pair of folding doors admitted us, amongst
others, into the open and extensive burying-place
which surrounds the Minster, or Cathedral Church
of Glasgow. The pile is of a gloomy and massive,
rather than of an elegant, style of Gothic architecture; but its peculiar character is so strongly
preserved, and so well suited with the accompaniments that surround it, that the impression of the
first view was awful and solemn in the extreme. I
was indeed so much struck, that I resisted for a few
minutes all Andrew's efforts to drag me into the
interior of the building, so deeply was I engaged in
surveying its outward character.

Situated in a populous and considerable town,
this ancient and massive pile has the appearance of
the most sequestered solitude. High walls divide
it from the buildings of the city on one side; on
the other, it is bounded by a ravine, at the bottom

of which, and invisible to the eye, murmurs a wandering rivulet, adding, by its gentle noise, to the imposing solemnity of the scene. On the opposite side of the ravine rises a steep bank, covered with fir-trees closely planted, whose dusky shade extends itself over the cemetery with an appropriate and gloomy effect. The churchyard itself had a peculiar character; for though in reality extensive, it is small in proportion to the number of respectable inhabitants who are interred within it, and whose graves are almost all covered with tombstones. There is therefore no room for the long rank grass, which, in most cases, partially clothes the surface of those retreats, where the wicked cease from troubling, and the weary are at rest. The broad flat monumental stones are placed so close to each other, that the precincts appear to be flagged with them, and, though roofed only by the heavens, resemble the floor of one of our old English churches, where the pavement is covered with sepulchral inscriptions. The contents of these sad records of mortality, the vain sorrows which they preserve, the stern lesson which they teach of the nothingness of humanity, the extent of ground which they so closely cover, and their uniform and melancholy tenor, reminded me of the roll of the prophet, which was 'written within and without, and there was written therein lamentations and mourning and woe.'

The Cathedral itself corresponds in impressive majesty with these accompaniments. We feel that its appearance is heavy, yet that the effect produced would be destroyed were it lighter or more ornamental. It is the only metropolitan church in Scotland, excepting, as I am informed, the cathedral of Kirkwall, in the Orkneys, which remained uninjured at the Reformation; and Andrew Fairservice, who saw with great pride the effect which it produced upon my mind, thus accounted for its preservation. 'Ah! it's a brave kirk—nane o' yere whigmaleeries and curliewurlies and open-steek hems about it—a' solid, weel-jointed mason-wark, that will stand as lang as the warld, keep hands and gunpowther aff it. It had amaist a doun-come lang syne at the Reformation, when they pu'd doun the kirks of St. Andrews and Perth, and there-awa', to cleanse them o' Papery, and idolatry, and image worship, and surplices, and sic like rags o' the muckle hure that sitteth on seven hills, as if ane wasna braid eneugh for her auld hinder end. Sae the commons o' Renfrew, and o' the Barony, and the Gorbals, and a' about, they behoved to come into Glasgow ae fair morning, to try their hand on purging the High Kirk o' Popish nick-nackets. But the townsmen o' Glasgow, they were feared their auld edifice might slip the girths in gaun through siccan rough physic, sae they rang the common bell, and assembled the train-bands wi' took o' drum—by good luck, the worthy James Rabat was Dean o' Guild that year—(and a gude mason he was himsell, made him the keener to keep up the auld bigging,) and the trades assembled, and offered downright battle to the commons, rather than their kirk should coup the crans, as others

had done elsewhere. It wasna for luve o' Paperie
—na, na!—nane could ever say that o' the trades
o' Glasgow—Sae they sune came to an agreement
to take a' the idolatrous statues of sants (sorrow
be on them) out o' their neuks—And sae the bits
o' stane idols were broken in pieces by Scripture
warrant, and flung into the Molendinar burn, and
the auld kirk stood as crouse as a cat when the flaes
are kaimed aff her, and a'body was alike pleased.
And I hae heard wise folk say, that if the same had
been done in ilka kirk in Scotland, the Reform wad
just hae been as pure as it is e'en now, and we wad
hae mair Christian-like kirks; for I hae been sae
lang in England, that naething will drived out o'
my head, that the dog-kennel at Osbaldistone Hall
is better that mony a house o' God in Scotland.'

Thus saying, Andrew led the way into the place
of worship.

CHAPTER XX

It strikes an awe
And terror on my aching sight; the tombs
And monumental caves of death look cold,
And shoot a chillness to the trembling heart.
MOURNING BRIDE.

NOTWITHSTANDING the impatience of my conductor, I could not forbear to pause and gaze for some minutes on the exterior of the building, rendered more impressively dignified by the solitude which ensued when its hitherto open gates were closed, after having, as it were, devoured the multitudes which had lately crowded the churchyard, but now, enclosed within the building, were engaged, as the choral swell of voices from within announced to us, in the solemn exercises of devotion. The sound of so many voices, united by the distance into one harmony, and freed from those harsh discordances which jar the ear when heard more near, combining with the murmuring brook, and the wind which sung among the old firs, affected me with a sense of sublimity. All nature, as invoked by the Psalmist whose verses they chanted, seemed united in offering that solemn praise in which trembling is mixed with joy as she addresses her Maker. I had heard the service of high mass in France, celebrated with all the eclat which the choicest music, the richest dresses, the most imposing ceremonies, could confer on it; yet it fell short in effect of the simplicity of the Presbyterian worship. The devotion, in which every one took a share, seemed so superior to that which was recited by musicians, as a lesson which they had learned by rote, that it gave the Scottish worship all the advantage of reality over acting.

As I lingered to catch more of the solemn sound, Andrew, whose impatience became ungovernable, pulled me by the sleeve—'Come awa, sir—Come awa, we maunna be late o' gaun in to disturb the worship; if we bide here, the searchers will be on us, and carry us to the guard-house for being idlers in kirk-time.'

Thus admonished, I followed my guide, but not, as I had supposed, into the body of the cathedral. 'This gate—this gate, sir!' he exclaimed, dragging me off as I made towards the main entrance of the building, — 'There's but cauldrife law-wark gaun on yonder—carnal morality, as dow'd and as fusionless as rue leaves at Yule — Here's the real savour of doctrine.'

So saying, we entered a small low-arched door, secured by a wicket, which a grave-looking person seemed on the point of closing, and descended several steps as if into the funeral vaults beneath the church. It was even so; for in these subterranean precincts, why chosen for such a purpose I knew not, was established a very singular place of worship.

ROB ROY

Conceive, Tresham, an extensive range of low-browed, dark, and twilight vaults, such as are used for sepulchres in other countries, and had long been dedicated to the same purpose in this, a portion of which was seated with pews, and used as a church. The part of the vaults thus occupied, though capable of containing a congregation of many hundreds, bore a small proportion to the darker and more extensive caverns which yawned around what may be termed the inhabited space. In those waste regions of oblivion, dusky banners and tattered escutcheons indicated the graves of those who were once, doubtless, ' princes in Israel.' Inscriptions, which could only be read by the painful antiquary, in language as obsolete as the act of devotional charity which they implored, invited the pas-sengers to pray for the souls of those whose bodies rested beneath. Surrounded by these re-ceptacles of the last remains of mortality, I found a numerous congregation engaged in the act of prayer. The Scotch perform this duty in a stand-ing, instead of a kneeling posture, more, perhaps, to take as broad a distinction as possible from the ritual of Rome than for any better reason, since I have observed that in their family worship, as doubt-less in their private devotions, they adopt, in their immediate address to the Deity, that posture which other Christians use as the humblest and most reverential. Standing, therefore, the men being uncovered, a crowd of several hundreds of both sexes, and all ages, listened with great reverence and attention to the extempore, at least the unwritten, prayer of an aged clergyman,* who was very popular in the city. Educated in the same religious persuasion, I seriously bent my mind to join in the devotion of the day, and it was not till the congregation resumed their seats that my attention was diverted to the consideration of the appearance of all around me.

At the conclusion of the prayer, most of the men put on their hats or bonnets, and all who had the happiness to have seats sate down. Andrew and I were not of this number, having been too late of entering the church to secure such accommodation. We stood among a number of other persons in the same situation, forming a sort of ring around the seated part of the congregation. Behind and around us were the vaults I have already described; before us the devout audience, dimly shown by the light which streamed on their faces through one or two low Gothic windows, such as give air and light to charnel-houses. By this were seen the usual variety of countenances, which are generally turned towards a Scotch pastor on such occasions, almost all composed to attention, unless where a father or mother here and there recalls the wandering eyes of a lively child, or disturbs the slumbers

---

* I have in vain laboured to discover this gentleman's name, and the period of his incumbency. I do not, however, despair to see these points, with some others which may elude my sagacity, satisfactorily elucidated by one or other of the periodical publications which have devoted their pages to explanatory commentaries on my former volumes ; and whose research and ingenuity claim my peculiar gratitude, for having discovered many persons and circumstances connected with my narratives, of which I myself never so much as dreamed.

of a dull one. The high-boned and harsh countenance of the nation, with the expression of intelligence and shrewdness which it frequently exhibits, is seen to more advantage in the act of devotion, or in the ranks of war, than on lighter and more cheerful occasions of assemblage. The discourse of the preacher was well qualified to call forth the various feelings and faculties of his audience.

Age and infirmities had impaired the powers of a voice originally strong and sonorous. He read his text with a pronunciation somewhat inarticulate; but when he closed the Bible, and commenced his sermon, his tones gradually strengthened, as he entered with vehemence into the arguments which he maintained. They related chiefly to the abstract points of the Christian faith, subjects grave, deep, and fathomless by mere human reason, but for which, with equal ingenuity and propriety, he sought a key in liberal quotations from the inspired writings. My mind was unprepared to coincide in all his reasoning, nor was I sure that in some instances I rightly comprehended his positions. But nothing could be more impressive than the eager enthusiastic manner of the good old man, and nothing more ingenious than his mode of reasoning. The Scotch, it is well known, are more remarkable for the exercise of their intellectual powers, than for the keenness of their feelings; they are, therefore, more moved by logic than by rhetoric, and more attracted by acute and argumentative reasoning on doctrinal points, than influenced by the enthusiastic appeals to the heart and to the passions, by which popular preachers in other countries win the favour of their hearers.

Among the attentive group which I now saw, might be distinguished various expressions similar to those of the audience in the famous cartoon of Paul preaching at Athens. Here sat a zealous and intelligent Calvinist, with brows bent just as much as to indicate profound attention; lips slightly compressed; eyes fixed on the minister, with an expression of decent pride, as if sharing the triumph of his argument; the forefinger of the right hand touching successively those of the left, as the preacher, from argument to argument, ascended towards his conclusion. Another, with fiercer and sterner look, intimated at once his contempt of all who doubted the creed of his pastor, and his joy at the appropriate punishment denounced against them. A third, perhaps belonging to a different congregation, and present only by accident or curiosity, had the appearance of internally impeaching some link of the reasoning; and you might plainly read, in the slight motion of his head, his doubts as to the soundness of the preacher's argument. The greater part listened with a calm satisfied countenance, expressive of a conscious merit in being present, and in listening to such an ingenious discourse, although, perhaps, unable entirely to comprehend it. The women in general belonged to this last division of the audience; the old, however, seeming more grimly intent upon the abstract doctrines laid before them; while the younger females permitted their eyes occasionally to make a modest circuit around the congregation ; and some of them, Tresham, (if my vanity did not greatly deceive me,) contrived to distinguish your friend and servant, as a handsome young stranger, and an Englishman. As to the rest of the congregation, the stupid gaped, yawned, or slept, till awakened by the application of their more zealous neighbours' heels to their shins ; and the idle indicated their inattention by the wandering of their eyes, but dared give no more decided token of weariness. Amid the Lowland costume of coat and cloak, I could here and there discern a Highland plaid, the wearer of which, resting on his basket-hilt, sent his eyes among the audience with the unrestrained curiosity of savage wonder ; and who, in all probability, was inattentive to the sermon, for a very pardonable reason—because he did not understand the language in which it was delivered. The martial and wild look, however, of these stragglers, added a kind of character which the congregation could not have exhibited without them. They were more numerous, Andrew afterwards observed, owing to some cattlefair in the neighbourhood.

Such was the group of countenances, rising tier on tier, discovered to my critical inspection by such sunbeams as forced their way through the narrow Gothic lattices of the Laigh Kirk of Glasgow ; and, having illuminated the attentive congregation, lost themselves in the vacuity of the vaults behind, giving to the nearer part of their labyrinth a sort of imperfect twilight, and leaving their recesses in an utter darkness, which gave them the appearance of being interminable.

I have already said that I stood with others in the exterior circle, with my face to the preacher, and my back to those vaults which I have so often mentioned. My position rendered me particularly obnoxious to any interruption which arose from any slight noise occurring amongst these retiring arches, where the least sound was multiplied by a thousand echoes. The occasional sound of rain-drops, which, admitted through some cranny in the ruined roof, fell successively, and plashed upon the pavement beneath, caused me to turn my head more than once to the place from whence it seemed to proceed; and when my eyes took that direction, I found it difficult to withdraw them; such is the pleasure our imagination receives from the attempt to penetrate as far as possible into an intricate labyrinth, imperfectly lighted, and exhibiting objects which irritate our curiosity, only because they acquire a mysterious interest from being undefined and dubious. My eyes became habituated to the gloomy atmosphere to which I directed them, and insensibly my mind became more interested in their discoveries than in the metaphysical subtleties which the preacher was enforcing.

My father had often checked me for this wandering mood of mind, arising perhaps from an excitability of imagination to which he was a stranger; and the finding myself at present solicited by these temptations to inattention, recalled the time when I used to walk, led by his hand, to Mr. Shower's chapel, and the earnest injunctions which he then laid on me to redeem the time, because the days were evil. At present, the picture which my thoughts suggested, far from fixing my attention, destroyed the portion I had yet left, by conjuring up to my recollection the peril in which his affairs now stood. I endeavoured, in the lowest whisper I could frame, to request Andrew to obtain information, whether any of the gentlemen of the firm of MacVittie and Co. were at present in the congregation. But Andrew, wrapped in profound attention to the sermon, only replied to my suggestion by hard punches with his elbow, as signals to me to remain silent. I next strained my eyes, with equally bad success, to see if, among the sea of up-turned faces which bent their eyes on the pulpit as a common centre, I could discover the sober and business-like physiognomy of Owen. But not among the broad beavers of the Glasgow citizens, or the yet broader-brimmed Lowland bonnets of the peasants of Lanarkshire, could I see any thing resembling the decent periwig, starched ruffles, or the uniform suit of light brown garments, appertaining to the head clerk of the establishment of Osbaldistone and Tresham. My anxiety now returned on me with such violence, as to overpower not only the novelty of the scene around me, by which it had hitherto been diverted, but moreover my sense of decorum. I pulled Andrew hard by the sleeve, and intimated my wish to leave the church, and pursue my investigation as I could. Andrew, obdurate in the Laigh Kirk of Glasgow as on the mountains of Cheviot, for some

time deigned me no answer; and it was only when
he found I could not otherwise be kept quiet that
he condescended to inform me, that, being once in
the church, we could not leave it till service was
over, because the doors were locked so soon as the
prayers began. Having thus spoken in a brief and
peevish whisper, Andrew again assumed the air of
intelligent and critical importance, and attention to
the preacher's discourse.

While I endeavoured to make a virtue of necessity, and recall my attention to the sermon, I was
again disturbed by a singular interruption. A voice
from behind whispered distinctly in my ear, ' You
are in danger in this city.'—I turned round as if
mechanically.

One or two starched and ordinary - looking
mechanics stood beside and behind me, stragglers,
who, like ourselves, had been too late in obtaining
entrance. But a glance at their faces satisfied me,
though I could hardly say why, that none of these
was the person who had spoken to me. Their
countenances seemed all composed to attention to
the sermon, and not one of them returned any
glance of intelligence to the inquisitive and startled
look with which I surveyed them. A massive round
pillar, which was close behind us, might have concealed the speaker the instant he uttered his mysterious caution; but wherefore it was given in such a
place, or to what species of danger it directed my
attention, or by whom the warning was uttered,
were points on which my imagination lost itself
in conjecture. It would, however, I concluded, be

repeated, and I resolved to keep my countenance turned towards the clergyman, that the whisperer might be tempted to renew his communication under the idea that the first had passed unobserved.

My plan succeeded. I had not resumed the appearance of attention to the preacher for five minutes, when the same voice whispered, 'Listen—but do not look back.' I kept my face in the same direction. 'You are in danger in this place,' the voice proceeded; 'so am I—Meet me to-night on the Brigg, at twelve preceesely—keep at home till the gloaming, and avoid observation.'

Here the voice ceased, and I instantly turned my head. But the speaker had, with still greater promptitude, glided behind the pillar, and escaped my observation. I was determined to catch a sight of him, if possible; and, extricating myself from the outer circle of hearers, I also stepped behind the column. All there was empty; and I could only see a figure wrapped in a mantle, whether a Lowland cloak, or Highland plaid, I could not distinguish, which traversed, like a phantom, the dreary vacuity of vaults which I have described.

I made a mechanical attempt to pursue the mysterious form, which glided away, and vanished in the vaulted cemetery, like the spectre of one of the numerous dead who rested within its precincts. I had little chance of arresting the course of one obviously determined not to be spoken with; but that little chance was lost by my stumbling and falling before I had made three steps from the column. The obscurity which occasioned my misfortune covered my disgrace; which I accounted rather lucky, for the preacher, with that stern authority which the Scottish ministers assume for the purpose of keeping order in their congregations, interrupted his discourse, to desire the 'proper officer' to take into custody the causer of this disturbance in the place of worship. As the noise, however, was not repeated, the beadle, or whatever else he was called, did not think it necessary to be rigorous in searching out the offender; so that I was enabled, without attracting farther observation, to place myself by Andrew's side in my original position. The service proceeded, and closed without the occurrence of any thing else worthy of notice.

As the congregation departed and dispersed, my friend Andrew exclaimed, 'See, yonder is worthy Mr. MacVittie and Mrs. MacVittie, and Miss Alison MacVittie, and Mr. Thamas MacFin, that they say is to marry Miss Alison, if a' bowls row right—she 'll hae a hantle siller, if she 's no that bonny.'

My eyes took the direction he pointed out. Mr. MacVittie was a tall, thin, elderly man, with hard features, thick grey eyebrows, light eyes, and, as I imagined, a sinister expression of countenance, from which my heart recoiled. I remembered the warning I had received in the church, and hesitated to address this person, though I could not allege to myself any rational ground of dislike or suspicion.

I was yet in suspense, when Andrew, who mistook my hesitation for bashfulness, proceeded to exhort me to lay it aside. 'Speak till him—speak till him, Mr. Francis—he 's no provost yet, though they say he'll be my lord neist year. Speak till him, then—he'll gie ye a decent answer for as rich as he is, unless ye were wanting siller frae him—they say he's dour to draw his purse.'

It immediately occurred to me, that if this merchant were really of the churlish and avaricious disposition which Andrew intimated, there might be some caution necessary in making myself known, as I could not tell how accounts might stand between my father and him. This consideration came in aid of the mysterious hint which I had received, and the dislike which I had conceived at the man's countenance. Instead of addressing myself directly to him, as I had designed to have done, I contented myself with desiring Andrew to inquire at Mr. MacVittie's house the address of Mr. Owen, an English gentleman; and I charged him not to mention the person from whom he received the commission, but to bring me the result to the small inn where we lodged. This Andrew promised to do. He said something of the duty of my attending the evening service; but added, with a causticity natural to him, that 'in troth, if folk couldna keep their legs still, but wad needs be couping the creels ower through-stanes, as if they wad raise the very dead folk wi' the clatter, a kirk wi' a chimley in 't was fittest for them.'

CHAPTER XXI

On the Rialto, every night at twelve,
I take my evening's walk of meditation:
There we two will meet.
VENICE PRESERVED.

FULL of sinister augury, for which, however, I could assign no satisfactory cause, I shut myself up in my apartment at the inn, and having dismissed Andrew, after resisting his importunity to accompany him to St. Enoch's Kirk,* where, he said, 'a soul-searching divine was to haud forth,' I set myself seriously to consider what were best to be done. I never was, what is properly called, superstitious; but I suppose all men, in situations of peculiar doubt and difficulty, when they have exercised their reason to little purpose, are apt, in a sort of despair, to abandon the reins to their imagination, and be guided either altogether by chance, or by those whimsical impressions which take possession of the mind, and to which we give way as if to involuntary impulses. There was something so singularly repulsive in the hard features of the Scotch trader, that I could not resolve to put myself into his hands without transgressing every caution which could be derived from the rules of physiognomy; while, at the same time,

---

* This I believe to be an anachronism, as Saint Enoch's Church was not built at the date of the story.

the warning voice, the form which flitted away like a vanishing shadow through those vaults, which might be termed 'the valley of the shadow of death,' had something captivating for the imagination of a young man, who, you will farther please to remember, was also a young poet.

If danger was around me, as the mysterious communication intimated, how could I learn its nature, or the means of averting it, but by meeting my unknown counsellor, to whom I could see no reason for imputing any other than kind intentions. Rashleigh and his machinations occurred more than once to my remembrance; but so rapid had my journey been, that I could not suppose him apprized of my arrival in Glasgow, much less prepared to play off any stratagem against my person. In my temper also I was bold and confident, strong and active in person, and in some measure accustomed to the use of arms, in which the French youth of all kinds were then initiated. I did not fear any single opponent; assassination was neither the vice of the age nor of the country; the place selected for our meeting was too public to admit any suspicion of meditated violence. In a word, I resolved to meet my mysterious counsellor on the bridge, as he had requested, and to be afterwards guided by circumstances. Let me not conceal from you, Tresham, what at the time I endeavoured to conceal from myself—the subdued, yet secretly-cherished hope, that Diana Vernon might—by what chance I knew not—through what means I could not guess—have some connexion with this strange and dubious intimation, conveyed at a time and place, and in a manner so surprising. She alone—whispered this insidious thought—she alone knew of my journey; from her own account, she possessed friends and influence in Scotland; she had furnished me with a talisman, whose power I was to invoke when all other aid failed me: who, then, but Diana Vernon, possessed either means, knowledge, or inclination for averting the dangers, by which, as it seemed, my steps were surrounded? This flattering view of my very doubtful case pressed itself upon me again and again. It insinuated itself into my thoughts, though very bashfully, before the hour of dinner; it displayed its attractions more boldly during the course of my frugal meal, and became so courageously intrusive during the succeeding half hour, (aided perhaps by the flavour of a few glasses of most excellent claret,) that, with a sort of desperate attempt to escape from a delusive seduction, to which I felt the danger of yielding, I pushed my glass from me, threw aside my dinner, seized my hat, and rushed into the open air with the feeling of one who would fly from his own thoughts. Yet perhaps I yielded to the very feelings from which I seemed to fly, since my steps insensibly led me to the bridge over the Clyde, the place assigned for the rendezvous by my mysterious monitor.

Although I had not partaken of my repast until the hours of evening church-service were over,—in which, by the way, I complied with the religious scruples of my landlady, who hesitated to dress a hot dinner between sermons, and also with the admonition of my unknown friend, to keep my apartment till twilight,—several hours had still to pass away betwixt the time of my appointment and that at which I reached the assigned place of meeting. The interval, as you will readily credit, was wearisome enough; and I can hardly explain to you how it passed away. Various groups of persons, all of whom, young and old, seemed impressed with a reverential feeling of the sanctity of the day, passed along the large open meadow which lies on the northern bank of the Clyde, and serves at once as a bleaching-field and pleasure-walk for the inhabitants, or paced with slow steps the long bridge which communicates with the southern district of the county. All that I remember of them was the general, yet not unpleasing, intimation of a devotional character impressed on each little party, formally assumed perhaps by some, but sincerely characterising the greater number, which hushed the petulant gaiety of the young into a tone of more quiet, yet more interesting, interchange of sentiments, and suppressed the vehement argument and protracted disputes of those of more advanced age. Notwithstanding the numbers who passed me, no general sound of the human voice was heard; few turned again to take some minutes' voluntary exercise, to which the leisure of the evening, and the beauty of the surrounding scenery, seemed to invite them: all hurried to their homes and resting-places. To one accustomed to the mode of spending Sunday evenings abroad, even among the French Calvinists, there seemed something Judaical, yet at the same time striking and affecting, in this mode of keeping the Sabbath holy. Insensibly, I felt my mode of sauntering by the side of the river, and crossing successively the various persons who were passing homeward, and without tarrying or delay, must expose me to observation at least, if not to censure, and I slunk out of the frequented path, and found a trivial occupation for my mind in marshalling my revolving walk in such a manner as should least render me obnoxious to observation. The different alleys lined out through this extensive meadow, and which are planted with trees, like the Park of St. James's in London, gave me facilities for carrying into effect these childish manœuvres.

As I walked down one of these avenues, I heard, to my surprise, the sharp and conceited voice of Andrew Fairservice, raised by a sense of self-consequence to a pitch somewhat higher than others seemed to think consistent with the solemnity of the day. To slip behind the row of trees under which I walked was perhaps no very dignified proceeding; but it was the easiest mode of escaping his observation, and perhaps his impertinent assiduity, and still more intrusive curiosity. As he passed, I heard him communicate to a grave-looking man, in a black coat, a slouched hat, and Geneva cloak, the following sketch of a character, which my self-love, while revolting against it as a caricature, could not, nevertheless, refuse to recognise as a likeness.

'Ay, ay, Mr. Hammorgaw, it's e'en as I tell ye.

He's no a'thegether sae void o' sense neither; he has a gloaming sight o' what's reasonable—that is ance and awa—a glisk and nae mair—but he's crack-brained and cockle-headed about his nipperty-tipperty poetry nonsense—He'll glowr at an auld-warld barkit aik-snag as if it were a queez-maddam in full bearing; and a naked craig, wi' a burn jawing ower't, is unto him as a garden garnisht with flowering knots and choice pot-herbs; then, he wad rather claver wi' a daft quean they ca' Diana Vernon (weel I wot they might ca' her Diana of the Ephesians, for she's little better than a heathen—better? she's waur—a Roman—a mere Roman)—he'll claver wi' her, or ony ither idle slut, rather than hear what might do him gude a' the days of his life, frae you or me, Mr. Hammorgaw, or ony ither sober and sponsible person. Reason, sir, is what he canna endure—he's a' for your vanities and volubilities; and he ance tell'd me, (puir blinded creature,) that the Psalms of David were excellent poetry! as if the holy Psalmist thought o' rattling rhymes in a blether, like his ain silly clinkum-clankum things that he ca's verse. Gude help him! twa lines o' Davie Lindsay wad ding a' he ever clerkit.'

While listening to this perverted account of my temper and studies, you will not be surprised if I meditated for Mr. Fairservice the unpleasant surprise of a broken pate on the first decent opportunity. His friend only intimated his attention by 'Ay, ay!' and 'Is't e'en sae?' and such like expressions of interest, at the proper breaks in Mr. Fairservice's harangue, until at length, in answer to some observation of greater length, the import of which I only collected from my trusty guide's reply, honest Andrew answered, 'Tell him a bit o' my mind, quoth ye?—Wha wad be fule then but Andrew?—He's a red-wud deevil, man!—He's like Giles Heathertap's auld boar; ye need but shake a clout at him to make him turn and gore. Bide wi' him, say ye?—Troth, I kenna what for I bide wi' him mysell—But the lad's no a bad lad after a'; and he needs some carefu' body to look after him. He hasna the right grip o' his hand— the gowd slips through't like water, man; and it's no that ill a thing to be near him when his purse is in his hand, and it's seldom out o't. And then he's come o' gude kith and kin—My heart warms to the puir thoughtless callant, Mr. Hammorgaw— and then the penny fee——'

In the latter part of this instructive communication, Mr. Fairservice lowered his voice to a tone better beseeming the conversation in a place of public resort on a Sabbath evening, and his companion and he were soon beyond my hearing. My feelings of hasty resentment soon subsided under the conviction, that, as Andrew himself might have said, 'A hearkener always hears a bad tale of himself,' and that whoever should happen to overhear their character discussed in their own servants'-hall, must prepare to undergo the scalpel of some such anatomist as Mr. Fairservice. The incident was so far useful, as, including the feelings to which it gave rise, it sped away a part of the time which hung so heavily on my hand.

Evening had now closed, and the growing darkness gave to the broad, still, and deep expanse of the brimful river, first a hue sombre and uniform, then a dismal and turbid appearance, partially lighted by a waning and pallid moon. The massive and ancient bridge which stretches across the Clyde, was now but dimly visible, and resembled that which Mirza, in his unequalled vision, has described as traversing the valley of Bagdad. The low-browed arches, seen as imperfectly as the dusky current which they bestrode, seemed rather caverns which swallowed up the gloomy waters of the river, than apertures contrived for their passage. With the advancing night the stillness of the scene increased. There was yet a twinkling light occasionally seen to glide along by the stream, which conducted home one or two of the small parties, who, after the abstinence and religious duties of the day, had partaken of a social supper, the only meal at which the rigid Presbyterians made some advance to sociality on the Sabbath. Occasionally, also, the hoofs of a horse were heard, whose rider, after spending the Sunday in Glasgow, was directing his steps towards his residence in the country. These sounds and sights became gradually of more rare occurrence. At length they altogether ceased, and I was left to enjoy my solitary walk on the shores of the Clyde in solemn silence, broken only by the tolling of the successive hours from the steeples of the churches.

But as the night advanced, my impatience at the uncertainty of the situation in which I was placed increased every moment, and became nearly ungovernable. I began to question whether I had been imposed upon by the trick of a fool, the raving of a madman, or the studied machination of a villain, and paced the little quay or pier adjoining the entrance to the bridge in a state of incredible anxiety and vexation. At length the hour of twelve o'clock swung its summons over the city from the belfry of the metropolitan church of St. Mungo, and was answered and vouched by all the others like dutiful diocesans. The echoes had scarcely ceased to repeat the last sound, when a human form—the first I had seen for two hours—appeared passing along the bridge from the southern shore of the river. I advanced to meet him with a feeling as if my fate depended on the result of the interview, so much had my anxiety been wound up by protracted expectation. All that I could remark of the passenger as we advanced towards each other was, that his frame was rather beneath than above the middle-size, but apparently strong, thick-set, and muscular; his dress a horseman's wrapping coat. I slackened my pace, and almost paused as I advanced, in expectation that he would address me. But to my inexpressible disappointment, he passed without speaking, and I had no pretence for being the first to address one, who, notwithstanding his appearance at the very hour of appointment, might nevertheless be an absolute stranger. I stopped when he had passed me, and looked after him, uncertain whether I ought not to follow him. The stranger walked on till near the northern end of the bridge, then paused, looked back, and, turning round, again advanced towards me. I resolved that this time he should not have the apology for silence proper to apparitions, who, it is vulgarly supposed, cannot speak until they are spoken to. 'You walk late, sir,' said I, as we met a second time.

'I bide tryste,' was the reply, 'and so I think do you, Mr. Osbaldistone.'

'You are then the person who requested to meet me here at this unusual hour?'

'I am,' he replied. 'Follow me, and you shall know my reasons.'

'Before following you, I must know your name and purpose,' I answered.

'I am a man,' was the reply; 'and my purpose is friendly to you.'

'A man!' I repeated. 'That is a very brief description.'

'It will serve for one who has no other to give,' said the stranger. 'He that is without name, without friends, without coin, without country, is still at least a man; and he that has all these is no more.'

'Yet this is still too general an account of yourself, to say the least of it, to establish your credit with a stranger.'

'It is all I mean to give, howsoe'er; you may choose to follow me, or to remain without the information I desire to afford you.'

'Can you not give me that information here?' I demanded.

'You must receive it from your eyes, not from

my tongue—you must follow me, or remain in ignorance of the information which I have to give you.'

There was something short, determined, and even stern in the man's manner, not certainly well calculated to conciliate undoubting confidence.

' What is it you fear?' he said impatiently. ' To whom, think ye, is your life of such consequence, that they should seek to bereave ye of it?'

' I fear nothing,' I replied firmly, though somewhat hastily. ' Walk on—I attend you.'

We proceeded, contrary to my expectation, to re-enter the town, and glided like mute spectres, side by side, up its empty and silent streets. The high and gloomy stone fronts, with the variegated ornaments and pediments of the windows, looked yet taller and more sable by the imperfect moonshine. Our walk was for some minutes in perfect silence. At length my conductor spoke.

' Are you afraid?'

' I retort your own words,' I replied; ' wherefore should I fear?'

' Because you are with a stranger—perhaps an enemy, in a place where you have no friends and many enemies.'

' I neither fear you nor them; I am young, active, and armed.'

' I am not armed,' replied my conductor; ' but no matter, a willing hand never lacked weapon. You say you fear nothing; but if you knew who was by your side, perhaps you might underlie a tremor.'

'And why should I?' replied I. 'I again repeat, I fear nought that you can do.'

'Nought that I can do?—Be it so. But do you not fear the consequences of being found with one, whose very name whispered in this lonely street would make the stones themselves rise up to apprehend him—on whose head half the men in Glasgow would build their fortune as on a found treasure, had they the luck to grip him by the collar—the sound of whose apprehension were as welcome at the Cross of Edinburgh as ever the news of a field stricken and won in Flanders?'

'And who then are you, whose name should create so deep a feeling of terror?' I replied.

'No enemy of yours, since I am conveying you to a place, where, were I myself recognised and identified, iron to the heels, and hemp to the craig, would be my brief dooming.'

I paused and stood still on the pavement, drawing back so as to have the most perfect view of my companion which the light afforded, and which was sufficient to guard me against any sudden motion of assault.

'You have said,' I answered, 'either too much or too little—too much to induce me to confide in you as a mere stranger, since you avow yourself a person amenable to the laws of the country in which we are—and too little, unless you could show that you are unjustly subjected to their rigour.'

As I ceased to speak, he made a step towards me. I drew back instinctively, and laid my hand on the hilt of my sword.

'What,' said he, 'on an unarmed man, and your friend ?'

'I am yet ignorant if you are either the one or the other,' I replied ; 'and, to say the truth, your language and manner might well entitle me to doubt both.'

'It is manfully spoken,' replied my conductor; 'and I respect him whose hand can keep his head. —I will be frank and free with you—I am conveying you to prison.'

'To prison !' I exclaimed ; 'by what warrant, or for what offence ?—You shall have my life sooner than my liberty — I defy you, and I will not follow you a step farther.'

'I do not,' he said, 'carry you there as a prisoner. I am,' he added, drawing himself haughtily up, 'neither a messenger nor sheriff's officer; I carry you to see a prisoner from whose lips you will learn the risk in which you presently stand. *Your* liberty is little risked by the visit; mine is in some peril; but that I readily encounter on your account, for I care not for risk, and I love a free young blood, that kens no protector but the cross o' the sword.'

While he spoke thus, we had reached the principal street, and were pausing before a large building of hewn stone, garnished, as I thought I could perceive, with gratings of iron before the windows.

'Muckle,' said the stranger, whose language became more broadly national as he assumed a tone of colloquial freedom — 'Muckle wad the provost and bailies o' Glasgow gie to hae him sitting with iron garters to his hose within their tolbooth, that now stands wi' his legs as free as the red-deer's on the outside on 't. And little wad it avail them; for an if they had me there wi' a stane's weight o' iron at every ancle, I would show them a toom room and a lost lodger before to-morrow—But come on, what stint ye for ?'

As he spoke thus, he tapped at a low wicket, and was answered by a sharp voice, as of one awakened from a dream or reverie,—'Fa's tat ?—Wha's that, I wad say ?—and fat a deil want ye at this hour at e'en ?—Clean again rules—clean again rules, as they ca' them.'

The protracted tone in which the last words were uttered, betokened that the speaker was again composing himself to slumber. But my guide spoke in a loud whisper, 'Dougal, man ! hae ye forgotten Ha nun Gregarach ?'

'Deil a bit, deil a bit,' was the ready and lively response, and I heard the internal guardian of the prison-gate bustle up with great alacrity. A few words were exchanged between my conductor and the turnkey, in a language to which I was an absolute stranger. The bolts revolved, but with a caution which marked the apprehension that the noise might be overheard, and we stood within the vestibule of the prison of Glasgow, a small, but strong guard-room, from which a narrow staircase led upwards, and one or two low entrances conducted to apartments on the same level with the outward gate, all secured with the jealous strength of wickets, bolts, and bars. The walls, otherwise naked, were not unsuitably garnished with iron fetters, and other uncouth implements, which might be designed for purposes still more inhuman, interspersed with partisans, guns, pistols of antique manufacture, and other weapons of defence and offence.

At finding myself so unexpectedly, fortuitously, and, as it were, by stealth, introduced within one of the legal fortresses of Scotland, I could not help recollecting my adventure in Northumberland, and fretting at the strange incidents which again, without any demerits of my own, threatened to place me in a dangerous and disagreeable collision with the laws of a country, which I visited only in the capacity of a stranger.

CHAPTER XXII

' Look round thee, young Astolpho: Here's the place
Which men (for being poor) are sent to starve in;—
Rude remedy, I trow, for sore disease.
Within these walls, stifled by damp and stench,
Doth Hope's fair torch expire; and at the snuff,
Ere yet 'tis quite extinct, rude, wild, and wayward,
The desperate revelries of wild despair,
Kindling their hell-born cressets, light to deeds
That the poor captive would have died ere practised,
Till bondage sunk his soul to his condition.'

THE PRISON, SCENE III. ACT I.

AT my first entrance I turned an eager glance towards my conductor; but the lamp in the vestibule was too low in flame to give my curiosity any satisfaction by affording a distinct perusal of his features. As the turnkey held the light in his hand, the beams fell more full on his own scarce less interesting figure. He was a wild shock-headed looking animal, whose profusion of red hair covered and obscured his features, which were otherwise only characterised by the extravagant joy that affected him at the sight of my guide. In my experience I have met nothing so absolutely resembling my idea of a very uncouth, wild, and ugly savage, adoring the idol of his tribe. He grinned, he shivered, he laughed, he was near crying, if he did not actually cry. He had a ' Where shall I go ?

59

—What can I do for you?' expression of face; the complete, surrendered, and anxious subservience and devotion of which it is difficult to describe, otherwise than by the awkward combination which I have attempted. The fellow's voice seemed choking in his ecstasy, and only could express itself in such interjections as 'Oigh, oigh,—Ay, ay—it's lang since she's seen ye!' and other exclamations equally brief, expressed in the same unknown tongue in which he had communicated with my conductor while we were on the outside of the jail door. My guide received all this excess of joyful gratulation much like a prince too early accustomed to the homage of those around him to be much moved by it, yet willing to requite it by the usual forms of royal courtesy. He extended his hand graciously towards the turnkey, with a civil inquiry of 'How's a' wi' you, Dougal?'

'Oigh, oigh!' exclaimed Dougal, softening the sharp exclamations of his surprise as he looked around with an eye of watchful alarm—'Oigh, to see you here—to see you here—Oigh, what will come o' ye gin the bailies suld come to get witting —ta filthy, gutty hallions, tat they are?'

My guide placed his finger on his lip, and said, 'Fear nothing, Dougal; your hands shall never draw a bolt on me.'

'Tat sall they no,' said Dougal; 'she suld—she wad—that is, she wishes them hacked aff by the elbows first—But when are ye gaun yonder again? and ye'll no forget to let her ken—she's your puir cousin, God kens, only seven times removed.'

'I will let you ken, Dougal, as soon as my plans are settled.'

'And, by her sooth, when you do, an it were twal o' the Sunday at e'en, she'll fling her keys at the provost's head or she gie them anither turn, and that or ever Monday morning begins—see if she winna.'

My mysterious stranger cut his acquaintance's ecstasies short by again addressing him, in what I afterwards understood to be the Irish, Earse, or Gaelic, explaining, probably, the services which he required at his hand. The answer, 'Wi' a' her heart —wi' a' her soul,' with a good deal of indistinct muttering in a similar tone, intimated the turnkey's acquiescence in what he proposed. The fellow trimmed his dying lamp, and made a sign to me to follow him.

'Do you not go with us?' said I, looking to my conductor.

'It is unnecessary,' he replied; 'my company may be inconvenient for you, and I had better remain to secure our retreat.'

'I do not suppose you mean to betray me to danger,' said I.

'To none but what I partake in doubly,' answered the stranger, with a voice of assurance which it was impossible to mistrust.

I followed the turnkey, who, leaving the inner wicket unlocked behind him, led me up a *turnpike*, (so the Scotch call a winding stair,) then along a narrow gallery,—then opening one of several doors which led into the passage, he ushered me into a small apartment, and casting his eye on the pallet bed which occupied one corner, said with an under voice, as he placed the lamp on a little deal table, ' She 's sleeping.'

' She !—who ?—can it be Diana Vernon in this abode of misery ? '

I turned my eye to the bed, and it was with a mixture of disappointment oddly mingled with pleasure, that I saw my first suspicion had deceived me. I saw a head neither young nor beautiful, garnished with a grey beard of two days' growth, and accommodated with a red nightcap. The first glance put me at ease on the score of Diana Vernon; the second, as the slumberer awoke from a heavy sleep, yawned, and rubbed his eyes, presented me with features very different indeed — even those of my poor friend Owen. I drew back out of view an instant, that he might have time to recover himself; fortunately recollecting that I was but an intruder on these cells of sorrow, and that any alarm might be attended with unhappy consequences.

Meantime, the unfortunate formalist, raising himself from the pallet-bed with the assistance of one hand, and scratching his cap with the other, exclaimed, in a voice in which as much peevishness as he was capable of feeling contended with drowsiness, ' I 'll tell you what, Mr. Dugwell, or whatever your name may be, the sum total of the matter is, that if my natural rest is to be broken in this manner, I must complain to the lord mayor.'

' Shentlemans to speak wi' her,' replied Dougal,

resuming the true dogged sullen tone of a turnkey, in exchange for the shrill clang of Highland congratulation with which he had welcomed my mysterious guide; and, turning on his heel, he left the apartment.

It was some time before I could prevail upon the unfortunate sleeper awakening to recognise me; and when he did so, the distress of the worthy creature was extreme, at supposing, which he naturally did, that I had been sent thither as a partner of his captivity.

'O, Mr. Frank, what have you brought yourself and the house to?—I think nothing of myself, that am a mere cipher, so to speak; but you, that was your father's sum total—his omnium—you that might have been the first man in the first house in the first city, to be shut up in a nasty Scotch jail, where one cannot even get the dirt brushed off their clothes!'

He rubbed, with an air of peevish irritation, the once stainless brown coat, which had now shared some of the impurities of the floor of his prison-house,—his habits of extreme punctilious neatness acting mechanically to increase his distress.

'O Heaven be gracious to us!' he continued. 'What news this will be on 'Change! There has not the like come there since the battle of Almanza, where the total of the British loss was summed up to five thousand men killed and wounded, besides a floating balance of missing—but what will that be to the news that Osbaldistone and Tresham have stopped!'

I broke in on his lamentations to acquaint him, that I was no prisoner, though scarce able to account for my being in that place at such an hour. I could only silence his inquiries by persisting in those which his own situation suggested; and at length obtained from him such information as he was able to give me. It was none of the most distinct; for however clear-headed in his own routine of commercial business, Owen, you are well aware, was not very acute in comprehending what lay beyond that sphere.

The sum of his information was, that of two correspondents of my father's firm at Glasgow, where, owing to engagements in Scotland formerly alluded to, he transacted a great deal of business, both my father and Owen had found the house of MacVittie, MacFin and Company, the most obliging and accommodating. They had deferred to the great English house on every possible occasion; and in their bargains and transactions acted, without repining, the part of the jackall, who only claims what the lion is pleased to leave him. However small the share of profit allotted to them, it was always, as they expressed it, 'enough for the like of them'; however large the portion of trouble, 'they were sensible they could not do too much to deserve the continued patronage and good opinion of their honoured friends in Crane Alley.'

The dictates of my father were to MacVittie and MacFin the laws of the Medes and Persians, not to be altered, innovated, or even discussed; and the punctilios exacted by Owen in their business transactions, for he was a great lover of form, more especially when he could dictate it *ex cathedra*, seemed scarce less sanctimonious in their eyes. This tone of deep and respectful observance went all currently down with Owen; but my father looked a little closer into men's bosoms, and whether suspicious of this excess of deference, or, as a lover of brevity and simplicity in business, tired with these gentlemen's long-winded professions of regard, he had uniformly resisted their desire to become his sole agents in Scotland. On the contrary, he transacted many affairs through a correspondent of a character perfectly different,— a man whose good opinion of himself amounted to self-conceit, and who, disliking the English in general as much as my father did the Scotch, would hold no communication but on a footing of absolute equality; jealous, moreover; captious occasionally; as tenacious of his own opinions in point of form as Owen could be of his; and totally indifferent, though the authority of all Lombard-Street had stood against his own private opinion.

As these peculiarities of temper rendered it difficult to transact business with Mr. Nicol Jarvie, —as they occasioned at times disputes and coldness between the English house and their correspondent, which were only got over by a sense of mutual interest,—as, moreover, Owen's personal vanity sometimes suffered a little in the discussions to which they gave rise, you cannot be surprised, Tresham, that our old friend threw at all times the weight of his influence in favour of the civil, discreet, accommodating concern of MacVittie and MacFin, and spoke of Jarvie as a petulant, conceited Scotch pedlar, with whom there was no dealing.

It was also not surprising, that in these circumstances, which I only learned in detail some time afterwards, Owen, in the difficulties to which the house was reduced by the absence of my father, and the disappearance of Rashleigh, should, on his arrival in Scotland, which took place two days before mine, have recourse to the friendship of those correspondents, who had always professed themselves obliged, gratified, and devoted to the service of his principal. He was received at Messrs. MacVittie and MacFin's counting-house in the Gallowgate, with something like the devotion a Catholic would pay to his tutelar saint. But, alas! this sunshine was soon overclouded, when, encouraged by the fair hopes which it inspired, he opened the difficulties of the house to his friendly correspondents, and requested their counsel and assistance. MacVittie was almost stunned by the communication; and MacFin, ere it was completed, was already at the ledger of their firm, and deeply engaged in the very bowels of the multitudinous accounts between their house and that of Osbaldistone and Tresham, for the purpose of discovering on which side the balance lay. Alas! the scale depressed considerably against the English firm; and the faces of MacVittie and MacFin, hitherto only blank and doubtful, became now ominous, grim, and lowering. They met Mr. Owen's request of countenance and assistance, with a counter-demand of instant security against imminent hazard of eventual loss; and at length, speaking more plainly, required that a deposit of assets, destined for other purposes, should be placed in their hands for that purpose. Owen repelled this demand with great indignation, as dishonourable to his constituents, unjust to the other creditors of Osbaldistone and Tresham, and very ungrateful on the part of those by whom it was made.

The Scotch partners gained, in the course of this controversy, what is very convenient to persons who are in the wrong, an opportunity and pretext for putting themselves in a violent passion, and for taking, under the pretext of the provocation they had received, measures to which some sense of decency, if not of conscience, might otherwise have deterred them from resorting.

Owen had a small share, as I believe is usual, in the house to which he acted as head clerk, and was therefore personally liable for all its obligations. This was known to Messrs. MacVittie and MacFin; and, with a view of making him feel their power, or rather in order to force him, at this emergency, into those measures in their favour, to which he had expressed himself so repugnant, they had recourse to a summary process of arrest and imprisonment, which it seems the law of Scotland (therein surely liable to much abuse) allows to a creditor, who finds his conscience at liberty to make oath that the debtor meditates departing from the realm. Under such a warrant had poor Owen been confined to durance on the day preceding that when I was so strangely guided to his prison-house.

Thus possessed of the alarming outline of facts, the question remained, what was to be done? and it was not of easy determination. I plainly perceived the perils with which we were surrounded, but it was more difficult to suggest any remedy. The warning which I had already received seemed to intimate, that my own personal liberty might be endangered by an open appearance in Owen's behalf. Owen entertained the same apprehension, and, in the exaggeration of his terror, assured me that a Scotchman, rather than run the risk of losing a farthing by an Englishman, would find law for arresting his wife, children, man-servant, maid-servant, and stranger within his household. The laws concerning debt, in most countries, are so unmercifully severe, that I could not altogether disbelieve his statement; and my arrest, in the present circumstances, would have been a *coup-de-grace* to my father's affairs. In this dilemma, I asked Owen if he had not thought of having recourse to my father's other correspondent in Glasgow, Mr. Nicol Jarvie?

'He had sent him a letter,' he replied, 'that morning; but if the smooth-tongued and civil house in the Gallowgate had used him thus, what was to be expected from the cross-grained crab-stock in the Salt-Market? You might as well ask a broker to give up his per centage, as expect a favour from him without the *per contra*. He had not even,' Owen said, 'answered his letter, though it was put into his hand that morning as he went to church.' And here the despairing man-of-figures threw himself down on his pallet, exclaiming,—

' My poor dear master!—My poor dear master! O, Mr. Frank, Mr. Frank, this is all your obstinacy! —But God forgive me for saying so to you in your distress! It's God's disposing, and man must submit.'

My philosophy, Tresham, could not prevent my sharing in the honest creature's distress, and we mingled our tears, the more bitter on my part, as the perverse opposition to my father's will, with which the kind-hearted Owen forbore to upbraid me, rose up to my conscience as the cause of all this affliction.

In the midst of our mingled sorrow, we were disturbed and surprised by a loud knocking at the outward door of the prison. I ran to the top of the staircase to listen, but could only hear the voice of the turnkey, alternately in a high tone, answering to some person without, and in a whisper, addressed to the person who had guided me hither: ' She's coming—she's coming,' aloud; then in a low key, ' O hon-a-ri! O hon-a-ri! what 'll she do now?— Gang up ta stair, and hide yoursell ahint ta Sassenach shentleman's ped.—She's coming as fast as she can—Ahellanay! it's my lord provosts, and ta pailies, and ta guard—and ta captain's coming toon stairs too—Got pless her! gang up or he meets her.— She's coming—she's coming—ta lock 's sair roosted.'

While Dougal unwillingly, and with as much delay as possible, undid the various fastenings to give admittance to those without, whose impatience became clamorous, my guide ascended the winding stair, and sprang into Owen's apartment, into which

I followed him.   He cast his eyes hastily round as if looking for a place of concealment, then said to me, 'Lend me your pistols—yet it's no matter, I can do without them—Whatever you see, take no heed, and do not mix your hand in another man's feud—This gear's mine, and I must manage it as I dow; but I have been as hard bested, and worse, than I am even now.'

As the stranger spoke these words, he stripped from his person the cumbrous upper coat in which he was wrapt, confronted the door of the apartment, on which he fixed a keen and determined glance, drawing his person a little back to concentrate his force, like a fine horse brought up to the leaping-bar. I had not a moment's doubt that he meant to extricate himself from his embarrassment, whatever might be the cause of it, by springing full upon those who should appear when the doors opened, and forcing his way through all opposition into the street; and such was the appearance of strength and agility displayed in his frame, and of determination in his look and manner, that I did not doubt a moment but that he might get clear through his opponents, unless they employed fatal means to stop his purpose.

It was a period of awful suspense betwixt the opening of the outward gate and that of the door of the apartment, when there appeared—no guard with bayonets fixed, or watch with clubs, bills, or partisans, but a good-looking young woman, with grogram petticoats, tucked up for trudging through the streets, and holding a lantern in her hand.   This female ushered in a more important personage, in form stout, short, and somewhat corpulent; and by dignity, as it soon appeared, a magistrate, bob-wigged, bustling, and breathless with peevish impatience. My conductor, at his appearance, drew back as if to escape observation; but he could not elude the penetrating twinkle with which this dignitary reconnoitred the whole apartment.

'A bonny thing it is, and a beseeming, that I should be kept at the door half an hour, Captain Stanchells,' said he, addressing the principal jailor, who now showed himself at the door as if in attendance on the great man, 'knocking as hard to get into the tolbooth as ony body else wad to get out of it, could that avail them, poor fallen creatures!— And how 's this ?—how 's this ?—strangers in the jail after lock-up hours, and on the Sabbath evening!— I shall look after this, Stanchells, you may depend on 't—Keep the door locked, and I 'll speak to these gentlemen in a gliffing—But first I maun hae a crack wi' an auld acquaintance here.—Mr. Owen, Mr. Owen, how 's a' wi' ye, man ?'

'Pretty well in body, I thank you, Mr. Jarvie,' drawled out poor Owen, 'but sore afflicted in spirit.'

'Nae doubt, nae doubt—ay, ay—it 's an awfu' whummle—and for ane that held his head sae high too—human nature, human nature—Ay, ay, we 're a' subject to a downcome. Mr. Osbaldistone is a gude honest gentleman; but I aye said he was ane o' them wad make a spune or spoil a horn, as my father the worthy deacon used to say. The

deacon used to say to me, " Nick—young Nick,"
(his name was Nicol as weel as mine; sae folk ca'd
us in their daffin' young Nick and auld Nick)—
" Nick," said he, " never put out your arm farther
than ye can draw it easily back again." I hae said
sae to Mr. Osbaldistone, and he didna seem to take
it a'thegether sae kind as I wished—but it was weel
meant—weel meant.'

This discourse, delivered with prodigious volubility, and a great appearance of self-complacency,
as he recollected his own advice and predictions,
gave little promise of assistance at the hands of
Mr. Jarvie. Yet it soon appeared rather to proceed
from a total want of delicacy than any deficiency of
real kindness; for when Owen expressed himself
somewhat hurt that these things should be recalled
to memory in his present situation, the Glaswegian
took him by the hand, and bade him ' Cheer up a
gliff! D'ye think I wad hae comed out at twal
o'clock at night, and amaist broken the Lord's-day,
just to tell a fa'en man o' his backslidings ? Na, na,
that's no Bailie Jarvie's gate, nor was 't his worthy
father's the deacon afore him. Why, man ! it's my
rule never to think on warldly business on the
Sabbath, and though I did a' I could to keep your
note that I gat this morning out o' my head, yet I
thought mair on it a' day, than on the preaching—
And it's my rule to gang to my bed wi' the yellow
curtains preceesely at ten o'clock — unless I were
eating a haddock wi' a neighbour, or a neighbour
wi' me—ask the lass-quean there, if it isna a funda-
mental rule in my household; and here hae I sitten

up reading gude books, and gaping as if I wad swallow St. Enox Kirk, till it chappit twal, whilk was a lawfu' hour to gie a look at my ledger just to see how things stood between us; and then, as time and tide wait for no man, I made the lass get the lantern, and came slipping my ways here to see what can be dune anent your affairs. Bailie Jarvie can command entrance into the tolbooth at ony hour, day or night; sae could my father the deacon in his time, honest man, praise to his memory.'

Although Owen groaned at the mention of the ledger, leading me grievously to fear that here also the balance stood in the wrong column; and although the worthy magistrate's speech expressed much self-complacency, and some ominous triumph in his own superior judgment, yet it was blended with a sort of frank and blunt good-nature, from which I could not help deriving some hopes. He requested to see some papers he mentioned, snatched them hastily from Owen's hand, and sitting on the bed, to 'rest his shanks,' as he was pleased to express the accommodation which that posture afforded him, his servant girl held up the lantern to him, while, pshawing, muttering, and sputtering, now at the imperfect light, now at the contents of the packet, he ran over the writings it contained.

Seeing him fairly engaged in this course of study, the guide who had brought me hither seemed disposed to take an unceremonious leave. He made a sign to me to say nothing, and intimated, by his change of posture, an intention to glide towards the door in such a manner as to attract the least possible observation. But the alert magistrate (very different from my old acquaintance Mr. Justice Inglewood) instantly detected and interrupted his purposes. 'I say, look to the door, Stanchells— shut and lock it, and keep watch on the outside.'

The stranger's brow darkened, and he seemed for an instant again to meditate the effecting his retreat by violence; but ere he had determined, the door closed, and the ponderous bolt revolved. He muttered an exclamation in Gaelic, strode across the floor, and then, with an air of dogged resolution, as if fixed and prepared to see the scene to an end, sate himself down on the oak table and whistled a strathspey.

Mr. Jarvie, who seemed very alert and expeditious in going through business, soon showed himself master of that which he had been considering, and addressed himself to Mr. Owen in the following strain: 'Weel, Mr. Owen, weel—your house are awin certain sums to Messrs. MacVittie and MacFin (shame fa' their souple snouts! they made that and mair out o' a bargain about the aik-woods at Glen-Cailziechat, that they took out atween my teeth—wi' help o' your gude word, I maun needs say, Mr. Owen—but that makes nae odds now.)—Weel, sir, your house awes them this siller; and for this, and relief of other engagements they stand in for you, they hae putten a double turn o' Stanchells' muckle key on ye.—Weel, sir, ye awe this siller—and maybe ye awe some mair to some other body too—maybe ye awe some to mysell, Bailie Nicol Jarvie.'

'I cannot deny, sir, but the balance may of this date be brought out against us, Mr. Jarvie,' said Owen; 'but you'll please to consider——'

'I hae nae time to consider e'enow, Mr. Owen—Sae near Sabbath at e'en, and out o' ane's warm bed at this time o' night, and a sort o''drow in the air besides—there's nae time for considering—But, sir, as I was saying, ye awe me money—it winna deny—ye awe me money, less or mair, I'll stand by it—But then, Mr. Owen, I canna see how you, an active man that understands business, can redd out the business ye're come down about, and clear us a' aff—as I have gritt·hope ye will—if ye're keepit lying here in the tolbooth of Glasgow.—Now, sir, if you can find caution *judicio sisti*, that is, that ye winna flee the country, but appear and relieve your caution when ca'd for in our legal courts, ye may be set at liberty this very morning.'

'Mr. Jarvie,' said Owen, 'if any friend would become surety for me to that effect, my liberty might be usefully employed, doubtless, both for the house and all connected with it.'

'Aweel, sir,' continued Jarvie, 'and doubtless such a friend wad expect ye to appear when ca'd on, and relieve him o' his engagement.'

'And I should do so as certainly, bating sickness or death, as that two and two make four.'

'Aweel, Mr. Owen,' resumed the citizen of Glasgow, 'I dinna misdoubt ye, and I'll prove it, sir—I'll prove it. I am a carefu' man, as is weel kend, and industrious, as the hale town can testify; and I can win my crowns, and keep my crowns, and count my crowns, wi' ony body in the Saut-Market, or it may be in the Gallowgate. And I 'm a prudent man, as my father the deacon was before me; but rather than an honest civil gentleman, that understands business, and is willing to do justice to all men, should lie by the heels this gate, unable to help himsell or ony body else—why, conscience, man! I 'll be your bail mysell—But ye 'll mind it 's a bail *judicio sisti*, as our town-clerk says, not *judicatum solvi*; ye 'll mind that, for there 's muckle difference.'

Mr. Owen assured him, that as matters then stood, he could not expect any one to become security for the actual payment of the debt, but that there was not the most distant cause for apprehending loss from his failing to present himself when lawfully called upon.

' I believe ye—I believe ye. Eneugh said—eneugh said. We 'se hae your legs loose by break-fast-time,—And now let 's hear what thir chamber chiels o' yours hae to say for themselves, or how, in the name of unrule, they got here at this time o' night.'

CHAPTER XXIII

Hame came our gudeman at e'en,
And hame came he,
And there he saw a man
Where a man suldna be.
'How's this now, kimmer?
How's this? quo he,—
How came this carle here
Without the leave o' me?'
OLD SONG.

THE magistrate took the light out of his servant-maid's hand, and advanced to his scrutiny, like Diogenes in the street of Athens, lantern-in-hand, and probably with as little expectation as that of the cynic, that he was likely to encounter any especial treasure in the course of his researches. The first whom he approached was my mysterious guide, who, seated on a table as I have already described him, with his eyes firmly fixed on the wall, his features arranged into the utmost inflexibility of expression, his hands folded on his breast with an air betwixt carelessness and defiance, his heel patting against the foot of the table, to keep time with the tune which he continued to whistle, submitted to Mr. Jarvie's investigation with an air of absolute confidence and assurance, which, for a moment, placed at fault the memory and sagacity of the acute and anxious investigator.

'Ah!—Eh!—Oh!' exclaimed the Bailie. 'My conscience!—it's impossible—and yet—no!—Conscience, it canna be!—and yet again—Deil hae me! that I suld say sae—Ye robber—ye cateran—ye born deevil that ye are, to a' bad ends and nae gude ane—can this be you?'

'E'en as ye see, Bailie,' was the laconic answer.

'Conscience! if I am na clean bumbaized—*you*, ye cheat-the-wuddy rogue, *you* here on your venture in the tolbooth o' Glasgow?—What d'ye think's the value o' your head?'

'Umph?—why, fairly weighed, and Dutch weight, it might weigh down one provost's, four bailies', a town-clerk's, six deacons', besides stentmasters'——'

'Ah, ye reiving villain!' interrupted Mr. Jarvie. 'But tell ower your sins, and prepare ye, for if I say the word——'

'True, Bailie,' said he who was thus addressed, folding his hands behind him with the utmost *nonchalance*, 'but ye will never say that word.'

'And why suld I not, sir?' exclaimed the magistrate—'Why suld I not? Answer me that—why suld I not?'

'For three sufficient reasons, Bailie Jarvie.— First, for auld langsyne;—second, for the sake of the auld wife ayont the fire at Stuckavrallachan, that made some mixture of our bluids, to my own proper shame be it spoken! that has a cousin wi' accounts, and yarn winnles, and looms, and shuttles, like a mere mechanical person;—and lastly, Bailie, because if I saw a sign o' your betraying me, I

would plaster that wa' with your harns ere the hand of man could rescue you!'

'Ye're a bauld desperate villain, sir,' retorted the undaunted Bailie; 'and ye ken that I ken ye to be sae, and that I wadna stand a moment for my ain risk.'

'I ken weel,' said the other, 'ye hae gentle bluid in your veins, and I wad be laith to hurt my ain kinsman. But I'll gang out here as free as I came in, or the very wa's o' Glasgow tolbooth shall tell o't these ten years to come.'

'Weel, weel,' said Mr. Jarvie, 'bluid's thicker than water; and it liesna in kith, kin, and ally, to see motes in ilk other's een if other een see them no. It wad be sair news to the auld wife below the Ben of Stuckavrallachan, that you, ye Hieland limmer, had knockit out my harns, or that I had kilted you up in a tow. But ye'll own, ye dour deevil, that were it no your very sell, I wad hae grippit the best man in the Hielands.'

'Ye wad hae tried, cousin,' answered my guide, 'that I wot weel; but I doubt ye wad hae come aff wi' the short measure; for we gang-there-out Hieland bodies are an unchancy generation when you speak to us o' bondage. We downa bide the coercion of gude braid-claith about our hinderlans; let a be breeks o' freestone, and garters o' iron.'

'Ye'll find the stane breeks and the airn garters, ay, and the hemp cravat, for a' that, neighbour,' replied the Bailie. 'Nae man in a civilized country ever played the pliskies ye hae done—but e'en pickle in your ain pock-neuk — I hae gien ye warning.'

'Well, cousin,' said the other, 'ye'll wear black at my burial?'

'Deil a black cloak will be there, Robin, but the corbies and the hoodie-craws, I'se gie ye my hand on that. But whar's the gude thousand pund Scots that I lent ye, man, and when am I to see it again?'

'Where it is,' replied my guide, after the affectation of considering for a moment, 'I cannot justly tell—probably where last year's snaw is.'

'And that's on the tap of Schehallion, ye Hieland dog,' said Mr. Jarvie; 'and I look for payment frae you where ye stand.'

'Ay,' replied the Highlander, 'but I keep neither snaw nor dollars in my sporran. And as to when you'll see it—why, just when the king enjoys his ain again, as the auld sang says.'

'Warst of a', Robin,' retorted the Glaswegian,— 'I mean, ye disloyal traitor—Warst of a'!—Wad ye bring popery in on us, and arbitrary power, and a foist and a warming-pan, and the set forms, and the curates, and the auld enormities o' surplices and cearments? Ye had better stick to your auld trade o' theft-boot, black-mail, spreaghs, and gillravaging —better stealing nowte than ruining nations.'

'Hout, man, whisht wi' your whiggery,' answered the Celt, 'we hae kend ane anither mony a lang day. I'se take care your counting-room is no cleaned out when the Gillon-a-naillie *

---

* The lads with the kilts or petticoats.

come to redd up the Glasgow buiths, and clear them o' their auld shop-wares. And, unless it just fa' in the preceese way o' your duty, ye maunna see me oftener, Nicol, than I am disposed to be seen.'

'Ye are a dauring villain, Rob,' answered the Bailie; 'and ye will be hanged, that will be seen and heard tell o'; but I'se ne'er be the ill bird and foul my nest, set apart strong necessity and the skreigh of duty, which no man should hear and be inobedient.—And wha the deevil's this?' he continued, turning to me—'Some gillravager that ye hae listed, I daur say. He looks as if he had a bauld heart to the highway, and a lang craig for the gibbet.'

'This, good Mr. Jarvie,' said Owen, who, like myself, had been struck dumb during this strange recognition, and no less strange dialogue, which took place betwixt these extraordinary kinsmen —'This, good Mr. Jarvie, is young Mr. Frank Osbaldistone, only child of the head of our house, who should have been taken into our firm at the time Mr. Rashleigh Osbaldistone, his cousin, had the luck to be taken into it'—(Here Owen could not suppress a groan)—'But, howsoever——'

'O, I have heard of that smaik,' said the Scotch merchant, interrupting him; 'it is he whom your principal, like an obstinate auld fule, wad make a merchant o', wad he or wad he no, and the lad turned a strolling stage-player, in pure dislike to the labour an honest man should live by.—Weel, sir, what say you to your handiwark? Will Hamlet the Dane, or Hamlet's ghost, be good security for Mr. Owen, sir?'

'I don't deserve your taunt,' I replied, 'though I respect your motive, and am too grateful for the assistance you have afforded Mr. Owen, to resent it. My only business here was to do what I could (it is perhaps very little) to aid Mr. Owen in the management of my father's affairs. My dislike of the commercial profession is a feeling of which I am the best and sole judge.'

'I protest,' said the Highlander, 'I had some respect for this callant even before I kend what was in him; but now I honour him for his contempt of weavers and spinners, and sic-like mechanical persons and their pursuits.'

'Ye're mad, Rob,' said the Bailie—'mad as a March hare,—though wherefore a hare suld be mad at March mair than at Martinmas, is mair than I can weel say. Weavers! Deil shake ye out o' the web the weaver craft made. Spinners!—ye'll spin and wind yoursell a bonny pirn. And this young birkie here, that ye're hoying and hounding on the shortest road to the gallows and the deevil, will his stage-plays and his poetries help him here, d'ye think, ony mair than your deep oaths and drawn dirks, ye reprobate that ye are?—Will *Tityre tu patulæ*, as they ca' it, tell him where Rashleigh Osbaldistone is? or Macbeth, and all his kernes and galla-glasses, and your awn to boot, Rob, procure him five thousand pounds to answer the bills which fall due ten days hence, were they a' rouped at the

Cross, basket-hilts, Andra-Ferraras, leather targets, brogues, brochan, and sporrans?'

'Ten days?' I answered, and instinctively drew out Diana Vernon's packet; and the time being elapsed during which I was to keep the seal sacred, I hastily broke it open. A sealed letter fell from a blank enclosure, owing to the trepidation with which I opened the parcel. A slight current of wind, which found its way through a broken pane of the window, wafted the letter to Mr. Jarvie's feet, who lifted it, examined the address with unceremonious curiosity, and, to my astonishment, handed it to his Highland kinsman, saying, 'Here's a wind has blown a letter to its right owner, though there were ten thousand chances against its coming to hand.'

The Highlander, having examined the address, broke the letter open without the least ceremony. I endeavoured to interrupt his proceeding.

'You must satisfy me, sir,' said I, 'that the letter is intended for you before I can permit you to peruse it.'

'Make yourself quite easy, Mr. Osbaldistone,' replied the mountaineer, with great composure;— 'remember Justice Inglewood, Clerk Jobson, Mr. Morris—above all, remember your vera humble servant, Robert Cawmil, and the beautiful Diana Vernon. Remember all this, and doubt no longer that the letter is for me.'

I remained astonished at my own stupidity. Through the whole night, the voice, and even the features of this man, though imperfectly seen, haunted me with recollections to which I could assign no exact local or personal associations. But now the light dawned on me at once,—this man was Campbell himself. His whole peculiarities flashed on me at once,—the deep strong voice,— the inflexible, stern, yet considerate cast of features, —the Scottish brogue, with its corresponding dialect and imagery, which, although he possessed the power at times of laying them aside, recurred at every moment of emotion, and gave pith to his sarcasm, or vehemence to his expostulation. Rather beneath the middle size than above it, his limbs were formed upon the very strongest model that is consistent with agility, while, from the remarkable ease and freedom of his movements, you could not doubt his possessing the latter quality in a high degree of perfection. Two points in his person interfered with the rules of symmetry—his shoulders were so broad in proportion to his height, as, notwithstanding the lean and lathy appearance of his frame, gave him something the air of being too square in respect to his stature; and his arms, though round, sinewy, and strong, were so very long as to be rather a deformity. I afterwards heard that this length of arm was a circumstance on which he prided himself; that when he wore his native Highland garb, he could tie the garters of his hose without stooping; and that it gave him great advantage in the use of the broadsword, at which he was very dexterous. But certainly this want of symmetry destroyed the claim he might otherwise have set up, to be accounted a very handsome man; it gave something wild, irregular, and, as it were, unearthly, to his appearance, and reminded me involuntarily, of the tales which Mabel used to tell of the old Picts who ravaged Northumberland in ancient times, who, according to her tradition, were a sort of half-goblin, half-human beings, distinguished, like this man, for courage, cunning, ferocity, the length of their arms, and the squareness of their shoulders.

When, however, I recollected the circumstances in which we formerly met, I could not doubt that the billet was most probably designed for him. He had made a marked figure among those mysterious personages over whom Diana seemed to exercise an influence, and from whom she experienced an influence in her turn. It was painful to think that the fate of a being so amiable was involved in that of desperadoes of this man's description; yet it seemed impossible to doubt it. Of what use, however, could this person be to my father's affairs?— I could think only of one. Rashleigh Osbaldistone had, at the instigation of Miss Vernon, certainly found means to produce Mr. Campbell when his presence was necessary to exculpate me from Morris's accusation—Was it not possible that her influence, in like manner, might prevail on Campbell to produce Rashleigh? Speaking on this supposition, I requested to know where my dangerous kinsman was, and when Mr. Campbell had seen him. The answer was indirect.

'It's a kittle cast she has gien me to play; but

yet it's fair play, and I winna baulk her. Mr. Osbaldistone, I dwell not very far from hence— my kinsman can show you the way—Leave Mr. Owen to do the best he can in Glasgow—do you come and see me in the glens, and it's like I may pleasure you, and stead your father in his extremity. I am but a poor man; but wit's better than wealth —and cousin,' (turning from me to address Mr. Jarvie,) 'if ye daur venture sae muckle as to eat a dish of Scotch collops, and a leg o' red-deer venison wi' me, come ye wi' this Sassenach gentleman as far as Drymen or Bucklivie, or the Clachan of Aberfoil will be better than ony o' them, and I'll hae somebody waiting to weise ye the gate to the place where I may be for the time—What say ye, man?—There's my thumb, I'll ne'er beguile thee.'

'Na, na, Robin,' said the cautious burgher, 'I seldom like to leave the Gorbals; I have nae freedom to gang amang your wild hills, Robin, and your kilted red-shanks—it disna become my place, man.'

'The devil damn your place and you baith!' reiterated Campbell. 'The only drap o' gentle bluid that's in your body was our great grand-uncle's that was justified at Dumbarton, and you set yourself up to say ye wad derogate frae your place to visit me!—Hark thee, man, I owe thee a day in harst—I'll pay up your thousan' pund Scots, plack and bawbee, gin ye'll be an honest fallow for ance, and just daiker up the gate wi' this Sassenach.'

'Hout awa' wi' your gentility,' replied the Bailie; 'carry your gentle bluid to the Cross, and see what ye'll buy wi't.—But, if I *were* to come, wad ye really and soothfastly pay me the siller?'

'I swear to ye,' said the Highlander, 'upon the halidome of him that sleeps beneath the grey stane at Inch-Cailleach.'*

'Say nae mair, Robin,—say nae mair—We'll see what may be dune.—But ye maunna expect me to gang ower the Highland line—I'll gae beyond the line at no rate. Ye maun meet me about Bucklivie or the Clachan of Aberfoil, and dinna forget the needful.'

'Nae fear—nae fear,' said Campbell, 'I'll be as true as the steel blade that never failed its master. —But I must be budging, cousin, for the air o' Glasgow tolbooth is no that ower salutary to a Highlander's constitution.'

'Troth,' replied the merchant, 'and if my duty were to be dune, ye couldna change your atmosphere, as the minister ca's it, this ae wee while.— Ochon, that I sud ever be concerned in aiding and abetting an escape frae justice! it will be a shame and disgrace to me and mine, and my very father's memory, for ever.'

'Hout tout, man, let that flee stick in the wa',' answered his kinsman; 'when the dirt's dry it will rub out—Your father, honest man, could look ower a friend's fault as weel as anither.'

'Ye may be right, Robin,' replied the Bailie,

---

* Inch-Cailleach is an island in Lochlomond, where the clan of Mac-Gregor were wont to be interred, and where their sepulchres may still be seen. It formerly contained a nunnery; hence the name Inch-Cailleach, or the Island of Old Women.

after a moment's reflection; 'he was a considerate man the deacon; he kend we had a' our frailties, and he lo'ed his friends — Ye'll no hae forgotten him, Robin?' This question he put in a softened tone, conveying as much at least of the ludicrous as the pathetic.

'Forgotten him!' replied his kinsman, 'what suld ail me to forget him?—a wapping weaver he was, and wrought my first pair o' hose.—But come awa, kinsman,

> 'Come fill up my cup, come fill up my cann,
> Come saddle my horses, and call up my man;
> Come open your gates, and let me gae free,
> I daurna stay langer in bonny Dundee.'

'Whisht, sir!' said the magistrate, in an authoritative tone—'lilting and singing sae near the latter end o' the Sabbath! This house may hear ye sing anither tune yet—Aweel, we hae a' backslidings to answer for—Stanchells, open the door.'

The jailor obeyed, and we all sallied forth. Stanchells looked with some surprise at the two strangers, wondering, doubtless, how they came into these premises without his knowledge; but Mr. Jarvie's 'Friends o' mine, Stanchells — friends o' mine,' silenced all disposition to inquiries. We now descended into the lower vestibule, and hollowed more than once for Dougal, to which summons no answer was returned; when Campbell observed, with a sardonic smile, 'That if Dougal was the lad he kent him, he would scarce wait to get thanks for his ain share of the night's wark, but was in all probability on the full trot to the pass of Ballamaha——'

'And left us—and, abune a', me, mysell, locked up in the tolbooth a' night!' exclaimed the Bailie, in ire and perturbation. 'Ca' for fore-hammers, sledge-hammers, pinches, and coulters; send for Deacon Yettlin, the smith, and let him ken that Bailie Jarvie's shut up in the tolbooth by a Hieland blackguard, whom he'll hang up as high as Haman——'

'When ye catch him,' said Campbell, gravely; 'but stay, the door is surely not locked.'

Indeed, on examination, we found that the door was not only left open, but that Dougal in his retreat had, by carrying off the keys along with him, taken care that no one should exercise his office of porter in a hurry.

'He has glimmerings o' common sense now, that creature Dougal,' said Campbell; 'he kend an open door might hae served me at a pinch.'

We were by this time in the street.

'I tell you, Robin,' said the magistrate, 'in my puir mind, if ye live the life ye do, ye shuld hae ane o' your gillies door-keeper in every jail in Scotland, in case o' the warst.'

'Ane o' my kinsmen a bailie in ilka burgh will just do as weel, cousin Nicol—so, gude-night or gude-morning to ye; and forget not the Clachan of Aberfoil.'

And without waiting for an answer, he sprung to the other side of the street, and was lost in darkness. Immediately on his disappearance, we heard him give a low whistle of peculiar modulation; which was instantly replied to.

'Hear to the Hieland deevils,' said Mr. Jarvie; 'they think themselves on the skirts of Benlomond already, where they may gang whewing and whistling about without minding Sunday or Saturday.' Here he was interrupted by something which fell with a heavy clash on the street before us—'Gude guide us! what's this mair o't?—Mattie, haud up the lantern—Conscience! if it isna the keys—Weel, that's just as weel—they cost the burgh siller, and there might hae been some clavers about the loss o' them—O, an Bailie Grahame were to get word o' this night's job, it wad be a sair hair in my neck!'

As we were still but a few steps from the tolbooth door, we carried back these implements of office, and consigned them to the head jailor, who, in lieu of the usual mode of making good his post by turning the keys, was keeping sentry in the vestibule till the arrival of some assistant, whom he had summoned in order to replace the Celtic fugitive Dougal.

Having discharged this piece of duty to the burgh, and my road lying the same way with the honest magistrate's, I profited by the light of his lantern, and he by my arm, to find our way through the streets, which, whatever they may now be, were then dark, uneven, and ill-paved. Age is easily propitiated by attentions from the young. The Bailie expressed himself interested in me, and added, 'That since I was nane o' that play-acting and play-ganging generation, whom his saul hated, he wad be glad if I wad eat a reisted haddock, or a fresh herring, at breakfast wi' him the morn, and meet my friend, Mr. Owen, whom, by that time, he would place at liberty.'

'My dear sir,' said I, when I had accepted of the invitation with thanks, 'how could you possibly connect me with the stage?'

'I watna,' replied Mr. Jarvie; 'it was a bletherin' phrasin' chield they ca' Fairservice, that cam at e'en to get an order to send the crier through the toun for ye at skreigh o' day the morn. He tell't me whae ye were, and how ye were sent frae your father's house, because ye wadna be a dealer, and that ye mightna disgrace your family wi' ganging on the stage. Ane Hammorgaw, our precentor, brought him here, and said he was an auld acquaintance; but I sent them baith awa, wi' a flae in their lug for bringing me sic an errand on sic a night. But I see he's a fule-creature a'thegither, and clean mista'en about ye. I like ye, man,' he continued; 'I like a lad that will stand by his friends in trouble —I aye did it mysell, and sae did the deacon my father, rest and bless him! But ye suldna keep ower muckle company wi' Hielandmen and thae wild cattle. Can a man touch pitch and no be defiled?—aye mind that. Nae doubt, the best and wisest may err—Once, twice, and thrice have I backslidden, man, and dune three things this night —my father wadna hae believed his een if he could hae looked up and seen me do them.'

He was by this time arrived at the door of his

own dwelling. He paused, however, on the threshold, and went on in a solemn tone of deep contrition,—'Firstly, I hae thought my ain thoughts on the Sabbath—Secondly, I hae gien security for an Englishman—and, in the third and last place, well-a-day! I hae let an ill-doer escape from the place of imprisonment — But there's balm in Gilead, Mr. Osbaldistone—Mattie, I can let mysell in—see Mr. Osbaldistone to Luckie Flyter's, at the corner o' the wynd.—Mr. Osbaldistone'—in a whisper— 'ye'll offer nae incivility to Mattie — she's an honest man's daughter, and a near cousin o' the Laird o' Limmerfield's.'

CHAPTER XXIV

' Will it please your worship to accept of my poor service ? I beseech that I may feed upon your bread, though it be the brownest, and drink of your drink, though it be of the smallest ; for I will do your worship as much service for forty shillings as another man shall for three pounds.'

GREENE'S TU QUOQUE.

I REMEMBERED the honest Bailie's parting charge, but did not conceive there was any incivility in adding a kiss to the half-crown with which I remunerated Mattie's attendance; nor did her ' Fie for shame, sir,' express any very deadly resentment of the affront. Repeated knocking at Mrs. Flyter's gate awakened in due order, first, one or two stray dogs, who began to bark with all their might; next two or three night-capped heads, which were thrust out of the neighbouring windows to reprehend me for disturbing the solemnity of the Sunday night by that untimely noise. While I trembled lest the thunders of their wrath might dissolve in showers like that of Xantippe, Mrs. Flyter herself awoke, and began, in a tone of objurgation not unbecoming the philosophical spouse of Socrates, to scold one or two loiterers in her kitchen, for not hastening to the door to prevent a repetition of my noisy summons.

These worthies were, indeed, nearly concerned

in the fracas which their laziness occasioned, being no other than the faithful Mr. Fairservice, with his friend Mr. Hammorgaw, and another person, whom I afterwards found to be the town-crier, who were sitting over a cog of ale, as they called it, (at my expense, as my bill afterwards informed me,) in order to devise the terms and style of a proclamation to be made through the streets the next day, in order that 'the unfortunate young gentleman,' as they had the impudence to qualify me, might be restored to his friends without farther delay. It may be supposed that I did not suppress my displeasure at this impertinent interference with my affairs; but Andrew set up such ejaculations of transport at my arrival, as fairly drowned my expressions of resentment. His raptures, perchance, were partly political; and the tears of joy which he shed had certainly their source in that noble fountain of emotion, the tankard. However, the tumultuous glee which he felt, or pretended to feel at my return, saved Andrew the broken head which I had twice destined him; first, on account of the colloquy he had held with the precentor on my affairs; and, secondly, for the impertinent history he had thought proper to give of me to Mr. Jarvie. I however contented myself with slapping the door of my bedroom in his face as he followed me, praising Heaven for my safe return, and mixing his joy with admonitions to me to take care how I walked my own ways in future. I then went to bed, resolving my first business in the morning should be to discharge this troublesome, pedantic, self-conceited coxcomb,

who seemed so much disposed to constitute himself
rather a preceptor than a domestic.

Accordingly in the morning I resumed my purpose, and calling Andrew into my apartment,
requested to know his charge for guiding and
attending me as far as Glasgow. Mr. Fairservice
looked very blank at this demand, justly considering it as a presage to approaching dismission.

'Your honour,' he said, after some hesitation,
'wunna think—wunna think——'

'Speak out, you rascal, or I'll break your head,'
said I, as Andrew, between the double risk of losing
all by asking too much, or a part, by stating his
demand lower than what I might be willing to
pay, stood gasping in the agony of doubt and
calculation.

Out it came with a bolt, however, at my threat;
as the kind violence of a blow on the back sometimes delivers the windpipe from an intrusive
morsel. 'Aughteen pennies sterling per diem—
that is by the day — your honour wadna think
unconscionable.'

'It is double what is usual, and treble what you
merit, Andrew; but there's a guinea for you, and
get about your business.'

'The Lord forgie us! Is your honour mad?'
exclaimed Andrew.

'No; but I think you mean to make me so—
I give you a third above your demand, and you
stand staring and expostulating there as if I were
cheating you.—Take your money, and go about
your business.'

'Gude safe us!' continued Andrew, 'in what can I hae offended your honour?—Certainly a' flesh is but as flowers of the field; but if a bed of camomile hath value in medicine, of a surety the use of Andrew Fairservice to your honour is nothing less evident—it's as muckle as your life's worth to part wi' me.'

'Upon my honour,' replied I, 'it is difficult to say whether you are more knave or fool.—So you intend then to remain with me whether I like it or no?'

'Troth, I was e'en thinking sae,' replied Andrew, dogmatically; 'for if your honour disna ken when ye hae a gude servant, I ken when I hae a gude master, and the deil be in my feet gin I leave ye —and there's the brief and the lang o't,—besides I hae received nae regular warning to quit my place.'

'Your place, sir!' said I; 'why, you are no hired servant of mine, you are merely a guide, whose knowledge of the country I availed myself of on my road.'

'I am no just a common servant, I admit, sir,' remonstrated Mr. Fairservice; 'but your honour kens I quitted a gude place at an hour's notice, to comply with your honour's solicitations. A man might make honestly and wi' a clear conscience, twenty sterling pounds per annum, weel counted siller, o' the garden at Osbaldistone Hall, and I wasna likely to gie up a' that for a guinea, I trow— I reckoned on staying wi' your honour to the term's end at the least o't; and I account upon my wage, board-wage, fee and bountith, ay, to that length o't at the least.'

'Come, come, sir,' replied I, 'these impudent pretensions won't serve your turn; and if I hear any more of them, I shall convince you, that Squire Thorncliff is not the only one of my name that can use his fingers.'

While I spoke thus, the whole matter struck me as so ridiculous, that, though really angry, I had some difficulty to forbear laughing at the gravity with which Andrew supported a plea so utterly extravagant. The rascal, aware of the impression he had made on my muscles, was encouraged to perseverance. He judged it safer, however, to take his pretensions a peg lower, in case of overstraining at the same time both his plea and my patience.

'Admitting that my honour could part with a faithful servant, that had served me and mine by day and night for twenty years, in a strange place, and at a moment's warning, he was weel assured,' he said, 'it wasna in my heart, nor in no true gentleman's, to pit a puir lad like himsell, that had come forty or fifty, or say a hundred miles out o' his road purely to bear my honour company, and that had nae hauding but his penny-fee, to sic a hardship as this comes to.'

I think it was you, Will, who once told me, that, to be an obstinate man, I am in certain things the most gullable and malleable of mortals. The fact is, that it is only contradiction which makes me peremptory, and when I do not feel myself called on to give battle to any proposition, I am always willing to grant it, rather than give myself much trouble. I knew this fellow to be a greedy, tiresome, meddling coxcomb; still, however, I must have some one about me in the quality of guide and domestic, and I was so much used to Andrew's humour, that on some occasions it was rather amusing. In the state of indecision to which these reflections led me, I asked Fairservice if he knew the roads, towns, etc., in the north of Scotland, to which my father's concerns with the proprietors of Highland forests were likely to lead me. I believe if I had asked him the road to the terrestrial paradise, he would have at that moment undertaken to guide me to it; so that I had reason afterwards to think myself fortunate in finding that his actual knowledge did not fall very much short of that which he asserted himself to possess. I fixed the amount of his wages, and reserved to myself the privilege of dismissing him when I chose, on paying him a week in advance. I gave him finally a severe lecture on his conduct of the preceding day, and then dismissed him, rejoicing at heart, though somewhat crestfallen in countenance, to rehearse to his friend, the precentor, who was taking his morning draught in the kitchen, the mode in which he had ' cuitled up the daft young English squire.'

Agreeable to appointment, I went next to Bailie Nicol Jarvie's, where a comfortable morning's repast was arranged in the parlour, which served as an apartment of all hours, and almost all work, to that honest gentleman. The bustling and benevolent magistrate had been as good as his word. I

found my friend Owen at liberty, and, conscious of
the refreshments and purification of brush and basin,
was of course a very different person from Owen a
prisoner, squalid, heart-broken, and hopeless. Yet
the sense of pecuniary difficulties arising behind,
before, and around him, had depressed his spirit,
and the almost paternal embrace which the good
man gave me, was embittered by a sigh of the
deepest anxiety. And when he sate down, the
heaviness in his eye and manner, so different from
the quiet composed satisfaction which they usually
exhibited, indicated that he was employing his arith-
metic in mentally numbering up the days, the hours,
the minutes, which yet remained as an interval
between the dishonour of bills and the downfall of
the great commercial establishment of Osbaldistone
and Tresham. It was left to me, therefore, to do
honour to our landlord's hospitable cheer,—to his
tea, right from China, which he got in a present
from some eminent ship's-husband at Wapping,—
to his coffee, from a snug plantation of his own, as
he informed us with a wink, called Salt-Market
Grove, in the Island of Jamaica,—to his English
toast and ale, his Scotch dried salmon, his Lochfine
herrings, and even to the double damask tablecloth,
' wrought by no hand, as you may guess,' save that
of his deceased father the worthy Deacon Jarvie.

Having conciliated our good-humoured host by
those little attentions which are great to most men,
I endeavoured in my turn to gain from him some
information which might be useful for my guidance,
as well as for the satisfaction of my curiosity. We

had not hitherto made the least allusion to the transactions of the preceding night, a circumstance which
made my question sound somewhat abrupt, when,
without any previous introduction of the subject, I
took advantage of a pause when the history of the
tablecloth ended, and that of the napkins was about
to commence, to inquire, 'Pray, by the by, Mr.
Jarvie, who may this Mr. Robert Campbell be
whom we met with last night?'

The interrogatory seemed to strike the honest
magistrate, to use the vulgar phase, 'all of a heap,'
and instead of answering, he returned the question,
—'Whae's Mr. Robert Campbell?—ahem—ahay!
—Whae's Mr. Robert Campbell, quo' he?'

'Yes,' said I, 'I mean who, and what is he?'

'Why, he's—ahay!—he's—ahem!—Where did
ye meet with Mr. Robert Campbell, as ye ca'
him?'

'I met him by chance,' I replied, 'some months
ago, in the north of England.'

'Ou then, Mr. Osbaldistone,' said the Bailie
doggedly, 'ye'll ken as muckle about him as I do.'

'I should suppose not, Mr. Jarvie,' I replied;
'you are his relation it seems, and his friend.'

'There is some cousin-red between us, doubtless,'
said the Bailie reluctantly, 'but we hae seen little
o' ilk other since Rob gae up the cattle-line o' dealing, poor fallow! he was hardly guided by them
might hae used him better—and they haena made
their plack a bawbee o't neither. There's mony
ane this day wad rather they had never chased puir
Robin frae the Cross o' Glasgow—there's mony ane

wad rather see him again at the tail o' three hundred kyloes, than at the head o' thirty waur cattle.'

'All this explains nothing to me, Mr. Jarvie, of Mr. Campbell's rank, habits of life, and means of subsistence,' I replied.

'Rank?' said Mr. Jarvie; 'he's a Hieland gentleman, nae doubt—better rank need nane to be;— and for habit, I judge he wears the Hieland habit amang the hills, though he has breeks on when he comes to Glasgow;—and as for his subsistence, what needs we care about his subsistence, sae lang as he asks naething frae us, ye ken. But I hae nae time for clavering about him e'en now, because we maun look into your father's concerns wi' a' speed.'

So saying, he put on his spectacles, and sate down to examine Mr. Owen's states, which the other thought it most prudent to communicate to him without reserve. I knew enough of business to be aware that nothing could be more acute and sagacious than the views which Mr. Jarvie entertained of the matters submitted to his examination; and, to do him justice, it was marked by much fairness and even liberality. He scratched his ear indeed repeatedly, on observing the balance which stood at the debit of Osbaldistone and Tresham in account with himself personally.

'It may be a dead loss,' he observed; 'and, conscience! whate'er ane o' your Lombard-street goldsmiths may say to it, it's a snell ane in the Saut-Market o' Glasgow. It will be a heavy deficit —a staff out o' my bicker, I trow. But what then?

—I trust the house wunna coup the crans for a'
that's come and gane yet; and if it does, I'll
never bear sae base a mind as thae corbies in the
Gallowgate—an I am to lose by ye, I'se ne'er
deny I hae won by ye mony a fair pund sterling
—Sae, an it come to the warst, I'se e'en lay the
head o' the sow to the tail o' the grice.' *

I did not altogether understand the proverbial
arrangement with which Mr. Jarvie consoled himself, but I could easily see that he took a kind and
friendly interest in the arrangement of my father's
affairs, suggested several expedients, approved several
plans proposed by Owen, and, by his countenance
and counsel, greatly abated the gloom upon the
brow of that afflicted delegate of my father's
establishment.

As I was an idle spectator on this occasion, and,
perhaps, as I showed some inclination more than
once to return to the prohibited, and, apparently,
the puzzling subject of Mr. Campbell, Mr. Jarvie
dismissed me with little formality, with an advice
to 'gang up the gate to the college, where I wad
find some chields could speak Greek and Latin
weel,—at least they got plenty o' siller for doing
deil haet else, if they didna do that; and where I
might read a spell o' the worthy Mr. Zachary
Boyd's translation o' the Scriptures—better poetry
need nane to be, as he had been tell'd by them
that kend, or suld hae kend, about sic things.'
But he seasoned this dismission with a kind and

---

* Anglicé, the head of the sow to the tail of the pig.

hospitable invitation, 'to come back and take part o' his family-chack, at ane preceesely—there wad be a leg o' mutton, and, it might be, a tup's head, for they were in season'; but, above all, I was to return at 'ane o'clock preceesely—it was the hour he and the deacon his father aye dined at—they pat it aff for naething nor for naebody.'

CHAPTER XXV

So stands the Thracian herdsman with his spear
Full in the gap, and hopes the hunted bear;
And hears him in the rustling wood, and sees
His course at distance by the bending trees,
And thinks—Here comes my mortal enemy,
And either he must fall in fight, or I.
                    PALAMON AND ARCITE.

I TOOK the route towards the college, as recommended by Mr. Jarvie, less with the intention of seeking for any object of interest or amusement, than to arrange my own ideas, and meditate on my future conduct. I wandered from one quadrangle of old-fashioned buildings to another, and from thence to the College-yards, or walking ground, where, pleased with the solitude of the place, most of the students being engaged in their classes, I took several turns, pondering on the waywardness of my own destiny.

I could not doubt, from the circumstances attending my first meeting with this person Campbell, that he was engaged in some strangely desperate courses; and the reluctance with which Mr. Jarvie alluded to his person or pursuits, as well as all the scene of the preceding night, tended to confirm these suspicions. Yet to this man Diana Vernon had not, it would seem, hesitated to address herself in my behalf; and the conduct of the magistrate himself towards him showed an odd mixture of kindness, and even respect, with pity and censure. Something there must be uncommon in Campbell's situation and character; and what was still more extraordinary, it seemed that his fate was doomed to have influence over, and connexion with my own. I resolved to bring Mr. Jarvie to close quarters on the first proper opportunity, and learn as much as was possible on the subject of this mysterious person, in order that I might judge whether it was possible for me, without prejudice to my reputation, to hold that degree of farther correspondence with him, to which he seemed to invite.

While I was musing on these subjects, my attention was attracted by three persons who appeared at the upper end of the walk through which I was sauntering, seemingly engaged in very earnest conversation. That intuitive impression which announces to us the approach of whomsoever we love or hate with intense vehemence, long before a more indifferent eye can recognise their persons, flashed upon my mind the sure conviction that the midmost of these three men was Rashleigh Osbaldistone. To address him was my first impulse; my second was, to watch him until he was alone, or at least to reconnoitre his companions before confronting him. The party was still at such distance, and engaged in such deep discourse, that I had time to step unobserved to the other side of a small hedge, which imperfectly screened the alley in which I was walking.

It was at this period the fashion of the young and gay to wear, in their morning walks, a scarlet cloak, often laced and embroidered, above their other dress, and it was the trick of the time for gallants occasionally to dispose it so as to muffle a part of the face. The imitating this fashion, with the degree of shelter which I received from the hedge, enabled me to meet my cousin, unobserved by him or the others, except perhaps as a passing stranger. I was not a little startled at recognising in his companions that very Morris on whose account I had been summoned before Justice Inglewood, and Mr. MacVittie the merchant, from whose starched and severe aspect I had recoiled on the preceding day.

A more ominous conjunction to my own affairs, and those of my father, could scarce have been formed. I remembered Morris's false accusation against me, which he might be as easily induced to renew as he had been intimidated to withdraw; I recollected the inauspicious influence of Mac-Vittie over my father's affairs, testified by the imprisonment of Owen; and I now saw both these men combined with one, whose talents for mischief I deemed little inferior to those of the great author of all ill, and my abhorrence of whom almost amounted to dread.

When they had passed me for some paces, I turned and followed them unobserved. At the end of the walk they separated, Morris and MacVittie leaving the gardens, and Rashleigh returning alone through the walks. I was now determined to confront him, and demand reparation for the injuries he had done my father, though in what form redress was likely to be rendered remained to be known. This, however, I trusted to chance; and, flinging back the cloak in which I was muffled, I passed through a gap of the low hedge, and presented myself before Rashleigh, as, in a deep reverie, he paced down the avenue.

Rashleigh was no man to be surprised or thrown off his guard by sudden occurrences. Yet he did not find me thus close to him, wearing undoubtedly in my face the marks of that indignation which was glowing in my bosom, without visibly starting at an apparition so sudden and so menacing.

'You are well met, sir,' was my commencement; 'I was about to take a long and doubtful journey in quest of you.'

'You know little of him you sought then,' replied Rashleigh, with his usual undaunted composure. 'I am easily found by my friends — still more easily by my foes;—your manner compels me to ask in which class I must rank Mr. Francis Osbaldistone?'

'In that of your foes, sir,' I answered; 'in that of your mortal foes, unless you instantly do justice to your benefactor, my father, by accounting for his property.'

'And to whom, Mr. Osbaldistone,' answered Rashleigh, 'am I, a member of your father's commercial establishment, to be compelled to give any account of my proceedings in those concerns, which are in every respect identified with my own?— Surely not to a young gentleman whose exquisite taste for literature would render such discussions disgusting and unintelligible.'

'Your sneer, sir, is no answer; I will not part with you until I have full satisfaction concerning the fraud you meditate — you shall go with me before a magistrate.'

'Be it so,' said Rashleigh, and made a step or two as if to accompany me; then pausing, proceeded:— 'Were I inclined to do as you would have me, you should soon feel which of us had most reason to dread the presence of a magistrate. But I have no wish to accelerate your fate. Go, young man! amuse yourself in your world of poetical imaginations, and leave the business of life to those who understand and can conduct it.'

His intention, I believe, was to provoke me, and he succeeded. 'Mr. Osbaldistone,' I said, 'this tone of calm insolence shall not avail you. You ought to be aware that the name we both bear never submitted to insult, and shall not in my person be exposed to it.'

'You remind me,' said Rashleigh, with one of his blackest looks, 'that it was dishonoured in my person!—and you remind me also by whom! Do you think I have forgotten the evening at Osbaldistone Hall, when you cheaply and with impunity played the bully at my expense? For that insult —never to be washed out but by blood!—for the various times you have crossed my path, and always to my prejudice — for the persevering folly with which you seek to traverse schemes, the importance of which you neither know nor are capable of estimating,—for all these, sir, you owe me a long account, for which there shall come an early day of reckoning.'

'Let it come when it will,' I replied, 'I shall be willing and ready to meet it. Yet you seem to have forgotten the heaviest article—that I had the pleasure to aid Miss Vernon's good sense and virtuous feeling in extricating her from your infamous toils.'

I think his dark eyes flashed actual fire at this home-taunt, and yet his voice retained the same calm expressive tone with which he had hitherto conducted the conversation.

'I had other views with respect to you, young man,' was his answer; 'less hazardous for you, and more suitable to my present character and former education. But I see you will draw on yourself the personal chastisement your boyish insolence so well merits. Follow me to a more remote spot, where we are less likely to be interrupted.'

I followed him accordingly, keeping a strict eye on his motions, for I believed him capable of the very worst actions. We reached an open spot in a sort of wilderness, laid out in the Dutch taste, with clipped hedges, and one or two statues. I was on my guard, and it was well with me that I was so; for Rashleigh's sword was out and at my breast ere I could throw down my cloak, or get my weapon unsheathed, so that I only saved my life by springing a pace or two backwards. He had some advantage in the difference of our weapons; for his sword, as I recollect, was longer than mine, and had one of those bayonet or three-cornered blades which are now generally worn; whereas, mine was what we then called a Saxon blade—narrow, flat, and two-edged, and scarcely so manageable as that of my enemy. In other respects we were pretty equally matched; for what advantage I might possess in superior address and agility, was fully counter-balanced by Rashleigh's great strength and coolness. He fought, indeed, more like a fiend than a man—with concentrated spite and desire of blood, only allayed by that cool consideration which made his worst actions appear yet worse from the air of deliberate premeditation which seemed to accompany them. His obvious malignity of purpose never for a moment threw him off his guard, and he exhausted every feint and stratagem proper to the science of defence; while, at the same time, he meditated the most desperate catastrophe to our rencounter.

On my part, the combat was at first sustained with more moderation. My passions, though hasty, were not malevolent; and the walk of two or three minutes' space gave me time to reflect that Rashleigh was my father's nephew, the son of an uncle, who after his fashion had been kind to me, and that his falling by my hand could not but occasion much family distress. My first resolution, therefore, was to attempt to disarm my antagonist; a manœuvre in which, confiding in my superiority of skill and practice, I anticipated little difficulty. I found, however, I had met my match; and one or two foils which I received, and from the consequences of which I narrowly escaped, obliged me to observe more caution in my mode of fighting. By degrees I became exasperated at the rancour with which Rashleigh sought my life, and returned his passes with an inveteracy resembling in some degree his own; so that the combat had all the appearance of being destined to have a tragic issue. That issue had nearly taken place at my expense. My foot slipped in a full lounge which I made at my adversary, and I could not so far recover myself as completely to parry the thrust with which my pass was repaid. Yet it took but partial effect, running through my waistcoat, grazing my ribs, and passing through my coat behind. The hilt of Rashleigh's sword, so great was the vigour of his thrust, struck against my breast with such force as to give me great pain, and confirm me in the momentary belief that I was mortally wounded. Eager for revenge, I grappled with my enemy, seizing with my left hand the hilt of his sword, and shortening my own with the purpose of running him through the body. Our death-grapple was interrupted by a man who forcibly threw himself between us, and pushing us separate from each other, exclaimed, in a loud and commanding voice, 'What! the sons of those fathers who sucked the same breast shedding each other's bluid as it were strangers'!—By the hand of my father, I will cleave to the brisket the first man that mints another stroke!'

I looked up in astonishment. The speaker was no other than Campbell. He had a basket-hilted broadsword drawn in his hand, which he made to whistle around his head as he spoke, as if for the purpose of enforcing his mediation. Rashleigh and I stared in silence at this unexpected intruder, who proceeded to exhort us alternately: 'Do you, Maister Francis, opine that ye will re-establish your father's credit by cutting your kinsman's thrapple, or getting your ain sneckit instead thereof in the College-yards of Glasgow?—Or do you, Mr. Rashleigh, think men will trust their lives and fortunes wi' ane, that, when in point of trust and in point of confidence wi' a great political interest, gangs about brawling like a drunken gillie?—Nay, never look gash or grim at me, man—if ye 're angry, ye ken how to turn the buckle o' your belt behind you.'

'You presume on my present situation,' replied Rashleigh, 'or you would have hardly dared to interfere where my honour is concerned.'

'Hout, tout, tout!—Presume?—And what for should it be presuming?—Ye may be the richer man, Mr. Osbaldistone, as is maist likely; and ye may be the mair learned man, whilk I dispute not: but I reckon ye are neither a prettier man nor a better gentleman than mysell—and it will be news to me when I hear ye are as gude. And *dare* too? —Muckle daring there's about it—I trow here I stand, that hae slashed as het a haggis as ony o' the twa o' ye, and thought nae muckle o' my morning's wark when it was dune. If my foot were on the heather as it 's on the causeway, or this pickle gravel, that 's little better, I hae been waur mistrysted than if I were set to gie ye baith your ser'ing o't.'

Rashleigh had by this time recovered his temper

completely. ' My kinsman,' he said, ' will acknowledge he forced this quarrel on me. It was none of
my seeking. I am glad we are interrupted before
I chastised his forwardness more severely.'

' Are ye hurt, lad ? ' inquired Campbell of me,
with some appearance of interest.

' A very slight scratch,' I answered, ' which my
kind cousin would not long have boasted of had not
you come between us.'

' In troth, and that 's true, Maister Rashleigh,'
said Campbell; ' for the cauld iron and your best
bluid were like to hae become acquaint when I
mastered Mr. Frank's right hand. But never look
like a sow playing upon a trump for the luve o'
that, man—come and walk wi' me. I hae news
to tell ye, and ye 'll cool and come to yoursell, like
MacGibbon's crowdy, when he set it out at the
window-bole.'

' Pardon me, sir,' said I. ' Your intentions have
seemed friendly to me on more occasions than one ;
but I must not, and will not, quit sight of this
person, until he yields up to me those means of
doing justice to my father's engagements, of which
he has treacherously possessed himself.'

' Ye 're daft, man,' replied Campbell, ' it will serve
ye naething to follow us e'enow ; ye hae just enow
o' ae man, wad ye bring twa on your head, and
might bide quiet ? '

' Twenty,' I replied, ' if it be necessary.'

I laid my hand on Rashleigh's collar, who made
no resistance, but said, with a sort of scornful smile,
' You hear him, MacGregor ! he rushes on his fate

—will it be my fault if he falls into it?—The warrants are by this time ready, and all is prepared.'

The Scotchman was obviously embarrassed. He looked around, and before, and behind him, and then said: 'The ne'er a bit will I yield my consent to his being ill-guided, for standing up for the father that got him—and I gie God's malison and mine to a' sort o' magistrates, justices, bailies, sheriffs, sheriff-officers, constables, and sic-like black cattle, that hae been the plagues o' puir auld Scotland this hunder year;—it was a merry warld when every man held his ain gear wi' his ain grip, and when the country side wasna fashed wi' warrants and poindings and apprizings, and a' that cheatery craft. And ance mair I say it, my conscience winna see this puir thoughtless lad ill-guided, and especially wi' that sort o' trade. I wad rather ye fell till 't again, and fought it out like douce honest men.'

'Your conscience, MacGregor!' said Rashleigh; 'you forget how long you and I have known each other.'

'Yes, my conscience,' reiterated Campbell, or MacGregor, or whatever was his name; 'I hae such a thing about me, Maister Osbaldistone; and therein it may weel chance that I hae the better o' you. As to our knowledge of each other,—if ye ken what I am, ye ken what usage it was made me what I am; and, whatever you may think, I would not change states with the proudest of the oppressors that hae driven me to tak the heather-bush for a beild. What *you* are, Maister Rashleigh, and what excuse ye hae for being *what* you are, is between your ain heart and the lang day.—And now, Maister Francis, let go his collar; for he says truly, that ye are in mair danger from a magistrate than he is, and were your cause as straight as an arrow, he wad find a way to put you wrang—So let go his craig, as I was saying.'

He seconded his words with an effort so sudden and unexpected, that he freed Rashleigh from my hold, and securing me, notwithstanding my struggles, in his own Herculean gripe, he called out, 'Take the bent, Mr. Rashleigh. Make ae pair o' legs worth twa pair o' hands; ye hae dune that before now.'

'You may thank this gentleman, kinsman,' said Rashleigh, 'if I leave any part of my debt to you unpaid; and if I quit you now, it is only in the hope we shall soon meet again without the possibility of interruption.'

He took up his sword, wiped it, sheathed it, and was lost among the bushes.

The Scotchman, partly by force, partly by remonstrance, prevented my following him; indeed, I began to be of opinion my doing so would be to little purpose.

'As I live by bread,' said Campbell, when, after one or two struggles in which he used much forbearance towards me, he perceived me inclined to stand quiet, 'I never saw sae daft a callant! I wad hae gien the best man in the country the breadth o' his back gin he had gien me sic a kemping as ye hae dune. What wad ye do?—Wad ye follow the wolf to his den?—I tell ye, man, he has the auld trap set for ye—He has got the collector-creature Morris to bring up a' the auld story again, and ye maun look for nae help frae me here, as ye got at Justice Inglewood's—It isna good for my health to come in the gate o' the whigamore bailie bodies. Now gang your ways hame, like a gude bairn— jouk and let the jaw gae by—Keep out o' sight o' Rashleigh, and Morris, and that MacVittie animal —Mind the Clachan of Aberfoil, as I said before, and, by the word of a gentleman, I wunna see ye wranged. But keep a calm sough till we meet again—I maun gae and get Rashleigh out o' the town afore waur comes o't, for the neb o' him's never out o' mischief—Mind the Clachan of Aberfoil.'

He turned upon his heel, and left me to meditate on the singular events which had befallen me. My first care was to adjust my dress and re-assume my cloak, disposing it so as to conceal the blood which flowed down my right side. I had scarcely accomplished this, when, the classes of the College being dismissed, the gardens began to be filled with parties of the students. I therefore left them as soon as possible; and in my way towards Mr. Jarvie's, whose dinner hour was now approaching, I stopped at a small unpretending shop, the sign of which intimated the indweller to be Christopher Nielson, surgeon and apothecary. I requested of a little boy who was pounding some stuff in a mortar, that he would procure me an audience of this learned pharmacopolist. He opened the door of the back-shop, where I found a lively elderly man, who shook his head incredulously at some idle account I gave him of having been wounded accidentally by the button breaking off my antagonist's foil while I was engaged in a fencing match. When he had applied some lint and somewhat else he thought proper to the trifling wound I had received, he observed, ' There never was button on the foil that made this hurt. Ah! young blood! young blood!—But we surgeons are a secret generation—If it werena for hot blood and ill blood, what would become of the twa learned faculties ? '

With which moral reflection he dismissed me; and I experienced very little pain or inconvenience afterwards from the scratch I had received.

CHAPTER XXVI

An iron race the mountain-cliffs maintain,
Foes to the gentler genius of the plain.
*   *   *   *   *   *   *
Who, while their rocky ramparts round they see,
The rough abode of want and liberty,
As lawless force from confidence will grow,
Insult the plenty of the vales below.

GRAY.

' WHAT made ye sae late ? ' said Mr. Jarvie, as
I entered the dining-parlour of that honest gentleman ; ' it is chappit ane the best feck o' five
minutes by-gane. Mattie has been twice at the
door wi' the dinner, and weel for you it was a tup's
head, for that canna suffer by delay. A sheep's
head ower muckle boiled is rank poison, as my
worthy father used to say—he likit the lug o' ane
weel, honest man.'

I made a suitable apology for my breach of
punctuality, and was soon seated at table, where
Mr. Jarvie presided with great glee and hospitality,
compelling, however, Owen and myself to do rather
more justice to the Scottish dainties with which his
board was charged, than was quite agreeable to our
southern palates. I escaped pretty well, from having
those habits of society which enable one to elude
this species of well-meant persecution. But it was

118

ridiculous enough to see Owen, whose ideas of politeness were more rigorous and formal, and who was willing, in all acts of lawful compliance, to evince his respect for the friend of the firm, eating, with rueful complaisance, mouthful after mouthful of singed wool, and pronouncing it excellent, in a tone in which disgust almost overpowered civility.

When the cloth was removed, Mr. Jarvie compounded with his own hands a very small bowl of brandy-punch, the first which I had ever the fortune to see.

'The limes,' he assured us, 'were from his own little farm yonder-awa,' (indicating the West Indies with a knowing shrug of his shoulders,) 'and he had learned the art of composing the liquor from auld Captain Coffinkey, who acquired it,' he added in a whisper, 'as maist folk thought, amang the Buccaniers. But it's excellent liquor,' said he, helping us round; 'and good ware has aften come frae a wicked market. And as for Captain Coffinkey, he was a decent man when I kent him, only he used to swear awfully—But he's dead, and gaen to his account, and I trust he's accepted—I trust he's accepted.'

We found the liquor exceedingly palatable, and it led to a long conversation between Owen and our host on the opening which the Union had afforded to trade between Glasgow and the British colonies in America and the West Indies, and on the facilities which Glasgow possessed of making up *sortable* cargoes for that market. Mr. Jarvie answered some objection which Owen made on the difficulty of sorting a cargo for America, without buying from England, with vehemence and volubility.

'Na, na, sir, we stand on our ain bottom—we pickle in our ain pock-neuk—We hae our Stirling serges, Musselburgh stuffs, Aberdeen hose, Edinburgh shalloons, and the like, for our woollen or worsted goods — and we hae linens of a' kinds better and cheaper than you hae in Lunnon itsell— and we can buy your north o' England wares, as Manchester wares, Sheffield wares, and Newcastle earthen-ware, as cheap as you can at Liverpool— And we are making a fair spell at cottons and muslins—Na, na! let every herring hing by its ain head, and every sheep by its ain shank, and ye'll find, sir, us Glasgow folk no sae far ahint but what we may follow.—This is but poor entertainment for you, Mr. Osbaldistone,' (observing that I had been for some time silent,) 'but ye ken cadgers maun aye be speaking about cart-saddles.'

I apologized, alleging the painful circumstances of my own situation, and the singular adventures of the morning, as the causes of my abstraction and absence of mind. In this manner I gained what I sought — an opportunity of telling my story distinctly and without interruption. I only omitted mentioning the wound I had received, which I did not think worthy of notice. Mr. Jarvie listened with great attention and apparent interest, twinkling his little grey eyes, taking snuff, and only interrupting me by brief interjections. When I came to the account of the rencounter, at which Owen folded his hands and cast up his eyes to Heaven, the very image of woful surprise, Mr. Jarvie broke in upon the narration with 'Wrang now—clean wrang— to draw a sword on your kinsman is inhibited by the laws o' God and man; and to draw a sword on the streets of a royal burgh, is punishable by fine and imprisonment—and the College-yards are nae better privileged—they should be a place of peace and quietness, I trow. The College didna get gude £600 a-year out o' bishops' rents, (sorrow fa' the brood o' bishops and their rents too!) nor yet a lease o' the Archbishoprick o' Glasgow the sell o't, that they suld let folk tuilzie in their yards, or the wild callants bicker there wi' snaw-ba's as they whiles do, that when Mattie and I gae through, we are fain to make a baik and a bow, or rin the risk o' our harns being knocked out—it suld be looked to.*— But come awa wi' your tale—what fell neist?'

On my mentioning the appearance of Mr. Campbell, Jarvie arose in great surprise, and paced the room, exclaiming, 'Robin again!—Robert's mad —clean wud, and waur—Rob will be hanged and disgrace a' his kindred, and that will be seen and heard tell o'. My father the deacon wrought him his first hose—odd, I am thinking Deacon Three-plie, the rape-spinner, will be twisting his last cravat. Ay, ay, puir Robin is in a fair way o'

---

* The boys in Scotland used formerly to make a sort of Saturnalia in a snow-storm, by pelting passengers with snow-balls. But those exposed to that annoyance were excused from it on the easy penalty of a baik (curtsey) from a female, or a bow from a man. It was only the refractory who underwent the storm.

being hanged—But come awa—come awa—let's hear the lave o't.'

I told the whole story as pointedly as I could; but Mr. Jarvie still found something lacking to make it clear, until I went back, though with considerable reluctance, on the whole story of Morris, and of my meeting with Campbell at the house of Justice Inglewood. Mr. Jarvie inclined a serious ear to all this, and remained silent for some time after I had finished my narrative.

'Upon all these matters I am now to ask your advice, Mr. Jarvie, which, I have no doubt, will point out the best way to act for my father's advantage and my own honour.'

'Ye're right, young man—ye're right,' said the Bailie. 'Aye take the counsel of those who are aulder and wiser than yoursell, and binna like the godless Rehoboam, who took the advice o' a wheen beardless callants, neglecting the auld counsellors who had sate at the feet o' his father Solomon, and, as it was weel put by Mr. Meiklejohn, in his lecture on the chapter, were doubtless partakers of his sapience. But I maun hear naething about honour—we ken naething here but about credit. Honour is a homicide and a bloodspiller, that gangs about making frays in the street; but Credit is a decent honest man, that sits at hame and makes the pat play.'

'Assuredly, Mr. Jarvie,' said our friend Owen, 'credit is the sum total; and if we can but save that, at whatever discount——'

'Ye are right, Mr. Owen—ye are right; ye speak

weel and wisely; and I trust bowls will row right, though they are a wee ajee e'enow. But touching Robin, I am of opinion he will befriend this young man if it is in his power. He has a gude heart, puir Robin; and though I lost a matter o' twa hunder punds wi' his former engagements, and haena muckle expectation ever to see back my thousand pund Scots that he promises me e'enow, yet I will never say but what Robin means fair by a' men.'

'I am then to consider him,' I replied, 'as an honest man?'

'Umph!' replied Jarvie, with a precautionary sort of cough,—' Ay, he has a kind o' Hieland honesty—he's honest after a sort, as they say. My father the deacon used aye to laugh when he tauld me how that by-word came up. Ane Captain Costlett was cracking crouse about his loyalty to King Charles, and Clerk Pettigrew (ye'll hae heard mony a tale about him) asked him after what manner he served the king, when he was fighting again him at Wor'ster in Cromwell's army; and Captain Costlett was a ready body, and said that he served him *after a sort*. My honest father used to laugh weel at that sport—and sae the by-word came up.'

'But do you think,' I said, 'that this man will be able to serve me after a sort, or should I trust myself to this place of rendezvous which he has given me?'

'Frankly and fairly, it's worth trying. Ye see yoursell there's some risk in your staying here. This bit body Morris has gotten a custom-house place doun at Greenock—that's a port on the Firth doun by here; and tho' a' the warld kens him to be but a twa-leggit creature, wi' a goose's head and a hen's heart, that goes about on the quay plaguing folk about permits, and cockits, and dockits, and a' that vexatious trade, yet if he lodge an information —ou, nae doubt a man in magisterial duty maun attend to it, and ye might come to be clapped up between four wa's, whilk wad be ill-convenient to your father's affairs.'

'True,' I observed; 'yet what service am I likely to render him by leaving Glasgow, which, it is probable, will be the principal scene of Rashleigh's machinations, and committing myself to the doubtful faith of a man of whom I know little but that he fears justice, and has doubtless good reasons for doing so; and that for some secret, and probably dangerous purpose, he is in close league and alliance with the very person who is like to be the author of our ruin?'

'Ah! but ye judge Rob hardly,' said the Bailie, —'ye judge him hardly, puir chield; and the truth is, that ye ken naething about our hill country, or Hielands, as we ca' them. They are clean anither set frae the like o' huz; there's nae bailie-courts amang them—nae magistrates that dinna bear the sword in vain, like the worthy deacon that's awa —and, I may say't, like mysell and other present magistrates in this city—But it's just the laird's command, and the loon maun loup; and the never another law hae they but the length o' their dirks — the broadsword's pursuer, or plaintiff, as you Englishers ca' it, and the target is defender; the

stoutest head bears langest out — and there's a
Hieland plea for ye.'

Owen groaned deeply; and I allow that the
description did not greatly increase my desire to
trust myself in a country so lawless as he described
these Scottish mountains.

'Now, sir,' said Jarvie, 'we speak little o' thae
things, because they are familiar to oursells; and
where's the use o' vilifying ane's country, and bringing a discredit on ane's kin, before southrons and
strangers? It's an ill bird that files its ain nest.'

'Well, sir, but as it is no impertinent curiosity
of mine, but real necessity, that obliges me to make
these inquiries, I hope you will not be offended at
my pressing for a little farther information. I have
to deal, on my father's account, with several gentlemen of these wild countries, and I must trust your
good sense and experience for the requisite lights
upon the subject.'

This little morsel of flattery was not thrown out
in vain.

'Experience!' said the Bailie, 'I hae had experience, nae doubt, and I hae made some calculations
—Ay, and to speak quietly among oursells, I hae
made some perquisitions through Andrew Wylie,
my auld clerk; he's wi' MacVittie and Co. now
—but he whiles drinks a gill on the Saturday after-
noon wi' his auld master. And since ye say ye are
willing to be guided by the Glasgow weaver-body's
advice, I am no the man that will refuse it to the
son of an auld correspondent, and my father the
deacon was nane sic afore me. I have whiles

thought o' letting my lights burn before the Duke of Argyle, or his brother Lord Ilay, (for wherefore should they be hidden under a bushel?) but the like o' thae grit men wadna mind the like o' me, a puir wabster-body—they think mair o' wha says a thing than o' what the thing is that's said. The mair's the pity—mair's the pity. Not that I wad speak ony ill of this MacCallum More—" Curse not the rich in your bed-chamber," saith the son of Sirach, for a bird of the air shall carry the clatter, and pint-stoups hae lang lugs.'

I interrupted these prolegomena, in which Mr. Jarvie was apt to be somewhat diffuse, by praying him to rely upon Mr. Owen and myself as perfectly secret and safe confidents.

' It's no for that,' he replied, ' for I fear nae man —what for suld I ?—I speak nae treason—Only thae Hielandmen hae lang grips, and I whiles gang a wee bit up the glens to see some auld kinsfolks, and I wadna willingly be in bad blude wi' ony o' their clans. Howsumever, to proceed—Ye maun understand I found my remarks on figures, whilk, as Mr. Owen here weel kens, is the only true demonstrable root of human knowledge.'

Owen readily assented to a proposition so much in his own way, and our orator proceeded.

' These Hielands of ours, as we ca' them, gentlemen, are but a wild kind of warld by themsells, full of heights and howes, woods, caverns, lochs, rivers, and mountains, that it wad tire the very deevil's wings to flee to the tap o' them. And in this country, and in the isles, whilk are little better, or, to speak the truth, rather waur than the mainland, there are about twa hunder and thirty parochines, including the Orkneys, where, whether they speak Gaelic or no, I wotna, but they are an uncivilized people.—Now, sirs, I sall haud ilk parochine at the moderate estimate of eight hunder examinable persons, deducting children under nine years of age, and then adding one-fifth to stand for bairns of nine years auld, and under, the whole population will reach to the sum of—let us add one-fifth to 800 to be the multiplier, and 230 being the multiplicand——'

'The product,' said Mr. Owen, who entered delightedly into these statistics of Mr. Jarvie, 'will be 230,000.'

'Right, sir — perfectly right; and the military array of this Hieland country, were a' the menfolk between aughteen and fifty-six brought out that could bear arms, couldna come weel short of fifty-seven thousand five hundred men. Now, sir, it's a sad and awfu' truth, that there is neither wark, nor the very fashion nor appearance of wark, for the tae half of thae puir creatures; that is to say, that the agriculture, the pasturage, the fisheries, and every species of honest industry about the country, cannot employ the one moiety of the population, let them work as lazily as they like, and they do work as if a pleugh or a spade burnt their fingers. Aweel, sir, this moiety of unemployed bodies, amounting to——'

'To one hundred and fifteen thousand souls,' said Owen, 'being the half of the above product.'

'Ye hae't, Maister Owen—ye hae't—whereof there may be twenty-eight thousand seven hundred able-bodied gillies fit to bear arms, and that do bear arms, and will touch or look at nae honest means of livelihood even if they could get it—which, lack-a-day, they cannot.'

'But is it possible,' said I, 'Mr. Jarvie, that this can be a just picture of so large a portion of the island of Britain?'

'Sir, I'll make it as plain as Peter Pasley's pike-staff— I will allow that ilk parochine, on an average, employs fifty pleughs, whilk is a great proportion in sic miserable soil as thae creatures hae to labour, and that there may be pasture eneugh for pleugh-horses, and owsen, and forty or fifty cows; now, to take care o' the pleughs and cattle, we'se allow seventy-five families of six lives in ilk family, and we'se add fifty mair to make even numbers, and ye hae five hundred souls, the tae half o' the population employed and maintained in a sort o' fashion, wi' some chance of sour-milk and crowdie; but I wad be glad to ken what the other five hundred are to do?'

'In the name of God!' said I, 'what *do* they do, Mr. Jarvie? It makes me shudder to think of their situation.'

'Sir,' replied the Bailie, 'ye wad maybe shudder mair if ye were living near-hand them. For, admitting that the tae half of them may make some little thing for themsells honestly in the Lowlands by shearing in harst, droving, hay-making, and the like; ye hae still mony hundreds and thousands o' lang-legged Hieland gillies that will neither work nor want, and maun gang thigging and sorning* about on their acquaintance, or live by doing the laird's bidding, be't right or be't wrang. And mair especially, mony hundreds o' them come down to the borders of the low country, where there's gear to grip, and live by stealing, reiving, lifting cows, and the like depredations! A thing deplorable in ony Christian country—the mair especially, that they take pride in it, and reckon driving a spreagh (whilk is, in plain Scotch, stealing a herd of nowte) a gallant, manly action, and mair befitting of pretty† men (as sic reivers will ca' themsells) than to win a day's wage by ony honest thrift. And the lairds are as bad as the loons; for if they dinna bid them gae reive and harry, the deil a bit they forbid them; and they shelter them, or let them shelter themsells, in their woods, and mountains, and strongholds, whenever the thing's dune. And every ane o' them will maintain as mony o' his ain name, or his clan, as we say, as he can rap and rend means for; or, whilk's the same thing, as mony as can in ony fashion, fair or foul, mainteen themsells—and there they are wi' gun and pistol, dirk and dourlach, ready to disturb the peace o' the country whenever the laird likes; and that's the

---

* *Thigging* and *sorning* was a kind of genteel begging, or rather something between begging and robbing, by which the needy in Scotland used to extort cattle, or the means of subsistence, from those who had any to give.

† The word *pretty* is, or was, used in Scotch, in the sense of the German *prachtig*, and meant a gallant, alert fellow, prompt and ready at his weapons.

grievance of the Hielands, whilk are, and hae been for this thousand years by-past, a bike o' the maist lawless unchristian limmers that ever disturbed a douce, quiet, Godfearing neighbourhood, like this o' ours in the west here.'

'And this kinsman of yours, and friend of mine, is he one of those great proprietors who maintain the household troops you speak of?' I inquired.

'Na, na,' said Bailie Jarvie; 'he's nane o' your great grandees o' chiefs, as they ca' them, neither. Though he is weel born, and lineally descended frae auld Glenstrae—I ken his lineage—indeed he is a near kinsman, and, as I said, of gude gentle Hieland blude, though ye may think weel that I care little about that nonsense—it's a' moonshine in water—waste threads and thrums, as we say— but I could show ye letters frae his father, that was the third aff Glenstrae, to my father Deacon Jarvie, (peace be wi' his memory!) beginning, Dear Deacon, and ending, your loving kinsman to command,—they are amaist a' about borrowed siller, sae the gude deacon, that's dead and gane, keepit them as documents and evidents—He was a carefu' man.'

'But if he is not,' I resumed, 'one of their chiefs or patriarchal leaders, whom I have heard my father talk of, this kinsman of yours has, at least, much to say in the Highlands, I presume?'

'Ye may say that—nae name better kend between the Lennox and Breadalbane. Robin was ance a weel-doing, pains-taking drover, as ye wad see amang ten thousand — It was a pleasure to see him in his belted plaid and brogues, wi' his target at his back, and claymore and dirk at his belt, following a hundred Highland stots, and a dozen o' the gillies, as rough and ragged as the beasts they drave. And he was baith civil and just in his dealings, and if he thought his chapman had made a hard bargain, he wad gie him a luck-penny to the mends. I hae kend him gie back five shillings out o' the pund sterling.'

'Twenty-five per cent,' said Owen — 'a heavy discount.'

'He wad gie it though, sir, as I tell ye; mair especially if he thought the buyer was a puir man, and couldna stand by a loss. But the times cam hard, and Rob was venturesome. It wasna my faut — it wasna my faut; he canna wyte me. I aye tauld him o't—And the creditors, mair especially some grit neighbours o' his, grippit to his living and land; and they say his wife was turned out o' the house to the hill-side, and sair misguided to the boot. Shamefu'! shamefu'!—I am a peacefu' man and a magistrate, but if ony ane had guided sae muckle as my servant quean, Mattie, as it's like they guided Rob's wife, I think it suld hae set the shabble* that my father the deacon had at Bothwell Brig a-walking again. Weel, Rob cam hame, and fand desolation, God pity us! where he left plenty; he looked east, west, south, north, and saw neither hauld nor hope—neither beild nor shelter; sae he e'en pu'd the bonnet ower his brow,

---

* Cutlass.

belted the broadsword to his side, took to the brae-side, and became a broken-man.'*

The voice of the good citizen was broken by his contending feelings. He obviously, while he professed to contemn the pedigree of his Highland kinsman, attached a secret feeling of consequence to the connexion, and he spoke of his friend in his prosperity with an overflow of affection, which deepened his sympathy for his misfortunes, and his regret for their consequences.

'Thus tempted, and urged by despair,' said I, seeing Mr. Jarvie did not proceed in his narrative, 'I suppose your kinsman became one of those depredators you have described to us?'

'No sae bad as that,' said the Glaswegian,— 'no a'thegither and outright sae bad as that; but he became a levier of black-mail, wider and farther than ever it was raised in our day, a' through the Lennox and Menteith, and up to the gates o' Stirling Castle.'

'Black-mail?—I do not understand the phrase,' I remarked.

'Ou, ye see, Rob soon gathered an unco band o' blue-bonnets at his back, for he comes o' a rough name when he's kent by his ain, and a name that's held its ain for mony a lang year, baith again king and parliament, and kirk too, for aught I ken—an auld and honourable name, for as sair as it has been worried and hadden down and oppressed. My mother was a MacGregor—I carena wha kens it—

---

* An outlaw.

And the Rob had soon a gallant band; and as it grieved him (he said) to see sic *hership*, and waste, and depredation to the south o' the Hieland line, why, if ony heritor or farmer wad pay him four punds Scots out of each hundred punds of valued rent, whilk was doubtless a moderate consideration, Rob engaged to keep them scaithless—let them send to him if they lost sae muckle as a single cloot by thieving, and Rob engaged to get them again, or pay the value—and he aye keepit his word —I canna deny but he keepit his word—a' men allow Rob keeps his word.'

'This is a very singular contract of assurance,' said Mr. Owen.

'It's clean again our statute law, that must be owned,' said Jarvie, 'clean again law; the levying and the paying black-mail are baith punishable : but if the law canna protect my barn and byre, whatfor suld I no engage wi' a Hieland gentleman that can ?—answer me that.'

'But,' said I, 'Mr. Jarvie, is this contract of black-mail, as you call it, completely voluntary on the part of the landlord or farmer who pays the insurance ? or what usually happens, in case any one refuses payment of this tribute ?'

'Aha, lad!' said the Bailie, laughing, and putting his finger to his nose, 'ye think ye hae me there. Troth, I wad advise ony friends o' mine to gree wi' Rob; for, watch as they like, and do what they like, they are sair apt to be harried* when the lang

---

* Plundered.

nights come on. Some o' the Grahame and Cohoon gentry stood out; but what then?—they lost their haill stock the first winter; sae maist folks now think it best to come into Rob's terms. He's easy wi' a' body that will be easy wi' him; but if ye thraw him, ye had better thraw the deevil.'

'And by his exploits in these vocations,' I continued, 'I suppose he has rendered himself amenable to the laws of the country?'

'Amenable?—ye may say that; his craig wad ken the weight o' his hurdies if they could get haud o' Rob. But he has gude friends amang the grit folks; and I could tell ye o' ae grit family that keeps him up as far as they decently can, to be a thorn in the side of another. And then he's sic an auld-farran lang-headed chield as never took up the trade o' cateran in our time; mony a daft reik he has played—mair than wad fill a book, and a queer ane it wad be—as gude as Robin Hood, or William Wallace—a' fu' o' venturesome deeds and escapes, sic as folk tell ower at a winter-ingle in the daft days. It's a queer thing o' me, gentlemen, that am a man o' peace mysell, and a peacefu' man's son, for the deacon my father quarrelled wi' nane out o' the town-council—it's a queer thing, I say, but I think the Hieland blude o' me warms at thae daft tales, and whiles I like better to hear them than a word o' profit, gude forgie me!—But they are vanities—sinfu' vanities—and, moreover, again the statute law—again the statute and gospel law.'

I now followed up my investigation, by inquiring what means of influence this Mr. Robert Campbell could possibly possess over my affairs, or those of my father.

'Why, ye are to understand,' said Mr. Jarvie in a very subdued tone—' I speak amang friends, and under the rose—Ye are to understand, that the Hielands hae been keepit quiet since the year aughty-nine — that was Killiecrankie year. But how hae they been keepit quiet, think ye? By siller, Mr. Owen—by siller, Mr. Osbaldistone. King William caused Breadalbane distribute twenty thousand gude punds sterling amang them, and it's said the auld Hieland Earl keepit a lang lug o't in his ain sporran. And then Queen Anne, that's dead, gae the chiefs bits o' pensions, sae they had wherewith to support their gillies and caterans that work nae wark, as I said afore; and they lay by quiet eneugh, saving some spreagherie on the Lowlands, whilk is their use and wont, and some cutting o' thrapples amang themsells, that nae civilized body kens or cares ony thing anent.— Weel, but there's a new warld come up wi' this King George, (I say, God bless him, for ane,)— there's neither like to be siller nor pensions gaun amang them; they haena the means o' mainteening the clans that eat them up, as ye may guess frae what I said before; their credit's gane in the Lowlands; and a man that can whistle ye up a thousand or feifteen hundred linking lads to do his will, wad hardly get fifty punds on his band at the Cross o' Glasgow—This canna stand lang—there will be an outbreak for the Stewarts—there will be an outbreak—they will come down on the Low Country

like a flood, as they did in the waefu' wars o'
Montrose, and that will be seen and heard tell o'
ere a twalmonth gangs round.'

'Yet still,' I said, 'I do not see how this concerns
Mr. Campbell, much less my father's affairs.'

'Rob can levy five hundred men, sir, and therefore war suld concern him as muckle as maist folk,'
replied the Bailie; 'for it is a faculty that is far less
profitable in time o' peace. Then, to tell ye the
truth, I doubt he has been the prime agent between
some o' our Hieland chiefs and the gentlemen in
the north o' England. We a' heard o' the public
money that was taen frae the chield Morris somewhere about the fit o' Cheviot by Rob and ane o'
the Osbaldistone lads; and, to tell ye the truth,
word gaed that it was yoursell, Mr. Francis, and
sorry was I that your father's son suld hae taen to
sic practices—Na, ye needna say a word about it
—I see weel I was mistaen; but I wad believe ony
thing o' a stage-player, whilk I concluded ye to be.
But now, I doubtna, it has been Rashleigh himsell,
or some other o' your cousins—they are a' tarr'd
wi' the same stick—rank jacobites and papists, and
wad think the government siller and government
papers lawfu' prize. And the creature Morris is
sic a cowardly caitiff, that to this hour he daurna
say that it was Rob took the portmanteau aff him;
and troth he's right, for your custom-house and
excise cattle are ill liket on a' sides, and Rob might
get a back-handed lick at him, before the Board,
as they ca't, could help him.'

'I have long suspected this, Mr. Jarvie,' said I,

' and perfectly agree with you ; but as to my father's affairs——'

' Suspected it ? — it 's certain — it 's certain — I ken them that saw some of the papers that were taen aff Morris—it 's needless to say where. But to your father's affairs—Ye maun think that in thae twenty years by-gane, some o' the Hieland lairds and chiefs hae come to some sma' sense o' their ain interest—your father and others hae bought the woods of Glen-Disseries, Glen Kissoch, Tober-na-Kippoch, and mony mair besides, and your father's house has granted large bills in payment,—and as the credit o' Osbaldistone and Tresham was gude —for I 'll say before Mr. Owen's face as I wad behind his back, that, bating misfortunes o' the Lord's sending, nae men could be mair honourable in business—the Hieland gentlemen, holders o' thae bills, hae found credit in Glasgow and Edinburgh —(I might amaist say in Glasgow wholly, for it 's little the pridefu' Edinburgh folk do in real business)—for all, or the greater part of the contents o' thae bills.—So that—Aha ! d'ye see me now ? '

I confessed I could not quite follow his drift.

' Why,' said he, ' if these bills are not paid, the Glasgow merchant comes on the Hieland lairds, whae hae deil a boddle o' siller, and will like ill to spew up what is item a' spent—They will turn desperate—five hundred will rise that might hae sitten at hame — the deil will gae ower Jock Wabster — and the stopping of your father's house will hasten the outbreak that 's been sae lang biding us.'

'You think, then,' said I, surprised at this singular view of the case, 'that Rashleigh Osbaldistone has done this injury to my father, merely to accelerate a rising in the Highlands, by distressing the gentlemen to whom these bills were originally granted?'

'Doubtless — doubtless—it has been one main reason, Mr. Osbaldistone. I doubtna but what the ready money he carried off wi' him might be another. But that makes comparatively but a sma' part o' your father's loss, though it might make the maist part o' Rashleigh's direct gain. The assetts he carried off are of nae mair use to him than if he were to light his pipe wi' them. He tried if MacVittie and Co. wad gie him siller on them— that I ken by Andro Wylie—but they were ower auld cats to draw that strae afore them—they keepit aff and gae fair words. Rashleigh Osbaldistone is better kend than trusted in Glasgow, for he was here about some jacobitical papistical troking in seventeen hundred and seven, and left debt ahint him. Na, na, he canna pit aff the paper here; folk will misdoubt him how he came by it. Na, na, he 'll hae the stuff safe at some o' their haulds in the Hielands, and I daur say my cousin Rob could get at it gin he liked.'

'But would he be disposed to serve us in this pinch, Mr. Jarvie?' said I. 'You have described him as an agent of the Jacobite party, and deeply connected in their intrigues; will he be disposed for my sake, or, if you please, for the sake of justice, to make an act of restitution, which, supposing it in his power, would, according to your view of the case, materially interfere with their plans?'

'I canna preceesely speak to that—the grandees among them are doubtfu' o' Rob, and he's doubtfu' o' them—and he's been weel friended wi' the Argyle family, wha stand for the present model of government.—If he was freed o' his hornings and captions, he wad rather be on Argyle's side than he wad be on Breadalbane's, for there's auld ill-will between the Breadalbane family and his kin and name. The truth is, that Rob is for his ain hand, as Henry Wynd feught*—he'll take the side that suits him best; if the deil was laird, Rob wad be for being tenant, and ye canna blame him, puir fallow, considering his circumstances. But there's ae thing sair again ye—Rob has a grey mear in his stable at hame.'

'A grey mare?' said I. 'What is that to the purpose?'

'The wife, man—the wife,—an awfu' wife she is. She downa bide the sight o' a kindly Scot, if he come frae the Lowlands, far less of an Inglisher, and she'll be keen for a' that can set up King James, and ding down King George.'

---

* Two great clans fought out a quarrel with thirty men of a side, in presence of the king, on the North Inch of Perth, on or about the year 1392; a man was amissing on one side, whose room was filled by a little bandy-legged citizen of Perth. This substitute, Henry Wynd—or, as the Highlanders called him, *Gow Chrom*, that is, the bandy-legged smith —fought well, and contributed greatly to the fate of the battle, without knowing which side he fought on—so, to fight for your own hand, like Henry Wynd, passed into a proverb.

'It is very singular,' I replied, 'that the mercantile transactions of London citizens should become involved with revolutions and rebellions.'

'Not at a', man—not at a',' returned Mr. Jarvie, 'that's a' your silly prejudications. I read whiles in the lang dark nights, and I hae read in Baker's Chronicle that the merchants o' London could gar the Bank of Genoa break their promise to advance a mighty sum to the King of Spain, whereby the sailing of the Grand Spanish Armada was put aff for a haill year—What think you of that, sir?'

'That the merchants did their country golden service, which ought to be honourably remembered in our histories.'

'I think sae too; and they wad do weel, and deserve weel baith o' the state and o' humanity, that wad save three or four honest Hieland gentlemen frae louping heads ower heels into destruction, wi' a' their puir sackless* followers, just because they canna pay back the siller they had reason to count upon as their ain—and save your father's credit—and my ain gude siller that Osbaldistone and Tresham awes me into the bargain—I say if ane could manage a' this, I think it suld be done and said unto him, even if he were a puir ca'-the-shuttle body, as unto one whom the king delighteth to honour.'

'I cannot pretend to estimate the extent of public gratitude,' I replied; 'but our own thankfulness,

---

* Sackless, that is, innocent.

Mr. Jarvie, would be commensurate with the extent of the obligation.'

' Which,' added Mr. Owen, ' we would endeavour to balance with a *per contra*, the instant our Mr. Osbaldistone returns from Holland.'

' I doubtna—I doubtna—he is a very worthy gentleman, and a sponsible, and wi' some o' my lights might do muckle business in Scotland—Weel, sir, if these assetts could be redeemed out o' the hands o' the Philistines, they are gude paper—they are the right stuff when they are in the right hands, and that's yours, Mr. Owen.—And I 'se find ye three men in Glasgow, for as little as ye may think o' us, Mr. Owen, — that's Sandie Steenson in the Trade's-Land, and John Pirie in Candleriggs, and another, that sall be nameless at this present, sall advance what soums are sufficient to secure the credit of your house, and seek nae better security.'

Owen's eyes sparkled at this prospect of extrication; but his countenance instantly fell on recollecting how improbable it was that the recovery of the assetts, as he technically called them, should be successfully achieved.

' Dinna despair, sir — dinna despair,' said Mr. Jarvie; ' I hae taen sae muckle concern wi' your affairs already, that it maun een be ower shoon ower boots wi' me now. I am just like my father the deacon, (praise be wi' him!) I canna meddle wi' a friend's business, but I aye end wi' making it my ain—Sae, I 'll een pit on my boots the morn, and be jogging ower Drymen-Muir wi' Mr. Frank here;

and if I canna mak Rob hear reason, and his wife too, I dinna ken wha can—I hae been a kind freend to them afore now, to say naething o' ower-looking him last night, when naming his name wad hae cost him his life—I 'll be hearing o' this in the council maybe frae Bailie Grahame, and MacVittie, and some o' them. They hae coost up my kindred to Rob to me already—set up their nashgabs! I tauld them I wad vindicate nae man's faults; but set apart what he had done again the law o' the country, and the hership o' the Lennox, and the misfortune o' some folk losing life by him, he was an honester man than stude on ony o' their shanks —And whatfor suld I mind their clavers?—If Rob is an outlaw, to himsell be it said—there is nae laws now about reset of intercommuned persons, as there was in the ill times o' the last Stewarts—I trow I hae a Scotch tongue in my head—if they speak, I 'se answer.'

It was with great pleasure that I saw the Bailie gradually surmount the barriers of caution, under the united influence of public spirit and good-natured interest in our affairs, together with his natural wish to avoid loss and acquire gain, and not a little harmless vanity. Through the combined operation of these motives he at length arrived at the doughty resolution of taking the field in person, to aid in the recovery of my father's property. His whole information led me to believe, that if the papers were in possession of this Highland adventurer, it might be possible to induce him to surrender what he could not keep with any prospect of personal advantage; and I was conscious that the presence of his kinsman was likely to have considerable weight with him. I therefore cheerfully acquiesced in Mr. Jarvie's proposal, that we should set out early next morning.

That honest gentleman was indeed as vivacious and alert in preparing to carry his purpose into execution, as he had been slow and cautious in forming it. He roared to Mattie to 'air his trot-cosey, to have his jack-boots greased and set before the kitchen-fire all night, and to see that his beast be corned, and a' his riding gear in order.' Having agreed to meet him at five o'clock next morning, and having settled that Owen, whose presence could be of no use to us upon this expedition, should await our return at Glasgow, we took a kind farewell of this unexpectedly zealous friend. I installed Owen in an apartment in my lodgings, contiguous to my own, and, giving orders to Andrew Fairservice to attend me next morning at the hour appointed, I retired to rest with better hopes than it had lately been my fortune to entertain.

CHAPTER XXVII

Far as the eye could reach no tree was seen,
Earth, clad in russet, scorn'd the lively green;
No birds, except as birds of passage, flew;
No bee was heard to hum, no dove to coo;
No streams, as amber smooth—as amber clear,
Were seen to glide, or heard to warble here.
PROPHECY OF FAMINE.

It was in the bracing atmosphere of a harvest morning, that I met by appointment Fairservice, with the horses, at the door of Mr. Jarvie's house, which was but little space distant from Mrs. Flyter's hotel. The first matter which caught my attention was, that whatever were the deficiencies of the pony which Mr. Fairservice's legal adviser, Clerk Touthope, generously bestowed upon him in exchange for Thorncliff's mare, he had contrived to part with it, and procure in its stead an animal with so curious and complete a lameness, that it seemed only to make use of three legs for the purpose of progression, while the fourth appeared as if meant to be flourished in the air by way of accompaniment. 'What do you mean by bringing such a creature as that here, sir? and where is the pony you rode to Glasgow upon?' were my very natural and impatient inquiries.

'I sell't it, sir. It was a slink beast, and wad

144

hae eaten its head aff, standing at Luckie Flyter's at livery. And I hae bought this on your honour's account. It's a grand bargain—cost but a pund sterling the foot — that's four a'thegither. The stringhalt will gae aff when it's gaen a mile ; it's a weel-kend ganger ; they ca' it Souple Tam.'

' On my soul, sir !' said I, ' you will never rest till my supple-jack and your shoulders become acquainted. If you do not go instantly and procure the other brute, you shall pay the penalty of your ingenuity.'

Andrew, notwithstanding my threats, continued to battle the point, as he said it would cost him a guinea of rue-bargain to the man who had bought his pony before he could get it back again. Like a true Englishman, though sensible I was duped by the rascal, I was about to pay his exaction rather than lose time, when forth sallied Mr. Jarvie, cloaked, mantled, hooded, and booted, as if for a Siberian winter, while two apprentices, under the immediate direction of Mattie, led forth the decent ambling steed which had the honour on such occasions to support the person of the Glasgow magistrate. Ere he ' clombe to the saddle,' an expression more descriptive of the Bailie's mode of mounting than that of the knights-errant to whom Spenser applies it, he inquired the cause of the dispute betwixt my servant and me. Having learned the nature of honest Andrew's manœuvre, he instantly cut short all debate by pronouncing, that if Fairservice did not forthwith return the three-legged palfrey, and produce the more useful quadruped which he had discarded, he would send him to prison, and amerce him in half his wages. 'Mr. Osbaldistone,' said he, 'contracted for the service of both your horse and you—twa brutes at ance—ye unconscionable rascal!—but I 'se look weel after you during this journey.'

'It will be nonsense fining me,' said Andrew doughtily, 'that hasna a grey groat to pay a fine wi'—it 's ill taking the breeks aff a Hielandman.'

'If ye hae nae purse to fine, ye hae flesh to pine,' replied the Bailie, 'and I will look weel to ye getting your deserts the tae way or the tither.'

To the commands of Mr. Jarvie, therefore, Andrew was compelled to submit, only muttering between his teeth, 'Ower mony maisters — ower mony maisters, as the paddock said to the harrow, when every tooth gae her a tig.'

Apparently he found no difficulty in getting rid of Supple Tam, and recovering possession of his former Bucephalus, for he accomplished the exchange without being many minutes absent; nor did I hear further of his having paid any smart-money for breach of bargain.

We now set forward, but had not reached the top of the street in which Mr. Jarvie dwelt, when a loud hallooing, and breathless call of 'Stop, stop!' was heard behind us. We stopped accordingly, and were overtaken by Mr. Jarvie's two lads, who bore two parting tokens of Mattie's care for her master. The first was conveyed in the form of a voluminous silk handkerchief, like the main-sail of one of his own West-Indiamen, which Mrs. Mattie particularly desired he would put about his neck, and which, thus entreated, he added to his other integuments. The second youngster brought only a verbal charge (I thought I saw the rogue disposed to laugh as he delivered it) on the part of the housekeeper, that her master would take care of the waters. 'Pooh! pooh! silly hussy,' answered Mr. Jarvie; but added, turning to me, 'it shows a kind heart though—it shows a kind heart in sae young a quean—Mattie's a carefu' lass.' So speaking, he pricked the sides of his palfrey, and we left the town without farther interruption.

While we paced easily forward, by a road which conducted us north-eastward from the town, I had an opportunity to estimate and admire the good qualities of my new friend. Although, like my father, he considered commercial transactions the most important objects of human life, he was not wedded to them so as to undervalue more general knowledge. On the contrary, with much oddity and vulgarity of manner,—with a vanity which he made much more ridiculous by disguising it now and then under a thin veil of humility, and devoid as he was of all the advantages of a learned education, Mr. Jarvie's conversation showed tokens of a shrewd, observing, liberal, and, to the extent of its opportunities, a well-improved mind. He was a good local antiquary, and entertained me, as we passed along, with an account of remarkable events which had formerly taken place in the scenes through which we passed. And as he was well acquainted with the ancient history of his district, he saw with the prospective eye of an enlightened patriot, the buds of many of those future advantages, which have only blossomed and ripened within these few years. I remarked also, and with great pleasure, that although a keen Scotchman, and abundantly zealous for the honour of his country, he was disposed to think liberally of the sister kingdom. When Andrew Fairservice (whom, by the way, the Bailie could not abide) chose to impute the accident of one of the horses casting his shoe to the deteriorating influence of the Union, he incurred a severe rebuke from Mr. Jarvie.

'Whisht, sir!—whisht! it's ill-scraped tongues like yours, that make mischief atween neighbourhoods and nations. There's naething sae gude on this side o' time but it might hae been better, and that may be said o' the Union. Nane were keener against it than the Glasgow folk, wi' their rabblings and their risings, and their mobs, as they ca' them now-a-days. But it's an ill wind blaws naebody gude—Let ilka ane roose the ford as they find it— I say, Let Glasgow flourish! whilk is judiciously and elegantly putten round the town's arms, by way of by-word.—Now, since St. Mungo catched herrings in the Clyde, what was ever like to gar us flourish like the sugar and tobacco-trade? Will ony body tell me that, and grumble at the treaty that opened us a road west-awa yonder?'

Andrew Fairservice was far from acquiescing in these arguments of expedience, and even ventured to enter a grumbling protest, 'That it was an unco change to hae Scotland's laws made in England;

and that, for his share, he wadna for a' the herring-barrels in Glasgow, and a' the tobacco-casks to boot, hae gien up the riding o' the Scots Parliament, or sent awa our crown, and our sword, and our sceptre, and Mons Meg,* to be keepit by thae English pock-puddings in the Tower o' Lunnon. What wad Sir William Wallace, or auld Davie Lindsay, hae said to the Union, or them that made it ?'

The road which we travelled, while diverting the way with these discussions, had become wild and open, as soon as we had left Glasgow a mile or two behind us, and was growing more dreary as we advanced. Huge continuous heaths spread before, behind, and around us in hopeless barrenness, now level and interspersed with swamps, green with treacherous verdure, or sable with turf, or, as they call them in Scotland, peat-bogs, and now swelling into huge heavy ascents, which wanted the dignity and form of hills, while they were still more toilsome to the passenger. There were neither trees nor bushes to relieve the eye from the russet livery of absolute sterility. The very heath was of that stinted imperfect kind which has little or no flower, and affords the coarsest and meanest covering, which, as far as my experience enables me to judge, mother Earth is ever arrayed in. Living thing we saw none, except occasionally a few straggling sheep of a strange diversity of colours, as black, bluish, and orange. The sable hue predominated, however,

---

* See Note F. Mons Meg.

in their faces and legs. The very birds seemed to shun these wastes, and no wonder, since they had an easy method of escaping from them; at least I only heard the monotonous and plaintive cries of the lapwing and curlew, which my companions denominated the peasweep and whaup.

At dinner, however, which we took about noon, at a most miserable alehouse, we had the good fortune to find that these tiresome screamers of the morass were not the only inhabitants of the moors. The goodwife told us, that 'the gudeman had been at the hill'; and well for us that he had been so, for we enjoyed the produce of his *chasse* in the shape of some broiled moor-game, a dish which gallantly eked out the ewe-milk cheese, dried salmon, and oaten bread, being all besides that the house afforded. Some very indifferent two-penny ale, and a glass of excellent brandy, crowned our repast; and as our horses had, in the meantime, discussed their corn, we resumed our journey with renovated vigour.

I had need of all the spirits a good dinner could give, to resist the dejection which crept insensibly on my mind, when I combined the strange uncertainty of my errand with the disconsolate aspect of the country through which it was leading me. Our road continued to be, if possible, more waste and wild than that we had travelled in the forenoon. The few miserable hovels that showed some marks of human habitation, were now of still rarer occurrence; and at length, as we began to ascend an uninterrupted swell of moorland, they totally disappeared. The only exercise which my imagination received was, when some particular turn of the road gave us a partial view, to the left, of a large assemblage of dark-blue mountains stretching to the north and north-west, which promised to include within their recesses, a country as wild perhaps, but certainly differing greatly in point of interest, from that which we now travelled. The peaks of this screen of mountains were as wildly varied and distinguished as the hills which we had seen on the right were tame and lumpish; and while I gazed on this Alpine region, I felt a longing to explore its recesses, though accompanied with toil and danger, similar to that which a sailor feels when he wishes for the risks and animation of a battle or a gale, in exchange for the insupportable monotony of a protracted calm. I made various inquiries of my friend Mr. Jarvie, respecting the names and positions of these remarkable mountains; but it was a subject on which he had no information, or did not choose to be communicative. 'They 're the Hieland hills— the Hieland hills—Ye 'll see and hear eneugh about them before ye see Glasgow Cross again—I downa look at them—I never see them but they gar me grew.—It 's no for fear—no for fear, but just for grief, for the puir blinded half-starved creatures that inhabit them—But say nae mair about it—it 's ill speaking o' Hielandmen sae near the line. I hae kend mony an honest man wadna hae ventured this length without he had made his last will and testament—Mattie had ill-will to see me set awa on this ride, and grat awee, the sillie tawpie; but it 's nae mair ferlie to see a woman greet than to see a goose gang barefit.'

I next attempted to lead the discourse on the character and history of the person whom we were going to visit; but on this topic Mr. Jarvie was totally inaccessible, owing perhaps in part to the attendance of Mr. Andrew Fairservice, who chose to keep so close in our rear that his ears could not fail to catch every word which was spoken, while his tongue assumed the freedom of mingling in our conversation as often as he saw an opportunity. For this he occasionally incurred Mr. Jarvie's reproof.

' Keep back, sir, as best sets ye,' said the Bailie, as Andrew pressed forward to catch the answer to some question I had asked about Campbell.— ' Ye wad fain ride the fore-horse, an ye wist how —That child 's aye for being out o' the cheese-fat he was moulded in.—Now, as for your questions, Mr. Osbaldistone, now that child 's out of ear-shot, I 'll just tell ye it 's free to you to speer, and it 's free to me to answer, or no—Gude I canna sae muckle o' Rob, puir chield; ill I winna say o' him, for, forby that he 's my cousin, we 're coming near his ain country, and there may be ane o' his gillies ahint every whin-bush for what I ken—And if ye 'll be guided by my advice, the less ye speak about him, or where we are gaun, or what we are gaun to do, we 'll be the mair likely to speed us in our errand. For it 's like we may fa' in wi' some o' his unfreends —there are e'en ower mony o' them about—and his bonnet sits even on his brow yet for a' that; but I doubt they 'll be upsides wi' Rob at the last—air day or late day, the fox's hide finds aye the flaying knife.'

'I will certainly,' I replied, 'be entirely guided by your experience.'

'Right, Mr. Osbaldistone—right,—but I maun speak to this gabbling skyte too, for bairns and fules speak at the Cross what they hear at the ingle side.—D' ye hear, you, Andrew—What's your name—Fairservice!'

Andrew, who at the last rebuff had fallen a good way behind, did not choose to acknowledge the summons.

'Andrew, ye scoundrel!' repeated Mr. Jarvie; 'here, sir! here!'

'Here is for the dog,' said Andrew, coming up sulkily.

'I 'll gie you dog's wages, ye rascal, if ye dinna attend to what I say t' ye—We are gaun into the Hielands a bit——'

'I judged as muckle,' said Andrew.

'Haud your peace, ye knave, and hear what I have to say till ye—We are gaun a bit into the Hielands——'

'Ye tauld me sae already,' replied the incorrigible Andrew.

'I 'll break your head,' said the Bailie, rising in wrath, 'if ye dinna haud your tongue.'

'A hadden tongue,' replied Andrew, 'makes a slabbered mouth.'

It was now necessary I should interfere, which I did by commanding Andrew, with an authoritative tone, to be silent at his peril.

153

'I am silent,' said Andrew. 'I 'se do a' your lawfu' bidding without a nay-say.—My puir mither used aye to tell me,

> " Be it better, be it worse,
> Be ruled by him that has the purse."

Say ye may e'en speak as lang as ye like, baith the tane and the tither o' you, for Andrew.'

Mr. Jarvie took the advantage of his stopping after quoting the above proverb, to give him the requisite instructions.

'Now, sir, it 's as muckle as your life 's worth— that wad be dear o' little siller, to be sure—but it is as muckle as a' our lives are worth, if ye dinna mind what I say to ye. In this public whar we are gaun to, and whar it is like we may hae to stay a' night, men o' a' clans and kindred—Hieland and Lawland—tak up their quarters—And whiles there are mair drawn dirks than open Bibles amang them, when the usquebaugh gets uppermost. See ye neither meddle nor mak, nor gie nae offence wi' that clavering tongue o' yours, but keep a calm sough, and let ilka cock fight his ain battle.'

'Muckle needs to tell me that,' said Andrew contemptuously, 'as if I had never seen a Hieland-man before, and kend nae how to manage them. Nae man alive can cuitle up Donald better than mysell—I hae bought wi' them, sauld wi' them, eaten wi' them, drucken wi' them——'

'Did ye ever fight wi' them?' said Mr. Jarvie.

'Na, na,' answered Andrew, 'I took care o' that; it wad ill hae set me, that am an artist and

half a scholar to my trade, to be fighting amang a
wheen kilted loons that dinna ken the name o' a
single herb or flower in braid Scots, let abee in the
Latin tongue.'

'Then,' said Mr. Jarvie, 'as ye wad keep either
your tongue in your mouth, or your lugs in your
head, (and ye might miss them, for as saucy members as they are,) I charge ye to say nae word,
gude or bad, that ye can weel get by, to ony body
that may be in the Clachan. And ye 'll specially
understand that ye 're no to be bleezing and blast-
ing about your master's name and mine, or saying
that this is Mr. Bailie Nicol Jarvie o' the Saut-
Market, son o' the worthy Deacon Nicol Jarvie,
that a'body has heard about; and this is Mr. Frank
Osbaldistone, son of the managing partner of the
great house of Osbaldistone and Tresham, in the
City.'

'Eneuch said,' answered Andrew—'eneuch said!
What need ye think I wad be speaking about
your names for ?—I hae mony things o' mair importance to speak about, I trow.'

'It's thae very things of importance that I am
feared for, ye blethering goose; ye maunna speak
ony thing, gude or bad, that ye can by any possibility help.'

'If ye dinna think me fit,' replied Andrew, in
a huff, 'to speak like ither folk, gie me my wages
and my board-wages, and I 'se gae back to Glasgow
—There's sma' sorrow at our parting, as the auld
mear said to the broken cart.'

Finding Andrew's perverseness again rising to

a point which threatened to occasion me inconvenience, I was under the necessity of explaining to him, that he might return if he thought proper, but that in that case I would not pay him a single farthing for his past services. The argument *ad crumenam*, as it has been called by jocular logicians, has weight with the greater part of mankind, and Andrew was in that particular far from affecting any trick of singularity. He 'drew in his horns,' to use the Bailie's phrase, on the instant, professed no intention whatever to disoblige, and a resolution to be guided by my commands, whatever they might be.

Concord being thus happily restored to our small party, we continued to pursue our journey. The road, which had ascended for six or seven English miles, began now to descend for about the same space, through a country which, neither in fertility nor interest, could boast any advantage over that which we had passed already, and which afforded no variety, unless when some tremendous peak of a Highland mountain appeared at a distance. We continued, however, to ride on without pause; and even when night fell and overshadowed the desolate wilds which we traversed, we were, as I understood from Mr. Jarvie, still three miles and a bittock distant from the place where we were to spend the night.

CHAPTER XXVIII

Baron of Bucklivie,
May the foul fiend drive ye,
And a' to pieces rive ye,
For building sic a town,
Where there's neither horse meat, nor man's meat, nor a chair to sit
down.

SCOTTISH POPULAR RHYMES ON A BAD INN.

THE night was pleasant, and the moon afforded us good light for our journey. Under her rays, the ground over which we passed assumed a more interesting appearance than during the broad daylight, which discovered the extent of its wasteness. The mingled light and shadows gave it an interest which naturally did not belong to it; and, like the effect of a veil flung over a plain woman, irritated our curiosity on a subject which had in itself nothing gratifying.

The descent, however, still continued, turned, winded, left the more open heaths, and got into steeper ravines, which promised soon to lead us to the banks of some brook or river, and ultimately made good their presage. We found ourselves at length on the bank of a stream, which rather resembled one of my native English rivers than those I had hitherto seen in Scotland. It was narrow, deep, still, and silent; although the imperfect light, as it gleamed on its placid waters, showed also that we were now among the lofty mountains which formed its cradle. 'That's the Forth,' said the Bailie, with an air of reverence, which I have observed the Scotch usually pay to their distinguished rivers. The Clyde, the Tweed, the Forth, the Spey, are usually named by those who dwell on their banks with a sort of respect and pride, and I have known duels occasioned by any word of disparagement. I cannot say I have the least quarrel with this sort of harmless enthusiasm. I received my friend's communication with the importance which he seemed to think appertained to it. In fact, I was not a little pleased, after so long and dull a journey, to approach a region which promised to engage the imagination. My faithful squire, Andrew, did not seem to be quite of the same opinion, for he received the solemn information, 'That is the Forth,' with a 'Umph!—an he had said that's the public-house, it wad hae been mair to the purpose.'

The Forth, however, as far as the imperfect light permitted me to judge, seemed to merit the admiration of those who claimed an interest in its stream. A beautiful eminence of the most regular round shape, and clothed with copsewood of hazels, mountain-ash, and dwarf-oak, intermixed with a few magnificent old trees, which, rising above the underwood, exposed their forked and bared branches to the silver moonshine, seemed to protect the sources from which the river sprung. If I could trust the tale of my companion, which, while professing to disbelieve every word of it, he told under his breath, and with an air of something like intimidation, this hill, so regularly formed, so richly verdant, and garlanded with such a beautiful variety of ancient trees and thriving copsewood, was held by the neighbourhood to contain, within its unseen caverns, the palaces of the fairies; a race of airy beings, who formed an intermediate class between men and demons, and who, if not positively malignant to humanity, were yet to be avoided and feared, on account of their capricious, vindictive, and irritable disposition.*

'They ca' them,' said Mr. Jarvie, in a whisper, '*Daoine Schie*, whilk signifies, as I understand, men of peace; meaning thereby to make their gudewill. And we may e'en as weel ca' them that too, Mr. Osbaldistone, for there's nae gude in speaking ill o' the laird within his ain bounds.' But he added presently after, on seeing one or two lights which twinkled before us, 'It's deceits o' Satan, after a', and I fearna to say it—for we are near the manse now, and yonder are the lights in the Clachan of Aberfoil.'

I own I was well pleased at the circumstance to which Mr. Jarvie alluded; not so much that it set his tongue at liberty, in his opinion, with all safety to declare his real sentiments with respect to the *Daoine Schie*, or fairies, as that it promised some hours' repose to ourselves and our horses, of which, after a ride of fifty miles and upwards, both stood in some need.

---

* See Note G.   Fairy Superstition.

We crossed the infant Forth by an old-fashioned stone bridge, very high and very narrow. My conductor, however, informed me, that to get through this deep and important stream, and to clear all its tributary dependencies, the general pass from the Highlands to the southward lay by what was called the Fords of Frew, at all times deep and difficult of passage, and often altogether unfordable. Beneath these fords there was no pass of general resort until so far east as the bridge of Stirling; so that the river of Forth forms a defensible line betwixt the Highlands and Lowlands of Scotland, from its source nearly to the Frith, or inlet of the ocean, in which it terminates. The subsequent events which we witnessed led me to recall with attention what the shrewdness of Bailie Jarvie suggested, in his proverbial expression, that 'Forth bridles the wild Highlandman.'

About half a mile's riding, after we crossed the bridge, placed us at the door of the public-house where we were to pass the evening. It was a hovel rather worse than better than that in which we had dined; but its little windows were lighted up, voices were heard from within, and all intimated a prospect of food and shelter, to which we were by no means indifferent. Andrew was the first to observe that there was a peeled willow-wand placed across the half-open door of the little inn. He hung back, and advised us not to enter. 'For,' said Andrew, 'some of their chiefs and grit men are birling at the usquebaugh in by there, and dinna want to be disturbed; and the least we'll get,

if we gang ram-stam in on them, will be a broken
head, to learn us better havings, if we dinna come
by the length of a cauld dirk in our wame, whilk is
just as likely.'

I looked at the Bailie, who acknowledged, in a
whisper, 'that the gowk had some reason for singing,
ance in the year.'

Meantime a staring half-clad wench or two came
out of the inn and the neighbouring cottages, on
hearing the sound of our horses' feet. No one bade
us welcome, nor did any one offer to take our
horses, from which we had alighted; and to our
various inquiries, the hopeless response of 'Ha niel
Sassenach,' was the only answer we could extract.
The Bailie, however, found (in his experience) a way
to make them speak English. 'If I gie ye a bawbee,' said he to an urchin of about ten years old,
with a fragment of a tattered plaid about him,
'will you understand Sassenach?'

'Ay, ay, that will I,' replied the brat, in very
decent English.

'Then gang and tell your mammy, my man, there's
twa Sassenach gentlemen come to speak wi' her.'

The landlady presently appeared, with a lighted
piece of split fir blazing in her hand. The turpen-
tine in this species of torch (which is generally dug
from out the turf-bogs) makes it blaze and sparkle
readily, so that it is often used in the Highlands
in lieu of candles. On this occasion such a torch
illuminated the wild and anxious features of a
female, pale, thin, and rather above the usual size,
whose soiled and ragged dress, though aided by a

plaid or tartan screen, barely served the purposes of decency, and certainly not those of comfort. Her black hair, which escaped in uncombed elf-locks from under her coif, as well as the strange and embarrassed look with which she regarded us, gave me the idea of a witch disturbed in the midst of her unlawful rites. She plainly refused to admit us into the house. We remonstrated anxiously, and pleaded the length of our journey, the state of our horses, and the certainty that there was not another place where we could be received nearer than Callander, which the Bailie stated to be seven Scots miles distant. How many these may exactly amount to in English measurement, I have never been able to ascertain, but I think the double *ratio* may be pretty safely taken as a medium computation. The obdurate hostess treated our expostulation with contempt.—'Better gang farther than fare waur,' she said, speaking the Scottish Lowland dialect, and being indeed a native of the Lennox district,—'Her house was taen up wi' them wadna like to be intruded on wi' strangers.—She didna ken wha mair might be there—redcoats, it might be, frae the garrison.' (These last words she spoke under her breath, and with very strong emphasis.) 'The night,' she said, 'was fair abune head—a night amang the heather wad caller our bloods— we might sleep in our claes as mony a gude blade does in the scabbard—there wasna muckle flow-moss in the shaw, if we took up our quarters right, and we might pit up our horses to the hill, naebody wad say naething against it.'

'But, my good woman,' said I, while the Bailie groaned and remained undecided, 'it is six hours since we dined, and we have not taken a morsel since. I am positively dying with hunger, and I have no taste for taking up my abode supperless among these mountains of yours. I positively must enter; and make the best apology you can to your guests for adding a stranger or two to their number. —Andrew, you will see the horses put up.'

The Hecate looked at me with surprise, and then ejaculated, 'A wilfu' man will hae his way—them that will to Cupar maun to Cupar!—To see thae English belly-gods—he has had ae fu' meal the day already, and he 'll venture life and liberty rather than he 'll want a het supper! Set roasted beef and pudding on the opposite side o' the pit o' Tophet, and an Englishman will mak a spang at it—But I wash my hands o't—Follow me, sir,' (to Andrew,) 'and I 'se show ye where to pit the beasts.'

I own I was somewhat dismayed at my landlady's expressions, which seemed to be ominous of some approaching danger. I did not, however, choose to shrink back after having declared my resolution, and accordingly I boldly entered the house; and after narrowly escaping breaking my shins over a turf back and a salting tub, which stood on either side of the narrow exterior passage, I opened a crazy half-decayed door, constructed not of plank, but of wicker, and, followed by the Bailie, entered into the principal apartment of this Scottish caravan-sary.

The interior presented a view which seemed

singular enough to southern eyes. The fire, fed
with blazing turf and branches of dried wood, blazed
merrily in the centre; but the smoke, having no
means to escape but through a hole in the roof,
eddied round the rafters of the cottage, and hung
in sable folds at the height of about five feet from
the floor. The space beneath was kept pretty
clear, by innumerable currents of air which rushed
towards the fire from the broken panel of basket-
work which served as a door, from two square holes,
designed as ostensible windows, through one of
which was thrust a plaid, and through the other a
tattered great-coat; and moreover, through various
less distinguishable apertures, in the walls of the
tenement, which, being built of round stones and
turf, cemented by mud, let in the atmosphere at
innumerable crevices.

At an old oaken table, adjoining to the fire, sat
three men, guests apparently, whom it was impossible to regard with indifference. Two were in the
Highland dress; the one, a little dark-complexioned
man, with a lively, quick, and irritable expression
of features, wore the trews, or close pantaloons,
wove out of a sort of chequered stocking stuff. The
Bailie whispered me, that ' he behoved to be a man
of some consequence, for that naebody but their
Duinhéwassels wore the trews; they were ill to
weave exactly to their Highland pleasure.'

The other mountaineer was a very tall, strong
man, with a quantity of reddish hair, freckled face,
high cheek-bones, and long chin—a sort of caricature of the national features of Scotland. The

tartan which he wore differed from that of his companion, as it had much more scarlet in it, whereas the shades of black and dark-green predominated in the chequers of the other. The third, who sate at the same table, was in the Lowland dress,—a bold, stout-looking man, with a cast of military daring in his eye and manner, his riding-dress showily and profusely laced, and his cocked hat of formidable dimensions. His hanger and a pair of pistols lay on the table before him. Each of the Highlanders had their naked dirks stuck upright in the board beside him,—an emblem, I was afterwards informed, but surely a strange one, that their compotation was not to be interrupted by any brawl. A mighty pewter measure, containing about an English quart of usquebaugh, a liquor nearly as strong as brandy, which the Highlanders distil from malt, and drink undiluted in excessive quantities, was placed before these worthies. A broken glass, with a wooden foot, served as a drinking cup to the whole party, and circulated with a rapidity, which, considering the potency of the liquor, seemed absolutely marvellous. These men spoke loudly and eagerly together, sometimes in Gaelic, at other times in English. Another Highlander, wrapt in his plaid, reclined on the floor, his head resting on a stone, from which it was only separated by a wisp of straw, and slept, or seemed to sleep, without attending to what was going on around him. He also was probably a stranger, for he lay in full dress, and accoutred with the sword and target, the usual arms of his countrymen when on a journey. Cribs there were of different dimensions beside the walls, formed, some of fractured boards, some of shattered wicker-work or plaited boughs, in which slumbered the family of the house, men, women, and children, their places of repose only concealed by the dusky wreaths of vapour which arose above, below, and around them.

Our entrance was made so quietly, and the carousers I have described were so eagerly engaged in their discussions, that we escaped their notice for a minute or two. But I observed the High-lander who lay beside the fire raise himself on his elbow as we entered, and, drawing his plaid over the lower part of his face, fix his look on us for a few seconds, after which he resumed his recumbent posture, and seemed again to betake himself to the repose which our entrance had interrupted.

We advanced to the fire, which was an agreeable spectacle after our late ride, during the chillness of an autumn evening among the mountains, and first attracted the attention of the guests who had preceded us, by calling for the landlady. She approached, looking doubtfully and timidly, now at us, now at the other party, and returned a hesitating and doubtful answer to our request to have something to eat.

'She didna ken,' she said, 'she wasna sure there was ony thing in the house,' and then modified her refusal with the qualification,— 'that is, ony thing fit for the like of us.'

I assured her we were indifferent to the quality of our supper; and looking round for the means of accommodation, which were not easily to be found, I arranged an old hen-coop as a seat for Mr. Jarvie, and turned down a broken tub to serve for my own. Andrew Fairservice entered presently afterwards, and took a place in silence behind our backs. The natives, as I may call them, continued staring at us with an air as if confounded by our assurance, and we, at least I myself, disguised as well as we could, under an appearance of indifference, any secret anxiety we might feel concerning the mode in which we were to be received by those whose privacy we had disturbed.

At length, the lesser Highlander, addressing himself to me, said, in very good English, and in a tone of great haughtiness, 'Ye make yourself at home, sir, I see.'

'I usually do so,' I replied, 'when I come into a house of public entertainment.'

'And did she na see,' said the taller man, 'by the white wand at the door, that gentlemans had taken up the public-house on their ain business?'

'I do not pretend to understand the customs of this country; but I am yet to learn,' I replied, 'how three persons should be entitled to exclude all other travellers from the only place of shelter and refreshment for miles round.'

'There's nae reason for't, gentlemen,' said the Bailie; 'we mean nae offence—but there's neither law nor reason for't—but as far as a stoup o' gude brandy wad make up the quarrel, we, being peaceable folk, wad be willing——'

'Damn your brandy, sir!' said the Lowlander,

adjusting his cocked-hat fiercely upon his head; 'we desire neither your brandy nor your company,' and up he rose from his seat. His companions also arose, muttering to each other, drawing up their plaids, and snorting and snuffing the air after the manner of their countrymen when working themselves into a passion.

'I tauld ye what wad come, gentlemen,' said the landlady, 'an ye wad hae been tauld — get awa wi' ye out o' my house, and make nae disturbance here—there's nae gentleman be disturbed at Jeanie MacAlpine's an she can hinder. A wheen idle English loons, gaun about the country under cloud o' night, and disturbing honest peaceable gentlemen that are drinking their drap drink at the fireside!'

At another time I should have thought of the old Latin adage,

'Dat veniam corvis, vexat censura columbas——'

But I had not any time for classical quotation, for there was obviously a fray about to ensue, at which, feeling myself indignant at the inhospitable insolence with which I was treated, I was totally indifferent, unless on the Bailie's account, whose person and qualities were ill qualified for such an adventure. I started up, however, on seeing the others rise, and dropped my cloak from my shoulders, that I might be ready to stand on the defensive.

'We are three to three,' said the lesser Highlander, glancing his eyes at our party; 'if ye be pretty men, draw!' and, unsheathing his broad-sword, he advanced on me. I put myself in a posture of defence, and, aware of the superiority of my weapon, a rapier or small-sword, was little afraid of the issue of the contest. The Bailie behaved with unexpected mettle. As he saw the gigantic Highlander confront him with his weapon drawn, he tugged for a second or two at the hilt of his *shabble*, as he called it; but finding it loth to quit the sheath, to which it had long been secured by rust and disuse, he seized, as a substitute, on the red-hot coulter of a plough which had been em-ployed in arranging the fire by way of a poker, and brandished it with such effect, that at the first pass he set the Highlander's plaid on fire, and compelled him to keep a respectful distance till he could get it extinguished. Andrew, on the contrary, who ought to have faced the Lowland champion, had, I grieve to say it, vanished at the very commence-ment of the fray. But his antagonist, crying, 'Fair play! fair play!' seemed courteously disposed to take no share in the scuffle. Thus we commenced our rencontre on fair terms as to numbers. My own aim was, to possess myself, if possible, of my antagonist's weapon; but I was deterred from closing for fear of the dirk which he held in his left hand, and used in parrying the thrusts of my rapier. Meantime the Bailie, notwithstanding the success of his first onset, was sorely bested. The weight of his weapon, the corpulence of his person, the very effervescence of his own passions, were rapidly exhausting both his strength and his breath, and he was almost at the mercy of his antagonist, when up started the sleeping Highlander from the floor on which he reclined, with his naked sword and target in his hand, and threw himself between the discomfited magistrate and his assailant, exclaiming, 'Her nainsell has eaten the town pread at the Cross o' Glasgow, and py her troth she 'll fight for Bailie Sharvie at the Clachan of Aberfoil—tat will she e'en!' And seconding his words with deeds, this unexpected auxiliary made his sword whistle about the ears of his tall countryman, who, nothing abashed, returned his blows with interest. But being both accoutred with round targets made of wood, studded with brass, and covered with leather, with which they readily parried each other's strokes, their combat was attended with much more noise and clatter than serious risk of damage. It appeared, indeed, that there was more of bravado than of serious attempt to do us any injury; for the Lowland gentleman, who, as I mentioned, had stood aside for want of an antagonist when the brawl commenced, was now pleased to act the part of moderator and peace-maker.

'Haud your hands—haud your hands—eneugh done—eneugh done!—the quarrel's no mortal. The strange gentlemen have shown themselves men of honour, and gien reasonable satisfaction. I 'll stand on mine honour as kittle as ony man, but I hate unnecessary bloodshed.'

It was not, of course, my wish to protract the fray — my adversary seemed equally disposed to sheath his sword — the Bailie, gasping for breath, might be considered as *hors de combat*, and our two sword-and-buckler men gave up their contest with as much indifference as they had entered into it.

'And now,' said the worthy gentleman who acted as umpire, 'let us drink and gree like honest fellows—The house will haud us a'. I propose that this good little gentleman that seems sair forfoughen, as I may say, in this tuilzie, shall send for a tass o' brandy, and I 'll pay for another, by way of archilowe,* and then we 'll birl our bawbees a' round about, like brethren.'

'And fa's to pay my new ponnie plaid,' said the larger Highlander, 'wi' a hole burnt in 't ane might put a kail-pat through? Saw ever ony body a decent gentleman fight wi' a firebrand before?'

'Let that be nae hinderance,' said the Bailie, who had now recovered his breath, and was at once disposed to enjoy the triumph of having behaved with spirit, and avoid the necessity of again resorting to such hard and doubtful arbitrement;—'Gin I hae broken the head,' he said, 'I sall find the plaister. A new plaid sall ye hae, and o' the best —your ain clan-colours, man—an ye will tell me where it can be sent t' ye frae Glasco.'

'I needna name my clan—I am of a king's clan, as is weel kend,' said the Highlander; 'but ye may tak a bit o' the plaid—figh, she smells like a singit sheep's head!—and that 'll learn ye the sett —and a gentleman, that 's a cousin o' my ain, that carries eggs doun frae Glencroe, will ca' for 't about

---

* Archilowe, of unknown derivation, signifies a peace-offering.

Martimas, an ye will tell her where ye bide. But, honest gentleman, neist time ye fight, an ye hae ony respect for your athversary, let it be wi' your sword, man, since ye wear ane, and no wi' thae het culters and fireprands, like a wild Indian.'

' Conscience ! ' replied the Bailie, ' every man maun do as he dow—my sword hasna seen the light since Bothwell Brigg, when my father, that's dead and gane, ware it; and I kenna weel if it was forthcoming than either, for the battle was o' the briefest—At ony rate, it's glewed to the scabbard now beyond my power to part them; and, finding that, I e'en grippit at the first thing I could make a fend wi'. I trow my fighting days is done, though I like ill to take the scorn, for a' that.—But where's the honest lad that tuik my quarrel on himsell sae frankly ?—I 'se bestow a gill o' aquavitæ on him, an I suld never ca' for anither.'

The champion for whom he looked around was, however, no longer to be seen. He had escaped, unobserved by the Bailie, immediately when the brawl was ended, yet not before I had recognised, in his wild features and shaggy red hair, our acquaintance Dougal, the fugitive turnkey of the Glasgow jail. I communicated this observation in a whisper to the Bailie, who answered in the same tone, ' Weel, weel, I see that him that ye ken o' said very right. There *is* some glimmering o' common sense about that creature Dougal ; I maun see and think o' something will do him some gude.'

Thus saying, he sat down, and fetching one or

two deep aspirations, by way of recovering his breath, called to the landlady; ' I think, Luckie, now that I find that there's nae hole in my wame, whilk I had muckle reason to doubt frae the doings o' your house, I wad be the better o' something to pit intill 't.'

The dame, who was all officiousness so soon as the storm had blown over, immediately undertook to broil something comfortable for our supper. Indeed, nothing surprised me more, in the course of the whole matter, than the extreme calmness with which she and her household seemed to regard the martial tumult that had taken place. The good woman was only heard to call to some of her assistants, ' Steek the door—steek the door!—Kill or be killed, let naebody pass out till they hae paid the lawin.' And as for the slumberers in those lairs by the wall, which served the family for beds, they only raised their shirtless bodies to look at the fray, ejaculated, ' Oigh! oigh!' in the tone suitable to their respective sex and ages, and were, I believe, fast asleep again, ere our swords were well returned to their scabbards.

Our landlady, however, now made a great bustle to get some victuals ready, and, to my surprise, very soon began to prepare for us, in the frying-pan, a savoury mess of venison collops, which she dressed in a manner that might well satisfy hungry men, if not epicures. In the meantime the brandy was placed on the table, to which the Highlanders, however partial to their native strong waters, showed no objection, but much the contrary; and the Lowland gentleman, after the first cup had passed round, became desirous to know our profession, and the object of our journey.

'We are bits o' Glasgow bodies, if it please your honour,' said the Bailie, with an affectation of great humility, 'travelling to Stirling to get in some siller that is awing us.'

I was so silly as to feel a little disconcerted at the unassuming account which he chose to give of us; but I recollected my promise to be silent, and allow the Bailie to manage the matter his own way. And really, when I recollected, Will, that I had not only brought the honest man a long journey from home, which even in itself had been some inconvenience, (if I were to judge from the obvious pain and reluctance with which he took his seat or arose from it,) but had also put him within a hair's-breadth of the loss of his life, I could hardly refuse him such a compliment. The spokesman of the other party, snuffing up his breath through his nose, repeated the words with a sort of sneer;—'You Glasgow tradesfolks hae naething to do but to gang frae the tae end o' the west o' Scotland to the ither, to plague honest folks that may chance to be awee ahint the hand, like me.'

'If our debtors were a' sic honest gentlemen as I believe you to be, Garschattachin,' replied the Bailie, 'conscience! we might save ourselves a labour, for they wad come to seek us.'

'Eh! what! how!' exclaimed the person whom he had addressed, 'as I shall live by bread, (not forgetting beef and brandy,) it's my auld friend

Nicol Jarvie, the best man that ever counted doun merks on a band till a distressed gentleman. Were ye na coming up my way?—were ye na coming up the Endrick to Garschattachin?'

'Troth no, Maister Galbraith,' replied the Bailie, 'I had other eggs on the spit—and I thought ye wad be saying I cam to look about the annual rent that's due on the bit heritable band that's between us.'

'Damn the annual rent!' said the laird, with an appearance of great heartiness,—'Deil a word o' business will you or I speak, now that ye're sae near my country—To see how a trot-cosey and a joseph can disguise a man—that I suldna ken my auld feal friend the deacon!'

'The bailie, if ye please,' resumed my companion; 'but I ken what gars ye mistak—the band was granted to my father that's happy, and he was deacon; but his name was Nicol as weel as mine. I dinna mind that there's been a payment of principal sum or annual rent on it in my day, and doubtless that has made the mistake.'

'Weel, the devil take the mistake and all that occasioned it!' replied Mr. Galbraith. 'But I am glad ye are a bailie. Gentlemen, fill a brimmer —this is my excellent friend, Bailie Nicol Jarvie's health—I kend him and his father these twenty years. Are ye a' cleared kelty aff?—Fill anither. Here's to his being sune provost—I say provost— Lord Provost Nicol Jarvie!—and them that affirms there's a man walks the Hie-street o' Glasgow that's fitter for the office, they will do weel not to let me,

Duncan Galbraith of Garschattachin, hear them say sae—that's all.' And therewith Duncan Galbraith martially cocked his hat, and placed it on one side of his head with an air of defiance.

The brandy was probably the best recommendation of these complimentary toasts to the two Highlanders, who drank them without appearing anxious to comprehend their purport. They commenced a conversation with Mr. Galbraith in Gaelic, which he talked with perfect fluency, being, as I afterwards learned, a near neighbour to the Highlands.

'I kend that Scant-o'-grace weel eneugh frae the very outset,' said the Bailie, in a whisper to me; 'but when blude was warm, and swords were out at ony rate, wha kens what way he might hae thought o' paying his debts? it will be lang or he does it in common form. But he's an honest lad, and has a warm heart too; he disna come often to the Cross o' Glasgow, but mony a buck and blackcock he sends us doun frae the hills. And I can want my siller weel eneugh. My father the deacon had a great regard for the family of Garschattachin.'

Supper being now nearly ready, I looked round for Andrew Fairservice; but that trusty follower had not been seen by any one since the beginning of the rencontre. The hostess, however, said that she believed our servant had gone into the stable, and offered to light me to the place, saying that 'no entreaties of the bairns or hers could make him give any answer; and that truly she caredna to gang into the stable hersell at this hour. She was a lone woman, and it was weel kend how the Brownie of Ben-ye-gask guided the gudewife of Ardnagowan; and it was aye judged there was a Brownie in our stable, which was just what garr'd me gie ower keeping an hostler.'

As, however, she lighted me towards the miserable hovel into which they had crammed our unlucky steeds, to regale themselves on hay, every fibre of which was as thick as an ordinary goose-quill, she plainly showed me that she had another reason for drawing me aside from the company than that which her words implied. 'Read that,' she said, slipping a piece of paper into my hand as we arrived at the door of the shed; 'I bless God I am rid o't. Between sogers and Saxons, and caterans and cattle-lifters, and hership and bluidshed, an honest woman wad live quieter in hell than on the Highland line.'

So saying, she put the pine-torch into my hand, and returned into the house.

CHAPTER XXIX

Bagpipes, not lyres, the Highland hills adorn,
MacLean's loud hollo, and MacGregor's horn.
JOHN COOPER'S REPLY TO ALLAN RAMSAY.

I STOPPED in the entrance of the stable, if indeed
a place be entitled to that name where horses were
stowed away along with goats, poultry, pigs, and
cows, under the same roof with the mansion-house;
although, by a degree of refinement unknown to the
rest of the hamlet, and which I afterwards heard
was imputed to an overpride on the part of Jeanie
MacAlpine, our landlady, the apartment was accommodated with an entrance different from that used
by her biped customers. By the light of my torch,
I deciphered the following billet, written on a wet,
crumpled, and dirty piece of paper, and addressed,
'For the honoured hands of Mr. F. O., a Saxon
young gentleman—These.' The contents were as
follows:

'SIR,
'There are night-hawks abroad, so that I cannot
give you and my respected kinsman, B. N. J., the
meeting at the Clachan of Aberfoil, whilk was my
purpose. I pray you to avoid unnecessary communication with those you may find there, as it may

178

give future trouble. The person who gives you this is faithful, and may be trusted, and will guide you to a place where, God willing, I may safely give you the meeting, when I trust my kinsman and you will visit my poor house, where, in despite of my enemies, I can still promise sic cheer as ane Hielandman may gie his friends, and where we will drink a solemn health to a certain D. V., and look to certain affairs whilk I hope to be your aidance in; and I rest, as is wont among gentlemen, your servant to command, **R. M. C.'**

I was a good deal mortified at the purport of this letter, which seemed to adjourn to a more distant place and date the service which I had hoped to receive from this man Campbell. Still, however, it was some comfort to know that he continued to be in my interest, since without him I could have no hope of recovering my father's papers. I resolved, therefore, to obey his instructions; and, observing all caution before the guests, to take the first good opportunity I could find to procure from the land-lady directions how I was to obtain a meeting with this mysterious person.

My next business was to seek out Andrew Fair-service, whom I called several times by name, without receiving any answer, surveying the stable all round, at the same time, not without risk of setting the premises on fire, had not the quantity of wet litter and mud so greatly counterbalanced two or three bunches of straw and hay. At length my repeated cries of 'Andrew Fairservice—Andrew!

Fool—Ass, where are you?' produced a doleful
'Here,' in a groaning tone, which might have
been that of the Brownie itself. Guided by this
sound, I advanced to the corner of a shed, where,
ensconced in the angle of the wall, behind a barrel
full of the feathers of all the fowls which had died
in the cause of the public for a month past, I found
the manful Andrew; and partly by force, partly by
command and exhortation, compelled him forth into
the open air. The first words he spoke were, 'I
am an honest lad, sir.'

'Who the devil questions your honesty?' said
I; 'or what have we to do with it at present? I
desire you to come and attend us at supper.'

'Yes,' reiterated Andrew, without apparently
understanding what I said to him, 'I am an honest
lad, whatever the Bailie may say to the contrary.
I grant the warld and the warld's gear sits ower
near my heart whiles, as it does to mony a ane
—But I am an honest lad; and, though I spak o'
leaving ye in the muir, yet God knows it was
far frae my purpose, but just like idle things folk
says when they're driving a bargain, to get it as
far to their ain side as they can—And I like your
honour weel for sae young a lad, and I wadna part
wi' ye lightly.'

'What the deuce are you driving at now?' I
replied. 'Has not every thing been settled again
and again to your satisfaction? And are you to
talk of leaving me every hour, without either rhyme
or reason?'

'Ay, but I was only making fashion before,'

replied Andrew; 'but it's come on me in sair earnest now—Lose or win, I daur gae nae farther wi' your honour; and if ye'll tak my foolish advice, ye'll bide by a broken tryste, rather than gang forward yoursell—I hae a sincere regard for ye, and I'm sure ye'll be a credit to your friends if ye live to saw out your wild aits, and get some mair sense and steadiness—But I can follow ye nae farther, even if ye suld founder and perish from the way for lack of guidance and counsel — to gang into Rob Roy's country is a mere tempting o' Providence.'

'Rob Roy?' said I, in some surprise; 'I know no such person. What new trick is this, Andrew?'

'It's hard,' said Andrew — 'very hard, that a man canna be believed when he speaks Heaven's truth, just because he's whiles owercome, and tells lees a little when there is necessary occasion. Ye needna ask whae Rob Roy is, the reiving lifter that he is—God forgie me! I hope naebody hears us— when ye hae a letter frae him in your pouch. I heard ane o' his gillies bid that auld rudas jaud of a gudewife gie ye that. They thought I didna understand their gibberish; but, though I canna speak it muckle, I can gie a gude guess at what I hear them say—I never thought to hae tauld ye that, but in a fright a' things come out that suld be keepit in. O, Maister Frank, a' your uncle's follies, and a' your cousins' pliskies, were naething to this!—Drink clean cap-out, like Sir Hildebrand; begin the blessed morning with brandy sops, like Squire Percie; swagger, like Squire Thorncliff; rin wud amang the lasses, like Squire John; gamble, like Richard; win souls to the pope and the deevil, like Rashleigh; rive, rant, break the Sabbath, and do the pope's bidding, like them a' put thegither— But, merciful Providence! take care o' your young bluid, and gang nae near Rob Roy!'

Andrew's alarm was too sincere to permit me to suppose he counterfeited. I contented myself, however, with telling him, that I meant to remain in the alehouse that night, and desired to have the horses well looked after. As to the rest, I charged him to observe the strictest silence upon the subject of his alarm, and he might rely upon it I would not incur any serious danger without due precaution. He followed me with a dejected air into the house, observing between his teeth, 'Man suld be served afore beast—I haena had a morsel in my mouth, but the rough legs o' that auld muircock, this haill blessed day.'

The harmony of the company seemed to have suffered some interruption since my departure, for I found Mr. Galbraith and my friend the Bailie high in dispute.

'I'll hear nae sic language,' said Mr. Jarvie, as I entered, 'respecting the Duke o' Argyle and the name o' Campbell. He's a worthy public-spirited nobleman, and a credit to the country, and a friend and benefactor to the trade o' Glasgow.'

'I'll say naething against MacCallum More and the Slioch-nan-Diarmid,' said the lesser Highlander, laughing. 'I live on the wrang side of Glencroe to quarrel with Inverara.'

'Our loch ne'er saw the Cawmil lymphads,'* said the bigger Highlander. 'She'll speak her mind and fear naebody—She doesna value a Cawmil mair as a Cowan, and ye may tell MacCallum More that Allan Iverach said sae—It's a far cry to Lochow.'†

Mr. Galbraith, on whom the repeated pledges which he had quaffed had produced some influence, slapped his hand on the table with great force, and said in a stern voice, 'There's a bloody debt due by that family, and they will pay it one day—The banes of a loyal and a gallant Grahame hae lang rattled in their coffin for vengeance on thae Dukes of Guile and Lords for Lorn. There ne'er was treason in Scotland but a Cawmil was at the bottom o't; and now that the wrang side's uppermost, wha but the Cawmils for keeping down the right? But this warld winna last lang, and it will be time to sharp the maiden‡ for shearing o' craigs and thrapples. I hope to see the auld rusty lass linking at a bluidy harst again.'

'For shame, Garschattachin!' exclaimed the Bailie; 'fy for shame, sir; wad ye say sic things before a magistrate, and bring yoursell into trouble? —How d'ye think to mainteen your family and satisfy your creditors, (mysell and others,) if ye gang on in that wild way, which cannot but bring

---

* *Lymphads.* The galley which the family of Argyle and others of the Clan-Campbell carry in their arms.

† Lochow and the adjacent districts formed the original seat of the Campbells. The expression of a 'far cry to Lochow' was proverbial.

‡ A rude kind of guillotine formerly used in Scotland.

you under the law, to the prejudice of a' that's
connected wi' ye ? '

' D—n my creditors,' retorted the gallant Galbraith, ' and you, if ye be ane o' them. I say there
will be a new warld sune—And we shall hae nae
Cawmils cocking their bonnet sae hie, and hounding
their dogs where they daurna come themsells, nor.
protecting thieves, nor murderers, and oppressors,
to harry and spoil better men and mair loyal clans
than themsells.'

The Bailie had a great mind to have continued
the dispute, when the savoury vapour of the broiled
venison, which our landlady now placed before us,
proved so powerful a mediator, that he betook himself to his trencher with great eagerness, leaving
the strangers to carry on the dispute among themselves.

' And tat's true,' said the taller Highlander,
whose name I found was Stewart, ' for we suldna
be plagued and worried here wi' meetings to pit
down Rob Roy, if the Cawmils didna gie him
refutch. I was ane o' thirty o' my ain name—
part Glenfinlas, and part men that came down
frae Appine. We shased the MacGregors as ye
wad shase rae-deer, till we came into Glenfalloch's
country, and the Cawmils raise and wadna let us
pursue nae farder, and sae we lost our labour; but
her wad gie twa and a plack to be as near Rob as
she was tat day.'

It seemed to happen very unfortunately, that in
every topic of discourse which these warlike gentlemen introduced, my friend the Bailie found some

matter of offence. 'Ye'll forgie me speaking my mind, sir; but ye wad maybe hae gien the best bowl in your bonnet to hae been as far awa frae Rob as ye are e'en now—Odd, my het pleugh-culter wad hae been naething to his claymore.'

'She had better speak nae mair about her culter, or, by G—, her will gar her eat her words, and twa handfuls o' cauld steel to drive them ower wi'!' And, with a most inauspicious and menacing look, the mountaineer laid his hand on his dagger.

'We'll hae nae quarrelling, Allan,' said his shorter companion; 'and if the Glasgow gentleman has ony regard for Rob Roy, he'll maybe see him in cauld irons the night, and playing tricks on a tow the morn; for this country has been ower lang plagued wi' him, and his race is near-hand run —And it's time, Allan, we were ganging to our lads.'

'Hout awa, Inverashalloch,' said Galbraith. 'Mind the auld saw, man—It's a bauld moon, quoth Bennygask—another pint, quoth Lesley—we'll no start for another chappin.'

'I hae had chappins eneugh,' said Inverashalloch; 'I'll drink my quart of usquebaugh or brandy, wi' ony honest fellow, but the deil a drap mair, when I hae wark to do in the morning. And, in my puir thinking, Garschattachin, ye had better be thinking to bring up your horsemen to the Clachan before day, that we may a' start fair.'

'What the deevil are ye in sic a hurry for?' said Garschattachin; 'meat and mass never hindered wark. An it had been my directing, deil a bit o' me wad hae fashed ye to come down the glens to help us. The garrison and our ain horse could hae taen Rob Roy easily eneugh. There's the hand,' he said, holding up his own, 'should lay him on the green, and never ask a Hielandman o' ye a' for his help.'

'Ye might hae loot us bide still where we were, then,' said Inverashalloch. 'I didna come sixty miles without being sent for. But an ye'll hae my opinion, I redd ye keep your mouth better steekit, if ye hope to speed. Shored folk live lang, and sae may him ye ken o'. The way to catch a bird is no to fling your bannet at her. And also thae gentlemen hae heard some things they suldna hae heard, an the brandy hadna been ower bauld for your brain, Major Galbraith.—Ye needna cock your hat and bully wi' me, man, for I will not bear it.'

'I hae said it,' said Galbraith, with a solemn air of drunken gravity, 'that I will quarrel no more this night either with broadcloth or tartan. When I am off duty, I'll quarrel with you or ony man in the Hielands or Lowlands, but not on duty—no—no.—I wish we heard o' these red-coats.—If it had been to do ony thing against King James, we wad hae seen them lang syne—but when it's to keep the peace o' the country, they can lie as lound as their neighbours.'

As he spoke, we heard the measured footsteps of a body of infantry on the march; and an officer, followed by two or three files of soldiers, entered the apartment. He spoke in an English accent, which was very pleasant to my ears, now so long accustomed to the varying brogue of the Highland and Lowland Scotch.

'You are, I suppose, Major Galbraith, of the squadron of Lennox Militia, and these are the two Highland gentlemen with whom I was appointed to meet in this place?'

They assented, and invited the officer to take some refreshments, which he declined.

'I have been too late, gentlemen, and am desirous to make up time. I have orders to search for and arrest two persons guilty of treasonable practices.'

'We'll wash our hands o' that,' said Inverashalloch. 'I came here wi' my men to fight against the red MacGregor that killed my cousin seven times removed, Duncan MacLaren in Invernenty;* but I will hae nothing to do touching honest gentlemen that may gaun through the country on their ain business.'

'Nor I neither,' said Iverach.

Major Galbraith took up the matter more solemnly, and, premising his oration with a hiccup, spoke to the following purpose:

'I shall say nothing against King George, Captain, because, as it happens, my commission may rin in his name—but one commission being good, sir, does not make another bad; and some think that

---

* This, as appears from the introductory matter to this Tale, is an anachronism. The slaughter of MacLaren, a retainer of the chief of Appine, by the MacGregors, did not take place till after Rob Roy's death, since it happened in 1736.

James may be just as good a name as George. There's the king that is—and there's the king that suld of right be—I say, an honest man may and suld be loyal to them both, Captain.—But I am of the Lord Lieutenant's opinion for the time, as it becomes a militia officer and a depute-lieutenant,— and about treason and all that, it's lost time to speak of it—least said is sunest mended.'

' I am sorry to see how you have been employing your time, sir,' replied the English officer,—as indeed the honest gentleman's reasoning had a strong relish of the liquor he had been drinking,—' and I could wish, sir, it had been otherwise on an occasion of this consequence. I would recommend to you to try to sleep for an hour — Do these gentlemen belong to your party?'—looking at the Bailie and me, who, engaged in eating our supper, had paid little attention to the officer on his entrance.

' Travellers, sir,' said Galbraith—' lawful travellers by sea and land, as the prayer-book hath it.'

' My instructions,' said the Captain, taking a light to survey us closer, ' are to place under arrest an elderly and a young person, and I think these gentlemen answer nearly the description.'

' Take care what you say, sir,' said Mr. Jarvie; ' it shall not be your red coat nor your laced hat shall protect you, if you put any affront on me. I 'se convene ye baith in an action of scandal and false imprisonment—I am a free burgess and a magistrate o' Glasgow; Nicol Jarvie is my name, sae was my father's afore me—I am a bailie, be praised for the honour, and my father was a deacon.'

' He was a prick-eared cur,' said Major Galbraith, ' and fought agane the King at Bothwell Brigg.'

' He paid what he ought and what he bought, Mr. Galbraith,' said the Bailie, ' and was an honester man than ever stude on your shanks.'

' I have no time to attend to all this,' said the officer; ' I must positively detain you, gentlemen, unless you can produce some respectable security that you are loyal subjects.'

' I desire to be carried before some civil magistrate,' said the Bailie,—' the sherra or the judge of the bounds—I am not obliged to answer every red-coat that speers questions at me.'

' Well, sir, I shall know how to manage you if you are silent—And you, sir,' (to me) ' what may your name be ? '

' Francis Osbaldistone, sir.'

' What, a son of Sir Hildebrand Osbaldistone, of Northumberland ? '

' No, sir,' interrupted the Bailie; ' a son of the great William Osbaldistone, of the House of Osbaldistone and Tresham, Crane-Alley, London.'

' I am afraid, sir,' said the officer, ' your name only increases the suspicions against you, and lays me under the necessity of requesting that you will give up what papers you have in charge.'

I observed the Highlanders look anxiously at each other when this proposal was made. ' I had none,' I replied, ' to surrender.'

The officer commanded me to be disarmed and searched. To have resisted would have been madness. I accordingly gave up my arms, and submitted to a search, which was conducted as civilly as an operation of the kind well could. They found nothing except the note which I had received that night through the hand of the landlady.

'This is different from what I expected,' said the officer; 'but it affords us good grounds for detaining you. Here I find you in written communication with the outlawed robber, Robert MacGregor Campbell, who has been so long the plague of this district—How do you account for that?'

'Spies of Rob!' said Inverashalloch—'we wad serve them right to strap them up till the neist tree.'

'We are gaun to see after some gear o' our ain, gentlemen,' said the Bailie, 'that's fa'en into his hands by accident—there's nae law agane a man looking after his ain, I hope?'

'How did you come by this letter?' said the officer, addressing himself to me.

I could not think of betraying the poor woman who had given it to me, and remained silent.

'Do you know any thing of it, fellow?' said the officer, looking at Andrew, whose jaws were chattering like a pair of castanets at the threats thrown out by the Highlander.

'O ay, I ken a' about it—It was a Hieland loon gied the letter to that lang-tongued jaud the gudewife there—I'll be sworn my maister kend naething about it. But he's wilfu' to gang up the hills and speak wi' Rob; and O, sir, it wad be a charity just to send a wheen o' your red-coats to see him safe back to Glasgow again whether he will or no—And ye can keep Mr. Jarvie as lang as ye like—He's responsible eneugh for ony fine ye may lay on him—and so's my master for that matter—for me, I'm just a puir gardener lad, and no worth your steering.'

'I believe,' said the officer, 'the best thing I can do is to send these persons to the garrison under an escort. They seem to be in immediate correspondence with the enemy, and I shall be in no respect answerable for suffering them to be at liberty.—Gentlemen, you will consider yourselves as my prisoners. So soon as dawn approaches I will send you to a place of security. If you be the persons you describe yourselves, it will soon appear, and you will sustain no great inconvenience from being detained a day or two.—I can hear no remonstrances,' he continued, turning away from the Bailie, whose mouth was open to address him, 'the service I am on gives me no time for idle discussions.'

'Aweel — aweel, sir,' said the Bailie, 'you're welcome to a tune on your ain fiddle; but see if I dinna gar ye dance till't afore a's dune.'

An anxious consultation now took place between the officer and the Highlanders, but carried on in so low a tone, that it was impossible to catch the sense. So soon as it was concluded they all left the house. At their departure, the Bailie thus expressed himself: 'Thae Hielandmen are o' the westland clans, and just as light-handed as their neighbours, an a' tales be true, and yet ye see they hae brought them frae the head o' Argyleshire to make war wi' puir Rob for some auld ill-will that they hae at him and his sirname—And there's the Grahames, and the Buchanans, and the Lennox gentry, a' mounted and in order.—It's weel kend their quarrel—and I dinna blame them—naebody likes to lose his kye—and then there's sodgers, puir things, hoyed out frae the garrison at a'body's bidding—Puir Rob will hae his hands fu' by the time the sun comes ower the hill. Weel — it's wrang for a magistrate to be wishing ony thing agane the course o' justice, but deil o' me an I wad break my heart to hear that Rob had gien them a' their paiks!'

CHAPTER XXX

General,
Hear me, and mark me well, and look upon me
Directly in my face—my woman's face—
See if one fear, one shadow of a terror,
One paleness dare appear, but from my anger,
To lay hold on your mercies.

BONDUCA.

WE were permitted to slumber out the remainder of the night in the best manner that the miserable accommodations of the alehouse permitted. The Bailie, fatigued with his journey and the subsequent scenes, less interested also in the event of our arrest, which to him could only be a matter of temporary inconvenience, perhaps less nice than habit had rendered me about the cleanliness or decency of his couch, tumbled himself into one of the cribs which I have already described, and soon was heard to snore soundly. A broken sleep, snatched by intervals, while I rested my head upon the table, was my only refreshment. In the course of the night I had occasion to observe, that there seemed to be some doubt and hesitation in the motions of the soldiery. Men were sent out as if to obtain intelligence, and returned apparently without bringing any satisfactory information to their commanding officer. He was obviously eager and anxious, and again dispatched small parties of two or three men, some of whom, as I could understand from what the others whispered to each other, did not return again to the Clachan.

The morning had broken, when a corporal and two men rushed into the hut, dragging after them, in a sort of triumph, a Highlander, whom I immediately recognised as my acquaintance the ex-turnkey. The Bailie, who started up at the noise with which they entered, immediately made the same discovery, and exclaimed, 'Mercy on us! they hae grippit the puir creature Dougal—Captain, I will put in bail—sufficient bail, for that Dougal creature.'

To this offer, dictated undoubtedly by a grateful recollection of the late interference of the Highlander in his behalf, the Captain only answered, by requesting Mr. Jarvie to 'mind his own affairs, and remember that he was himself for the present a prisoner.'

'I take you to witness, Mr. Osbaldistone,' said the Bailie, who was probably better acquainted with the process in civil than in military cases, 'that he has refused sufficient bail. It's my opinion that the creature Dougal will have a good action of wrongous imprisonment and damages agane him, under the Act seventeen hundred and one, and I'll see the creature righted.'

The officer, whose name I understood was Thornton, paying no attention to the Bailie's threats or expostulations, instituted a very close inquiry into Dougal's life and conversation, and compelled him to admit, though with apparent reluctance, the successive facts,—that he knew Rob Roy Mac-

Gregor—that he had seen him within these twelve months — within these six months — within this month—within this week; in fine, that he had parted from him only an hour ago. All this detail came like drops of blood from the prisoner, and was, to all appearance, only extorted by the threat of an halter and the next tree, which Captain Thornton assured him should be his doom, if he did not give direct and special information.

'And now, my friend,' said the officer, 'you will please inform me how many men your master has with him at present.'

Dougal looked in every direction except at the querist, and began to answer, 'She canna just be sure about that.'

'Look at me, you Highland dog,' said the officer, 'and remember your life depends on your answer. How many rogues had that outlawed scoundrel with him when you left him?'

'Ou, no aboon sax rogues when I was gane.'

'And where are the rest of his banditti?'

'Gane wi' the Lieutenant agane ta westland carles.'

'Against the westland clans?' said the Captain. 'Umph—that is likely enough; and what rogue's errand were you dispatched upon?'

'Just to see what your honour and ta gentlemen red-coats were doing doun here at ta Clachan.'

'The creature will prove fause-hearted after a',' said the Bailie, who by this time had planted himself close behind me; 'it's lucky I didna pit mysell to expenses anent him.'

'And now, my friend,' said the Captain, 'let us

understand each other. You have confessed yourself a spy, and should string up to the next tree—
but come, if you will do me one good turn, I will
do you another. You, Donald—you shall just in
the way of kindness carry me and a small party
to the place where you left your master, as I wish
to speak a few words with him on serious affairs;
and I 'll let you go about your business, and give
you five guineas to boot.'

'Oigh! oigh!' exclaimed Dougal, in the extremity of distress and perplexity, 'she canna do
tat—she canna do tat—she 'll rather be hanged.'

'Hanged, then, you shall be, my friend,' said the
officer; 'and your blood be upon your own head.
—Corporal Cramp, do you play Provost-Marshal—
away with him!'

The corporal had confronted poor Dougal for
some time, ostentatiously twisting a piece of cord
which he had found in the house into the form
of a halter. He now threw it about the culprit's
neck, and, with the assistance of two soldiers, had
dragged Dougal as far as the door, when, overcome
with the terror of immediate death, he exclaimed,
'Shentlemans, stops—stops!—She 'll do his honour's
bidding—stops!'

'Awa wi' the creature!' said the Bailie, 'he
deserves hanging mair now than ever—awa wi'
him, corporal—why dinna ye tak him awa?'

'It 's my belief and opinion, honest gentleman,'
said the corporal, 'that if you were going to be
hanged yourself, you would be in no such d—d
hurry.'

This by-dialogue prevented my hearing what passed between the prisoner and Captain Thornton, but I heard the former snivel out, in a very subdued tone, 'And ye'll ask her to gang nae farther than just to show ye where the MacGregor is?—Ohon! ohon!'

'Silence your howling, you rascal—No; I give you my word I will ask you to go no farther.—Corporal, make the men fall-in in front of the houses. Get out these gentlemen's horses; we must carry them with us. I cannot spare any men to guard them here.—Come, my lads, get under arms.'

The soldiers bustled about, and were ready to move. We were led out, along with Dougal, in the capacity of prisoners. As we left the hut, I heard our companion in captivity remind the Captain of 'ta foive kuineas.'

'Here they are for you,' said the officer, putting gold into his hand; 'but observe, that if you attempt to mislead me, I will blow your brains out with my own hand.'

'The creature,' said the Bailie, 'is waur than I judged him—it is a warldly and a perfidious creature—O the filthy lucre of gain that men gies themsells up to! My father the deacon used to say, the penny siller slew mair souls than the naked sword slew bodies.'

The landlady now approached, and demanded payment of her reckoning, including all that had been quaffed by Major Galbraith and his Highland friends. The English officer remonstrated, but

Mrs. MacAlpine declared, if she 'hadna trusted to his honour's name being used in their company, she wad never hae drawn them a stoup o' liquor; for Mr. Galbraith, she might see him again, or she might no, but weel did she wot she had sma' chance of seeing her siller—and she was a puir widow, had naething but her custom to rely on.'

Captain Thornton put a stop to her remonstrances by paying the charge, which was only a few English shillings, though the amount sounded very formidable in Scottish denominations. The generous officer would have included Mr. Jarvie and me in this general acquittance; but the Bailie disregarding an intimation from the landlady, to 'make as muckle of the Inglishers as we could, for they were sure to gie us plague eneugh,' went into a formal accounting respecting our share of the reckoning, and paid it accordingly. The Captain took the opportunity to make us some slight apology for detaining us. 'If we were loyal and peaceable subjects,' he said, 'we would not regret being stopped for a day, when it was essential to the king's service; if otherwise, he was acting according to his duty.'

We were compelled to accept an apology which it would have served no purpose to refuse, and we sallied out to attend him on his march.

I shall never forget the delightful sensation with which I exchanged the dark, smoky, smothering atmosphere of the Highland hut, in which we had passed the night so uncomfortably, for the refreshing fragrance of the morning air, and the glorious beams of the rising sun, which, from a tabernacle of purple and golden clouds, were darted full on such a scene of natural romance and beauty as had never before greeted my eyes. To the left lay the valley, down which the Forth wandered on its easterly course, surrounding the beautiful detached hill, with all its garland of woods. On the right, amid a profusion of thickets, knolls, and crags, lay the bed of a broad mountain lake, lightly curled into tiny waves by the breath of the morning breeze, each glittering in its course under the influence of the sunbeams. High hills, rocks, and banks, waving with natural forests of birch and oak, formed the borders of this enchanting sheet of water; and, as their leaves rustled to the wind and twinkled in the sun, gave to the depth of solitude a sort of life and vivacity. Man alone seemed to be placed in a state of inferiority, in a scene where all the ordinary features of nature were raised and exalted. The miserable little *bourocks*, as the Bailie termed them, of which about a dozen formed the village called the Clachan of Aberfoil, were composed of loose stones, cemented by clay instead of mortar, and thatched by turfs, laid rudely upon rafters formed of native and unhewn birches and oaks from the woods around. The roofs approached the ground so nearly, that Andrew Fairservice observed we might have ridden over the village the night before, and never found out we were near it, unless our horses' feet had 'gane through the riggin'.'

From all we could see, Mrs. MacAlpine's house, miserable as were the quarters it afforded, was still by far the best in the hamlet; and I dare say (if my description gives you any curiosity to see it) you will hardly find it much improved at the present day, for the Scotch are not a people who speedily admit innovation, even when it comes in the shape of improvement.*

The inhabitants of these miserable dwellings were disturbed by the noise of our departure; and as our party of about twenty soldiers drew up in rank before marching off, we were reconnoitred by many a beldam from the half-opened door of her cottage. As these sibyls thrust forth their grey heads, imperfectly covered with close caps of flannel, and showed their shrivelled brows, and long skinny arms, with various gestures, shrugs, and muttered expressions in Gaelic addressed to each other, my imagination recurred to the witches of Macbeth, and I imagined I read in the features of these crones the malevolence of the weird sisters. The little children also, who began to crawl forth, some quite naked, and others very imperfectly covered with tatters of tartan stuff, clapped their tiny hands, and grinned at the English soldiers, with an expression

---

* I do not know how this might stand in Mr. Osbaldistone's day, but I can assure the reader, whose curiosity may lead him to visit the scenes of these romantic adventures, that the Clachan of Aberfoil now affords a very comfortable little inn. If he chances to be a Scottish antiquary, it will be an additional recommendation to him, that he will find himself in the vicinity of the Rev. Dr. Patrick Grahame, minister of the gospel at Aberfoil, whose urbanity in communicating information on the subject of national antiquities, is scarce exceeded even by the stores of legendary lore which he has accumulated.—*Orig. Note.* The respectable clergyman alluded to has been dead for some years.

of national hate and malignity which seemed beyond their years. I remarked particularly that there were no men, nor so much as a boy of ten or twelve years old, to be seen among the inhabitants of a village which seemed populous in proportion to its extent; and the idea certainly occurred to me, that we were likely to receive from them, in the course of our journey, more effectual tokens of ill-will than those which lowered on the visages, and dictated the murmurs, of the women and children.

It was not until we commenced our march that the malignity of the elder persons of the community broke forth into expressions. The last file of men had left the village, to pursue a small broken track, formed by the sledges in which the natives transported their peats and turfs, and which led through the woods that fringed the lower end of the lake, when a shrilly sound of female exclamation broke forth, mixed with the screams of children, the whooping of boys, and the clapping of hands with which the Highland dames enforce their notes, whether of rage or lamentation. I asked Andrew, who looked as pale as death, what all this meant.

'I doubt we'll ken that ower sune,' said he. 'Means?—It means that the Highland wives are cursing and banning the red-coats, and wishing ill-luck to them, and ilka ane that ever spoke the Saxon tongue. I have heard wives flyte in England and Scotland—it's nae marvel to hear them flyte ony gate—but sic ill-scrapit tongues as thae Hieland carlines'—and sic grewsome wishes, that men should be slaughtered like sheep—and that they may lapper

their hands to the elbows in their heart's blude—
and that they suld dee the death of Walter Cuming
of Guiyock,* wha hadna as muckle o' him left
thegither as would supper a messan-dog—sic awsome
language as that I ne'er heard out o' a human
thrapple;—and, unless the deil wad rise amang
them to gie them a lesson, I thinkna that their
talent at cursing could be amended. The warst o't
is, they bid us aye gang up the loch, and see what
we 'll land in.'

Adding Andrew's information to what I had
myself observed, I could scarce doubt that some
attack was meditated upon our party. The road,
as we advanced, seemed to afford every facility for
such an unpleasant interruption. At first it winded
apart from the lake through marshy meadow ground,
overgrown with copsewood, now traversing dark and
close thickets which would have admitted an ambuscade to be sheltered within a few yards of our
line of march, and frequently crossing rough mountain torrents, some of which took the soldiers up
to the knees, and ran with such violence, that
their force could only be stemmed by the strength
of two or three men holding fast by each other's
arms. It certainly appeared to me, though altogether unacquainted with military affairs, that a
sort of half-savage warriors, as I had heard the

---

* A great feudal oppressor, who, riding on some cruel purpose through
the forest of Guiyock, was thrown from his horse, and, his foot being
caught in the stirrup, was dragged along by the frightened animal till
he was torn to pieces. The expression, Walter of Guiyock's curse, is
proverbial.

Highlanders asserted to be, might, in such passes as these, attack a party of regular forces with great advantage. The Bailie's good sense and shrewd observation had led him to the same conclusion, as I understood from his requesting to speak with the Captain, whom he addressed nearly in the following terms:—' Captain, it's no to fleech ony favour out o' ye, for I scorn it—and it's under protest that I reserve my action and pleas of oppression and wrongous imprisonment;—but, being a friend to King George and his army, I take the liberty to speer—Dinna ye think ye might tak a better time to gang up this glen? If ye are seeking Rob Roy, he's kend to be better than half a hundred men strong when he's at the fewest; and if he brings in the Glengyle folk, and the Glenfinlas and Balquidder lads, he may come to gie you your kail through the reek; and it's my sincere advice, as a king's friend, ye had better tak back again to the Clachan, for thae women at Aberfoil are like the scarts and sea-maws at the Cumries, there's aye foul weather follows their skirling.'

' Make yourself easy, sir,' replied Captain Thornton, ' I am in the execution of my orders. And as you say you are a friend to King George, you will be glad to learn, that it is impossible that this gang of ruffians, whose license has disturbed the country so long, can escape the measures now taken to suppress them. The horse squadron of militia, commanded by Major Galbraith, is already joined by two or more troops of cavalry, which will occupy all the lower passes of this wild country;

three hundred Highlanders, under the two gentlemen you saw at the inn, are in possession of the upper part, and various strong parties from the garrison are securing the hills and glens in different directions. Our last accounts of Rob Roy correspond with what this fellow has confessed, that, finding himself surrounded on all sides, he had dismissed the greater part of his followers, with the purpose either of lying concealed, or of making his escape through his superior knowledge of the passes.'

'I dinna ken,' said the Bailie; 'there's mair brandy than brains in Garschattachin's head this morning—And I wadna, an I were you, Captain, rest my main dependence on the Hielandmen—hawks winna pike out hawks' een. They may quarrel amang themsells, and gie ilk ither ill names, and maybe a slash wi' a claymore; but they are sure to join in the lang run against a' civilized folk, that wear breeks on their hinder ends, and hae purses in their pouches.'

Apparently these admonitions were not altogether thrown away on Captain Thornton. He reformed his line of march, commanded his soldiers to unsling their firelocks and fix their bayonets, and formed an advanced and rear-guard, each consisting of a non-commissioned officer and two soldiers, who received strict orders to keep an alert look-out. Dougal underwent another and very close examination, in which he steadfastly asserted the truth of what he had before affirmed; and being rebuked on account of the suspicious and dangerous appearance of the route by which he was guiding them, he answered with a sort of testiness that seemed very natural, 'Her nainsell didna mak ta road—an shentlemans likit grand roads, she suld hae pided at Glasco.'

All this passed off well enough, and we resumed our progress.

Our route, though leading towards the lake, had hitherto been so much shaded by wood, that we only from time to time obtained a glimpse of that beautiful sheet of water. But the road now suddenly emerged from the forest ground, and, winding close by the margin of the loch, afforded us a full view of its spacious mirror, which now, the breeze having totally subsided, reflected in still magnificence the high dark heathy mountains, huge grey rocks, and shaggy banks, by which it is encircled. The hills now sunk on its margin so closely, and were so broken and precipitous, as to afford no passage except just upon the narrow line of the track which we occupied, and which was overhung with rocks, from which we might have been destroyed merely by rolling down stones, without much possibility of offering resistance. Add to this, that, as the road winded round every promontory and bay which indented the lake, there was rarely a possibility of seeing a hundred yards before us. Our commander appeared to take some alarm at the nature of the pass in which he was engaged, which displayed itself in repeated orders to his soldiers to be on the alert, and in many threats of instant death to Dougal, if he should be found to have led them into danger. Dougal received these threats with an air of stupid impenetrability, which might arise either from conscious innocence, or from dogged resolution.

'If shentlemans were seeking ta Red Gregarach,' he said, 'to be sure they couldna expect to find her without some wee danger.'

Just as the Highlander uttered these words, a halt was made by the corporal commanding the advance, who sent back one of the file who formed it, to tell the Captain that the path in front was occupied by Highlanders, stationed on a commanding point of particular difficulty. Almost at the same instant a soldier from the rear came to say, that they heard the sound of a bagpipe in the woods through which we had just passed. Captain Thornton, a man of conduct as well as courage, instantly resolved to force the pass in front, without waiting till he was assailed from the rear; and, assuring his soldiers that the bagpipes which they heard were those of the friendly Highlanders who were advancing to their assistance, he stated to them the importance of advancing and securing Rob Roy, if possible, before these auxiliaries should come up to divide with them the honour, as well as the reward which was placed on the head of this celebrated freebooter. He therefore ordered the rear-guard to join the centre, and both to close up to the advance, doubling his files, so as to occupy with his column the whole practicable part of the road, and to present such a front as its breadth admitted. Dougal, to whom he said in a whisper,

'You dog, if you have deceived me you shall die for it!' was placed in the centre, between two grenadiers, with positive orders to shoot him if he attempted an escape. The same situation was assigned to us, as being the safest, and Captain Thornton, taking his half-pike from the soldier who carried it, placed himself at the head of his little detachment, and gave the word to march forward.

The party advanced with the firmness of English soldiers. Not so Andrew Fairservice, who was frightened out of his wits; and not so, if truth must be told, either the Bailie or I myself, who, without feeling the same degree of trepidation, could not with stoical indifference see our lives exposed to hazard in a quarrel with which we had no concern. But there was neither time for remonstrance nor remedy.

We approached within about twenty yards of the spot where the advanced-guard had seen some appearance of an enemy. It was one of those promontories which run into the lake, and round the base of which the road had hitherto winded in the manner I have described. In the present case, however, the path, instead of keeping the water's edge, scaled the promontory by one or two rapid zigzags, carried in a broken track along the precipitous face of a slaty grey rock, which would otherwise have been absolutely inaccessible. On the top of this rock, only to be approached by a road so broken, so narrow, and so precarious, the corporal declared he had seen the bonnets and long-barrelled guns of several mountaineers, apparently couched among the long heath and brushwood which crested the eminence. Captain Thornton ordered him to move forward with three files, to dislodge the supposed ambuscade, while at a more slow but steady pace, he advanced to his support with the rest of his party.

The attack which he meditated was prevented by the unexpected apparition of a female upon the summit of the rock. 'Stand!' she said, with a commanding tone, 'and tell me what ye seek in MacGregor's country?'

I have seldom seen a finer or more commanding form than this woman. She might be between the term of forty and fifty years, and had a countenance which must once have been of a masculine cast of beauty; though now, imprinted with deep lines by exposure to rough weather, and perhaps by the wasting influence of grief and passion, its features were only strong, harsh, and expressive. She wore her plaid, not drawn around her head and shoulders, as is the fashion of the women in Scotland, but disposed around her body as the Highland soldiers wear theirs. She had a man's bonnet, with a feather in it, an unsheathed sword in her hand, and a pair of pistols at her girdle.

'It's Helen Campbell, Rob's wife,' said the Bailie, in a whisper of considerable alarm; 'and there will be broken heads amang us or it's lang.'

'What seek ye here?' she asked again of Captain Thornton, who had himself advanced to reconnoitre.

'We seek the outlaw, Rob Roy MacGregor

Campbell,' answered the officer, 'and make no war on women; therefore offer no vain opposition to the king's troops, and assure yourself of civil treatment.'

'Ay,' retorted the Amazon, 'I am no stranger to your tender mercies. Ye have left me neither name nor fame — my mother's bones will shrink aside in their grave when mine are laid beside them —Ye have left me and mine neither house nor hold, blanket nor bedding, cattle to feed us, or flocks to clothe us—Ye have taken from us all—all!—The very name of our ancestors have ye taken away, and now ye come for our lives.'

'I seek no man's life,' replied the Captain; 'I only execute my orders. If you are alone, good woman, you have nought to fear—if there are any with you so rash as to offer useless resistance, their own blood be on their own heads—Move forward, sergeant.'

'Forward — march,' said the non-commissioned officer. 'Huzza, my boys, for Rob Roy's head and a purse of gold!'

He quickened his pace into a run, followed by the six soldiers; but as they attained the first traverse of the ascent, the flash of a dozen of firelocks from various parts of the pass parted in quick succession and deliberate aim. The sergeant, shot through the body, still struggled to gain the ascent, raised himself by his hands to clamber up the face of the rock, but relaxed his grasp, after a desperate effort, and falling, rolled from the face of the cliff into the deep lake, where he perished. Of the soldiers three fell, slain or disabled; the others retreated on their main body, all more or less wounded.

'Grenadiers, to the front!' said Captain Thornton. —You are to recollect, that in those days this description of soldiers actually carried that destructive species of fire-work from which they derive their name. The four grenadiers moved to the front accordingly. The officer commanded the rest of the party to be ready to support them, and only saying to us, 'Look to your safety, gentlemen,' gave, in rapid succession, the word to the grenadiers: 'Open your pouches — handle your grenades—blow your matches—fall on.'

The whole advanced with a shout, headed by Captain Thornton, the grenadiers preparing to throw their grenades among the bushes where the ambuscade lay, and the musketeers to support them by an instant and close assault. Dougal, forgotten in the scuffle, wisely crept into the thicket which overhung that part of the road where we had first halted, which he ascended with the activity of a wild cat. I followed his example, instinctively recollecting that the fire of the Highlanders would sweep the open track. I clambered until out of breath; for a continued spattering fire, in which every shot was multiplied by a thousand echoes, the hissing of the kindled fusees of the grenades, and the successive explosion of those missiles, mingled with the huzzas of the soldiers, and the yells and cries of their Highland antagonists, formed a contrast which added—I do not shame to own it—

wings to my desire to reach a place of safety. The difficulties of the ascent soon increased so much that I despaired of reaching Dougal, who seemed to swing himself from rock to rock, and stump to stump, with the facility of a squirrel, and I turned down my eyes to see what had become of my other companions. Both were brought to a very awkward stand-still.

The Bailie, to whom I suppose fear had given a temporary share of agility, had ascended about twenty feet from the path, when his foot slipping, as he straddled from one huge fragment of rock to another, he would have slumbered with his father the deacon, whose acts and words he was so fond of quoting, but for a projecting branch of a ragged thorn, which, catching hold of the skirts of his riding coat, supported him in mid-air, where he dangled not unlike to the sign of the Golden Fleece over the door of a mercer in the Trongate of his native city.

As for Andrew Fairservice, he had advanced with better success, until he had attained the top of a bare cliff, which, rising above the wood, exposed him, at least in his own opinion, to all the dangers of the neighbouring skirmish, while, at the same time, it was of such precipitous and impracticable nature, that he dared neither to advance nor retreat. Footing it up and down upon the narrow space which the top of the cliff afforded, (very like a fellow at a country-fair dancing upon a trencher,) he roared for mercy in Gaelic and English alternately, according to the side on which the scale of victory seemed to predominate, while his exclamations were only answered by the groans of the Bailie, who suffered much, not only from apprehension, but from the pendulous posture in which he hung suspended by the loins.

On perceiving the Bailie's precarious situation, my first idea was to attempt to render him assistance; but this was impossible without the concurrence of Andrew, whom neither sign nor entreaty, nor command, nor expostulation, could inspire with courage to adventure the descent from his painful elevation, where, like an unskilful and obnoxious minister of state, unable to escape from the eminence to which he had presumptuously ascended, he continued to pour forth piteous prayers for mercy, which no one heard, and to skip to and fro, writhing his body into all possible antick shapes to avoid the balls which he conceived to be whistling around him.

In a few minutes this cause of terror ceased, for the fire at first so well sustained, now sunk at once, a sure sign that the conflict was concluded. To gain some spot from which I could see how the day had gone was now my object, in order to appeal to the mercy of the victors, who, I trusted, (whichever side might be gainers,) would not suffer the honest Bailie to remain suspended, like the coffin of Mahomet, between heaven and earth, without lending a hand to disengage him. At length, by dint of scrambling, I found a spot which commanded a view of the field of battle. It was indeed ended; and, as my mind already augured, from the place and circumstances attending the contest, it had terminated in the defeat of Captain Thornton. I saw a party of Highlanders in the act of disarming that officer, and the scanty remainder of his party. They consisted of about twelve men, most of whom were wounded, who, surrounded by treble their number, and without the power either to advance or retreat, exposed to a murderous and well-aimed fire, which they had no means of returning with effect, had at length laid down their arms by the order of their officer, when he saw that the road in his rear was occupied, and that protracted resistance would be only wasting the lives of his brave followers. By the Highlanders, who fought under cover, the victory was cheaply bought, at the expense of one man slain and two wounded by the grenades. All this I learned afterwards. At present I only comprehended the general result of the day, from seeing the English officer, whose face was covered with blood, stripped of his hat and arms, and his men, with sullen and dejected countenances, which marked their deep regret, enduring, from the wild and martial figures who surrounded them, the severe measures to which the laws of war subject the vanquished for security of the victors.

CHAPTER XXXI

'Woe to the vanquish'd!' was stern Brenno's word,
When sunk proud Rome beneath the Gallic sword—
'Woe to the vanquish'd!' when his massive blade
Bore down the scale against her ransom weigh'd;
And on the field of foughten battle still,
Woe knows no limit save the victor's will.
THE GAULLIAD.

I ANXIOUSLY endeavoured to distinguish Dougal among the victors. I had little doubt that the part he had played was assumed, on purpose to lead the English officer into the defile, and I could not help admiring the address with which the ignorant, and apparently half-brutal savage, had veiled his purpose, and the affected reluctance with which he had suffered to be extracted from him the false information which it must have been his purpose from the beginning to communicate. I foresaw we should incur some danger on approaching the victors in the first flush of their success, which was not unstained with cruelty, for one or two of the soldiers, whose wounds prevented them from rising, were poniarded by the victors, or rather by some ragged Highland boys who had mingled with them. I concluded, therefore, it would be unsafe to present ourselves without some mediator; and as Campbell, whom I now could not but identify with the celebrated freebooter Rob Roy, was nowhere to be seen, I resolved to claim the protection of his emissary, Dougal.

After gazing everywhere in vain, I at length retraced my steps to see what assistance I could individually render to my unlucky friend, when, to my great joy, I saw Mr. Jarvie delivered from his state of suspense; and though very black in the face, and much deranged in the garments, safely seated beneath the rock, in front of which he had been so lately suspended. I hastened to join him and offer my congratulations, which he was at first far from receiving in the spirit of cordiality with which they were offered. A heavy fit of coughing scarce permitted him breath enough to express the broken hints which he threw out against my sincerity.

'Uh! uh! uh! uh!—they say a friend—uh! uh!—a friend sticketh closer than a brither—uh! uh! uh!—When I came up here, Maister Osbaldistone, to this country, cursed of God and man —uh! uh!—Heaven forgie me for swearing—on nae man's errand but yours, d'ye think it was fair —uh! uh!—to leave me, first, to be shot or drowned atween red-wud Highlanders and redcoats; and next, to be hung up between heaven and earth, like an auld potato-bogle, without sae muckle as trying—uh! uh!—sae muckle as trying to relieve me?'

I made a thousand apologies, and laboured so hard to represent the impossibility of my affording him relief by my own unassisted exertions, that at length I succeeded, and the Bailie, who was as placable as hasty in his temper, extended his favour to me once more. I next took the liberty of asking him how he had contrived to extricate himself.

'Me extricate! I might hae hung there till the day of judgment, or I could hae helped mysell, wi' my head hinging down on the tae side, and my heels on the tother, like the yarn scales in the weigh-house. It was the creature Dougal that extricated me, as he did yestreen—he cuttit aff the tails o' my coat wi' his durk, and another gillie and him set me on my legs as cleverly as if I had never been aff them.—But to see what a thing gude braid claith is—had I been in ony o' your rotten French camlets now, or your drab-de-berries, it would hae screeded like an auld rag wi' sic a weight as mine.—But fair fa' the weaver that wrought the weft o't—I swung and bobbit yonder as safe as a gabbart * that's moored by a three-plie cable at the Broomie-law.'

I now inquired what had become of his pre-server.

'The creature,' so he continued to call the High-landman, 'contrived to let me ken there wad be danger in gaun near the leddy till he came back, and bade me stay here—I am o' the mind,' he continued, 'that he's seeking after you—it's a con-siderate creature—and troth, I wad swear he was right about the leddy as he ca's her, too—Helen

---

* A kind of lighter used in the river Clyde, probably from the French *gabare.*

Campbell was nane o' the maist douce maidens, nor meekest wives neither, and folk say that Rob himsell stands in awe o' her. I doubt she winna ken me, for it's mony years since we met—I am clear for waiting for the Dougal creature or we gang near her.'

I signified my acquiescence in this reasoning; but it was not the will of fate that day that the Bailie's prudence should profit himself or any one else.

Andrew Fairservice, though he had ceased to caper on the pinnacle upon the cessation of the firing, which had given occasion for his whimsical exercise, continued, as perched on the top of an exposed cliff, too conspicuous an object to escape the sharp eyes of the Highlanders, when they had time to look a little around them. We were apprized he was discovered, by a wild and loud halloo set up among the assembled victors, three or four of whom instantly plunged into the copsewood, and ascended the rocky side of the hill in different directions towards the place where they had discovered this whimsical apparition.

Those who arrived first within gunshot of poor Andrew, did not trouble themselves to offer him any assistance in the ticklish posture of his affairs, but levelling their long Spanish-barrelled guns, gave him to understand by signs, which admitted of no misconstruction, that he must contrive to come down and submit himself to their mercy, or be marked at from beneath, like a regimental target set up for ball-practice. With such a formidable hint for venturous exertion, Andrew Fairservice could no longer hesitate; the more imminent peril overcame his sense of that which seemed less inevitable, and he began to descend the cliff at all risks, clutching to the ivy and oak stumps, and projecting fragments of rock, with an almost feverish anxiety, and never failing, as circumstances left him a hand at liberty, to extend it to the plaided gentry below in an attitude of supplication, as if to deprecate the discharge of their levelled fire-arms. In a word, the fellow, under the influence of a counteracting motive for terror, achieved a safe descent from his perilous eminence, which, I verily believe, nothing but fear of instant death could have moved him to attempt. The awkward mode of Andrew's descent greatly amused the Highlanders below, who fired a shot or two while he was engaged in it, without the purpose of injuring him, as I believe, but merely to enhance the amusement they derived from his extreme terror, and the superlative exertions of agility to which it excited him.

At length he attained firm and comparatively level ground, or rather, to speak more correctly, his foot slipping at the last point of descent, he fell on the earth at his full length, and was raised by the assistance of the Highlanders, who stood to receive him, and who, ere he gained his legs, stripped him not only of the whole contents of his pockets, but of periwig, hat, coat, doublet, stockings, and shoes, performing the feat with such admirable celerity, that, although he fell on his back a well-clothed and decent burgher-seeming serving-man, he arose a forked, uncased, bald-pated, beggarly-looking scare-crow. Without respect to the pain which his un-defended toes experienced from the sharp encounter of the rocks over which they hurried him, those who had detected Andrew proceeded to drag him downward towards the road through all the inter-vening obstacles.

In the course of their descent, Mr. Jarvie and I became exposed to their lynx-eyed observation, and instantly half-a-dozen armed Highlanders thronged around us, with drawn dirks and swords pointed at our faces and throats, and cocked pistols pre-sented against our bodies. To have offered resist-ance would have been madness, especially as we had no weapons capable of supporting such a demon-stration. We therefore submitted to our fate; and, with great roughness on the part of those who assisted at our toilette, were in the act of being reduced to as unsophisticated a state (to use King Lear's phrase) as the plumeless biped Andrew Fair-service, who stood shivering between fear and cold at a few yards' distance. Good chance, however, saved us from this extremity of wretchedness; for, just as I had yielded up my cravat, (a smart Steinkirk, by the way, and richly laced,) and the Bailie had been disrobed of the fragments of his riding-coat — enter Dougal, and the scene was changed. By a high tone of expostulation, mixed with oaths and threats, as far as I could conjecture the tenor of his language from the violence of his gestures, he compelled the plunderers, however reluc-tant, not only to give up their further depredations on our property, but to restore the spoil they had already appropriated. He snatched my cravat from the fellow who had seized it, and twisted it (in the zeal of his restitution) around my neck with such suffocating energy, as made me think that he had not only been, during his residence at Glasgow, a substitute of the jailor, but must moreover have taken lessons as an apprentice of the hangman. He flung the tattered remnants of Mr. Jarvie's coat around his shoulders, and as more Highlanders began to flock towards us from the high road, he led the way downwards, directing and commanding the others to afford us, but particularly the Bailie, the assistance necessary to our decending with comparative ease and safety. It was, however, in vain that Andrew Fairservice employed his lungs in obsecrating a share of Dougal's protection, or at least his interference, to procure restoration of his shoes.

'Na, na,' said Dougal in reply, 'she's nae gentle body, I trow; her petters hae ganged parefoot, or she's muckle mista'en.' And, leaving Andrew to follow at his leisure, or rather at such leisure as the surrounding crowd were pleased to indulge him with, he hurried us down to the pathway in which the skirmish had been fought, and hastened to present us as additional captives to the female leader of his band.

We were dragged before her accordingly, Dougal fighting, struggling, screaming, as if he were the party most apprehensive of hurt, and repulsing, by threats and efforts, all those who attempted to take a nearer interest in our capture than he seemed to do himself. At length we were placed before the heroine of the day, whose appearance, as well as those of the savage, uncouth, yet martial figures who surrounded us, struck me, to own the truth, with considerable apprehension. I do not know if Helen MacGregor had personally mingled in the fray, and indeed I was afterwards given to understand the contrary; but the specks of blood on her brow, her hands and naked arms, as well as on the blade of the sword which she continued to hold in her hand—her flushed countenance, and the disordered state of the raven locks which escaped from under the red bonnet and plume that formed her head-dress, seemed all to intimate that she had taken an immediate share in the conflict. Her keen black eyes and features expressed an imagination inflamed by the pride of gratified revenge, and the triumph of victory. Yet there was nothing positively sanguinary, or cruel, in her deportment; and she reminded me, when the immediate alarm of the interview was over, of some of the paintings I had seen of the inspired heroines in the catholic churches of France. She was not, indeed, sufficiently beautiful for a Judith, nor had she the inspired expression of features which painters have given to Deborah, or to the wife of Heber the Kenite, at whose feet the strong oppressor of Israel, who dwelled in Harosheth of the Gentiles, bowed down, fell, and lay a dead man. Nevertheless, the enthusiasm by which she was agitated, gave her countenance and deportment, wildly dignified in themselves, an air which made her approach nearly to the ideas of those wonderful artists, who gave to the eye the heroines of Scripture history.

I was uncertain in what terms to accost a personage so uncommon, when Mr. Jarvie, breaking the ice with a preparatory cough, (for the speed with which he had been brought into her presence had again impeded his respiration,) addressed her as follows:—'Uh! uh! etc. etc., I am very happy to have this joyful opportunity,' (a quaver in his voice strongly belied the emphasis which he studiously laid on the word joyful)—' this *joyful* occasion,' he resumed, trying to give the adjective a more suitable accentuation, 'to wish my kinsman Robin's wife a very good morning—Uh! uh!—How's a' wi' ye' (by this time he had talked himself into his usual jog-trot manner, which exhibited a mixture of familiarity and self-importance)—'How's a' wi' ye this lang time?—Ye'll hae forgotten me, Mrs. MacGregor Campbell, as your cousin—uh! uh!—but ye'll mind my father, Deacon Nicol Jarvie, in the Saut Market o' Glasgow?—an honest man he was, and a sponsible, and respectit you and yours—Sae, as I said before, I am right glad to see you, Mrs. MacGregor Campbell, as my kinsman's wife. I wad crave the liberty of a kinsman to salute you, but that your gillies keep such a dolefu' fast haud o' my arms; and, to speak Heaven's truth and a magistrate's, ye wadna be the waur of a cogfu' o' water before ye welcomed your friends.'

There was something in the familiarity of this

introduction which ill suited the exalted state of temper of the person to whom it was addressed, then busied with distributing dooms of death, and warm from conquest in a perilous encounter.

'What fellow are you,' she said, 'that dare to claim kindred with the MacGregor, and neither wear his dress nor speak his language?—What are you, that have the tongue and the habit of the hound, and yet seek to lie down with the deer?'

'I dinna ken,' said the undaunted Bailie, 'if the kindred has ever been weel rede out to you yet, cousin—but it's kend and can be proved. My mother, Elspeth MacFarlane, was the wife of my father, Deacon Nicol Jarvie—peace be wi' them baith—and Elspeth was the daughter of Parlane MacFarlane, at the Sheeling o' Loch Sloy. Now, this Parlane MacFarlane, as his surviving daughter, Maggy MacFarlane, alias MacNab, wha married Duncan MacNab o' Stuckavrallachan, can testify, stood as near to your gudeman, Robin MacGregor, as in the fourth degree of kindred, for—'

The virago lopped the genealogical tree, by demanding haughtily, 'If a stream of rushing water acknowledged any relation with the portion withdrawn from it for the mean domestic uses of those who dwelt on its banks?'

'Vera true, kinswoman,' said the Bailie; 'but for a' that, the burn wad be glad to hae the mill-dam back again in simmer, when the chuckie stanes are white in the sun. I ken weel eneugh you Hieland folk haud us Glasgow people light and cheap for our language and our claes; but every

body speaks their native tongue that they learned
in infancy; and it would be a daft-like thing to
see me wi' my fat wame in a short Hieland coat,
and my puir short houghs gartered below the knee,
like ane o' your lang-legged gillies—Mair by token,
kinswoman,' he continued, in defiance of various
intimations by which Dougal seemed to recommend
silence, as well as of the marks of impatience which
the Amazon evinced at his loquacity, 'I wad hae
ye to mind that the king's errand whiles comes in
the cadger's gate, and that, for as high as ye may
think o' the gentleman, as it's right every wife should
honour her husband—there's Scripture warrant for
that—yet as high as ye haud him, as I was saying,
I hae been serviceable to Rob ere now;—forbye a
set o' pens I sent yoursell when ye was gaun to
be married, and when Rob was an honest weel-
doing drover, and nane o' this unlawfu' wark, wi'
fighting, and flashes, and fluf-gibs, disturbing the
king's peace and disarming his soldiers.'

He had apparently touched on a key which his
kinswoman could not brook. She drew herself
up to her full height, and betrayed the acuteness
of her feelings by a laugh of mingled scorn and
bitterness.

'Yes,' she said, 'you, and such as you, might
claim a relation to us when we stooped to be the
paltry wretches fit to exist under your dominion, as
your hewers of wood and drawers of water—to find
cattle for your banquets, and subjects for your laws
to oppress and trample on—But now we are free—
free by the very act which left us neither house nor

hearth, food nor covering—which bereaved me of all—of all—and makes me groan when I think I must still cumber the earth for other purposes than those of vengeance. And I will carry on the work this day has so well commenced, by a deed that shall break all bands between MacGregor and the Lowland churles. — Here — Allan—Dougal—bind these Sassenachs neck and heel together, and throw them into the Highland loch to seek for their Highland kinsfolk.'

The Bailie, alarmed at this mandate, was commencing an expostulation, which probably would have only inflamed the violent passions of the person whom he addressed, when Dougal threw himself between them, and in his own language, which he spoke with a fluency and rapidity strongly contrasted by the slow, imperfect, and idiot-like manner in which he expressed himself in English, poured forth what I doubt not was a very animated pleading in our behalf.

His mistress replied to him, or rather cut short his harangue, by exclaiming in English, (as if determined to make us taste in anticipation the full bitterness of death,) 'Base dog, and son of a dog, do you dispute my commands?—Should I tell ye to cut out their tongues and put them into each other's throats, to try which would there best knap Southron, or to tear out their hearts and put them into each other's breasts, to see which would there best plot treason against the MacGregor—and such things have been done of old in the day of revenge, when our fathers had wrongs to redress—Should I command you to do this, would it be your part to dispute my orders?'

'To be sure, to be sure,' Dougal replied, with accents of profound submission; 'her pleasure suld be done—tat's but reason—but an it were—tat is, an it could be thought the same to her to coup the ill-faured loon of ta red-coat Captain, and hims corporal Cramp, and twa three o' the red-coats into the loch, hersell wad do't wi' muckle mair great satisfaction than to hurt ta honest civil shentlemans as were friends to the Gregarach, and came up on the Chief's assurance, and not to do no treason, as hersell could testify.'

The lady was about to reply, when a few wild strains of a pibroch were heard advancing up the road from Aberfoil, the same probably which had reached the ears of Captain Thornton's rear-guard, and determined him to force his way onward rather than return to the village, on finding the pass occupied. The skirmish being of very short duration, the armed men who followed this martial melody, had not, although quickening their march when they heard the firing, been able to arrive in time sufficient to take any share in the rencontre. The victory, therefore, was complete without them, and they now arrived only to share in the triumph of their countrymen.

There was a marked difference betwixt the appearance of these new comers and that of the party by which our escort had been defeated, and it was greatly in favour of the former. Among the Highlanders who surrounded the Chieftainess, if I may presume to call her so without offence to grammar, were men in the extremity of age, boys scarce able to bear a sword, and even women—all, in short, whom the last necessity urges to take up arms; and it added a shade of bitter shame to the dejection which clouded Thornton's manly countenance, when he found that the numbers and position of a foe, otherwise so despicable, had enabled them to conquer his brave veterans. But the thirty or forty Highlanders who now joined the others, were all men in the prime of youth or manhood, active clean-made fellows, whose short hose and belted plaids set out their sinewy limbs to the best advantage. Their arms were as superior to those of the first party as their dress and appearance. The followers of the female Chief had axes, scythes, and other antique weapons, in aid of their guns, and some had only clubs, daggers, and long knives. But of the second party, most had pistols at the belt, and almost all had dirks hanging at the pouches which they wore in front. Each had a good gun in his hand, and a broadsword by his side, besides a stout round target, made of light wood, covered with leather, and curiously studded with brass, and having a steel pike screwed into the centre. These hung on their left shoulder during a march, or while they were engaged in exchanging fire with the enemy, and were worn on the left arm when they charged with sword in hand.

But it was easy to see that this chosen band had not arrived from a victory such as they found their ill-appointed companions possessed of. The pibroch sent forth occasionally a few wailing notes, expressive of a very different sentiment from triumph, and when they appeared before the wife of their Chieftain, it was in silence, and with downcast and melancholy looks. They paused when they approached her, and the pipes again sent forth the same wild and melancholy strain.

Helen rushed towards them with a countenance in which anger was mingled with apprehension. 'What means this, Allaster?' she said to the minstrel. 'Why a lament in the moment of victory?—Robert—Hamish—Where's the Mac-Gregor?—where's your father?'

Her sons, who led the band, advanced with slow and irresolute steps towards her, and murmured a few words in Gaelic, at hearing which she set up a shriek that made the rocks ring again, in which all the women and boys joined, clapping their hands and yelling, as if their lives had been expiring in the sound. The mountain echoes, silent since the military sounds of battle had ceased, had now to answer these frantic and discordant shrieks of sorrow, which drove the very night-birds from their haunts in the rocks, as if they were startled to hear orgies more hideous and ill-omened than their own, performed in the face of open day.

'Taken!' repeated Helen, when the clamour had subsided—'Taken!—captive!—and you live to say so?—Coward dogs! did I nurse you for this, that you should spare your blood on your father's enemies? or see him prisoner and come back to tell it?'

The sons of MacGregor, to whom this expostulation was addressed, were youths, of whom the eldest had hardly attained his twentieth year. *Hamish*, or James, the elder of these youths, was the tallest by a head, and much handsomer than his brother; his light-blue eyes, with a profusion of fair hair, which streamed from under his smart blue bonnet, made his whole appearance a most favourable specimen of the Highland youth. The younger was called Robert; but, to distinguish him from his father, the Highlanders added the epithet, *Oig*, or the young. Dark hair, and dark features, with a ruddy glow of health and animation, and a form strong and well-set beyond his years, completed the sketch of the young mountaineer.

Both now stood before their mother with countenances clouded with grief and shame, and listened, with the most respectful submission, to the reproaches with which she loaded them. At length, when her resentment appeared in some degree to subside, the eldest, speaking in English, probably that he might not be understood by their followers, endeavoured respectfully to vindicate himself and his brother from his mother's reproaches. I was so near him as to comprehend much of what he said; and, as it was of great consequence to me to be possessed of information in this strange crisis, I failed not to listen as attentively as I could.

'The MacGregor,' his son stated, 'had been called out upon a trysting with a Lowland hallion, who came with a token from'—he muttered the name very low, but I thought it sounded like my own.

—' The MacGregor,' he said, ' accepted of the invitation, but commanded the Saxon who brought the message to be detained, as a hostage that good faith should be observed to him. Accordingly he went to the place of appointment,' (which had some wild Highland name that I cannot remember,) ' attended only by Angus Breck and little Rory, commanding no one to follow him. Within half an hour Angus Breck came back with the doleful tidings that the MacGregor had been surprised and made prisoner by a party of Lennox militia, under Galbraith of Garschattachin.' He added, ' that Galbraith, on being threatened by MacGregor, who, upon his capture, menaced him with retaliation on the person of the hostage, had treated the threat with great contempt, replying, " Let each side hang his man; we 'll hang the thief, and your catherans may hang the gauger, Rob, and the country will be rid of two damned things at once, a wild Highlander and a revenue officer." Angus Breck, less carefully looked to than his master, contrived to escape from the hands of the captors, after having been in their custody long enough to hear this discussion and to bring off the news.'

' And did you learn this, you false-hearted traitor,' said the wife of MacGregor, ' and not instantly rush to your father's rescue to bring him off, or leave your body on the place ? '

The young MacGregor modestly replied, by representing the very superior force of the enemy, and stated, that as they made no preparation for leaving the country, he had fallen back up the glen with the purpose of collecting a band sufficient to attempt a rescue with some tolerable chance of success. At length he said, ' The militiamen would quarter, he understood, in the neighbouring house of Gartartan, or the old castle in the port of Monteith, or some other stronghold, which, although strong and defensible, was nevertheless capable of being surprised, could they but get enough of men assembled for the purpose.'

I understood afterwards that the rest of the freebooter's followers were divided into two strong bands, one destined to watch the remaining garrison of Inversnaid, a party of which, under Captain Thornton, had been defeated; and another to show front to the Highland clans who had united with the regular troops and Lowlanders in this hostile and combined invasion of that mountainous and desolate territory, which, lying between the lakes of Loch-Lomond, Loch-Katrine, and Loch-Ard, was at this time currently called Rob Roy's, or the MacGregor, country. Messengers were dispatched in great haste, to concentrate, as I supposed, their forces, with a view to the purposed attack on the Lowlanders; and the dejection and despair, at first visible on each countenance, gave place to the hope of rescuing their leader, and to the thirst of vengeance. It was under the burning influence of the latter passion that the wife of MacGregor commanded that the hostage exchanged for his safety should be brought into her presence. I believe her sons had kept this unfortunate wretch out of her sight, for fear of the consequences; but if it was so, their humane precaution only postponed his fate. They dragged forward at her summons a wretch already half dead with terror, in whose agonized features I recognised, to my horror and astonishment, my old acquaintance Morris.

He fell prostrate before the female Chief with an effort to clasp her knees, from which she drew back, as if his touch had been pollution, so that all he could do in token of the extremity of his humiliation, was to kiss the hem of her plaid. I never heard entreaties for life poured forth with such agony of spirit. The ecstasy of fear was such, that, instead of paralyzing his tongue, as on ordinary occasions, it even rendered him eloquent; and, with cheeks pale as ashes, hands compressed in agony, eyes that seemed to be taking their last look of all mortal objects, he protested, with the deepest oaths, his total ignorance of any design on the person of Rob Roy, whom he swore he loved and honoured as his own soul. In the inconsistency of his terror, he said, he was but the agent of others, and he muttered the name of Rashleigh. He prayed but for life—for life he would give all he had in the world: it was but life he asked—life, if it were to be prolonged under tortures and privations: he asked only breath, though it should be drawn in the damps of the lowest caverns of their hills.

It is impossible to describe the scorn, the loathing, and contempt, with which the wife of MacGregor regarded this wretched petitioner for the poor boon of existence.

'I could have bid you live,' she said, 'had life

been to you the same weary and wasting burden that it is to me—that it is to every noble and generous mind. But you—wretch! you could creep through the world unaffected by its various disgraces, its ineffable miseries, its constantly accumulating masses of crime and sorrow: you could live and enjoy yourself, while the noble-minded are betrayed—while nameless and birthless villains tread on the neck of the brave and the long-descended: you could enjoy yourself, like a butcher's dog in the shambles, battening on garbage, while the slaughter of the oldest and best went on around you! This enjoyment you shall not live to partake of; you shall die, base dog, and that before yon cloud has passed over the sun.'

She gave a brief command in Gaelic to her attendants, two of whom seized upon the prostrate suppliant, and hurried him to the brink of a cliff which overhung the flood. He set up the most piercing and dreadful cries that fear ever uttered —I may well term them dreadful, for they haunted my sleep for years afterwards. As the murderers, or executioners, call them as you will, dragged him along, he recognised me even in that moment of horror, and exclaimed, in the last articulate words I ever heard him utter, ' O, Mr. Osbaldistone, save me!—save me!'

I was so much moved by this horrid spectacle, that, although in momentary expectation of sharing his fate, I did attempt to speak in his behalf, but, as might have been expected, my interference was sternly disregarded. The victim was held fast by some, while others, binding a large heavy stone in a plaid, tied it round his neck, and others again eagerly stripped him of some part of his dress. Half-naked, and thus manacled, they hurled him into the lake, there about twelve feet deep, with a loud halloo of vindictive triumph, above which, however, his last death-shriek, the yell of mortal agony, was distinctly heard. The heavy burden splashed in the dark-blue waters, and the Highlanders, with their pole-axes and swords, watched an instant to guard, lest, extricating himself from the load to which he was attached, the victim might have struggled to regain the shore. But the knot had been securely bound; the wretched man sunk without effort; the waters, which his fall had disturbed, settled calmly over him, and the unit of that life for which he had pleaded so strongly, was for ever withdrawn from the sum of human existence.

CHAPTER XXXII

And be he safe restored ere evening set,
Or, if there's vengeance in an injured heart,
And power to wreak it in an armed hand,
Your land shall ache for 't.

OLD PLAY.

I KNOW not why it is, that a single deed of violence and cruelty affects our nerves more than when these are exercised on a more extended scale. I had seen that day several of my brave countrymen fall in battle—it seemed to me that they met a lot appropriate to humanity; and my bosom, though thrilling with interest, was affected with nothing of that sickening horror with which I beheld the unfortunate Morris put to death without resistance, and in cold blood. I looked at my companion, Mr. Jarvie, whose face reflected the feelings which were painted in mine. Indeed, he could not so suppress his horror, but that the words escaped him in a low and broken whisper,——

'I take up my protest against this deed, as a bloody and cruel murder—it is a cursed deed, and God will avenge it in his due way and time.'

'Then you do not fear to follow?' said the virago, bending on him a look of death, such as that with which a hawk looks at his prey ere he pounces.

'Kinswoman,' said the Bailie, 'nae man willingly wad cut short his thread of life before the end o' his pirn was fairly measured off on the yarn-winles—And I hae muckle to do, an I be spared, in this warld—public and private business, as weel that belanging to the magistracy as to my ain particular—and nae doubt I hae some to depend on me, as. puir Mattie, wha is an orphan—She's a far-awa cousin o' the Laird o' Limmerfield—Sae that, laying a' this thegither—skin for skin, yea all that a man hath will he give for his life.'

'And were I to set you at liberty,' said the imperious dame, 'what name would you give to the drowning of that Saxon dog?'

'Uh! uh!—hem! hem!' said the Bailie, clearing his throat as well as he could, 'I suld study to say as little on that score as might be—least said is sunest mended.'

'But if you were called on by the courts, as you term them, of justice,' she again demanded, 'what then would be your answer?'

The Bailie looked this way and that way, like a person who meditates an escape, and then answered in the tone of one who, seeing no means of accomplishing a retreat, determines to stand the brunt of battle,—'I see what you are driving me to the wa' about. But I'll tell you't plain, kinswoman, I behoved just to speak according to my ain conscience; and though your ain gudeman, that I wish had been here for his ain sake and mine, as weel as the puir Hieland creature Dougal, can tell ye that Nicol Jarvie can wink as hard at a friend's failings as ony body, yet I 'se tell ye, kinswoman, mine 's ne'er be the tongue to belie my thought; and sooner than say that yonder puir wretch was lawfully slaughtered, I wad consent to be laid beside him—though I think ye are the first Hieland woman wad mint sic a doom to her husband's kinsman but four times removed.'

It is probable that the tone of firmness assumed by the Bailie in his last speech was better suited to make an impression on the hard heart of his kinswoman than the tone of supplication he had hitherto assumed, as gems can be cut with steel, though they resist softer metals. She commanded us both to be placed before her. 'Your name,' she said to me, 'is Osbaldistone?—the dead dog, whose death you have witnessed, called you so.'

'My name *is* Osbaldistone,' was my answer.

'Rashleigh, then, I suppose, is your Christian name?' she pursued.

'No; my name is Francis.'

'But you know Rashleigh Osbaldistone?' she continued. 'He is your brother, if I mistake not, at least your kinsman and near friend.'

'He is my kinsman,' I replied, 'but not my friend. We were lately engaged together in a rencontre, when we were separated by a person whom I understand to be your husband. My blood is hardly yet dried on his sword, and the wound on my side is yet green. I have little reason to acknowledge him as a friend.'

'Then,' she replied, 'if a stranger to his intrigues, you can go in safety to Garschattachin and his party, without fear of being detained, and carry them a message from the wife of the Mac: Gregor ? '

I answered, ' That I knew no reasonable cause why the militia gentlemen should detain me ; that I had no reason, on my own account, to fear being in their hands ; and that if my going on her embassy would act as a protection to my friend and servant, who were here prisoners, I was ready to set out directly.' I took the opportunity to say, ' That I had come into this country on her husband's invitation, and his assurance that he would aid me in some important matters in which I was interested ; that my companion, Mr. Jarvie, had accompanied me on the same errand.'

' And I wish Mr. Jarvie's boots had been fu' o' boiling water when he drew them on for sic a purpose,' interrupted the Bailie.

' You may read your father,' said Helen Mac-Gregor, turning to her sons, ' in what this young Saxon tells us—Wise only when the bonnet is on his head, and the sword is in his hand, he never exchanges the tartan for the broad-cloth, but he runs himself into the miserable intrigues of the Lowlanders, and becomes again, after all he has suffered, their agent—their tool—their slave.'

' Add, madam,' said I, ' and their benefactor.'

' Be it so,' she said ; ' for it is the most empty title of them all, since he has uniformly sown benefits to reap a harvest of the most foul ingratitude.—But enough of this.—I shall cause you to be guided to the enemy's outposts—ask for their commander, and deliver him this message from me, Helen MacGregor;—that if they injure a hair of MacGregor's head, and if they do not set him at liberty within the space of twelve hours, there is not a lady in the Lennox but shall before Christmas cry the coronach for them she will be loath to lose, —there is not a farmer but shall sing well-a-wa over a burnt barnyard and an empty byre,—there is not a laird nor heritor shall lay his head on the pillow at night with the assurance of being a live man in the morning,—and, to begin as we are to end, so soon as the term is expired, I will send them this Glasgow Bailie, and this Saxon Captain, and all the rest of my prisoners, each bundled in a plaid, and chopped into as many pieces as there are checks in the tartan.'

As she paused in her denunciation, Captain Thornton, who was within hearing, added with great coolness, ' Present my compliments—Captain Thornton's, of the Royals, compliments — to the commanding officer, and tell him to do his duty and secure his prisoner, and not waste a thought upon me. If I have been fool enough to have been led into an ambuscade by these artful savages, I am wise enough to know how to die for it without disgracing the service. I am only sorry for my poor fellows,' he said, ' that have fallen into such butcherly hands.'

' Whisht ! whisht ! ' exclaimed the Bailie ; ' are ye weary o' your life ?—Ye'll gie *my* service to the commanding officer, Mr. Osbaldistone—Bailie Nicol Jarvie's service, a magistrate o' Glasgow, as his father the deacon was before him—and tell him, here are a wheen honest men in great trouble, and like to come to mair; and the best thing he can do for the common good, will be just to let Rob come his wa's up the glen, and nae mair about it— There's been some ill dune here already, but as it has lighted chiefly on the gauger, it winna be muckle worth making a stir about.'

With these very opposite injunctions from the parties chiefly interested in the success of my embassy, and with the reiterated charge of the wife of MacGregor, to remember and detail every word of her injunctions, I was at length suffered to depart; and Andrew Fairservice, chiefly, I believe, to get rid of his clamorous supplications, was permitted to attend me. Doubtful, however, that I might use my horse as a means of escape from my guides, or desirous to retain a prize of some value, I was given to understand that I was to perform my journey on foot, escorted by Hamish Mac-Gregor, the elder brother, who, with two followers, attended, as well to show me the way, as to reconnoitre the strength and position of the enemy. Dougal had been at first ordered on this party, but he contrived to elude the service, with the purpose, as we afterwards understood, of watching over Mr. Jarvie, whom, according to his wild principles of fidelity, he considered as entitled to his good offices, from having once acted in some measure as his patron or master.

After walking with great rapidity about an hour, we arrived at an eminence covered with brushwood, which gave us a commanding prospect down the valley, and a full view of the post which the militia occupied. Being chiefly cavalry, they had judiciously avoided any attempt to penetrate the pass which had been so unsuccessfully essayed by Captain Thornton. They had taken up their situation with some military skill, on a rising ground in the centre of the little valley of Aberfoil, through which the river Forth winds its earliest course, and which is formed by two ridges of hills, faced with barricades of limestone rock, intermixed with huge masses of brescia, or pebbles imbedded in some softer substance which has hardened around them like mortar; and surrounded by the more lofty mountains in the distance. These ridges, however, left the valley of breadth enough to secure the cavalry from any sudden surprise by the mountaineers, and they had stationed sentinels and outposts at proper distances from this main body, in every direction, so that they might secure full time to mount and get under arms upon the least alarm. It was not indeed expected at that time, that Highlanders would attack cavalry in an open plain, though late events have shown that they may do so with success.* When I first knew the Highlanders, they had almost a superstitious dread of a mounted trooper, the horse being so much more fierce and imposing in his appearance than the

---

* The affairs of Prestonpans and Falkirk are probably alluded to, which marks the time of writing the Memoirs as subsequent to 1745.

little *shelties* of their own hills, and moreover being trained, as the more ignorant mountaineers believed, to fight with his feet and his teeth.

The appearance of the picqueted horses, feeding in this little vale; the forms of the soldiers, as they sate, stood, or walked, in various groups in the vicinity of the beautiful river, and of the bare yet romantic ranges of rock which hedge in the landscape on either side, formed a noble foreground, while far to the eastward the eye caught a glance of the lake of Menteith; and Stirling Castle, dimly seen along with the blue and distant line of the Ochill Mountains, closed the scene.

After gazing on this landscape with great earnestness, young MacGregor intimated to me that I was to descend to the station of the militia and execute my errand to their commander, enjoining me at the same time, with a menacing gesture, neither to inform them who had guided me to that place, nor where I had parted from my escort. Thus tutored, I descended towards the military post, followed by Andrew, who, only retaining his breeches and stockings of the English costume, without a hat, bare-legged, with brogues on his feet, which Dougal had given him out of compassion, and having a tattered plaid to supply the want of all upper garments, looked as if he had been playing the part of a Highland Tom-of-Bedlam. We had not proceeded far before we became visible to one of the videttes, who, riding towards us, presented his carabine and commanded me to stand. I obeyed, and when the soldier came up, desired to be conducted to his commanding officer. I was immediately brought where a circle of officers, sitting upon the grass, seemed in attendance upon one of superior rank. He wore a cuirass of polished steel, over which were drawn the insignia of the ancient Order of the Thistle. My friend Garschattachin, and many other gentlemen, some in uniform, others in their ordinary dress, but all armed and well attended, seemed to receive their orders from this person of distinction. Many servants in rich liveries, apparently a part of his household, were also in waiting.

Having paid to this nobleman the respect which his rank appeared to demand, I acquainted him that I had been an involuntary witness to the king's soldiers having suffered a defeat from the Highlanders at the pass of Loch-Ard, (such I had learned was the name of the place where Mr. Thornton was made prisoner,) and that the victors threatened every species of extremity to those who had fallen into their power, as well as to the Low Country in general, unless their Chief, who had that morning been made prisoner, were returned to them uninjured. The Duke (for he whom I addressed was of no lower rank) listened to me with great composure, and then replied, that he should be extremely sorry to expose the unfortunate gentlemen who had been made prisoners to the cruelty of the barbarians into whose hands they had fallen, but that it was folly to suppose that he would deliver up the very author of all these disorders and offences, and so encourage his followers in their license. ' You may return to those who sent you,' he proceeded, ' and inform them, that I shall certainly cause Rob Roy Campbell, whom they call MacGregor, to be executed, by break of day, as an outlaw taken in arms, and deserving death by a thousand acts of violence; that I should be most justly held unworthy of my situation and commission did I act otherwise; that I shall know how to protect the country against their insolent threats of violence; and that if they injure a hair of the head of any of the unfortunate gentlemen whom an unlucky accident has thrown into their power, I will take such ample vengeance, that the very stones of their glens shall sing woe for it this hundred years to come ! '

I humbly begged leave to remonstrate respecting the honourable mission imposed on me, and touched upon the obvious danger attending it, when the noble commander replied, ' that, such being the case, I might send my servant.'

' The deil be in my feet,' said Andrew, without either having respect to the presence in which he stood, or waiting till I replied—' the deil be in my feet, if I gang my tae's length. Do the folk think I hae another thrapple in my pouch after John Highlandman's sneckit this ane wi' his joctaleg ? or that I can dive doun at the tae side of a Highland loch and rise at the tother, like a shell-drake ? Na, na—ilk ane for himsell, and God for us a'. Folk may just mak a page o' their ain age, and serve themsells till their bairns grow up, and gang their ain errands for Andrew. Rob Roy never came near the parish of Dreepdaily, to steal either pippin or pear frae me or mine.'

Silencing my follower with some difficulty, I represented to the Duke the great danger Captain Thornton and Mr. Jarvie would certainly be exposed to, and entreated he would make me the bearer of such modified terms as might be the means of saving their lives. I assured him I should decline no danger if I could be of service; but from what I had heard and seen, I had little doubt they would be instantly murdered should the chief of the outlaws suffer death.

The Duke was obviously much affected. 'It was a hard case,' he said, 'and he felt it as such; but he had a paramount duty to perform to the country—Rob Roy must die!'

I own it was not without emotion that I heard this threat of instant death to my acquaintance Campbell, who had so often testified his good-will towards me. Nor was I singular in the feeling, for many of those around the Duke ventured to express themselves in his favour. 'It would be more advisable,' they said, 'to send him to Stirling Castle, and there detain him a close prisoner, as a pledge for the submission and dispersion of his gang. It were a great pity to expose the country to be plundered, which, now that the long nights approached, it would be found very difficult to prevent, since it was impossible to guard every point, and the Highlanders were sure to select those that were left exposed.' They added, that there was great hardship in leaving the unfortunate prisoners to the almost certain doom of massacre denounced against them, which no one doubted would be executed in the first burst of revenge.

Garschattachin ventured yet farther, confiding in the honour of the nobleman whom he addressed, although he knew he had particular reasons for disliking their prisoner. 'Rob Roy,' he said, 'though a kittle neighbour to the Low Country, and particularly obnoxious to his Grace, and though he maybe carried the catheran trade farther than ony man o' his day, was an auld-farrand carle, and there might be some means found of making him hear reason; whereas his wife and sons were reckless fiends, without either fear or mercy about them, and, at the head of a' his limmer loons, would be a worse plague to the country than ever he had been.'

'Pooh! pooh!' replied his Grace, 'it is the very sense and cunning of this fellow which has so long maintained his reign — a mere Highland robber would have been put down in as many weeks as he has flourished years. His gang, without him, is no more to be dreaded as a permanent annoyance—it will no longer exist—than a wasp without its head, which may sting once perhaps, but is instantly crushed into annihilation.'

Garschattachin was not so easily silenced. 'I am sure, my Lord Duke,' he replied, 'I have no favour for Rob, and he as little for me, seeing he has twice cleaned out my ain byres, beside skaith amang my tenants; but, however——'

'But, however, Garschattachin,' said the Duke, with a smile of peculiar expression, 'I fancy you think such a freedom may be pardoned in a friend's friend, and Rob's supposed to be no enemy to Major Galbraith's friends over the water.'

'If it be so, my lord,' said Garschattachin, in the same tone of jocularity, 'it's no the warst thing I have heard of him. But I wish we heard some news from the clans, that we have waited for sae lang. I vow to God they'll keep a Hielandman's word wi' us — I never kend them better — it's ill drawing boots upon trews.'

'I cannot believe it,' said the Duke; 'these gentlemen are known to be men of honour, and I must necessarily suppose they are to keep their appointment. Send out two more horsemen to look for our friends. We cannot, till their arrival, pretend to attack the pass where Captain Thornton has suffered himself to be surprised, and which, to my knowledge, ten men on foot might make good against a regiment of the best horse in Europe— Meanwhile let refreshments be given to the men.'

I had the benefit of this last order, the more necessary and acceptable, as I had tasted nothing since our hasty meal at Aberfoil the evening before. The videttes who had been dispatched, returned without tidings of the expected auxiliaries, and sunset was approaching, when a Highlander belonging to the clans whose co-operation was expected, appeared as the bearer of a letter, which he delivered to the Duke with a most profound congé.

'Now will I wad a hogshead of claret,' said Garschattachin, 'that this is a message to tell us that these cursed Highlandmen, whom we have fetched here at the expense of so much plague and vexation, are going to draw off, and leave us to do our own business if we can.'

'It is even so, gentlemen,' said the Duke, reddening with indignation, after having perused the letter, which was written upon a very dirty scrap of paper, but most punctiliously addressed, 'For the much-honoured hands of Ane High and Mighty Prince, the Duke,' etc. etc. etc. 'Our allies,' continued the Duke, 'have deserted us, gentlemen, and have made a separate peace with the enemy.'

'It's just the fate of all alliances,' said Garschattachin; 'the Dutch were gaun to serve us the same gate, if we had not got the start of them at Utrecht.'

'You are facetious, sir,' said the Duke, with a frown which showed how little he liked the pleasantry, 'but our business is rather of a grave cast just now.—I suppose no gentleman would advise our attempting to penetrate farther into the country, unsupported either by friendly Highlanders, or by infantry from Inversnaid?'

A general answer announced that the attempt would be perfect madness.

'Nor would there be great wisdom,' the Duke added, 'in remaining exposed to a night-attack in this place. I therefore propose that we should retreat to the house of Duchray and that of Gartartan, and keep safe and sure watch and ward until morning. But before we separate, I will examine Rob Roy before you all, and make you sensible, by your own eyes and ears, of the extreme

unfitness of leaving him space for farther outrage.'
He gave orders accordingly, and the prisoner was
brought before him, his arms belted down above
the elbow, and secured to his body by a horse-girth
buckled tight behind him. Two non-commissioned
officers had hold of him, one on each side, and
two file of men with carabines and fixed bayonets
attended for additional security.

I had never seen this man in the dress of his
country, which set in a striking point of view the
peculiarities of his form. A shock-head of red hair,
which the hat and periwig of the Lowland costume
had in a great measure concealed, was seen beneath
the Highland bonnet, and verified the epithet of
Roy, or Red, by which he was much better known
in the Low Country than by any other, and is still,
I suppose, best remembered. The justice of the
appellation was also vindicated by the appearance
of that part of his limbs, from the bottom of his kilt
to the top of his short hose, which the fashion of
his country dress left bare, and which was covered
with a fell of thick, short, red hair, especially around
his knees, which resembled in this respect, as well
as from their sinewy appearance of extreme strength,
the limbs of a red-coloured Highland bull. Upon
the whole, betwixt the effect produced by the change
of dress, and by my having become acquainted with
his real and formidable character, his appearance
had acquired to my eyes something so much wilder
and more striking than it before presented, that I
could scarce recognise him to be the same person.

His manner was bold, unconstrained unless by

the actual bonds, haughty, and even dignified. He bowed to the Duke, nodded to Garschattachin and others, and showed some surprise at seeing me among the party.

'It is long since we have met, Mr. Campbell,' said the Duke.

'It is so, my Lord Duke; I could have wished it had been,' (looking at the fastening on his arms,) 'when I could have better paid the compliments I owe to your Grace—but there's a gude time coming.'

'No time like the time present, Mr. Campbell,' answered the Duke, 'for the hours are fast flying that must settle your last account with all mortal affairs. I do not say this to insult your distress; but you must be aware yourself that you draw near the end of your career. I do not deny that you may sometimes have done less harm than others of your unhappy trade, and that you may occasionally have exhibited marks of talent, and even of a disposition which promised better things. But you are aware how long you have been the terror and the oppressor of a peaceful neighbourhood, and by what acts of violence you have maintained and extended your usurped authority. You know, in short, that you have deserved death, and that you must prepare for it.'

'My lord,' said Rob Roy, 'although I may well lay my misfortunes at your Grace's door, yet I will never say that you yourself have been the wilful and witting author of them. My lord, if I had thought sae, your Grace would not this day have been sitting in judgment on me; for you have been three times within good rifle distance of me when you were thinking but of the red deer, and few people have kend me miss my aim. But as for them that have abused your Grace's ear, and set you up against a man that was ance as peacefu' a man as ony in the land, and made your name the warrant for driving me to utter extremity,—I have had some amends of them, and, for a' that your Grace now says, I expect to live to hae mair.'

'I know,' said the Duke, in rising anger, 'that you are a determined and impudent villain, who will keep his oath if he swears to mischief; but it shall be my care to prevent you. You have no enemies but your own wicked actions.'

'Had I called myself Grahame, instead of Campbell, I might have heard less about them,' answered Rob Roy, with dogged resolution.

'You will do well, sir,' said the Duke, 'to warn your wife and family and followers, to beware how they use the gentlemen now in their hands, as I will requite tenfold on them, and their kin and allies, the slightest injury done to any of his majesty's liege subjects.'

'My lord,' said Roy in answer, 'none of my enemies will allege that I have been a bloodthirsty man, and were I now wi' my folk, I could rule four or five hundred wild Hielanders as easy as your Grace those eight or ten lackeys and foot-boys. But if your Grace is bent to take the head away from a house, ye may lay your account there will be misrule amang the members.—However, come o't what like, there 's an honest man, a kinsman o' my ain, maun come by nae skaith.—Is there ony body here wad do a gude deed for MacGregor?—he may repay it, though his hands be now tied.'

The Highlander who had delivered the letter to the Duke replied, 'I'll do your will for you, MacGregor; and I'll gang back up the glen on purpose.'

He advanced, and received from the prisoner a message to his wife, which, being in Gaelic, I did not understand, but I had little doubt it related to some measures to be taken for the safety of Mr. Jarvie.

'Do you hear the fellow's impudence?' said the Duke; 'he confides in his character of a messenger. His conduct is of a piece with his masters', who invited us to make common cause against these freebooters, and have deserted us so soon as the MacGregors have agreed to surrender the Balquidder lands they were squabbling about.

> "No truth in plaids, no faith in tartan trews!
> Cameleon-like, they change a thousand hues."'

'Your great ancestor never said so, my lord,' answered Major Galbraith; 'and, with submission, neither would your Grace have occasion to say it, wad ye but be for beginning justice at the wellhead—Gie the honest man his mear again—Let every head wear its ain bannet, and the distractions o' the Lennox wad be mended wi' them o' the land.'

'Hush! hush! Garschattachin,' said the Duke; 'this is language dangerous for you to talk to any

one, and especially to me; but I presume you
reckon yourself a privileged person. Please to
draw off your party towards Gartartan; I shall
myself see the prisoner escorted to Duchray, and
send you orders to-morrow. You will please grant
no leave of absence to any of your troopers.'

' Here's auld ordering and counter-ordering,'
muttered Garschattachin between his teeth. ' But
patience! patience!—we may ae day play at Change
seats, the king's coming.'

The two troops of cavalry now formed, and prepared to march off the ground, that they might
avail themselves of the remainder of daylight to
get to their evening quarters. I received an
intimation rather than an invitation, to attend the
party; and I perceived, that, though no longer
considered as a prisoner, I was yet under some
sort of suspicion. The times were indeed so
dangerous,—the great party questions of Jacobite
and Hanoverian divided the country so effectually,
—and the constant disputes and jealousies between
the Highlanders and Lowlanders, besides a number
of inexplicable causes of feud which separated the
great leading families in Scotland from each other,
occasioned such general suspicion, that a solitary
and unprotected stranger was almost sure to meet
with something disagreeable in the course of his
travels.

I acquiesced, however, in my destination, with
the best grace I could, consoling myself with the
hope that I might obtain from the captive freebooter some information concerning Rashleigh and

his machinations. I should do myself injustice did I not add, that my views were not merely selfish. I was too much interested in my singular acquaintance not to be desirous of rendering him such services as his unfortunate situation might demand, or admit of his receiving.

CHAPTER XXXIII

And when he came to broken brigg,
He bent his bow and swam;
And when he came to grass growing,
Set down his feet and ran.

GIL MORRICE.

THE echoes of the rocks and ravines, on either side, now rang to the trumpets of the cavalry, which, forming themselves into two distinct bodies, began to move down the valley at a slow trot. That commanded by Major Galbraith soon took to the right hand, and crossed the Forth, for the purpose of taking up the quarters assigned them for the night, when they were to occupy, as I understood, an old castle in the vicinity. They formed a lively object while crossing the stream, but were soon lost in winding up the bank on the opposite side, which was clothed with wood.

We continued our march with considerable good order. To ensure the safe custody of the prisoner, the Duke had caused him to be placed on horseback behind one of his retainers, called, as I was informed, Ewan of Brigglands, one of the largest and strongest men who were present. A horse-belt, passed round the bodies of both, and buckled before the yeoman's breast, rendered it impossible

255

for Rob Roy to free himself from his keeper. I was directed to keep close beside them, and accommodated for the purpose with a troop-horse. We were as closely surrounded by the soldiers as the width of the road would permit, and had always at least one, if not two, on each side with pistol in hand. Andrew Fairservice, furnished with a Highland pony of which they had made prey somewhere or other, was permitted to ride among the other domestics, of whom a great number attended the line of march, though without falling into the ranks of the more regularly trained troopers.

In this manner we travelled for a certain distance, until we arrived at a place where we also were to cross the river. The Forth, as being the outlet of a lake, is of considerable depth, even where less important in point of width, and the descent to the ford was by a broken precipitous ravine, which only permitted one horseman to descend at once. The rear and centre of our small body halting on the bank while the front files passed down in succession, produced a considerable delay, as is usual on such occasions, and even some confusion; for a number of those riders, who made no proper part of the squadron, crowded to the ford without regularity, and made the militia cavalry, although tolerably well drilled, partake in some degree of their own disorder.

It was while we were thus huddled together on the bank that I heard Rob Roy whisper to the man behind whom he was placed on horseback, 'Your father, Ewan, wadna hae carried an auld friend to the shambles, like a calf, for a' the Dukes in Christendom.'

Ewan returned no answer, but shrugged, as one who would express by that sign that what he was doing was none of his own choice.

'And when the MacGregors come down the glen, and ye see toom faulds, a bluidy hearth-stane, and the fire flashing out between the rafters o' your house, ye may be thinking then, Ewan, that were your friend Rob to the fore, you would have had that safe which it will make your heart sair to lose.'

Ewan of Brigglands again shrugged and groaned, but remained silent.

'It's a sair thing,' continued Rob, sliding his insinuations so gently into Ewan's ear that they reached no other but mine, who certainly saw myself in no shape called upon to destroy his prospects of escape—'It's a sair thing, that Ewan of Brigglands, whom Roy MacGregor has helped with hand, sword, and purse, suld mind a gloom from a great man mair than a friend's life.'

Ewan seemed sorely agitated, but was silent. We heard the Duke's voice from the opposite bank call, 'Bring over the prisoner.'

Ewan put his horse in motion, and just as I heard Roy say, 'Never weigh a MacGregor's bluid against a broken whang o' leather, for there will be another accounting to gie for it baith here and hereafter,' they passed me hastily, and, dashing forward rather precipitately, entered the water.

'Not yet, sir—not yet,' said some of the troopers

to me, as I was about to follow, while others pressed forward into the stream.

I saw the Duke on the other side, by the waning light, engaged in commanding his people to get into order, as they landed dispersedly, some higher, some lower. Many had crossed, some were in the water, and the rest were preparing to follow, when a sudden splash warned me that MacGregor's eloquence had prevailed on Ewan to give him freedom and a chance for life. The Duke also heard the sound, and instantly guessed its meaning. 'Dog!' he exclaimed to Ewan as he landed, 'where is your prisoner?' and, without waiting to hear the apology which the terrified vassal began to falter forth, he fired a pistol at his head, whether fatally I know not, and exclaimed, 'Gentlemen, disperse and pursue the villain—An hundred guineas for him that secures Rob Roy!'

All became an instant scene of the most lively confusion. Rob Roy, disengaged from his bonds, doubtless by Ewan's slipping the buckle of his belt, had dropped off at the horse's tail, and instantly dived, passing under the belly of the troop-horse which was on his left hand. But as he was obliged to come to the surface an instant for air, the glimpse of his tartan plaid drew the attention of the troopers, some of whom plunged into the river with a total disregard to their own safety, rushing, according to the expression of their country, through pool and stream, sometimes swimming their horses, sometimes losing them and struggling for their own lives. Others less zealous, or more prudent, broke off in different directions, and galloped up and down the banks, to watch the places at which the fugitive might possibly land. The hollowing, the whooping, the calls for aid at different points, where they saw, or conceived they saw, some vestige of him they were seeking,—the frequent report of pistols and carabines, fired at every object which excited the least suspicion,—the sight of so many horsemen riding about, in and out of the river, and striking with their long broadswords at whatever excited their attention, joined to the vain exertions used by their officers to restore order and regularity; and all this in so wild a scene, and visible only by the imperfect twilight of an autumn evening, made the most extraordinary hubbub I had hitherto witnessed. I was indeed left alone to observe it, for our whole cavalcade had dispersed in pursuit, or at least to see the event of the search. Indeed, as I partly suspected at the time, and afterwards learned with certainty, many of those who seemed most active in their attempts to waylay and recover the fugitive, were, in actual truth, least desirous that he should be taken, and only joined in the cry to increase the general confusion, and to give Rob Roy a better opportunity of escaping.

Escape, indeed, was not difficult for a swimmer so expert as the freebooter, as soon as he had eluded the first burst of pursuit. At one time he was closely pressed, and several blows were made which flashed in the water around him; the scene much resembling one of the otter-hunts which I had seen at Osbaldistone-Hall, where the animal is detected by the hounds from his being necessitated to put his nose above the stream to vent or breathe, while he is enabled to elude them by getting under water again so soon as he has refreshed himself by respiration. MacGregor, however, had a trick beyond the otter; for he contrived, when very closely pursued, to disengage himself unobserved from his plaid, and suffer it to float down the stream, where in its progress it quickly attracted general attention; many of the horsemen were thus put upon a false scent, and several shots or stabs were averted from the party for whom they were designed.

Once fairly out of view, the recovery of the prisoner became almost impossible, since, in so many places, the river was rendered inaccessible by the steepness of its banks, or the thickets of alders, poplars, and birch, which, overhanging its banks, prevented the approach of horsemen. Errors and accidents had also happened among the pursuers, whose task the approaching night rendered every moment more hopeless. Some got themselves involved in the eddies of the stream, and required the assistance of their companions to save them from drowning. Others, hurt by shots or blows in the confused melée, implored help or threatened vengeance, and in one or two instances such accidents led to actual strife. The trumpets, therefore, sounded the retreat, announcing that the commanding officer, with whatsoever unwillingness, had for the present relinquished hopes of the important prize which had thus unexpectedly escaped his grasp, and the troopers began slowly, reluctantly, and brawling

with each other as they returned, again to assume their ranks. I could see them darkening, as they formed on the southern bank of the river, whose murmurs, long drowned by the louder cries of vengeful pursuit, were now heard hoarsely mingling with the deep, discontented, and reproachful voices of the disappointed horsemen.

Hitherto I had been as it were a mere spectator, though far from an uninterested one, of the singular scene which had passed. But now I heard a voice suddenly exclaim, 'Where is the English stranger?—It was he gave Rob Roy the knife to cut the belt.'

'Cleave the pock-pudding to the chafts!' cried one voice.

'Weize a brace of balls through his harn-pan!' said a second.

'Drive three inches of cauld airn into his breaskit!' shouted a third.

And I heard several horses galloping to and fro, with the kind purpose, doubtless, of executing these denunciations. I was immediately awakened to the sense of my situation, and to the certainty that armed men, having no restraint whatever on their irritated and inflamed passions, would probably begin by shooting or cutting me down, and afterwards investigate the justice of the action. Impressed by this belief, I leaped from my horse, and turning him loose, plunged into a bush of alder-trees, where, considering the advancing obscurity of the night, I thought there was little chance of my being discovered. Had I been near enough to the Duke to have invoked his personal protection, I would have done so; but he had already commenced his retreat, and I saw no officer on the left bank of the river of authority sufficient to have afforded protection, in case of my surrendering myself. I thought there was no point of honour which could require, in such circumstances, an unnecessary exposure of my life. My first idea, when the tumult began to be appeased, and the clatter of the horses' feet was heard less frequently in the immediate vicinity of my hiding-place, was to seek out the Duke's quarters, when all should be quiet, and give myself up to him, as a liege subject, who had nothing to fear from his justice, and a stranger, who had every right to expect protection and hospitality. With this purpose I crept out of my hiding-place, and looked around me.

The twilight had now melted nearly into darkness; few or none of the troopers were left on my side of the Forth, and of those who were already across it, I only heard the distant trample of the horses' feet, and the wailing and prolonged sound of their trumpets, which rung through the woods to recall stragglers. Here, therefore, I was left in a situation of considerable difficulty. I had no horse, and the deep and wheeling stream of the river, rendered turbid by the late tumult of which its channel had been the scene, and seeming yet more so under the doubtful influence of an imperfect moonlight, had no inviting influence for a pedestrian by no means accustomed to wade rivers, and who had lately seen horsemen weltering, in this dangerous passage, up to the very saddle-laps. At the same time, my prospect, if I remained on the side of the river on which I then stood, could be no other than of concluding the various fatigues of this day and the preceding night, by passing that which was now closing in, *al fresco* on the side of a Highland hill.

After a moment's reflection, I began to consider that Fairservice, who had doubtless crossed the river with the other domestics, according to his forward and impertinent custom of putting himself always among the foremost, could not fail to satisfy the Duke, or the competent authorities, respecting my rank and situation ; and that, therefore, my character did not require my immediate appearance, at the risk of being drowned in the river,—of being unable to trace the march of the squadron in case of my reaching the other side in safety,—or, finally, of being cut down, right or wrong, by some straggler, who might think such a piece of good service a convenient excuse for not sooner rejoining his ranks. I therefore resolved to measure my steps back to the little inn, where I had passed the preceding night. I had nothing to apprehend from Rob Roy. He was now at liberty, and I was certain, in case of my falling in with any of his people, the news of his escape would ensure me protection. I might thus also show, that I had no intention to desert Mr. Jarvie in the delicate situation in which he had engaged himself, chiefly on my account. And lastly, it was only in this quarter that I could hope to learn tidings concerning Rashleigh and my father's papers, which had been the original cause of an expedition so fraught with perilous adventure. I therefore abandoned all thoughts of crossing the Forth that evening; and, turning my back on the Fords of Frew, began to retrace my steps towards the little village of Aberfoil.

A sharp frost-wind, which made itself heard and felt from time to time, removed the clouds of mist which might otherwise have slumbered till morning on the valley; and, though it could not totally disperse the clouds of vapour, yet threw them in confused and changeful masses, now hovering round the heads of the mountains, now filling, as with a dense and voluminous stream of smoke, the various deep gullies where masses of the composite rock, or brescia, tumbling in fragments from the cliffs, have rushed to the valley, leaving each behind its course a rent and torn ravine resembling a deserted watercourse. The moon, which was now high, and twinkled with all the vivacity of a frosty atmosphere, silvered the windings of the river and the peaks and precipices which the mist left visible, while her beams seemed as it were absorbed by the fleecy whiteness of the mist, where it lay thick and condensed; and gave to the more light and vapoury specks, which were elsewhere visible, a sort of filmy transparency resembling the lightest veil of silver gauze. Despite the uncertainty of my situation, a view so romantic, joined to the active and inspiring influence of the frosty atmosphere, elevated my spirits while it braced my nerves. I felt an inclination to cast care away, and bid defiance to danger, and involuntarily whistled, by way of cadence to my steps, which my feeling of the cold led me to accelerate, and I felt the pulse of existence beat prouder and higher in proportion as I felt confidence in my own strength, courage, and resources. I was so much lost in these thoughts, and in the feelings which they excited, that two horsemen came up behind me without my hearing their approach, until one was on each side of me, when the left-hand rider, pulling up his horse, addressed me in the English tongue. ' So ho, friend, whither so late ? '

' To my supper and bed at Aberfoil,' I replied.

' Are the passes open ? ' he inquired, with the same commanding tone of voice.

' I do not know,' I replied ; ' I shall learn when I get there ; but,' I added, the fate of Morris recurring to my recollection, ' if you are an English stranger, I advise you to turn back till daylight ; there has been some disturbance in this neighbourhood, and I should hesitate to say it is perfectly safe for strangers.'

' The soldiers had the worst ?—had they not ? ' was the reply.

' They had indeed ; and an officer's party were destroyed or made prisoners.'

' Are you sure of that ? ' replied the horseman.

' As sure as that I hear you speak,' I replied. ' I was an unwilling spectator of the skirmish.'

' Unwilling ? ' continued the interrogator. ' Were you not engaged in it then ? '

' Certainly no,' I replied ; ' I was detained by the king's officer.'

'On what suspicion? and who are you? or what is your name?' he continued.

'I really do not know, sir,' said I, 'why I should answer so many questions to an unknown stranger. I have told you enough to convince you that you are going into a dangerous and distracted country. If you choose to proceed, it is your own affair; but as I ask you no questions respecting your name and business, you will oblige me by making no inquiries after mine.'

'Mr. Francis Osbaldistone,' said the other rider, in a voice the tones of which thrilled through every nerve of my body, 'should not whistle his favourite airs when he wishes to remain undiscovered.'

And Diana Vernon—for she, wrapped in a horseman's cloak, was the last speaker—whistled in playful mimicry the second part of the tune, which was on my lips when they came up.

'Good God!' I exclaimed, like one thunderstruck, 'can it be you, Miss Vernon, on such a spot—at such an hour—in such a lawless country—in such——'

'In such a masculine dress, you would say.—But what would you have?—The philosophy of the excellent Corporal Nym is the best after all—things must be as they may—*pauca verba.*'

While she was thus speaking, I eagerly took advantage of an unusually bright gleam of moonshine, to study the appearance of her companion; for it may be easily supposed, that finding Miss Vernon in a place so solitary, engaged in a journey so dangerous, and under the protection of one

gentleman only, were circumstances to excite every feeling of jealousy, as well as surprise. The rider did not speak with the deep melody of Rashleigh's voice; his tones were more high and commanding; he was taller, moreover, as he sate on horseback, than that first-rate object of my hate and suspicion. Neither did the stranger's address resemble that of any of my other cousins; it had that indescribable tone and manner by which we recognise a man of sense and breeding, even in the first few sentences he speaks.

The object of my anxiety seemed desirous to get rid of my investigation.

'Diana,' he said, in a tone of mingled kindness and authority, 'give your cousin his property, and let us not spend time here.'

Miss Vernon had in the meantime taken out a small case, and leaning down from her horse towards me, she said, in a tone in which an effort at her usual quaint lightness of expression contended with a deeper and more grave tone of sentiment, 'You see, my dear coz, I was born to be your better angel. Rashleigh has been compelled to yield up his spoil, and had we reached this same village of Aberfoil last night, as we purposed, I should have found some Highland sylph to have wafted to you all these representatives of commercial wealth. But there were giants and dragons in the way; and errant-knights and damsels of modern times, bold though they be, must not, as of yore, run into useless danger—Do not you do so either, my dear coz.'

'Diana,' said her companion, 'let me once more warn you that the evening waxes late, and we are still distant from our home.'

'I am coming, sir, I am coming—consider,' she added, with a sigh, 'how lately I have been subjected to control—besides, I have not yet given my cousin the packet—and bid him farewell—for ever.—Yes, Frank,' she said, '*for ever!*—there is a gulf between us—a gulf of absolute perdition—where we go, you must not follow—what we do, you must not share in—farewell—be happy!'

In the attitude in which she bent from her horse, which was a Highland pony, her face, not perhaps altogether unwillingly, touched mine—She pressed my hand, while the tear that trembled in her eye found its way to my cheek instead of her own. It was a moment never to be forgotten—inexpressibly bitter, yet mixed with a sensation of pleasure so deeply soothing and affecting, as at once to unlock all the flood-gates of the heart. It was *but* a moment, however; for, instantly recovering from the feeling to which she had involuntarily given way, she intimated to her companion she was ready to attend him, and putting their horses to a brisk pace, they were soon far distant from the place where I stood.

Heaven knows, it was not apathy which loaded my frame and my tongue so much, that I could neither return Miss Vernon's half embrace, nor even answer her farewell. The word, though it rose to my tongue, seemed to choke in my throat like the fatal *guilty*, which the delinquent who makes it his plea knows must be followed by the doom of death. The surprise—the sorrow, almost stupified me. I remained motionless with the packet in my hand, gazing after them, as if endeavouring to count the sparkles which flew from the horses' hoofs. I continued to look after even these had ceased to be visible, and to listen for their footsteps long after the last distant trampling had died in my ears. At length, tears rushed to my eyes, glazed as they were by the exertion of straining after what was no longer to be seen. I wiped them mechanically, and almost without being aware that they were flowing, but they came thicker and thicker. I felt the tightening of the throat and breast, the *hysterica passio* of poor Lear; and, sitting down by the wayside, I shed a flood of the first and most bitter tears which had flowed from my eyes since childhood.

CHAPTER XXXIV

I HAD scarce given vent to my feelings in this paroxysm, ere I was ashamed of my weakness. I remembered that I had been for some time endeavouring to regard Diana Vernon, when her idea intruded itself on my remembrance, as a friend, for whose welfare I should indeed always be anxious, but with whom I could have little further communication. But the almost unrepressed tenderness of her manner, joined to the romance of our sudden meeting where it was so little to have been expected, were circumstances which threw me entirely off my guard. I recovered, however, sooner than might have been expected, and without giving myself time accurately to examine my motives, I resumed the path on which I had been travelling when overtaken by this strange and unexpected apparition.

I am not, was my reflection, transgressing her injunction so pathetically given, since I am but pursuing my own journey by the only open route. If I have succeeded in recovering my father's property, it still remains incumbent on me to see my Glasgow friend delivered from the situation in which he has

270

involved himself on my account; besides, what other place of rest can I obtain for the night excepting at the little inn of Aberfoil? They also must stop there, since it is impossible for travellers on horseback to go farther—Well, then, we shall meet again—meet for the last time perhaps—but I shall see and hear her—I shall learn who this happy man is who exercises over her the authority of a husband—I shall learn if there remains, in the difficult course in which she seems engaged, any difficulty which my efforts may remove, or aught that I can do to express my gratitude for her generosity—for her disinterested friendship.—

As I reasoned thus with myself, colouring with every plausible pretext which occurred to my ingenuity, my passionate desire once more to see and converse with my cousin, I was suddenly hailed by a touch on the shoulder; and the deep voice of a Highlander, who, walking still faster than I, though I was proceeding at a smart pace, accosted me with, ' A braw night, Maister Osbaldistone—we have met at the mirk hour before now.'

There was no mistaking the tone of MacGregor; he had escaped the pursuit of his enemies, and was in full retreat to his own wilds and to his adherents. He had also contrived to arm himself, probably at the house of some secret adherent, for he had a musket on his shoulder, and the usual Highland weapons by his side. To have found myself alone with such a character in such a situation, and at this late hour in the evening, might not have been pleasant to me in any ordinary mood of mind; for, though habituated to think of Rob Roy in rather a friendly point of view, I will confess frankly that I never heard him speak but that it seemed to thrill my blood. The intonation of the mountaineers gives a habitual depth and hollowness to the sound of their words, owing to the guttural expression so common in their native language, and they usually speak with a good deal of emphasis. To these national peculiarities Rob Roy added a sort of hard indifference of accent and manner, expressive of a mind neither to be daunted, nor surprised, nor affected, by what passed before him, however dreadful, however sudden, however afflicting. Habitual danger, with unbounded confidence in his own strength and sagacity, had rendered him indifferent to fear; and the lawless and precarious life he led had blunted, though its dangers and errors had not destroyed, his feelings for others. And it was to be remembered, that I had very lately seen the followers of this man commit a cruel slaughter on an unarmed and suppliant individual.

Yet such was the state of my mind, that I welcomed the company of the outlaw leader as a relief to my own overstrained and painful thoughts; and was not without hopes, that through his means I might obtain some clew of guidance through the maze in which my fate had involved me. I therefore answered his greeting cordially, and congratulated him on his late escape in circumstances when escape seemed impossible.

'Ay,' he replied, 'there is as much between

the craig and the woodie* as there is between the cup and the lip. But my peril was less than you may think, being a stranger to this country. Of those that were summoned to take me, and to keep me, and to retake me again, there was a moiety, as cousin Nicol Jarvie calls it, that had nae will that I suld be either taen, or keepit fast, or retaen; and of t'other moiety, there was ae half was feared to stir me; and so I had only like the fourth part of fifty or sixty men to deal withal.'

'And enough too, I should think,' replied I.

'I dinna ken that,' said he; 'but I ken, that turn every ill-willer that I had amang them out upon the green before the Clachan of Aberfoil, I wad find them play with broadsword and target, one down and another come on.'

He now inquired into my adventures since we entered his country, and laughed heartily at my account of the battle we had in the inn, and at the exploits of the Bailie with the red-hot poker.

'Let Glasgow Flourish!' he exclaimed. 'The curse of Cromwell on me, if I wad hae wished better sport than to see cousin Nicol Jarvie singe Iverach's plaid, like a sheep's head between a pair of tongs. But my cousin Jarvie,' he added more gravely, 'has some gentleman's bluid in his veins, although he has been unhappily bred up to a peaceful and mechanical craft, which could not but blunt any pretty man's spirit. — Ye may estimate the

---

* *i.e.* The throat and the withy. Twigs of willow, such as bind fagots, were often used for halters in Scotland and Ireland, being a sage economy of hemp.

reason why I could not receive you at the Clachan of Aberfoil, as I purposed. They had made a fine hosenet for me when I was absent twa or three days at Glasgow, upon the king's business—but I think I broke up the league about their lugs—they 'll no be able to hound one clan against another as they hae dune.—I hope soon to see the day when a' Hielandmen will stand shouther to shouther.—But what chanced next ? '

I gave him an account of the arrival of Captain Thornton and his party, and the arrest of the Bailie and myself, under pretext of our being suspicious persons ; and upon his more special inquiry, I recollected the officer had mentioned that, besides my name sounding suspicious in his ears, he had orders to secure an old and young person, resembling our description. This again moved the outlaw's risibility.

' As man lives by bread,' he said, ' the buzzards have mistaen my friend the Bailie for his Excellency, and you for Diana Vernon—O, the most egregious night-howlets ! '

' Miss Vernon ? ' said I, with hesitation, and trembling for the answer—' Does she still bear that name ?—She passed but now, along with a gentleman who seemed to use a style of authority.'

' Ay, ay ! ' answered Rob, ' she 's under lawfu' authority now ; and full time, for she was a daft hempie—But she 's a mettle quean. It 's a pity his Excellency is a thought eldern. The like o' yoursell, or my son Hamish, wad be mair sortable in point of years.'

Here, then, was a complete downfall of those castles of cards which my fancy had, in despite of my reason, so often amused herself with building. Although in truth I had scarcely anything else to expect, since I could not suppose that Diana could be travelling in such a country, at such an hour, with any but one who had a legal title to protect her, I did not feel the blow less severely when it came, and MacGregor's voice, urging me to pursue my story, sounded in my ears without conveying any exact import to my mind.

'You are ill,' he said, at length, after he had spoken twice without receiving an answer; 'this day's wark has been ower muckle for ane doubtless unused to sic things.'

The tone of kindness in which this was spoken recalling me to myself, and to the necessities of my situation, I continued my narrative as well as I could.—Rob Roy expressed great exultation at the successful skirmish in the pass.

'They say,' he observed, 'that king's chaff is better than other folk's corn; but I think that canna be said o' king's soldiers, if they let themselves be beaten wi' a wheen auld carles that are past fighting, and bairns that are no come till 't, and wives wi' their rocks and distaffs, the very wally-draigles o' the country-side—and Dougal Gregor, too, wha wad hae thought there had been as muckle sense in his tatty pow, that ne'er had a better covering than his ain shaggy hassock of hair!—But say away—though I dread what's to come neist,—for my Helen's an incarnate devil when her bluid's up—puir thing, she has ower muckle reason.'

I observed as much delicacy as I could in communicating to him the usage we had received, but I obviously saw the detail gave him great pain.

'I wad rather than a thousand merks,' he said, 'that I had been at hame! To misguide strangers, and forbye a', my ain natural cousin, that had showed me sic kindness—I wad rather they had burned half the Lennox in their folly! But this comes o' trusting women and their bairns, that have neither measure nor reason in their dealings —however, it's a' owing to that dog of a gauger, wha betrayed me by pretending a message from your cousin Rashleigh, to meet him on the king's affairs, whilk I thought was very like to be anent Garschattachin and a party of the Lennox declaring themselves for King James. Faith, but I kend I was clean beguiled when I heard the Duke was there; and when they strapped the horse-girth ower my arms, I might hae judged what was biding me; for I kend your kinsman, being, wi' pardon, a slippery loon himsell, is prone to employ those of his ain kidney—I wish he mayna hae been at the bottom o' the ploy himsell—I thought the chield Morris looked devilish queer when I determined he should remain a wad, or hostage, for my safe back-coming. But I *am* come back, nae thanks to him, or them that employed him, and the question is, how the collector-loon is to win back himsell—I promise him it will not be without ransom.'

'Morris,' said I, 'has already paid the last ransom which mortal man can owe.'

'Eh! What?' exclaimed my companion hastily; 'What d'ye say? I trust it was in the skirmish he was killed?'

'He was slain in cold blood, after the fight was over, Mr. Campbell.'

'Cold blood?—Damnation!'—he said, muttering betwixt his teeth—'How fell that, sir?—Speak out, sir, and do not Maister or Campbell me— my foot is on my native heath, and my name is MacGregor!'

His passions were obviously irritated; but, without noticing the rudeness of his tone, I gave him a short and distinct account of the death of Morris. He struck the but of his gun with great vehemence against the ground, and broke out, 'I vow to God, such a deed might make one forswear kin, clan, country, wife, and bairns! — and yet the villain wrought long for it. And what is the difference between warsling below the water wi' a stane about your neck, and wavering in the wind wi' a tether round it?—it's but choking after a', and he drees the doom he ettled for me. I could have wished, though, they had rather putten a ball through him, or a dirk; for the fashion of removing him will give rise to mony idle clavers—But every wight has his weird, and we maun a' dee when our day comes —And naebody will deny that Helen MacGregor has deep wrongs to avenge.'

So saying, he seemed to dismiss the theme altogether from his mind, and proceeded to inquire how

I got free from the party in whose hands he had seen me.

My story was soon told; and I added the episode of my having recovered the papers of my father, though I dared not trust my voice to name the name of Diana.

'I was sure ye wad get them,' said MacGregor; 'the letter ye brought me contained his Excellency's pleasure to that effect; and nae doubt it was my will to have aided in it. And I asked ye up into this glen on the very errand. But it's like his Excellency has forgathered wi' Rashleigh sooner than I expected.'

The first part of this answer was what most forcibly struck me.

'Was the letter I brought you, then, from this person you call his Excellency? Who is he? and what is his rank and proper name?'

'I am thinking,' said MacGregor, 'that since ye dinna ken them already, they canna be o' muckle consequence to you, and sae I shall say naething on that score. But weel I wot the letter was frae his ain hand, or, having a sort of business of my ain on my hands, being, as ye weel may see, just as much as I can fairly manage, I canna say I would hae fashed mysell sae muckle about the matter.'

I now recollected the lights seen in the library —the various circumstances which had excited my jealousy—the glove—the agitation of the tapestry which covered the secret passage from Rashleigh's apartment; and, above all, I recollected that Diana retired, in order to write, as I then thought, the

billet to which I was to have recourse in case of
the last necessity. Her hours, then, were not spent
in solitude, but in listening to the addresses of some
desperate agent of Jacobitical treason, who was a
secret resident within the mansion of her uncle!
Other young women have sold themselves for gold,
or suffered themselves to be seduced from their first
love from vanity; but Diana had sacrificed my
affections and her own to partake the fortunes of
some desperate adventurer—to seek the haunts of
freebooters through midnight deserts, with no better
hopes of rank or fortune than that mimicry of
both which the mock court of the Stewarts at St.
Germains had in their power to bestow.

'I will see her,' I said internally, 'if it be possible,
once more. I will argue with her as a friend—as
a kinsman—on the risk she is incurring, and I will
facilitate her retreat to France, where she may, with
more comfort and propriety, as well as safety,
abide the issue of the turmoils which the political
trepanner, to whom she has united her fate, is
doubtless busied in putting into motion.

'I conclude, then,' I said to MacGregor, after
about five minutes' silence on both sides, 'that his
Excellency, since you give me no other name for
him, was residing in Osbaldistone Hall at the same
time with myself?'

'To be sure—to be sure—and in the young lady's
apartment, as best reason was.' This gratuitous
information was adding gall to bitterness. 'But
few,' added MacGregor, 'kend he was derned there,
save Rashleigh and Sir Hildebrand; for you were

out o' the question; and the young lads haena
wit eneugh to ca' the cat frae the cream—But it's
a bra' auld-fashioned house; and what I specially
admire, is the abundance o' holes and bores and
concealments—ye could put twenty or thirty men
in ae corner, and a family might live a week without finding them out—whilk, nae doubt, may on
occasion be a special convenience. I wish we had
the like o' Osbaldistone-Hall on the braes o' Craig
Royston—But we maun gar woods and caves serve
the like o' us puir Hieland bodies.'

'I suppose his Excellency,' said I, 'was privy to
the first accident which befell——'

I could not help hesitating a moment.

'Ye were going to say Morris,' said Rob Roy
coolly, for he was too much accustomed to deeds of
violence for the agitation he had at first expressed
to be of long continuance. 'I used to laugh heartily
at that reik, but I'll hardly hae the heart to do't
again, since the ill-far'd accident at the Loch—Na,
na, his Excellency kend nought o' that ploy—it was
a' managed atween Rashleigh and mysell. But the
sport that came after—and Rashleigh's shift o'
turning the suspicion aff himself upon you, that he
had nae grit favour to frae the beginning—and then
Miss Die, she maun hae us sweep up a' our spiders'
webs again, and set you out o' the Justice's claws
—and then the frightened craven, Morris, that was
scared out o' his seven senses by seeing the real
man when he was charging the innocent stranger
—and the gowk of a clerk—and the drunken carle
of a justice—Ohon! ohon!—mony a laugh that

job's gien me—and now, a' that I can do for the puir devil is to get some messes said for his soul.'

'May I ask,' said I, 'how Miss Vernon came to have so much influence over Rashleigh and his accomplices, as to derange your projected plan?'

'Mine? it was none of mine. No man can say I ever laid my burden on other folk's shoulders—it was a' Rashleigh's doings — But, undoubtedly, she had great influence wi' us baith on account of his Excellency's affection, as weel as that she kend far ower mony secrets to be lightlied in a matter o' that kind.—Deil tak him,' he ejaculated, by way of summing up, 'that gies women either secret to keep or power to abuse—fules shouldna hae chapping sticks.'

We were now within a quarter of a mile from the village, when three Highlanders, springing upon us with presented arms, commanded us to stand and tell our business. The single word *Gregaragh*, in the deep and commanding voice of my companion, was answered by a shout, or rather yell, of joyful recognition. One, throwing down his firelock, clasped his leader so fast round the knees, that he was unable to extricate himself, müttering, at the same time, a torrent of Gaelic gratulation, which every now and then rose into a sort of scream of gladness. The two others, after the first howling was over, set off literally with the speed of deers, contending which should first carry to the village, which a strong party of the MacGregors now occupied, the joyful news of Rob Roy's escape and return. The intelligence excited such shouts of jubilation that the very hills rung again, and young and old, men, women, and children, without distinction of sex or age, came running down the vale to meet us, with all the tumultuous speed and clamour of a mountain torrent. When I heard the rushing noise and yells of this joyful multitude approach us, I thought it a fitting precaution to remind MacGregor that I was a stranger, and under his protection. He accordingly held me fast by the hand, while the assemblage crowded around him with such shouts of devoted attachment, and joy at his return, as were really affecting; nor did he extend to his followers what all eagerly sought, the grasp, namely, of his hand, until he had made them understand that I was to be kindly and carefully used.

The mandate of the Sultan of Delhi could not have been more promptly obeyed. Indeed, I now sustained nearly as much inconvenience from their well-meant attentions as formerly from their rudeness. They would hardly allow the friend of their leader to walk upon his own legs, so earnest were they in affording me support and assistance upon the way; and at length, taking advantage of a slight stumble which I made over a stone, which the press did not permit me to avoid, they fairly seized upon me, and bore me in their arms in triumph towards Mrs. MacAlpine's.

On arrival before her hospitable wigwam, I found power and popularity had its inconveniences in the Highlands, as everywhere else; for, before Mac-Gregor could be permitted to enter the house where he was to obtain rest and refreshment, he was obliged to relate the story of his escape at least a dozen times over, as I was told by an officious old man, who chose to translate it at least as often for my edification, and to whom I was in policy obliged to seem to pay a decent degree of attention. The audience being at length satisfied, group after group departed to take their bed upon the heath, or in the neighbouring huts, some cursing the Duke and Garschattachin, some lamenting the probable danger of Ewan of Brigglands, incurred by his friendship to MacGregor, but all agreeing that the escape of Rob Roy himself lost nothing in comparison with the exploit of any one of their chiefs since the days of Dougal-Ciar, the founder of his line.

The friendly outlaw, now taking me by the arm, conducted me into the interior of the hut. My eyes roved round its smoky recesses in quest of Diana and her companion; but they were nowhere to be seen, and I felt as if to make inquiries might betray some secret motives, which were best concealed. The only known countenance upon which my eyes rested, was that of the Bailie, who, seated on a stool by the fireside, received, with a sort of reserved dignity, the welcomes of Rob Roy, the apologies which he made for his indifferent accommodation, and his inquiries after his health.

'I am pretty weel, kinsman,' said the Bailie, 'indifferent weel, I thank ye; and for accommodations, ane canna expect to carry about the Saut-Market at his tail, as a snail does his caup—and I

am blythe that ye hae gotten out o' the hands o'
your unfreends.'

'Weel, weel, then,' answered Roy, 'what is 't ails
ye, man?—a's weel that ends weel!—the warld
will last our day—come, take a cup o' brandy—
your father the deacon could tak ane at an orra
time.'

'It might be he might do sae, Robin, after fatigue
—whilk has been my lot mair ways than ane this
day. But,' he continued, slowly filling up a little
wooden stoup which might hold about three glasses,
'he was a moderate man of his bicker, as I am
mysell—Here's wussing health to ye, Robin,' (a
sip,) 'and your weelfare here and hereafter,' (another
taste,) 'and also to my cousin Helen—and to your
twa hopefu' lads, of whom mair anon.'

So saying, he drank up the contents of the cup
with great gravity and deliberation, while Mac-
Gregor winked aside to me, as if in ridicule of the
air of wisdom and superior authority which the
Bailie assumed towards him in their intercourse,
and which he exercised when Rob was at the head
of his armed clan, in full as great, or a greater
degree, than when he was at the Bailie's mercy in
the Tolbooth of Glasgow. It seemed to me, that
MacGregor wished me, as a stranger, to understand, that if he submitted to the tone which his
kinsman assumed, it was partly out of deference
to the rights of hospitality, but still more for the
jest's sake.

As the Bailie set down his cup he recognised me,
and giving me a cordial welcome on my return, he

waived farther communication with me for the present.

'I will speak to your matters anon; I maun begin, as in reason, wi' those of my kinsman.—I presume, Robin, there's naebody here will carry aught o' what I am gaun to say, to the town-council or elsewhere, to my prejudice or to yours?'

'Make yourself easy on that head, Cousin Nicol,' answered MacGregor; 'the tae half o' the gillies winna ken what ye say, and the tother winna care —besides, that I wad stow the tongue out o' the head o' ony o' them that suld presume to say ower again ony speech held wi' me in their presence.'

'Aweel, cousin, sic being the case, and Mr. Osbaldistone here being a prudent youth, and a safe friend—I'se plainly tell ye, ye are breeding up your family to gang an ill gate.'—Then clearing his voice with a preliminary hem, he addressed his kinsman, checking, as Malvolio proposed to do when seated in his state, his familiar smile with an austere regard of control.—'Ye ken yoursell ye haud light by the law—and for my cousin Helen, forbye that her reception o' me this blessed day, whilk I excuse on account of perturbation of mind, was muckle on the north side o' *friendly*, I say (out-putting this personal reason of complaint) I hae that to say o' your wife——'

'Say *nothing* of her, kinsman,' said Rob, in a grave and stern tone, 'but what is befitting a friend to say, and her husband to hear. Of me you are welcome to say your full pleasure.'

'Aweel, aweel,' said the Bailie, somewhat disconcerted, 'we'se let that be a pass-over—I dinna approve of making mischief in families—But here are your twa sons, Hamish and Robin, whilk signifies, as I'm gien to understand, James and Robert —I trust ye will call them sae in future—there comes nae gude o' Hamishes, and Eachines, and Angusses, except that they're the names ane aye chances to see in the indictments at the Western Circuits for cow-lifting, at the instance of his majesty's advocate for his majesty's interest — aweel, but the twa lads, as I was saying, they haena sae muckle as the ordinar grunds, man, of liberal education—they dinna ken the very multiplication-table itself, whilk is the root of a' usefu' knowledge, and they did naething but laugh and fleer at me when I tauld them my mind on their ignorance—It's my belief they can neither read, write, nor cipher, if sic a thing could be believed o' ane's ain connexions in a Christian land.'

'If they could, kinsman,' said MacGregor, with great indifference, 'their learning must have come o' free will, for whar the deil was I to get them a teacher?—wad ye hae had me put on the gate o' your Divinity-Hall at Glasgow College, "Wanted, a tutor for Rob Roy's bairns?"'

'Na, kinsman,' replied Mr. Jarvie, 'but ye might hae sent the lads whar they could hae learned the fear o' God, and the usages of civilized creatures. They are as ignorant as the kyloes ye used to drive to market, or the very English churls that ye sauld them to, and can do naething whatever to purpose.'

'Umph!' answered Rob; 'Hamish can bring doun a black-cock when he's on the wing wi' a single bullet, and Rob can drive a dirk through a twa-inch board.'

'Sae muckle the waur for them, cousin! Sae muckle the waur for them baith!' answered the Glasgow merchant in a tone of great decision; 'an they ken naething better than that, they had better no ken that neither. Tell me yoursell, Rob, what has a' this cutting, and stabbing, and shooting, and driving of dirks, whether through human flesh or fir deals, dune for yoursell? and werena ye a happier man at the tail o' your nowte-bestial, when ye were in an honest calling, than ever ye hae been since, at the head o' your Hieland kernes and gally-glasses?'

I observed that MacGregor, while his well-meaning kinsman spoke to him in this manner, turned and writhed his body like a man who indeed suffers pain, but is determined no groan shall escape his lips; and I longed for an opportunity to interrupt the well-meant, but, as it was obvious to me, quite mistaken strain, in which Jarvie addressed this extraordinary person. The dialogue, however, came to an end without my interference.

'And sae,' said the Bailie, 'I hae been thinking, Rob, that as it may be ye are ower deep in the black book to win a pardon, and ower auld to mend yoursell, that it wad be a pity to bring up twa hopefu' lads to sic a godless trade as your ain, and I wad blithely tak them for prentices at the loom, as I began mysell and my father the deacon afore me, though, praise to the Giver, I only trade now as wholesale dealer—And—and——'

He saw a storm gathering on Rob's brow, which probably induced him to throw in, as a sweetener of an obnoxious proposition, what he had reserved to crown his own generosity, had it been embraced as an acceptable one;—' and Robin, lad, ye needna look sae glum, for I'll pay the prentice-fee, and never plague ye for the thousand merks neither.'

' *Ceade millia diaoul*, hundred thousand devils!' exclaimed Rob, rising and striding through the hut. ' My sons weavers!—*Millia molligheart!* but I wad see every loom in Glasgow, beam, traddles, and shuttles, burnt in hell-fire sooner!'

With some difficulty I made the Bailie, who was preparing a reply, comprehend the risk and impropriety of pressing our host on this topic, and in a minute he recovered, or reassumed, his serenity of temper.

' But ye mean weel—ye mean weel,' said he; ' so gie me your hand, Nicol, and if ever I put my sons apprentice, I will gie you the refusal o' them. And, as you say, there's the thousand merks to be settled between us.—Here, Eachin MacAnaleister, bring me my sporran.'

The person he addressed, a tall, strong mountaineer, who seemed to act as MacGregor's lieutenant, brought from some place of safety a large leathern pouch, such as Highlanders of rank wear before them when in full dress, made of the skin of the sea otter, richly garnished with silver ornaments and studs.

' I advise no man to attempt opening this sporran till he has my secret,' said Rob Roy; and then
twisting one button in one direction, and another
in another, pulling one stud upward, and pressing
another downward, the mouth of the purse, which
was bound with massive silver-plate, opened and
gave admittance to his hand. He made me remark,
as if to break short the subject on which Bailie
Jarvie had spoken, that a small steel pistol was
concealed within the purse, the trigger of which was
connected with the mounting, and made part of the
machinery, so that the weapon would certainly be
discharged, and in all probability its contents lodged
in the person of any one, who, being unacquainted
with the secret, should tamper with the lock which
secured his treasure. ' This,' said he, touching the
pistol—' this is the keeper of my privy purse.'

The simplicity of the contrivance to secure a
furred pouch, which could have been ripped open
without any attempt on the spring, reminded me
of the verses in the Odyssey, where Ulysses, in a
yet ruder age, is content to secure his property by
casting a curious and involved complication of cord-
age around the sea-chest in which it was deposited.

The Bailie put on his spectacles to examine the
mechanism, and when he had done, returned it
with a smile and a sigh, observing, ' Ah ! Rob, had
ither folk's purses been as weel guarded, I doubt if
your sporran wad hae been as weel filled as it kythes
to be by the weight.'

' Never mind, kinsman,' said Rob, laughing, ' it
will aye open for a friend's necessity, or to pay a

just due—and here,' he added, pulling out a rouleau of gold, ' here is your ten hundred merks—count them, and see that you are full and justly paid.'

Mr. Jarvie took the money in silence, and weighing it in his hand for an instant, laid it on the table, and replied, ' Rob, I canna tak it—I downa intromit with it—there can nae gude come o't—I hae seen ower weel the day what sort of a gate your gowd is made in—ill-got gear ne'er prospered ; and, to be plain wi' you, I winna meddle wi't—it looks as there might be bluid on 't.'

' Troutsho ! ' said the outlaw, affecting an indifference which, perhaps, he did not altogether feel, ' it 's gude French gowd, and ne'er was in Scotchman's pouch before mine—look at them, man —they are a' louis d'ors, bright and bonnie as the day they were coined.'

' The waur, the waur—just sae muckle the waur, Robin,' replied the Bailie, averting his eyes from the money, though, like Cæsar on the Lupercal, his fingers seemed to itch for it — ' Rebellion is waur than witchcraft, or robbery either; there 's gospel warrant for 't.'

' Never mind the warrant, kinsman,' said the freebooter; ' you come by the gowd honestly, and in payment of a just debt—it came from the one king, you may gie it to the other, if ye like ; and it will just serve for a weakening of the enemy, and in the point where puir King James is weakest too, for, God knows, he has hands and hearts eneugh, but I doubt he wants the siller.'

' He 'll no get mony Hielanders, then, Robin,'

said Mr. Jarvie, as, again replacing his spectacles
on his nose, he undid the rouleau, and began to
count its contents.

'Nor Lowlanders neither,' said MacGregor, arch-
ing his eyebrow, and, as he looked at me, directing
a glance towards Mr. Jarvie, who, all unconscious
of the ridicule, weighed each piece with habitual
scrupulosity; and having told twice over the sum,
which amounted to the discharge of his debt,
principal and interest, he returned three pieces to
buy his kinswoman a gown, as he expressed himself,
and a brace more for the twa bairns, as he called
them, requesting they might buy any thing they
liked with them except gunpowder. The Highlander stared at his kinsman's unexpected generosity,
but courteously accepted his gift, which he deposited
for the time in his well-secured pouch.

The Bailie next produced the original bond for
the debt, on the back of which he had written a
formal discharge, which, having subscribed himself,
he requested me to sign as a witness. I did so,
and Bailie Jarvie was looking anxiously around for
another, the Scottish law requiring the subscription
of two witnesses to validate either a bond or acquittance. 'You will hardly find a man that can
write save ourselves within these three miles,' said
Rob, 'but I 'll settle the matter as easily'; and,
taking the paper from before his kinsman, he threw
it in the fire. Bailie Jarvie stared in his turn, but
his kinsman continued, 'That 's a Hieland settlement of accounts—the time might come, cousin,
were I to keep a' these charges and discharges,

that friends might be brought into trouble for having dealt with me.'

The Bailie attempted no reply to this argument, and our supper now appeared in a style of abundance, and even delicacy, which, for the place, might be considered as extraordinary. The greater part of the provisions were cold, intimating they had been prepared at some distance; and there were some bottles of good French wine to relish pasties of various sorts of game, as well as other dishes. I remarked that MacGregor, while doing the honours of the table with great and anxious hospitality, prayed us to excuse the circumstance that some particular dish or pasty had been infringed on before it was presented to us. 'You must know,' said he to Mr. Jarvie, but without looking towards me, 'you are not the only guests this night in the MacGregor's country, whilk, doubtless, ye will believe, since my wife and the twa lads would otherwise have been maist ready to attend to you, as weel beseems them.'

Bailie Jarvie looked as if he felt glad at any circumstance which occasioned their absence; and I should have been entirely of his opinion, had it not been that the outlaw's apology seemed to imply they were in attendance on Diana and her companion, whom even in my thoughts I could not bear to designate as her husband.

While the unpleasant ideas , arising from this suggestion counteracted the good effects of appetite, welcome, and good cheer, I remarked that Rob Roy's attention had extended itself to providing us better bedding than we had enjoyed the night before. Two of the least fragile of the bedsteads, which stood by the wall of the hut, had been stuffed with heath, then in full flower, so artificially arranged, that, the flowers being uppermost, afforded a mattress at once elastic and fragrant. Cloaks, and such bedding as could be collected, stretched over this vegetable couch, made it both soft and warm. The Bailie seemed exhausted by fatigue. I resolved to adjourn my communication to him until next morning ; and therefore suffered him to betake himself to bed so soon as he had finished a plentiful supper. Though tired and harassed, I did not myself feel the same disposition to sleep, but rather a restless and feverish anxiety, which led to some farther discourse betwixt me and MacGregor.

CHAPTER XXXV

A hopeless darkness settles o'er my fate;
I've seen the last look of her heavenly eyes,—
I've heard the last sound of her blessed voice,—
I've seen her fair form from my sight depart:
My doom is closed.

COUNT BASIL.

'I KEN not what to make of you, Mr. Osbaldistone,' said MacGregor, as he pushed the flask towards me. 'You eat not, you show no wish for rest; and yet you drink not, though that flask of Bourdeaux might have come out of Sir Hildebrand's ain cellar. Had you been always as abstinent, you would have escaped the deadly hatred of your cousin Rashleigh.'

'Had I been always prudent,' said I, blushing at the scene he recalled to my recollection, 'I should have escaped a worse evil—the reproach of my own conscience.'

MacGregor cast a keen and somewhat fierce glance on me, as if to read whether the reproof, which he evidently felt, had been intentionally conveyed. He saw that I was thinking of myself, not of him, and turned his face towards the fire with a deep sigh. I followed his example, and each remained for a few minutes wrapt in his own painful reverie. All in the hut were now asleep, or at least silent, excepting ourselves.

MacGregor first broke silence, in the tone of one who takes up his determination to enter on a painful subject. 'My cousin Nicol Jarvie means well,' he said, 'but he presses ower hard on the temper and situation of a man like me, considering what I have been—what I have been forced to become—and, above all, that which has forced me to become what I am.'

He paused; and, though feeling the delicate nature of the discussion in which the conversation was likely to engage me, I could not help replying, that I did not doubt his present situation had much which must be most unpleasant to his feelings. 'I should be happy to learn,' I added, 'that there is an honourable chance of your escaping from it.'

'You speak like a boy,' returned MacGregor, in a low tone that growled like distant thunder— 'like a boy, who thinks the auld gnarled oak can be twisted as easily as the young sapling. Can I forget that I have been branded as an outlaw,— stigmatised as a traitor,—a price set on my head as if I had been a wolf,—my family treated as the dam and cubs of the hill-fox, whom all may torment, vilify, degrade, and insult,—the very name which came to me from a long and noble line of martial ancestors, denounced, as if it were a spell to conjure up the devil with?'

As he went on in this manner, I could plainly see, that, by the enumeration of his wrongs, he was lashing himself up into a rage, in order to justify in his own eyes the errors they had led him into. In this he perfectly succeeded; his light grey eyes contracting alternately and dilating their pupils, until they seemed actually to flash with flame, while he thrust forward and drew back his foot, grasped the hilt of his dirk, extended his arm, clenched his fist, and finally rose from his seat.

' And they *shall* find,' he said, in the same muttered, but deep tone of stifled passion, ' that the name they have dared to proscribe — that the name of MacGregor—*is* a spell to raise the wild devil withal.—*They* shall hear of my vengeance, that would scorn to listen to the story of my wrongs —The miserable Highland drover, bankrupt, bare-footed,—stripped of all, dishonoured and hunted down, because the avarice of others grasped at more than that poor all could pay, shall burst on them in an awful change. They that scoffed at the grovelling worm, and trode upon him, may cry and howl when they see the stoop of the flying and fiery-mouthed dragon.—But why do I speak of all this ?' he said, sitting down again, and in a calmer tone —' Only ye may opine it frets my patience, Mr. Osbaldistone, to be hunted like an otter, or a sealgh, or a salmon upon the shallows, and that by my very friends and neighbours ; and to have as many sword-cuts made, and pistols flashed at me, as I had this day in the ford of Avondow, would try a saint's temper, much more a Highlander's, who are not famous for that gude gift, as ye may hae heard, Mr. Osbaldistone.— But ae thing bides wi' me o' what Nicol said.— I 'm vexed for the bairns—I 'm vexed when I think o' Hamish and Robert living their father's life.' And yielding to despondence on account of his sons, which he felt not upon his own, the father rested his head upon his hand.

I was much affected, Will. All my life long I have been more melted by the distress under which a strong, proud, and powerful mind is compelled to give way, than by the more easily excited sorrows of softer dispositions. The desire of aiding him rushed strongly on my mind, notwithstanding the apparent difficulty, and even impossibility, of the task.

'We have extensive connexions abroad,' said I; 'might not your sons, with some assistance—and they are well entitled to what my father's house can give—find an honourable resource in foreign service?'

I believe my countenance showed signs of sincere emotion; but my companion, taking me by the hand, as I was going to speak farther, said, 'I thank—I thank ye—but let us say nae mair o' this. I did not think the eye of man would again have seen a tear on MacGregor's eye-lash.' He dashed the moisture from his long grey eye-lash and shaggy red eye-brow with the back of his hand. 'To-morrow morning,' he said, 'we'll talk of this, and we will talk, too, of your affairs—for we are early starters in the dawn, even when we have the luck to have good beds to sleep in. Will ye not pledge me in a grace cup?' I declined the invitation.

'Then, by the soul of St. Maronoch! I must pledge myself,' and he poured out and swallowed at least half a quart of wine.

I laid myself down to repose, resolving to delay

my own inquiries until his mind should be in a more composed state. Indeed, so much had this singular man possessed himself of my imagination, that I felt it impossible to avoid watching him for some minutes after I had flung myself on my heath mattress to seeming rest. He walked up and down the hut, crossed himself from time to time, muttering over some Latin prayer of the Catholic church; then wrapped himself in his plaid, with his naked sword on one side, and his pistol on the other, so disposing the folds of his mantle, that he could start up at a moment's warning, with a weapon in either hand, ready for instant combat. In a few minutes his heavy breathing announced that he was fast asleep. Overpowered by fatigue, and stunned by the various unexpected and extraordinary scenes of the day, I, in my turn, was soon overpowered by a slumber deep and overwhelming, from which, notwithstanding every cause for watchfulness, I did not awake until the next morning.

When I opened my eyes, and recollected my situation, I found that MacGregor had already left the hut. I awakened the Bailie, who, after many a snort and groan, and some heavy complaints of the soreness of his bones, in consequence of the unwonted exertions of the preceding day, was at length able to comprehend the joyful intelligence, that the assets carried off by Rashleigh Osbaldistone had been safely recovered. The instant he understood my meaning he forgot all his grievances, and, bustling up in a great hurry, proceeded to compare the contents of the packet, which I put into his hands, with Mr. Owen's memorandums, muttering as he went on, 'Right, right—the real thing—Baillie and Whittington—where's Baillie and Whittington?—seven hundred, six, and eight—exact to a fraction — Pollock and Peelman — twenty-eight, seven—exact—Praise be blest!—Grub and Grinder—better men cannot be—three hundred and seventy—Gliblad—twenty; I doubt Gliblad's ganging—Slipprytongue — Slipprytongue's gaen — but they are sma' sums—sma' sums—the rest's a' right—Praise be blest! we have got the stuff, and may leave this doleful country. I shall never think on Loch-Ard but the thought will gar me grew again.'

'I am sorry, cousin,' said MacGregor, who entered the hut during the last observation, 'I have not been altogether in the circumstances to make your reception sic as I could have desired—natheless, if you would condescend to visit my puir dwelling——'

'Muckle obliged, muckle obliged,' answered Mr. Jarvie, very hastily. 'But we maun be ganging—we maun be jogging, Mr. Osbaldistone and me—business canna wait.'

'Aweel, kinsman,' replied the Highlander, 'ye ken our fashion — foster the guest that comes—further him that maun gang.—But ye cannot return by Drymen—I must set ye on Loch Lomond, and boat ye down to the Ferry o' Balloch, and send your nags round to meet ye there—It's a maxim of a wise man never to return by the same road he came, providing another's free to him.'

'Ay, ay, Rob,' said the Bailie, 'that's ane o' the maxims ye learned when ye were a drover— ye caredna to face the tenants where your beasts had been taking a rug of their moorland grass in the by-ganging—and I doubt your road's waur marked now than it was then.'

'The mair need not to travel it ower often, kinsman,' replied Rob; 'but I'se send round your nags to the ferry wi' Dougal Gregor, wha is converted for that purpose into the Bailie's man, coming—not, as ye may believe, from Aberfoil or Rob Roy's country, but on a quiet jaunt from Stirling.—See, here he is.'

'I wadna hae kend the creature,' said Mr. Jarvie; nor indeed was it easy to recognise the wild Highlander, when he appeared before the door of the cottage, attired in a hat, periwig, and riding-coat, which had once called Andrew Fairservice master, and mounted on the Bailie's horse, and leading mine. He received his last orders from his master to avoid certain places where he might be exposed to suspicion—to collect what intelligence he could in the course of his journey, and to await our coming at an appointed place, near the Ferry of Balloch.

At the same time, MacGregor invited us to accompany him upon our own road, assuring us that we must necessarily march a few miles before breakfast, and recommending a dram of brandy as a proper introduction to the journey, in which he was pledged by the Bailie, who pronounced it 'an unlawful and perilous habit to begin the day wi' spirituous liquors, except to defend the stomach (whilk was a tender part) against the morning mist; in whilk case his father the deacon had recommended a dram, by precept and example.'

'Very true, kinsman,' replied Rob, 'for which reason we, who are Children of the Mist, have a right to drink brandy from morning till night.'

The Bailie, thus refreshed, was mounted on a small Highland pony; another was offered for my use, which, however, I declined, and we resumed, under very different guidance and auspices, our journey of the preceding day.

Our escort consisted of MacGregor, and five or six of the handsomest, best armed, and most athletic mountaineers of his band, and whom he had generally in immediate attendance upon his own person.

When we approached the pass, the scene of the skirmish of the preceding day, and of the still more direful deed which followed it, MacGregor hastened to speak, as if it were rather to what he knew must be necessarily passing in my mind, than to any thing I had said—he spoke, in short, to my thoughts, and not to my words.

'You must think hardly of us, Mr. Osbaldistone, and it is not natural that it should be otherwise. But remember, at least, we have not been unprovoked—we are a rude and an ignorant, and it may be a violent and passionate, but we are not a cruel people—the land might be at peace and in law for us, did they allow us to enjoy the blessings of peaceful law.   But we have been a persecuted generation.'

'And persecution,' said the Bailie, 'maketh wise men mad.'

'What must it do then to men like us, living as our fathers did a thousand years since, and possessing scarce more lights than they did ?—Can we view their bluidy edicts against us—their hanging, heading, hounding, and hunting down an ancient and honourable name, as deserving better treatment than that which enemies give to enemies ?—Here I stand, have been in twenty frays, and never hurt man but when I was in het bluid ; and yet they wad betray me and hang me like a masterless dog, at the gate of ony great man that has an ill will at me.'

I replied, 'that the proscription of his name and family sounded in English ears as a very cruel and arbitrary law '; and having thus far soothed him, I resumed my propositions of obtaining military employment for himself, if he chose it, and his sons in foreign parts.   MacGregor shook me very cordially by the hand, and detaining me, so as to permit Mr. Jarvie to precede us, a manœuvre for which the narrowness of the road served as an excuse, he said to me, 'You are a kind-hearted and an honourable youth, and understand, doubtless, that which is due to the feelings of a man of honour. — But the heather that I have trod upon when living, must bloom ower me when I am dead —my heart would sink, and my arm would shrink and wither like fern in the frost, were I to lose sight of my native hills; nor has the world a scene that would console me for the loss of the rocks and cairns, wild as they are, that you see around us.— And Helen—what would become of her, were I to leave her the subject of new insult and atrocity? —or how could she bear to be removed from these scenes, where the remembrance of her wrongs is aye sweetened by the recollection of her revenge? —I was once so hard put at by my Great enemy, as I may well ca' him, that I was forced e'en to gie way to the tide, and removed myself and my people and family from our dwellings in our native land, and to withdraw for a time into MacCallum More's country — and Helen made a Lament on our departure, as weel as MacRimmon* himsell could hae framed it—and so piteously sad and wae-some, that our hearts amaist broke as we sate and listened to her—it was like the wailing of one that mourns for the mother that bore him—the tears came down the rough faces of our gillies as they hearkened — and I wad not have the same touch of heartbreak again, no, not to have all the lands that ever were owned by MacGregor.'

'But your sons,' I said, 'they are at the age when your countrymen have usually no objection to see the world?'

'And I should be content,' he replied, 'that they pushed their fortune in the French or Spanish

---

* The MacRimmons or MacCrimonds were hereditary pipers to the chiefs of MacLeod, and celebrated for their talents. The pibroch said to have been composed by Helen MacGregor is still in existence. See the Introduction to this Novel.

service, as is the wont of Scottish cavaliers of
honour, and last night your plan seemed feasible
enough—But I hae seen his Excellency this morning before ye were up.'

'Did he then quarter so near us?' said I, my
bosom throbbing with anxiety.

'Nearer than ye thought,' was MacGregor's
reply; 'but he seemed rather in some shape to
jalouse your speaking to the young leddy; and so
you see——'

'There was no occasion for jealousy,' I answered,
with some haughtiness; 'I should not have intruded
on his privacy.'

'But ye must not be offended, or look out from
amang your curls then, like a wild-cat out of an
ivy-tod, for ye are to understand that he wishes
most sincere weel to you, and has proved it. And
it's partly that whilk has set the heather on fire
e'en now.'

'Heather on fire?' said I, 'I do not understand
you.'

'Why,' resumed MacGregor, 'ye ken weel eneugh
that women and gear are at the bottom of a' the
mischief in this warld — I hae been misdoubting
your cousin Rashleigh since ever he saw that he
wasna to get Die Vernon for his marrow, and I
think he took grudge at his Excellency mainly on
that account. But then came the splore about
the surrendering your papers — and we hae now
gude evidence, that, sae soon as he was compelled
to yield them up, he rade post to Stirling, and tauld
the government all, and mair than all, that was gaun

doucely on amang us hill-folk; and, doubtless, that was the way that the country was laid to take his Excellency and the leddy, and to make sic an unexpected raid on me. And I hae as little doubt that the poor deevil Morris, whom he could gar believe ony thing, was egged on by him, and some of the Lowland gentry, to trepan me in the gate he tried to do. But if Rashleigh Osbaldistone were baith the last and best of his name; and granting that he and I ever forgather again, the fiend go down my weasand with a bare blade at his belt, if we part before my dirk and his best bluid are weel acquainted thegither!'

He pronounced the last threat with an ominous frown, and the appropriate gesture of his hand upon his dagger.

'I should almost rejoice at what has happened,' said I, 'could I hope that Rashleigh's treachery might prove the means of preventing the explosion of the rash and desperate intrigues, in which I have long suspected him to be a prime agent.'

'Trow ye na that,' said Rob Roy; 'traitor's word never yet hurt honest cause. He was ower deep in our secrets, that's true; and had it not been so, Stirling and Edinburgh Castles would have been baith in our hands by this time, or briefly hereafter, whilk is now scarce to be hoped for. But there are ower many engaged, and far ower gude a cause to be gien up for the breath of a traitor's tale, and that will be seen and heard of ere it be lang. And so, as I was about to say, the best of my thanks to you for your offer anent my sons, whilk last night

I had some thoughts to have embraced in their behalf. But I see that this villain's treason will convince our great folks that they must instantly draw to a head, and make a blow for it, or be taen in their houses, coupled up like hounds, and driven up to London like the honest noblemen and gentlemen in the year seventeen hundred and seven. Civil war is like a cockatrice; we have sitten hatching the egg that held it for ten years, and might hae sitten on for ten years mair, when in comes Rashleigh, and chips the shell, and out bangs the wonder amang us, and cries to fire and sword. Now in sic a matter I'll hae need o' a' the hands I can mak; and, nae disparagement to the Kings of France and Spain, whom I wish very weel to, King James is as gude a man as ony o' them, and has the best right to Hamish and Rob, being his natural-born subjects.'

I easily comprehended that these words boded a general national convulsion; and, as it would have been alike useless and dangerous to have combated the political opinions of my guide, at such a place and moment, I contented myself with regretting the promiscuous scene of confusion and distress likely to arise from any general exertion in favour of the exiled royal family.

'Let it come, man—let it come,' answered Mac-Gregor; 'ye never saw dull weather clear without a shower; and if the world is turned upside down, why, honest men have the better chance to cut bread out of it.'

I again attempted to bring him back to the

subject of Diana; but although on most occasions
and subjects he used a freedom of speech which I
had no great delight in listening to, yet upon that
alone, which was most interesting to me, he kept
a degree of scrupulous reserve, and contented himself with intimating, 'that he hoped the leddy would
be soon in a quieter country than this was like to
be for one while.' I was obliged to be content
with this answer, and to proceed in the hope that
accident might, as on a former occasion, stand my
friend, and allow me at least the sad gratification
of bidding farewell to the object who had occupied
such a share of my affections, so much beyond
even what I had supposed, till I was about to be
separated from her for ever.

We pursued the margin of the lake for about
six English miles, through a devious and beauti-
fully variegated path, until we attained a sort of
Highland farm, or assembly of hamlets, near the
head of that fine sheet of water, called, if I mistake not, Lediart, or some such name. Here a
numerous party of MacGregor's men were stationed
in order to receive us. The taste, as well as the
eloquence of tribes, in a savage, or, to speak more
properly, in a rude state, is usually just, because it
is unfettered by system and affectation; and of this
I had an example in the choice these mountaineers
had made of a place to receive their guests. It has
been said that a British monarch would judge well
to receive the embassy of a rival power in the cabin
of a man-of-war; and a Highland leader acted with
some propriety in choosing a situation, where the

natural objects of grandeur proper to his country might have the full effect on the minds of his guests.

We ascended about two hundred yards from the shores of the lake, guided by a brawling brook, and left on the right hand four or five Highland huts, with patches of arable land around them, so small as to show that they must have been worked with the spade rather than the plough, cut as it were out of the surrounding copsewood, and waving with crops of barley and oats. Above this limited space the hill became more steep; and on its edge we descried the glittering arms and waving drapery of about fifty of MacGregor's followers. They were stationed on a spot, the recollection of which yet strikes me with admiration. The brook, hurling its waters downwards from the mountain, had in this spot encountered a barrier rock, over which it had made its way by two distinct leaps. The first fall, across which a magnificent old oak, slanting out from the farther bank, partly extended itself as if to shroud the dusky stream of the cascade, might be about twelve feet high; the broken waters were received in a beautiful stone basin, almost as regular as if hewn by a sculptor; and after wheeling around its flinty margin, they made a second precipitous dash, through a dark and narrow chasm, at least fifty feet in depth, and from thence, in a hurried, but comparatively a more gentle course, escaped to join the lake.

With the natural taste which belongs to mountaineers, and especially to the Scottish Highlanders, whose feelings I have observed are often allied with the romantic and poetical, Rob Roy's wife and followers had prepared our morning repast, in a scene well calculated to impress strangers with some feelings of awe. They are also naturally a grave and proud people, and, however rude in our estimation, carry their ideas of form and politeness to an excess that would appear overstrained, except from the demonstration of superior force which accompanies the display of it; for it must be granted that the air of punctilious deference and rigid etiquette which would seem ridiculous in an ordinary peasant, has, like the salute of a *corps-de-garde*, a propriety when tendered by a Highlander completely armed. There was, accordingly, a good deal of formality in our approach and reception.

The Highlanders, who had been dispersed on the side of the hill, drew themselves together when we came in view, and, standing firm and motionless, appeared in close column behind three figures, whom I soon recognised to be Helen MacGregor and her two sons. MacGregor himself arranged his attendants in the rear, and requesting Mr. Jarvie to dismount where the ascent became steep, advanced slowly, marshalling us forward at the head of the troop. As we advanced, we heard the wild notes of the bagpipes, which lost their natural discord from being mingled with the dashing sound of the cascade. When we came close, the wife of MacGregor came forward to meet us: Her dress was studiously arranged in a more feminine taste than it had been on the preceding day, but her features wore the same lofty, unbending, and resolute character; and as she folded my friend the Bailie in an unexpected and apparently unwelcome embrace, I could perceive, by the agitation of his wig, his back, and the calves of his legs, that he felt much like to one who feels himself suddenly in the gripe of a she-bear, without being able to distinguish whether the animal is in kindness or in wrath.

'Kinsman,' she said, 'you are welcome — and you too, stranger,' she added, releasing my alarmed companion, who instinctively drew back and settled his wig, and addressing herself to me,—'You also are welcome. You came,' she added, 'to our unhappy country, when our bloods were chafed, and our hands were red. Excuse the rudeness that gave you a rough welcome, and lay it upon the evil times, and not upon us.' All this was said with the manners of a princess, and in the tone and style of a court. Nor was there the least tincture of that vulgarity, which we naturally attach to the Lowland Scottish. There was a strong provincial accentuation, but, otherwise, the language rendered by Helen MacGregor, out of the native and poetical Gaelic, into English, which she had acquired as we do learned tongues, but had probably never heard applied to the mean purposes of ordinary life, was graceful, flowing, and declamatory. Her husband, who had in his time played many parts, used a much less elevated and emphatic dialect,—but even *his* language rose in purity of expression, as you may have remarked, if I have been accurate in recording it, when the affairs which he discussed were of an agitating and important nature; and it appears to me in his case, and in that of some other Highlanders whom I have known, that, when familiar and facetious, they used the Lowland Scottish dialect, —when serious and impassioned, their thoughts arranged themselves in the idiom of their native language; and in the latter case, as they uttered the corresponding ideas in English, the expressions sounded wild, elevated, and poetical. In fact, the language of passion is almost always pure as well as vehement, and it is no uncommon thing to hear a Scotchman, when overwhelmed by a country-man with a tone of bitter and fluent upbraiding, reply by way of taunt to his adversary, 'You have gotten to your English.'

Be this as it may, the wife of MacGregor invited us to a refreshment spread out on the grass, which abounded with all the good things their mountains could offer, but it was clouded by the dark and undisturbed gravity which sat on the brow of our hostess, as well as by our deep and anxious recollection of what had taken place on the preceding day. It was in vain that the leader exerted himself to excite mirth: A chill hung over our minds as if the feast had been funereal; and every bosom felt light when it was ended.

'Adieu, cousin,' she said to Mr. Jarvie, as we rose from the entertainment; 'the best wish Helen MacGregor can give to a friend is, that he may see her no more.'

The Bailie struggled to answer, probably with some common-place maxim of morality; but the calm and melancholy sternness of her countenance bore down and disconcerted the mechanical and formal importance of the magistrate. He coughed, —hemmed,—bowed,—and was silent. 'For you, stranger,' she said, ' I have a token, from one whom you can never——'

'Helen,' interrupted MacGregor, in a loud and stern voice, 'what means this?—have you forgotten the charge?'

'MacGregor,' she replied, 'I have forgotten nought that is fitting for me to remember. It is not such hands as these,' and she stretched forth her long, sinewy, and bare arm, 'that are fitting to convey love-tokens, were the gift connected with aught but misery.—Young man,' she said, presenting me with a ring, which I well remembered as one of the few ornaments that Miss Vernon sometimes wore, 'this comes from one whom you will never see more. If it is a joyless token, it is well fitted to pass through the hands of one to whom joy can never be known. Her last words were— Let him forget me for ever.'

'And can she,' I said, almost without being conscious that I spoke, 'suppose that is possible?'

'All may be forgotten,' said the extraordinary female who addressed me,—'all—but the sense of dishonour, and the desire of vengeance.'

'*Seid suas!*' * cried the MacGregor, stamping

---

* ' Strike up. '

with impatience. The bagpipes sounded, and, with their thrilling and jarring tones, cut short our conference. Our leave of our hostess was taken by silent gestures; and we resumed our journey, with an additional proof on my part, that I was beloved by Diana, and was separated from her for ever.

CHAPTER XXXVI

Farewell to the land where the clouds love to rest,
Like the shroud of the dead, on the mountain's cold breast;
To the cataract's roar where the eagles reply,
And the lake her lone bosom expands to the sky.

OUR route lay through a dreary, yet romantic country, which the distress of my own mind prevented me from remarking particularly, and which, therefore, I will not attempt to describe. The lofty peak of Ben Lomond, here the predominant monarch of the mountains, lay on our right hand, and served as a striking land-mark. I was not awakened from my apathy, until, after a long and toilsome walk, we emerged through a pass in the hills, and Loch Lomond opened before us. I will spare you the attempt to describe what you would hardly comprehend without going to see it. But certainly this noble lake, boasting innumerable beautiful islands, of every varying form and outline which fancy can frame,—its northern extremity narrowing until it is lost among dusky and retreating mountains, — while, gradually widening as it extends to the southward, it spreads its base around the indentures and promontories of a fair and fertile land, affords one of the most surprising, beautiful, and sublime spectacles in nature. The eastern side,

314

peculiarly rough and rugged, was at this time the chief seat of MacGregor and his clan, to curb whom a small garrison had been stationed in a central position betwixt Loch Lomond and another lake. The extreme strength of the country, however, with the numerous passes, marshes, caverns, and other places of concealment or defence, made the establishment of this little fort seem rather an acknowledgment of the danger, than an effectual means of securing against it.

On more than one occasion, as well as on that which I witnessed, the garrison suffered from the adventurous spirit of the outlaw and his followers. These advantages were never sullied by ferocity when he himself was in command; for, equally good-tempered and sagacious, he understood well the danger of incurring unnecessary odium. I learnt with pleasure that he had caused the captives of the preceding day to be liberated in safety; and many traits of mercy, and even generosity, are recorded of this remarkable man on similar occasions.

A boat waited for us in a creek beneath a huge rock, manned by four lusty Highland rowers; and our host took leave of us with great cordiality, and even affection. Betwixt him and Mr. Jarvie, indeed, there seemed to exist a degree of mutual regard, which formed a strong contrast to their different occupations and habits. After kissing each other very lovingly, and when they were just in the act of parting, the Bailie, in the fulness of his heart, and with a faltering voice, assured his kinsman, 'that if ever an hundred pund, or even twa hundred, would put him or his family in a settled way, he need but just send a line to the Saut-Market'; and Rob, grasping his basket-hilt with one hand, and shaking Mr. Jarvie's heartily with the other, protested, ' that if ever any body should affront his kinsman, an he would but let him ken, he would stow his lugs out of his head, were he the best man in Glasgow.'

With these assurances of mutual aid and continued good-will, we bore away from the shore, and took our course for the south-western angle of the lake, where it gives birth to the river Leven. Rob Roy remained for some time standing on the rock from beneath which we had departed, conspicuous by his long gun, waving tartans, and the single plume in his cap, which in those days denoted the Highland gentleman and soldier; although I observe the present military taste has decorated the Highland bonnet with a quantity of black plumage, resembling that which is borne before funerals. At length, as the distance increased between us, we saw him turn and go slowly up the side of the hill, followed by his immediate attendants or body guard.

We performed our voyage for a long time in silence, interrupted only by the Gaelic chant which one of the rowers sung in low irregular measure, rising occasionally into a wild chorus, in which the others joined.

My own thoughts were sad enough; yet I felt something soothing in the magnificent scenery with which I was surrounded; and thought, in the enthusiasm of the moment, that had my faith been that

of Rome, I could have consented to live and die a
lonely hermit in one of the romantic and beautiful
islands amongst which our boat glided.

The Bailie had also his speculations, but they
were of somewhat a different complexion; as I
found when, after about an hour's silence, during
which he had been mentally engaged in the calculations necessary, he undertook to prove the possibility of draining the lake, and 'giving to plough
and harrow many hundred, ay, many a thousand
acres, from whilk no man could get earthly gude
e'enow, unless it were a gedd,* or a dish of perch
now and then.'

Amidst a long discussion, which he 'crammed
into mine ear against the stomach of my sense,' I
only remember, that it was part of his project to
preserve a portion of the lake just deep enough and
broad enough for the purposes of water-carriage, so
that coal-barges and gabbards should pass as easily
between Dunbarton and Glenfalloch as between
Glasgow and Greenock.

At length we neared our distant place of land-
ing, adjoining to the ruins of an ancient castle, and
just where the lake discharges its superfluous waters
into the Leven. There we found Dougal with
the horses. The Bailie had formed a plan with
respect to 'the creature,' as well as upon the draining of the lake; and, perhaps, in both cases, with
more regard to the utility than to the practical
possibility of his scheme. 'Dougal,' he said, 'ye

---

* A pike.

are a kindly creature, and hae the sense and feeling
o' what is due to your betters—and I'm e'en wae
for you, Dougal, for it canna be but that in the
life ye lead you suld get a Jeddart cast ae day,
suner or later. I trust, considering my services as
a magistrate, and my father the deacon's afore me,
I hae interest eneugh in the council to gar them
wink a wee at a waur faut than yours. Sae I hae
been thinking that if ye will gang back to Glasgow
wi' us, being a strong-backit creature, ye might be
employed in the warehouse till something better
suld cast up.'

'Her nainsell muckle obliged till the Bailie's
honour,' replied Dougal; 'but teil be in her shanks
fan she gangs on a causeway'd street, unless she
be drawn up the Gallowgate wi' tows, as she was
before.'

In fact, I afterwards learned that Dougal had
originally come to Glasgow as a prisoner, from
being concerned in some depredation, but had
somehow found such favour in the eyes of the
jailor, that, with rather overweening confidence, he
had retained him in his service as one of the turn-
keys; a task which Dougal had discharged with
sufficient fidelity, so far as was known, until overcome by his clannish prejudices on the unexpected
appearance of his old leader.

Astonished at receiving so round a refusal to
so favourable an offer, the Bailie, turning to me,
observed, that the 'creature was a natural - born
idiot.' I testified my own gratitude in a way which
Dougal much better relished, by slipping a couple

of guineas into his hand. He no sooner felt the
touch of the gold, than he sprung twice or thrice
from the earth with the agility of a wild buck,
flinging out first one heel and then another, in a
manner which would have astonished a French
dancing-master. He ran to the boatmen to show
them the prize, and a small gratuity made them
take part in his raptures. He then, to use a
favourite expression of the dramatic John Bunyan,
'went on his way, and I saw him no more.'

The Bailie and I mounted our horses, and proceeded on the road to Glasgow. When we had
lost the view of the lake, and its superb amphi-
theatre of mountains, I could not help expressing,
with enthusiasm, my sense of its natural beauties,
although I was conscious that Mr. Jarvie was a
very uncongenial spirit to communicate with on
such a subject.

'Ye are a young gentleman,' he replied, 'and an
Englishman, and a' this may be very fine to you;
but for me, wha am a plain man, and ken something o' the different values of land, I wadna gie
the finest sight we hae seen in the Hielands, for
the first keek o' the Gorbals o' Glasgow; and if
I were ance there, it suldna be every fule's errand,
begging your pardon, Mr. Francis, that suld take
me out o' sight o' Saint Mungo's steeple again!'

The honest man had his wish; for, by dint of
travelling very late, we arrived at his own house
that night, or rather on the succeeding morning.
Having seen my worthy fellow-traveller safely
consigned to the charge of the considerate and

officious Mattie, I proceeded to Mrs. Flyter's, in whose house, even at this unwonted hour, light was still burning. The door was opened by no less a person than Andrew Fairservice himself, who, upon the first sound of my voice, set up a loud shout of joyful recognition, and without uttering a syllable, ran up stairs towards a parlour on the second floor, from the windows of which the light proceeded. Justly conceiving that he went to announce my return to the anxious Owen, I followed him upon the foot. Owen was not alone,—there was another in the apartment,—it was my father.

The first impulse was to preserve the dignity of his usual equanimity,—' Francis, I am glad to see you.' — The next was to embrace me tenderly,— ' My dear—dear son ! '—Owen secured one of my hands, and wetted it with his tears, while he joined in gratulating my return. These are scenes which address themselves to the eye and to the heart, rather than to the ear. — My old eye-lids still moisten at the recollection of our meeting ; but your kind and affectionate feelings can well imagine what I should find it impossible to describe.

When the tumult of our joy was over, I learnt that my father had arrived from Holland shortly after Owen had set off for Scotland. Determined and rapid in all his movements, he only stopped to provide the means of discharging the obligations incumbent on his house. By his extensive resources, with funds enlarged, and credit fortified, by eminent success in his continental speculation, he easily accomplished what perhaps his absence alone rendered difficult, and set out for Scotland to exact justice from Rashleigh Osbaldistone, as well as to put order to his affairs in that country. My father's arrival in full credit, and with the ample means of supporting his engagements honourably, as well as benefiting his correspondents in future, was a stunning blow to MacVittie and Company, who had conceived his star set for ever. Highly incensed at the usage his confidential clerk and agent had received at their hands, Mr. Osbaldistone refused every tender of apology and accommodation ; and, having settled the balance of their account, announced to them, that, with all its numerous contingent advantages, that leaf of their ledger was closed for ever.

While he enjoyed this triumph over false friends, he was not a little alarmed on my account. Owen, good man, had not supposed it possible that a journey of fifty or sixty miles, which may be made with so much ease and safety in any direction from London, could be attended with any particular danger. But he caught alarm, by sympathy, from my father, to whom the country, and the lawless character of its inhabitants, were better known.

These apprehensions were raised to agony, when, a few hours before I arrived, Andrew Fairservice made his appearance, with a dismal and exaggerated account of the uncertain state in which he had left me. The nobleman with whose troops he had been a sort of prisoner, had, after examination, not only dismissed him, but furnished him with the means of returning rapidly to Glasgow, in order

to announce to my friends my precarious and unpleasant situation.

Andrew was one of those persons who have no
objection to the sort of temporary attention and
woful importance which attaches itself to the bearer
of bad tidings, and had therefore by no means
smoothed down his tale in the telling, especially
as the rich London merchant himself proved unexpectedly one of the auditors. He went at great
length into an account of the dangers I had escaped,
chiefly, as he insinuated, by means of his own experience, exertion, and sagacity.

'What was to come of me now, when my better
angel, in his (Andrew's) person, was removed from
my side, it was,' he said, 'sad and sair to conjecture;
that the Bailie was nae better than just naebody
at a pinch, or something waur, for he was a
conceited body—and Andrew hated conceit—but
certainly atween the pistols and the carabines of
the troopers, that rappit aff the tane after the tother
as fast as hail, and the dirks and claymores o' the
Hielanders, and the deep waters and weils o' the
Avondow, it was to be thought there wad be a puir
account of the young gentleman.'

This statement would have driven Owen to
despair, had he been alone and unsupported; but
my father's perfect knowledge of mankind enabled
him easily to appreciate the character of Andrew,
and the real amount of his intelligence. Stripped of
all exaggeration, however, it was alarming enough
to a parent. He determined to set out in person
to obtain my liberty, by ransom or negotiation, and

was busied with Owen till a late hour, in order to get through some necessary correspondence, and devolve on the latter some business which should be transacted during his absence; and thus it chanced that I found them watchers.

It was late ere we separated to rest, and, too impatient long to endure repose, I was stirring early the next morning. Andrew gave his attendance at my levee, as in duty bound, and, instead of the scarecrow figure to which he had been reduced at Aberfoil, now appeared in the attire of an undertaker, a goodly suit, namely, of the deepest mourning. It was not till after one or two queries, which the rascal affected as long as he could to misunderstand, that I found out he 'had thought it but decent to put on mourning, on account of my inexpressible loss; and as the broker at whose shop he had equipped himself, declined to receive the goods again, and as his own garments had been destroyed or carried off in my honour's service, doubtless I and my honourable father, whom Providence had blessed wi' the means, wadna suffer a puir lad to sit down wi' the loss; a stand o' claes was nae great matter to an Osbaldistone, (be praised for 't!) especially to an auld and attached servant o' the house.'

As there was something of justice in Andrew's plea of loss in my service, his finesse succeeded; and he came by a good suit of mourning, with a beaver and all things conforming, as the exterior signs of woe for a master who was alive and merry.

My father's first care, when he arose, was to visit

Mr. Jarvie, for whose kindness he entertained the most grateful sentiments, which he expressed in very few but manly and nervous terms. He explained the altered state of his affairs and offered the Bailie, on such terms as could not but be both advantageous and acceptable, that part in his concerns which had been hitherto managed by MacVittie and Company. The Bailie heartily congratulated my father and Owen on the changed posture of their affairs, and, without affecting to disclaim that he had done his best to serve them, when matters looked otherwise, he said, ' He had only just acted as he wad be done by—that, as to the extension of their correspondence, he frankly accepted it with thanks. Had MacVittie's folk behaved like honest men,' he said, ' he wad hae liked ill to hae come in ahint them, and out afore them, this gate. But it's otherwise, and they maun e'en stand the loss.'

The Bailie then pulled me by the sleeve into a corner, and, after again cordially wishing me joy, proceeded in rather an embarrassed tone.

' I wad heartily wish, Maister Francis, there suld be as little said as possible about the queer things we saw up yonder awa—There's nae gude, unless ane were judicially examinate, to say ony thing about that awfu' job o' Morris — and the members o' the council wadna think it creditable in ane of their body to be fighting wi' a wheen Hielandmen, and singeing their plaidens — And abune a', though I am a decent sponsible man, when I am on my right end, I canna but think I

324

maun hae made a queer figure without my hat and my periwig, hinging by the middle like bawdrons, or a cloak flung ower a cloak-pin. Bailie Grahame wad hae an unco hair in my neck an he got that tale by the end.'

I could not suppress a smile when I recollected the Bailie's situation, although I certainly thought it no laughing matter at the time. The good-natured merchant was a little confused, but smiled also when he shook his head. ' I see how it is— I see how it is. But say naething about it—there's a gude callant; and charge that lang-tongued, conceited, upsetting serving-man o' yours, to say naething neither. I wadna for ever sae muckle that even the lassock Mattie kend ony thing about it. I wad never hear an end o't.'

He was obviously relieved from his impending fears of ridicule, when I told him it was my father's intention to leave Glasgow almost immediately. Indeed he had now no motive for remaining, since the most valuable part of the papers carried off by Rashleigh had been recovered. For that portion which he had converted into cash and expended in his own or on political intrigues, there was no mode of recovering it but by a suit at law, which was forthwith commenced, and proceeded, as our law-agents assured us, with all deliberate speed.

We spent, accordingly, one hospitable day with the Bailie, and took leave of him, as this narrative now does. He continued to grow in wealth, honour, and credit, and actually rose to the highest civic honours in his native city. About two years

after the period I have mentioned, he tired of his
bachelor life, and promoted Mattie from her wheel
by the kitchen fire, to the upper end of his table,
in the character of Mrs. Jarvie.   Bailie Grahame,
the MacVitties, and others, (for all men have their
enemies, especially in the council of a royal burgh,)
ridiculed this transformation.   'But,' said Mr.
Jarvie, 'let them say their say.   I'll ne'er fash
mysell, nor lose my liking for sae feckless a matter
as a nine days' clash.   My honest father the deacon
had a byword,

> "Brent brow and lily skin,
> A loving heart, and a leal within,
> Is better than gowd or gentle kin."

Besides,' as he always concluded, 'Mattie was nae
ordinary lassock-quean; she was akin to the Laird
o' Limmerfield.'

Whether it was owing to her descent or her good
gifts, I do not presume to decide; but Mattie behaved excellently in her exaltation, and relieved the
apprehensions of some of the Bailie's friends, who
had deemed his experiment somewhat hazardous.
I do not know that there was any other incident
of his quiet and useful life worthy of being particularly recorded.

CHAPTER XXXVII

' Come ye hither, my "six" good sons,
    Gallant men I trow ye be,
How many of you, my children dear,
    Will stand by that good Earl and me ?'

' " Five" of them did answer make—
    " Five" of them spoke hastily,
O father, till the day we die,
    We 'll stand by that good Earl and thee." '
THE RISING IN THE NORTH.

ON the morning when we were to depart from Glasgow, Andrew Fairservice bounced into my apartment like a madman, jumping up and down, and singing, with more vehemence than tune,

' The kiln 's on fire—the kiln 's on fire—
The kiln 's on fire—she 's a' in a lowe.'

With some difficulty I prevailed on him to cease his confounded clamour, and explain to me what the matter was. He was pleased to inform me, as if he had been bringing the finest news imaginable, 'that the Hielands were clean broken out every man o' them, and that Rob Roy, and a' his breekless bands, wad be down upon Glasgow, or twentyfour hours o' the clock gaed round.'

'Hold your tongue,' said I, 'you rascal! You must be drunk or mad; and if there is any

327

truth in your news, is it a singing matter, you scoundrel?'

'Drunk or mad? nae doubt,' replied Andrew, dauntlessly; 'ane 's aye drunk or mad if he tells what grit folks dinna like to hear—Sing? odd, the clans will make us sing on the wrang side o' our mouth, if we are sae drunk or mad as to bide their coming.'

I rose in great haste, and found my father and Owen also on foot, and in considerable alarm.

Andrew's news proved but too true in the main. The great rebellion which agitated Britain in the year 1715 had already broken out, by the unfortunate Earl of Mar's setting up the standard of the Stewart family in an ill-omened hour, to the ruin of many honourable families, both in England and Scotland. The treachery of some of the Jacobite agents, (Rashleigh among the rest,) and the arrest of others, had made George the First's government acquainted with the extensive ramifications of a conspiracy long prepared, and which at last exploded prematurely, and in a part of the kingdom too distant to have any vital effect upon the country, which, however, was plunged into much confusion.

This great public event served to confirm and elucidate the obscure explanations I had received from MacGregor; and I could easily see why the westland clans, who were brought against him, should have waived their private quarrel, in consideration that they were all shortly to be engaged in the same public cause. It was a more melancholy reflection to my mind, that Diana Vernon was the wife of one of those who were most active in turning the world upside down, and that she was herself exposed to all the privations and perils of her husband's hazardous trade.

We held an immediate consultation on the measures we were to adopt in this crisis, and acquiesced in my father's plan, that we should instantly get the necessary passports, and make the best of our way to London. I acquainted my father with my wish to offer my personal service to the government in any volunteer corps, several being already spoken of. He readily acquiesced in my proposal; for, though he disliked war as a profession, yet upon principle, no man would have exposed his life more willingly in defence of civil and religious liberty.

We travelled in haste and in peril through Dumfries-shire and the neighbouring counties of England. In this quarter, gentlemen of the Tory interest were already in motion mustering men and horses, while the Whigs assembled themselves in the principal towns, armed the inhabitants, and prepared for civil war. We narrowly escaped being stopped on more occasions than one, and were often compelled to take circuitous routes to avoid the points where forces were assembling.

When we reached London, we immediately associated with those bankers and eminent merchants who agreed to support the credit of government, and to meet that run upon the funds, on which the conspirators had greatly founded their hopes of furthering their undertaking, by rendering the government, as it were, bankrupt. My father was chosen one of the members of this formidable body of the monied interest, as all had the greatest confidence in his zeal, skill, and activity. He was also the organ by which they communicated with government, and contrived, from funds belonging to his own house, or over which he had command, to find purchasers for a quantity of the national stock, which was suddenly flung into the market at a depreciated price when the rebellion broke out. I was not idle myself, but obtained a commission, and levied, at my father's expense, about two hundred men, with whom I joined General Carpenter's army.

The rebellion, in the meantime, had extended itself to England. The unfortunate Earl of Derwentwater had taken arms in the cause, along with General Foster. My poor uncle, Sir Hildebrand, whose estate was reduced to almost nothing by his own carelessness and the expense and debauchery of his sons and household, was easily persuaded to join that unfortunate standard. Before doing so, however, he exhibited a degree of precaution of which no one could have suspected him—he made his will!

By this document he devised his estates at Osbaldistone-Hall, and so forth, to his sons successively, and their male heirs, until he came to Rashleigh, whom, on account of the turn he had lately taken in politics, he detested with all his might,—he cut him off with a shilling, and settled the estate on me, as his next heir. I had always been rather a favourite of the old gentleman; but it is probable that, confident in the number of gigantic youths who now armed around him, he considered the destination as likely to remain a dead letter, which he inserted chiefly to show his displeasure at Rashleigh's treachery, both public and domestic. There was an article, by which he bequeathed to the niece of his late wife, Diana Vernon, now Lady Diana Vernon Beauchamp, some diamonds belonging to her late aunt, and a great silver ewer, having the arms of Vernon and Osbaldistone quarterly engraven upon it.

But Heaven had decreed a more speedy extinction of his numerous and healthy lineage than, most probably, he himself had reckoned on. In the very first muster of the conspirators at a place called Green-Rigg, Thorncliff Osbaldistone quarrelled about precedence with a gentleman of the Northumbrian border, to the full as fierce and intractable as himself. In spite of all remonstrances, they gave their commander a specimen of how far their discipline might be relied upon, by fighting it out with their rapiers, and my kinsman was killed on the spot. His death was a great loss to Sir Hildebrand, for, notwithstanding his infernal temper, he had a grain or two of more sense than belonged to the rest of the brotherhood, Rashleigh always excepted.

Perceval, the sot, died also in his calling. He had a wager with another gentleman, who, from his exploits in that line, had acquired the formidable epithet of Brandy Swalewell, which should drink the largest cup of strong liquor when King James was proclaimed by the insurgents at Morpeth. The exploit was something enormous. I forget the exact quantity of brandy which Percie swallowed, but it occasioned a fever, of which he expired at the end of three days, with the word, *water, water*, perpetually on his tongue.

Dickon broke his neck near Warrington Bridge, in an attempt to show off a foundered blood-mare, which he wished to palm upon a Manchester merchant who had joined the insurgents. He pushed the animal at a five-barred gate; she fell in the leap, and the unfortunate jockey lost his life.

Wilfred the fool, as sometimes befalls, had the best fortune of the family. He was slain at Proud Preston, in Lancashire, on the day that General Carpenter attacked the barricades, fighting with great bravery, though I have heard he was never able exactly to comprehend the cause of quarrel, and did not uniformly remember, on which king's side he was engaged. John also behaved very boldly in the same engagement, and received several wounds, of which he was not happy enough to die on the spot.

Old Sir Hildebrand, entirely broken-hearted by these successive losses, became, by the next day's surrender, one of the unhappy prisoners, and was lodged in Newgate with his wounded son John.

I was now released from my military duty, and lost no time, therefore, in endeavouring to relieve the distresses of these near relations. My father's

interest with government, and the general compassion excited by a parent who had sustained the
successive loss of so many sons within so short a
time, would have prevented my uncle and cousin
from being brought to trial for high treason; but
their doom was given forth from a greater tribunal.
John died of his wounds in Newgate, recommending to me, with his last breath, a cast of hawks
which he had at the Hall, and a black spaniel
bitch, called Lucy.

My poor uncle seemed beaten down to the very
earth by his family calamities, and the circumstances
in which he unexpectedly found himself. He said
little, but seemed grateful for such attentions as
circumstances permitted me to show him. I did
not witness his meeting with my father for the first
time for so many years, and under circumstances so
melancholy; but judging from my father's extreme
depression of spirits, it must have been melancholy
in the last degree. Sir Hildebrand spoke with great
bitterness against Rashleigh, now his only surviving
child; laid upon him the ruin of his house, and
the deaths of all his brethren, and declared, that
neither he nor they would have plunged into political
intrigue, but for that very member of his family
who had been the first to desert them. He once or
twice mentioned Diana, always with great affection;
and once he said, while I sate by his bedside —
' Nevoy, since Thorncliff and all of them are dead,
I am sorry you cannot have her.'

The expression affected me much at the time;
for it was a usual custom of the poor old Baronet's,

when joyously setting forth upon the morning's chase, to distinguish Thorncliff, who was a favourite, while he summoned the rest more generally; and the loud jolly tone in which he used to hollo, 'Call Thornie—call all of them,' contrasted sadly with the wobegone and self-abandoning note in which he uttered the disconsolate words which I have above quoted. He mentioned the contents of his will, and supplied me with an authenticated copy— the original he had deposited with my old acquaintance Mr. Justice Inglewood, who, dreaded by no one, and confided in by all as a kind of neutral person, had become, for aught I know, the depositary of half the wills of the fighting men of both factions in the county of Northumberland.

The greater part of my uncle's last hours were spent in the discharge of the religious duties of his church, in which he was directed by the chaplain of the Sardinian ambassador, for whom, with some difficulty, we obtained permission to visit him. I could not ascertain by my own observation, or through the medical attendants, that Sir Hildebrand Osbaldistone died of any formed complaint, bearing a name in the science of medicine. He seemed to me completely worn out and broken down by fatigue of body and distress of mind, and rather ceased to exist than died of any positive struggle; just as a vessel, buffeted and tossed by a succession of tempestuous gales, her timbers overstrained, and her joints loosened, will sometimes spring a leak and founder, when there are no apparent causes for her destruction.

It was a remarkable circumstance that my father, after the last duties were performed to his brother, appeared suddenly to imbibe a strong anxiety that I should act upon the will, and represent his father's house, which had hitherto seemed to be the thing in the world which had least charms for him. But formerly, he had been only like the fox in the fable, contemning what was beyond his reach; and, moreover, I doubt not that the excessive dislike which he entertained against Rashleigh (now Sir Rashleigh) Osbaldistone, who loudly threatened to attack his father Sir Hildebrand's will and settlement, corroborated my father's desire to maintain it.

'He had been most unjustly disinherited,' he said, 'by his own father — his brother's will had repaired the disgrace, if not the injury, by leaving the wreck of the property to Frank, the natural heir, and he was determined the bequest should take effect.'

In the meantime, Rashleigh was not altogether a contemptible personage as an opponent. The information he had given to government was critically well-timed, and his extreme plausibility, with the extent of his intelligence, and the artful manner in which he contrived to assume both merit and influence, had, to a certain extent, procured him patrons among ministers. We were already in the full tide of litigation with him on the subject of his pillaging the firm of Osbaldistone and Tresham; and, judging from the progress we made in that comparatively simple lawsuit, there was a chance that this second course of litigation might be drawn out beyond the period of all our natural lives.

To avert these delays as much as possible, my father, by the advice of his counsel learned in the law, paid off and vested in my person the rights to certain large mortgages, affecting Osbaldistone-Hall. Perhaps, however, the opportunity to convert a great share of the large profits which accrued from the rapid rise of the funds upon the suppression of the rebellion, and the experience he had so lately had of the perils of commerce, encouraged him to realize, in this manner, a considerable part of his property. At any rate, it so chanced, that, instead of commanding me to the desk, as I fully expected, having intimated my willingness to comply with his wishes, however they might destine me, I received his directions to go down to Osbaldistone - Hall, and take possession of it as the heir and representative of the family. I was directed to apply to Squire Inglewood for the copy of my uncle's will deposited with him, and take all necessary measures to secure that possession, which sages say makes nine points of the law.

At another time I should have been delighted with this change of destination. But now Osbaldistone-Hall was accompanied with many painful recollections. Still, however, I thought, that in that neighbourhood only I was likely to acquire some information respecting the fate of Diana Vernon. I had every reason to fear it must be far different from what I could have wished it. But I could obtain no precise information on the subject.

It was in vain that I endeavoured, by such acts of kindness as their situation admitted, to conciliate the confidence of some distant relations who were among the prisoners in Newgate. A pride which I could not condemn, and a natural suspicion of the Whig, Frank Osbaldistone, cousin to the double-distilled traitor Rashleigh, closed every heart and tongue, and I only received thanks, cold and extorted, in exchange for such benefits as I had power to offer. The arm of the law was also gradually abridging the numbers of those whom I endeavoured to serve, and the hearts of the survivors became gradually more contracted towards all whom they conceived to be concerned with the existing government. As they were led gradually, and by detachments, to execution, those who survived lost interest in mankind, and the desire of communicating with them. I shall long remember what one of them, Ned Shafton by name, replied to my anxious inquiry, whether there was any indulgence I could procure him? 'Mr. Frank Osbaldistone, I must suppose you mean me kindly, and therefore I thank you. But, by G—, men cannot be fattened like poultry, when they see their neighbours carried off day by day to the place of execution, and know that their own necks are to be twisted round in their turn.'

Upon the whole, therefore, I was glad to escape from London, from Newgate, and from the scenes which both exhibited, to breathe the free air of Northumberland. Andrew Fairservice had continued in my service more from my father's pleasure than my own.   At present there seemed a prospect that his local acquaintance with Osbaldistone-Hall and its vicinity might be useful; and, of course, he accompanied me on my journey, and I enjoyed the prospect of getting rid of him, by establishing him in his old quarters.   I cannot conceive how he could prevail upon my father to interest himself in him, unless it were by the art, which he possessed in no inconsiderable degree, of affecting an extreme attachment to his master, which theoretical attachment he made compatible in practice with playing all manner of tricks without scruple, providing only against his master being cheated by any one but himself.

We performed our journey to the North without any remarkable adventure, and we found the country, so lately agitated by rebellion, now peaceful and in good order.   The nearer we approached to Osbaldistone-Hall, the more did my heart sink at the thought of entering that deserted mansion; so that, in order to postpone the evil day, I resolved first to make my visit at Mr. Justice Inglewood's.

That venerable person had been much disturbed with thoughts of what he had been, and what he now was; and natural recollections of the past had interfered considerably with the active duty, which, in his present situation, might have been expected from him.   He was fortunate, however, in one respect: he had got rid of his clerk, Jobson, who had finally left him in dudgeon at his inactivity, and become legal assistant to a certain Squire Standish, who had lately commenced operations in those parts as a justice, with a zeal for King George and the Protestant succession, which, very different from the feelings of his old patron, Mr. Jobson had more occasion to restrain within the bounds of the law, than to stimulate to exertion.

Old Justice Inglewood received me with great courtesy, and readily exhibited my uncle's will, which seemed to be without a flaw. He was for some time in obvious distress, how he should speak and act in my presence; but when he found, that though a supporter of the present government upon principle, I was disposed to think with pity on those who had opposed it on a mistaken feeling of loyalty and duty, his discourse became a very diverting medley of what he had done, and what he had left undone,—the pains he had taken to prevent some squires from joining, and to wink at the escape of others, who had been so unlucky as to engage in the affair.

We were *tête-à-tête*, and several bumpers had been quaffed by the Justice's special desire, when, on a sudden, he requested me to fill a *bona fide* brimmer to the health of poor dear Die Vernon, the rose of the wilderness, the heath-bell of Cheviot, and the blossom that's transplanted to an infernal convent.

'Is not Miss Vernon married then?' I exclaimed, in great astonishment. 'I thought his Excellency——'

'Pooh! pooh! his Excellency and his Lordship's all a humbug now, you know—mere St. Germains titles—Earl of Beauchamp, and ambassador plenipotentiary from France, when the Duke Regent of Orleans scarce knew that he lived, I daresay. But you must have seen old Sir Frederick Vernon at the hall, when he played the part of Father Vaughan ?'

' Good Heavens ! then Vaughan was Miss Vernon's father !'

' To be sure he was,' said the Justice, coolly ; ' There's no use in keeping the secret now, for he must be out of the country by this time—otherwise, no doubt, it would be my duty to apprehend him.—Come, off with your bumper to my dear lost Die !

> And let her health go round, around, around,
>   And let her health go round ;
> For though your stocking be of silk,
>   Your knees near kiss the ground, aground, aground.' *

I was unable, as the reader may easily conceive, to join in the Justice's jollity. My head swam with the shock I had received. ' I never heard,' I said, ' that Miss Vernon's father was living.'

' It was not our government's fault that he is,' replied Inglewood, ' for the devil a man there is whose head would have brought more money. He was condemned to death for Fenwick's plot, and was thought to have had some hand in the Knightsbridge affair, in King William's time ; and as he had married in Scotland a relation of the house of Breadalbane, he possessed great influence with

---

* This pithy verse occurs, it is believed, in Shadwell's play of Bury Fair.

all their chiefs. There was a talk of his being demanded to be given up at the Peace of Ryswick, but he shammed ill, and his death was given publicly out in the French papers. But when he came back here on the old score, we old cavaliers knew him well,—that is to say, I knew him, not as being a cavalier myself, but no information being lodged against the poor gentleman, and my memory being shortened by frequent attacks of the gout, I could not have sworn to him, you know.'

'Was he, then, not known at Osbaldistone-Hall?' I inquired.

'To none but to his daughter, the old knight, and Rashleigh, who had got at that secret as he did at every one else, and held it like a twisted cord about poor Die's neck. I have seen her one hundred times she would have spit at him, if it had not been fear for her father, whose life would not have been worth five minutes' purchase if he had been discovered to the government—But don't mistake me, Mr. Osbaldistone; I say the government is a good, a gracious, and a just government; and if it has hanged one-half of the rebels, poor things, all will acknowledge they would not have been touched had they staid peaceably at home.'

Waiving the discussion of these political questions, I brought back Mr. Inglewood to his subject, and I found that Diana, having positively refused to marry any of the Osbaldistone family, and expressed her particular detestation of Rashleigh, he had from that time begun to cool in zeal for the cause of the Pretender; to which, as the youngest of six brethren, and bold, artful, and able, he had hitherto looked forward as the means of making his fortune. Probably the compulsion with which he had been forced to render up the spoils which he had abstracted from my father's counting-house by the united authority of Sir Frederick Vernon and the Scottish Chiefs, had determined his resolution to advance his progress by changing his opinions, and betraying his trust. Perhaps also, for few men were better judges where his interest was concerned, he considered their means and talents to be, as they afterwards proved, greatly inadequate to the important task of overthrowing an established government. Sir Frederick Vernon, or, as he was called among the Jacobites, his Excellency Viscount Beauchamp, had, with his daughter, some difficulty in escaping the consequences of Rashleigh's information. Here Mr. Inglewood's information was at fault; but he did not doubt, since we had not heard of Sir Frederick being in the hands of the government, he must be by this time abroad, where, agreeably to the cruel bond he had entered into with his brother-in-law, Diana, since she had declined to select a husband out of the Osbaldistone family, must be confined to a convent. The original cause of this singular agreement Mr. Inglewood could not perfectly explain; but he understood it was a family compact, entered into for the purpose of securing to Sir Frederick the rents of the remnant of his large estates, which had been vested in the Osbaldistone family by some legal manœuvre; in short, a family compact, in which, like many of those undertaken at that time of day, the feelings of the principal parties interested were no more regarded than if they had been a part of the live-stock upon the lands.

I cannot tell, such is the waywardness of the human heart, whether this intelligence gave me joy or sorrow. It seemed to me, that, in the knowledge that Miss Vernon was eternally divided from me, not by marriage with another, but by seclusion in a convent, in order to fulfil an absurd bargain of this kind, my regret for her loss was aggravated rather than diminished. I became dull, low-spirited, absent, and unable to support the task of conversing with Justice Inglewood, who in his turn yawned, and proposed to retire early. I took leave of him over night, determining the next day, before break-fast, to ride over to Osbaldistone-Hall.

Mr. Inglewood acquiesced in my proposal. ' It would be well,' he said, ' that I made my appearance there before I was known to be in the country, the more especially as Sir Rashleigh Osbaldistone was now, he understood, at Mr. Jobson's house, hatching some mischief doubtless.—They were fit company,' he added, ' for each other, Sir Rashleigh having lost all right to mingle in the society of men of honour; but it was hardly possible two such d—d rascals should collogue together without mischief to honest people.'

He concluded, by earnestly recommending a toast and tankard, and an attack upon his venison pasty, before I set out in the morning, just to break the cold air on the wolds.

CHAPTER XXXVIII

His master's gone, and no one now
Dwells in the halls of Ivor;
Men, dogs, and horses, all are dead,
He is the sole survivor.
                              Wordsworth.

THERE are few more melancholy sensations than those with which we regard scenes of past pleasure, when altered and deserted. In my ride to Osbaldistone-Hall, I passed the same objects which I had seen in company with Miss Vernon on the day of our memorable ride from Inglewood Place. Her spirit seemed to keep me company on the way; and, when I approached the spot where I had first seen her, I almost listened for the cry of the hounds and the notes of the horn, and strained my eye on vacant space, as if to descry the fair huntress again descend like an apparition from the hill. But all was silent, and all was solitary. When I reached the Hall, the closed doors and windows, the grass-grown pavement, the courts, which were now so silent, presented a strong contrast to the gay and bustling scene I had so often seen them exhibit, when the merry hunters were going forth to their morning sport, or returning to the daily festival. The joyous bark of the fox-hounds as they were uncoupled, the cries of the huntsman, the clang of the horses' hoofs, the loud laugh of the old knight at the head of his strong and numerous descendants, were all silenced now and for ever.

While I gazed round the scene of solitude and emptiness, I was inexpressibly affected, even by recollecting those whom, when alive, I had no reason to regard with affection. But the thought that so many youths of goodly presence, warm with life, health, and confidence, were within so short a time cold in the grave, by various yet all violent and unexpected modes of death, afforded a picture of mortality at which the mind trembled. It was little consolation to me that I returned a proprietor to the halls, which I had left almost like a fugitive. My mind was not habituated to regard the scenes around as my property, and I felt myself an usurper, at least an intruding stranger, and could hardly divest myself of the idea, that some of the bulky forms of my deceased kinsmen were, like the gigantic spectres of a romance, to appear in the gateway, and dispute my entrance.

While I was engaged in these sad thoughts, my follower, Andrew, whose feelings were of a very different nature, exerted himself in thundering alternately on every door in the building, calling, at the same time, for admittance, in a tone so loud as to intimate, that *he*, at least, was fully sensible of his newly acquired importance, as squire of the body to the new lord of the manor. At length, timidly and reluctantly, Anthony Syddall, my uncle's aged butler and major-domo, presented himself at a lower window, well fenced with iron bars, and inquired our business.

'We are come to tak your charge aff your hand, my auld friend,' said Andrew Fairservice; 'ye may gie up your keys as sune as ye like—ilka dog has his day. I 'll tak the plate and napery aff your hand. Ye hae had your ain time o't, Mr. Syddall; but ilka bean has its black, and ilka path has its puddle; and it will just set you henceforth to sit at the board-end, as weel as it did Andrew lang syne.'

Checking with some difficulty the forwardness of my follower, I explained to Syddall the nature of my right, and the title I had to demand admittance into the Hall, as into my own property. The old man seemed much agitated and distressed, and testified manifest reluctance to give me entrance, although it was couched in a humble and submissive tone. I allowed for the agitation of natural feelings, which really did the old man honour; but continued peremptory in my demand of admittance, explaining to him that his refusal would oblige me to apply for Mr. Inglewood's warrant, and a constable.

'We are come from Mr. Justice Inglewood's this morning,' said Andrew, to enforce the menace, 'and I saw Archie Rutledge, the constable, as I came up by—the country 's no to be lawless as it has been, Mr. Syddall, letting rebels and papists gang on as they best listed.'

The threat of the law sounded dreadful in the old man's ears, conscious as he was of the suspicion under which he himself lay, from his religion and his devotion to Sir Hildebrand and his sons. He undid, with fear and trembling, one of the postern entrances, which was secured with many a bolt and bar, and humbly hoped that I would excuse him for fidelity in the discharge of his duty.—I reassured him, and told him I had the better opinion of him for his caution.

'Sae have not I,' said Andrew; 'Syddall is an auld sneck-drawer; he wadna be looking as white as a sheet, and his knees knocking thegether, unless it were for something mair than he 's like to tell us.'

'Lord forgive you, Mr. Fairservice,' replied the butler, 'to say such things of an old friend and fellow-servant!—Where,'—following me humbly along the passage, 'where would it be your honour's pleasure to have a fire lighted? I fear me you will find the house very dull and dreary—But perhaps you mean to ride back to Inglewood Place to dinner?'

'Light a fire in the library,' I replied.

'In the library!'—answered the old man; 'nobody has sat there this many a day, and the room smokes, for the daws have built in the chimney this spring, and there were no young men about the Hall to pull them down.'

'Our ain reek 's better than other folk's fire,' said Andrew; 'his honour likes the library. He 's nane o' your Papishers, that delight in blinded ignorance, Mr. Syddall.'

Very reluctantly, as it appeared to me, the butler led the way to the library, and, contrary to what he

had given me to expect, the interior of the apartment looked as if it had been lately arranged, and
made more comfortable than usual. There was a
fire in the grate, which burned clearly, notwithstanding what Syddall had reported of the vent. Taking
up the tongs, as if to arrange the wood, but rather
perhaps to conceal his own confusion, the butler
observed, 'it was burning clear now, but had smoked
woundily in the morning.'

Wishing to be alone, till I recovered myself
from the first painful sensations which every thing
around me recalled, I desired old Syddall to call
the land-steward, who lived at about a quarter of
a mile from the Hall. He departed with obvious
reluctance. I next ordered Andrew to procure the
attendance of a couple of stout fellows upon whom
he could rely, the population around being Papists,
and Sir Rashleigh, who was capable of any
desperate enterprise, being in the neighbourhood.
Andrew Fairservice undertook this task with great
cheerfulness, and promised to bring me up from
Trinlay-Knowe, 'twa true-blue Presbyterians like
himsell, that would face and out-face baith the Pope,
the devil, and the Pretender—and blythe will I be
o' their company mysell, for the very last night that
I was at Osbaldistone-Hall, the blight be on ilka
blossom in my bit yard, if I didna see that very
picture' (pointing to the full-length portrait of Miss
Vernon's grandfather) 'walking by moonlight in
the garden! I tauld your honour I was fleyed wi'
a bogle that night, but ye wadna listen to me—
I aye thought there was witchcraft and deevilry

348

amang the Papishers, but I ne'er saw 't wi' bodily
een till that awfu' night.'

'Get along, sir,' said I, 'and bring the fellows
you talk of; and see they have more sense than
yourself, and are not frightened at their own
shadow.'

'I hae been counted as gude a man as my
neighbours ere now,' said Andrew, petulantly; 'but
I dinna pretend to deal wi' evil spirits.' And so he
made his exit, as Wardlaw the land-steward made
his appearance.

He was a man of sense and honesty, without
whose careful management my uncle would have
found it difficult to have maintained himself a
housekeeper so long as he did. He examined the
nature of my right of possession carefully, and
admitted it candidly. To any one else the succession would have been a poor one, so much was the
land encumbered with debt and mortgage. Most
of these, however, were already vested in my father's
person, and he was in a train of acquiring the rest;
his large gains, by the recent rise of the funds,
having made it a matter of ease and convenience
for him to pay off the debt which affected his
patrimony.

I transacted much necessary business with Mr.
Wardlaw, and detained him to dine with me. We
preferred taking our repast in the library, although
Syddall strongly recommended our removing to
the Stone-Hall, which he had put in order for the
occasion. Meantime Andrew made his appearance
with his true-blue recruits, whom he recommended

in the highest terms, as ' sober decent men, weel founded in doctrinal points, and, above all, as bold as lions.' I ordered them something to drink, and they left the room. I observed old Syddall shake his head as they went out, and insisted upon knowing the reason.

' I maybe cannot expect,' he said, ' that your honour should put confidence in what I say, but it is Heaven's truth for all that—Ambrose Wingfield is as honest a man as lives, but if there is a false knave in the country, it is his brother Lancie—the whole country knows him to be a spy for Clerk Jobson on the poor gentlemen that have been in trouble—But he's a dissenter, and I suppose that's enough now-a-days.'

Having thus far given vent to his feelings, to which, however, I was little disposed to pay attention, and having placed the wine on the table, the old butler left the apartment.

Mr. Wardlaw having remained with me until the evening was somewhat advanced, at length bundled up his papers, and removed himself to his own habitation, leaving me in that confused state of mind in which we can hardly say whether we desire company or solitude. I had not, however, the choice betwixt them; for I was left alone in the room, of all others most calculated to inspire me with melancholy reflections.

As twilight was darkening the apartment, Andrew had the sagacity to advance his head at the door, not to ask if I wished for lights, but to recommend them as a measure of precaution against the bogles which still haunted his imagination. I rejected his proffer somewhat peevishly, trimmed the wood-fire, and placing myself in one of the large leathern chairs which flanked the old Gothic chimney, I watched unconsciously the bickering of the blaze which I had fostered. 'And this,' said I alone, 'is the progress and the issue of human wishes! Nursed by the merest trifles, they are first kindled by fancy, nay, are fed upon the vapour of hope till they consume the substance which they inflame; and man, and his hopes, passions, and desires, sink into a worthless heap of embers and ashes!'

There was a deep sigh from the opposite side of the room, which seemed to reply to my reflections. I started up in amazement—Diana Vernon stood before me, resting on the arm of a figure so strongly resembling that of the portrait so often mentioned, that I looked hastily at the frame, expecting to see it empty. My first idea was, either that I had gone suddenly distracted, or that the spirits of the dead had arisen and been placed before me. A second glance convinced me of my being in my senses, and that the forms which stood before me were real and substantial. It was Diana herself, though paler and thinner than her former self; and it was no tenant of the grave who stood beside her, but Vaughan, or rather Sir Frederick Vernon, in a dress made to imitate that of his ancestor, to whose picture his countenance possessed a family resemblance. He was the first that spoke, for Diana kept her eyes fast fixed on the ground, and astonishment actually riveted my tongue to the roof of my mouth.

'We are your suppliants, Mr. Osbaldistone,' he said, 'and we claim the refuge and protection of your roof till we can pursue a journey, where dungeons and death gape for me at every step.'

'Surely,' I articulated with great difficulty—'Miss Vernon cannot suppose—you, sir, cannot believe, that I have forgot your interference in my difficulties, or that I am capable of betraying any one, much less you?'

'I know it,' said Sir Frederick; 'yet it is with the most inexpressible reluctance that I impose on you a confidence, disagreeable perhaps—certainly dangerous—and which I would have specially wished to have conferred on some one else. But my fate, which has chased me through a life of perils and escapes, is now pressing me hard, and I have no alternative.'

At this moment the door opened, and the voice of the officious Andrew was heard. 'A 'm bringin' in the caunles—Ye can light them gin ye like—Can do is easy carried about wi' ane.'

I ran to the door, which, as I hoped, I reached in time to prevent his observing who were in the apartment. I turned him out with hasty violence, shut the door after him, and locked it — then instantly remembering his two companions below, knowing his talkative humour, and recollecting Syddall's remark, that one of them was supposed to be a spy, I followed him as fast as I could to the servants' hall, in which they were assembled.

Andrew's tongue was loud as I opened the door, but my unexpected appearance silenced him.

'What is the matter with you, you fool?' said I; 'you stare and look wild, as if you had seen a ghost.'

'N—n—no—nothing,' said Andrew; 'but your worship was pleased to be hasty.'

'Because you disturbed me out of a sound sleep, you fool. Syddall tells me he cannot find beds for these good fellows to-night, and Mr. Wardlaw thinks there will be no occasion to detain them. Here is a crown-piece for them to drink my health, and thanks for their good-will.—You will leave the Hall immediately, my good lads.'

The men thanked me for my bounty, took the silver, and withdrew, apparently unsuspicious and contented. I watched their departure until I was sure they could have no further intercourse that night with honest Andrew. And so instantly had I followed on his heels, that I thought he could not have time to speak two words with them before I interrupted him. But it is wonderful what mischief may be done by only two words. On this occasion they cost two lives.

Having made these arrangements, the best which occurred to me upon the pressure of the moment, to secure privacy for my guests, I returned to report my proceedings, and added, that I had desired Syddall to answer every summons, concluding that it was by his connivance they had been secreted in the Hall. Diana raised her eyes to thank me for the caution.

'You now understand my mystery,' she said; 'you know, doubtless, how near and dear that relative is who has so often found shelter here; and will be no longer surprised, that Rashleigh, having such a secret at his command, should rule me with a rod of iron.'

Her father added, 'that it was their intention to trouble me with their presence as short a time as was possible.'

I entreated the fugitives to waive every consideration but what affected their safety, and to rely on my utmost exertions to promote it. This led to an explanation of the circumstances under which they stood.

'I always suspected Rashleigh Osbaldistone,' said Sir Frederick; 'but his conduct towards my unprotected child, which with difficulty I wrung from her, and his treachery in your father's affairs, made me hate and despise him. In our last interview I concealed not my sentiments, as I should in prudence have attempted to do; and in resentment of the scorn with which I treated him, he added treachery and apostasy to his catalogue of crimes. I at that time fondly hoped that his defection would be of little consequence. The Earl of Mar had a gallant army in Scotland, and Lord Derwentwater, with Forster, Kenmure, Winterton, and others, were assembling forces on the Border. As my connexions with these English nobility and gentry were extensive, it was judged proper that I should accompany a detachment of Highlanders, who, under Brigadier MacIntosh of Borlum, crossed the Frith of Forth, traversed the low country of Scotland, and united themselves on the Borders with the English insurgents. My daughter accompanied me through the perils and fatigues of a march so long and difficult.'

' And she will never leave her dear father ! ' exclaimed Miss Vernon, clinging fondly to his arm.

' I had hardly joined our English friends when I became sensible that our cause was lost. Our numbers diminished instead of increasing, nor were we joined by any except of our own persuasion. The Tories of the High Church remained in general undecided, and at length we were cooped up by a superior force in the little town of Preston. We defended ourselves resolutely one day. On the next, the hearts of our leaders failed, and they resolved to surrender at discretion. To yield myself up on such terms, were to have laid my head on the block. About twenty or thirty gentlemen were of my mind : We mounted our horses, and placed my daughter, who insisted on sharing my fate, in the centre of our little party. My companions, struck with her courage and filial piety, declared that they would die rather than leave her behind. We rode in a body down a street called Fishergate, which leads to a marshy ground or meadow, extending to the river Ribble, through which one of our party promised to show us a good ford. This marsh had not been strongly invested by the enemy, so that we had only an affair with a patrol of Honeywood's dragoons, whom we dispersed and cut to pieces. We crossed the river, gained the high road to Liverpool, and then dispersed to seek several places of concealment and safety. My fortune led me to Wales, where there are many gentlemen of my religious and political opinions. I could not, however, find a safe opportunity of escaping by sea, and found myself obliged again to draw towards the North. A well-tried friend has appointed to meet me in this neighbourhood, and guide me to a seaport on the Solway, where a sloop is prepared to carry me from my native country for ever. As Osbaldistone-Hall was for the present uninhabited, and under the charge of old Syddall, who had been our confident on former occasions, we drew to it as to a place of known and secure refuge. I resumed a dress which had been used with good effect to scare the superstitious rustics, or domestics, who chanced at any time to see me; and we expected from time to time to hear by Syddall of the arrival of our friendly guide, when your sudden coming hither, and occupying this apartment, laid us under the necessity of submitting to your mercy.'

Thus ended Sir Frederick's story, whose tale sounded to me like one told in a vision; and I could hardly bring myself to believe, that I saw his daughter's form once more before me in flesh and blood, though with diminished beauty and sunk spirits. The buoyant vivacity with which she had resisted every touch of adversity, had now assumed the air of composed and submissive, but dauntless resolution and constancy. Her father, though aware and jealous of the effect of her praises on my mind, could not forbear expatiating upon them.

'She has endured trials,' he said, 'which might have dignified the history of a martyr;—she has faced danger and death in various shapes;—she has undergone toil and privation, from which men of the strongest frame would have shrunk;—she has spent the day in darkness, and the night in vigil, and has never breathed a murmur of weakness or complaint. In a word, Mr. Osbaldistone,' he concluded, 'she is a worthy offering to that God, to whom,' crossing himself, 'I shall dedicate her, as all that is left dear or precious to Frederick Vernon.'

There was a silence after these words, of which I well understood the mournful import. The father of Diana was still as anxious to destroy my hopes of being united to her now, as he had shown himself during our brief meeting in Scotland.

'We will now,' said he to his daughter, 'intrude no farther on Mr. Osbaldistone's time, since we have acquainted him with the circumstances of the miserable guests who claim his protection.'

I requested them to stay, and offered myself to leave the apartment. Sir Frederick observed, that my doing so could not but excite my attendant's suspicion; and that the place of their retreat was in every respect commodious, and furnished by Syddall with all they could possibly want. 'We might perhaps have even contrived to remain there, concealed from your observation; but it would have been unjust to decline the most absolute reliance on your honour.'

'You have done me but justice,' I replied. 'To you, Sir Frederick, I am but little known; but

357

Miss Vernon, I am sure, will bear me witness that——'

'I do not want my daughter's evidence,' he said politely, but yet with an air calculated to prevent my addressing myself to Diana, 'since I am prepared to believe all that is worthy of Mr. Francis Osbaldistone. Permit us now to retire; we must take repose when we can, since we are absolutely uncertain when we may be called upon to renew our perilous journey.'

He drew his daughter's arm within his, and, with a profound reverence, disappeared with her behind the tapestry.

CHAPTER XXXIX

But now the hand of fate is on the curtain,
And gives the scene to light.

DON SEBASTIAN.

I FELT stunned and chilled as they retired. Imagination, dwelling on an absent object of affection, paints her not only in the fairest light, but in that in which we most desire to behold her. I had thought of Diana as she was, when her parting tear dropped on my cheek; when her parting token, received from the wife of MacGregor, augured her wish to convey into exile and conventual seclusion the remembrance of my affection. I saw her; and her cold passive manner, expressive of little except composed melancholy, disappointed, and, in some degree, almost offended me. In the egotism of my feelings I accused her of indifference — of insensibility. I upbraided her father with pride, with cruelty, with fanaticism; forgetting that both were sacrificing their interest, and Diana her inclination, to the discharge of what they regarded as their duty.

Sir Frederick Vernon was a rigid Catholic, who thought the path of salvation too narrow to be trodden by an heretic; and Diana, to whom her father's safety had been for many years the prin-

359

cipal and moving spring of thoughts, hopes, and actions, felt that she had discharged her duty in resigning to his will, not alone her property in the world, but the dearest affections of her heart. But it was not surprising that I could not, at such a moment, fully appreciate these honourable motives; yet my spleen sought no ignoble means of discharging itself.

'I am contemned, then,' I said, when left to run over the tenor of Sir Frederick's communications, 'I am contemned, and thought unworthy even to exchange words with her. Be it so; they shall not at least prevent me from watching over her safety. Here will I remain as an outpost, and, while under my roof at least, no danger shall threaten her, if it be such as the arm of one determined man can avert.'

I summoned Syddall to the library. He came, but came attended by the eternal Andrew, who, dreaming of great things in consequence of my taking possession of the Hall and the annexed estates, was resolved to lose nothing for want of keeping himself in view; and, as often happens to men who entertain selfish objects, overshot his mark, and rendered his attentions tedious and inconvenient.

His unrequired presence prevented me from speaking freely to Syddall, and I dared not send him away for fear of increasing such suspicions as he might entertain from his former abrupt dismissal from the library. 'I shall sleep here, sir,' I said, giving them directions to wheel nearer to the fire an old-fashioned day-bed, or settee. 'I have much to do, and shall go late to bed.'

Syddall, who seemed to understand my look, offered to procure me the accommodation of a mattress and some bedding. I accepted his offer, dismissed my attendant, lighted a pair of candles, and desired that I might not be disturbed till seven in the ensuing morning.

The domestics retired, leaving me to my painful and ill-arranged reflections, until nature, worn out, should require some repose.

I endeavoured forcibly to abstract my mind from the singular circumstances in which I found myself placed. Feelings which I had gallantly combated while the exciting object was remote, were now exasperated by my immediate neighbourhood to her whom I was so soon to part with for ever. Her name was written in every book which I attempted to peruse; and her image forced itself on me in whatever train of thought I strove to engage myself. It was like the officious slave of Prior's Solomon,—

> Abra was ready ere I named her name,
> And when I call'd another, Abra came.

I alternately gave way to these thoughts, and struggled against them, sometimes yielding to a mood of melting tenderness of sorrow which was scarce natural to me, sometimes arming myself with the hurt pride of one who had experienced what he esteemed unmerited rejection. I paced the library until I had chafed myself into a temporary fever. I then threw myself on the couch, and endeavoured to dispose myself to sleep; but it was in vain that I used every effort to compose myself—that I lay without movement of finger or of muscle, as still as if I had been already a corpse—that I endeavoured to divert or banish disquieting thoughts, by fixing my mind on some act of repetition or arithmetical process. My blood throbbed, to my feverish apprehension, in pulsations which resembled the deep and regular strokes of a distant fulling-mill, and tingled in my veins like streams of liquid fire.

At length I arose, opened the window, and stood by it for some time in the clear moonlight, receiving, in part at least, that refreshment and dissipation of ideas from the clear and calm scene, without which they had become beyond the command of my own volition. I resumed my place on the couch with a heart, Heaven knows, not lighter, but firmer, and more resolved for endurance. In a short time a slumber crept over my senses; still, however, though my senses slumbered, my soul was awake to the painful feelings of my situation, and my dreams were of mental anguish and external objects of terror.

I remember a strange agony, under which I conceived myself and Diana in the power of MacGregor's wife, and about to be precipitated from a rock into the lake; the signal was to be the discharge of a cannon, fired by Sir Frederick Vernon, who, in the dress of a cardinal, officiated at the ceremony. Nothing could be more lively than the impression which I received of this imaginary scene. I could paint, even at this moment, the mute

and courageous submission expressed in Diana's
features—the wild and distorted faces of the executioners, who crowded around us with 'mopping
and mowing'; grimaces ever changing, and each
more hideous than that which preceded. I saw the
rigid and inflexible fanaticism painted in the face
of the father—I saw him lift the fatal match—the
deadly signal exploded—It was repeated again and
again and again, in rival thunders, by the echoes
of the surrounding cliffs, and I awoke from fancied
horror to real apprehension.

The sounds in my dream were not ideal. They
reverberated on my waking ears, but it was two or
three minutes ere I could collect myself so as distinctly to understand that they proceeded from a
violent knocking at the gate. I leaped from my
couch in great apprehension, took my sword under
my arm, and hastened to forbid the admission of
any one. But my route was necessarily circuitous,
because the library looked not upon the quadrangle,
but into the gardens. When I had reached a
staircase, the windows of which opened upon the
entrance court, I heard the feeble and intimidated
tones of Syddall expostulating with rough voices,
which demanded admittance, by the warrant of
Justice Standish, and in the King's name, and
threatened the old domestic with the heaviest
penal consequences, if he refused instant obedience.
Ere they had ceased, I heard, to my unspeakable
provocation, the voice of Andrew bidding Syddall
stand aside, and let him open the door.

'If they come in King George's name, we have

naething to fear—we hae spent baith bluid and gowd for him—We dinna need to darn ourselves like some folks, Mr. Syddall — We are neither Papists nor Jacobites, I trow.'

It was in vain I accelerated my pace down stairs; I heard bolt after bolt withdrawn by the officious scoundrel, while all the time he was boasting his own and his master's loyalty to King George; and I could easily calculate that the party must enter before I could arrive at the door to replace the bars. Devoting the back of Andrew Fairservice to the cudgel so soon as I should have time to pay him his deserts, I ran back to the library, barricaded the door as I best could, and hastened to that by which Diana and her father entered, and begged for instant admittance. Diana herself undid the door. She was ready dressed, and betrayed neither perturbation nor fear.

'Danger is so familiar to us,' she said, 'that we are always prepared to meet it—My father is already up—he is in Rashleigh's apartment—We will escape into the garden, and thence by the postern-gate (I have the key from Syddall in case of need) into the wood—I know its dingles better than any one now alive—Keep them a few minutes in play.—And, dear, dear Frank, once more, fare thee well!'

She vanished like a meteor to join her father, and the intruders were rapping violently, and attempting to force the library door by the time I had returned into it.

'You robber dogs!' I exclaimed, wilfully mistaking the purpose of their disturbance, 'if you do not instantly quit the house I will fire my blunderbuss through the door.'

'Fire a fule's bauble!' said Andrew Fairservice; 'it's Mr. Clerk Jobson, with a legal warrant—'

'To search for, take, and apprehend,' said the voice of that execrable pettifogger, 'the bodies of certain persons in my warrant named, charged of high treason under the 13th of King William, chapter third.'

And the violence on the door was renewed. 'I am rising, gentlemen,' said I, desirous to gain as much time as possible—'commit no violence—give me leave to look at your warrant; and, if it is formal and legal, I shall not oppose it.'

'God save great George our King!' ejaculated Andrew. 'I tauld ye that ye would find nae Jacobites here.'

Spinning out the time as much as possible, I was at length compelled to open the door, which they would otherwise have forced.

Mr. Jobson entered, with several assistants, among whom I discovered the younger Wingfield, to whom, doubtless, he was obliged for his information, and exhibited his warrant, directed not only against Frederick Vernon, an attainted traitor, but also against Diana Vernon, spinster, and Francis Osbaldistone, gentleman, accused of misprision of treason. It was a case in which resistance would have been madness; I therefore, after capitulating for a few minutes' delay, surrendered myself a prisoner.

I had next the mortification to see Jobson go

straight to the chamber of Miss Vernon, and I learned that from thence, without hesitation or difficulty, he went to the room where Sir Frederick had slept. 'The hare has stolen away,' said the brute, 'but her form is warm—the greyhounds will have her by the haunches yet.'

A scream from the garden announced that he prophesied too truly. In the course of five minutes, Rashleigh entered the library with Sir Frederick Vernon and his daughter as prisoners. 'The fox,' he said, 'knew his old earth, but he forgot it could be stopped by a careful huntsman — I had not forgot the garden gate, Sir Frederick—or, if that title suits you better, most noble Lord Beauchamp.'

'Rashleigh,' said Sir Frederick, 'thou art a detestable villain!'

'I better deserved the name, Sir Knight, or my Lord, when, under the direction of an able tutor, I sought to introduce civil war into the bosom of a peaceful country. But I have done my best,' said he, looking upwards, 'to atone for my errors.'

I could hold no longer. I had designed to watch their proceedings in silence, but I felt that I must speak or die. 'If hell,' I said, 'has one complexion more hideous than another, it is where villainy is masked by hypocrisy.'

'Ha! my gentle cousin,' said Rashleigh, holding a candle towards me, and surveying me from head to foot; 'right welcome to Osbaldistone-Hall! —I can forgive your spleen—It is hard to lose an estate and a mistress in one night; for we shall take possession of this poor manor-house in the name of the lawful heir, Sir Rashleigh Osbaldistone.'

While Rashleigh braved it out in this manner, I could see that he put a strong force upon his feelings, both of anger and shame. But his state of mind was more obvious when Diana Vernon addressed him. 'Rashleigh,' she said, 'I pity you —for, deep as the evil is which you have laboured to do me, and the evil you have actually done, I cannot hate you so much as I scorn and pity you. What you have now done may be the work of an hour, but will furnish you with reflection for your life—of what nature I leave to your own conscience, which will not slumber for ever.'

Rashleigh strode once or twice through the room, came up to the side-table, on which wine was still standing, and poured out a large glass with a trembling hand; but when he saw that we observed his tremor, he suppressed it by a strong effort, and, looking at us with fixed and daring composure, carried the bumper to his head without spilling a drop.

'It is my father's old burgundy,' he said, looking to Jobson; 'I am glad there is some of it left—You will get proper persons to take care of the house and property in my name, and turn out the doating old butler, and that foolish Scotch rascal. Meanwhile, we will convey these persons to a more proper place of custody.—I have provided the old family coach for your convenience,' he said, 'though I am not ignorant that even the lady could brave the night air on foot or on horseback, were the errand more to her mind.'

Andrew wrung his hands. — 'I only said that my master was surely speaking to a ghaist in the library—and the villain Lancie to betray an auld friend, that sang aff the same Psalm-book wi' him every Sabbath for twenty years!'

He was turned out of the house, together with Syddall, without being allowed to conclude his lamentation. His expulsion, however, led to some singular consequences. Resolving, according to his own story, to go down for the night where Mother Simpson would give him a lodging for old acquaintance' sake, he had just got clear of the avenue, and into the old wood as it was called, though it was now used as pasture-ground rather than woodland, when he suddenly lighted on a drove of Scotch cattle, which were lying there to repose themselves after the day's journey. At this, Andrew was in no way surprised, it being the well-known custom of his countrymen, who take care of those droves, to quarter themselves after night upon the best unenclosed grass-ground they can find, and depart before daybreak to escape paying for their night's lodgings. But he was both surprised and startled, when a Highlander, springing up, accused him of disturbing the cattle, and refused him to pass forward till he had spoken to his master. The mountaineer conducted Andrew into a thicket, where he found three or four more of his country-men. 'And,' said Andrew, 'I saw sune they were ower mony men for the drove; and from the questions they put to me, I judged they had other tow on their rock.'

They questioned him closely about all that had passed at Osbaldistone-Hall, and seemed surprised and concerned at the report he made to them.

'And troth,' said Andrew, 'I tauld them a' I kend; for dirks and pistols were what I could never refuse information to in a' my life.'

They talked in whispers among themselves, and at length collected their cattle together, and drove them close up to the entrance of the avenue, which might be half a mile distant from the house. They proceeded to drag together some felled trees which lay in the vicinity, so as to make a temporary barricade across the road, about fifteen yards beyond the avenue. It was now near daybreak, and there was a pale eastern gleam mingled with the fading moonlight, so that objects could be discovered with some distinctness. The lumbering sound of a coach, drawn by four horses, and escorted by six men on horseback, was heard coming up the avenue. The Highlanders listened attentively. The carriage contained Mr. Jobson and his unfortunate prisoners. The escort consisted of Rashleigh, and several horsemen, peace-officers and their assistants. So soon as we had passed the gate at the head of the avenue, it was shut behind the cavalcade by a Highlandman, stationed there for that purpose. At the same time the carriage was impeded in its farther progress by the cattle, amongst which we were involved, and by the barricade in front. Two of the escort dismounted to remove the felled trees, which they might think were left there by accident or carelessness. The others began with their whips to drive the cattle from the road.

' Who dare abuse our cattle ? ' said a rough voice. —' Shoot him, Angus.'

Rashleigh instantly called out, ' A rescue — a rescue ! ' and, firing a pistol, wounded the man who spoke.

' *Claymore !* ' cried the leader of the Highlanders, and a scuffle instantly commenced. The officers of the law, surprised at so sudden an attack, and not usually possessing the most desperate bravery, made but an imperfect defence, considering the superiority of their numbers. Some attempted to ride back to the Hall, but on a pistol being fired from behind the gate, they conceived themselves surrounded, and at length galloped off in different directions. Rashleigh, meanwhile, had dismounted, and on foot had maintained a desperate and single-handed conflict with the leader of the band. The window of the carriage, on my side, permitted me to witness it. At length Rashleigh dropped.

' Will you ask forgiveness for the sake of God, King James, and auld friendship ? ' said a voice which I knew right well.

' No, never,' said Rashleigh, firmly.

' Then, traitor, die in your treason ! ' retorted MacGregor, and plunged his sword in his prostrate antagonist.

In the next moment he was at the carriage door

—handed out Miss Vernon, assisted her father and me to alight, and dragging out the attorney, head foremost, threw him under the wheel.

'Mr. Osbaldistone,' he said, in a whisper, 'you have nothing to fear—I must look after those who have—Your friends will soon be in safety—Farewell, and forget not the MacGregor.'

He whistled—his band gathered round him, and, hurrying Diana and her father along with him, they were almost instantly lost in the glades of the forest. The coachman and postilion had abandoned their horses, and fled at the first discharge of fire-arms; but the animals, stopped by the barricade, remained perfectly still; and well for Jobson that they did so, for the slightest motion would have dragged the wheel over his body. My first object was to relieve him, for such was the rascal's terror that he never could have risen by his own exertions. I next commanded him to observe, that I had neither taken part in the rescue, nor availed myself of it to make my escape, and enjoined him to go down to the Hall, and call some of his party, who had been left there, to assist the wounded. But Jobson's fears had so mastered and controlled every faculty of his mind, that he was totally incapable of moving. I now resolved to go myself, but in my way I stumbled over the body of a man, as I thought, dead or dying. It was, however, Andrew Fairservice, as well and whole as ever he was in his life, who had only taken this recumbent posture to avoid the slashes, stabs, and pistol-balls, which, for a moment or two, were flying in various directions. I was so glad to find him that I did not inquire how he came thither, but instantly commanded his assistance.

Rashleigh was our first object. He groaned when I approached him, as much through spite as through pain, and shut his eyes, as if determined, like Iago, to speak no word more. We lifted him into the carriage, and performed the same good office to another wounded man of his party, who had been left on the field. I then with difficulty made Jobson understand that he must enter the coach also, and support Sir Rashleigh upon the seat. He obeyed, but with an air as if he but half comprehended my meaning. Andrew and I turned the horses' heads round, and, opening the gate of the avenue, led them slowly back to Osbaldistone-Hall.

Some fugitives had already reached the Hall by circuitous routes, and alarmed its garrison by the news that Sir Rashleigh, Clerk Jobson, and all their escort, save they who escaped to tell the tale, had been cut to pieces at the head of the avenue, by a whole regiment of wild Highlanders. When we reached the mansion, therefore, we heard such a buzz as arises when bees are alarmed, and mustering in their hives. Mr. Jobson, however, who had now in some measure come to his senses, found voice enough to make himself known. He was the more anxious to be released from the carriage, as one of his companions (the peace-officer) had, to his inexpressible terror, expired by his side with a hideous groan.

Sir Rashleigh Osbaldistone was still alive, but so dreadfully wounded that the bottom of the coach was filled with his blood, and long traces of it left from the entrance-door into the Stone-Hall, where he was placed in a chair, some attempting to stop the bleeding with cloths, while others called for a surgeon, and no one seemed willing to go to fetch one.

'Torment me not,' said the wounded man. 'I know no assistance can avail me. I am a dying man.' He raised himself in his chair, though the damps and chill of death were already on his brow, and spoke with a firmness which seemed beyond his strength. 'Cousin Francis,' he said, 'draw near to me.' I approached him as he requested. —'I wish you only to know that the pangs of death do not alter one iota of my feelings towards you. I hate you!' he said, the expression of rage throwing a hideous glare into the eyes which were soon to be closed for ever—'I hate you with a hatred as intense, now while I lie bleeding and dying before you, as if my foot trod on your neck.'

'I have given you no cause, sir,' I replied, 'and for your own sake I could wish your mind in a better temper.'

'You *have* given me cause,' he rejoined —'in love, in ambition, in the paths of interest, you have crossed and blighted me at every turn. I was born to be the honour of my father's house—I have been its disgrace — and all owing to you. — My very patrimony has become yours — Take it,' he said, 'and may the curse of a dying man cleave to it!'

In a moment after he had uttered this frightful wish, he fell back in the chair; his eyes became glazed, his limbs stiffened, but the grin and glare of mortal hatred survived even the last gasp of life. I will dwell no longer on so painful a picture, nor say any more of the death of Rashleigh than that it gave me access to my rights of inheritance without farther challenge, and that Jobson found himself compelled to allow, that the ridiculous charge of misprision of high-treason was got up on an affidavit which he made with the sole purpose of favouring Rashleigh's views, and removing me from Osbaldistone-Hall. The rascal's name was struck off the list of attorneys, and he was reduced to poverty and contempt.

I returned to London when I had put my affairs in order at Osbaldistone-Hall, and felt happy to escape from a place which suggested so many painful recollections. My anxiety was now acute to learn the fate of Diana and her father. A French gentleman who came to London on commercial business, was entrusted with a letter to me from Miss Vernon, which put my mind at rest respecting their safety.

It gave me to understand, that the opportune appearance of MacGregor and his party was not fortuitous. The Scottish nobles and gentry, engaged in the insurrection, as well as those of England, were particularly anxious to further the escape of Sir Frederick Vernon, who, as an old and trusted agent of the house of Stewart, was possessed of matter enough to have ruined half Scotland. Rob

Roy, of whose sagacity and courage they had known so many proofs, was the person whom they pitched upon to assist his escape, and the place of meeting was fixed at Osbaldistone-Hall. You have already heard how nearly the plan had been disconcerted by the unhappy Rashleigh. It succeeded, however, perfectly ; for when once Sir Frederick and his daughter were again at large, they found horses prepared for them, and, by MacGregor's knowledge of the country,—for every part of Scotland, and of the north of England, was familiar to him,—were conducted to the western sea-coast, and safely embarked for France. The same gentleman told me, that Sir Frederick was not expected to survive for many months a lingering disease, the consequence of late hardships and privations. His daughter was placed in a convent, and although it was her father's wish she should take the veil, he was understood to refer the matter entirely to her own inclinations.

When these news reached me, I frankly told the state of my affections to my father, who was not a little startled at the idea of my marrying a Roman Catholic. But he was very desirous to see me 'settled in life,' as he called it ; and he was sensible that, in joining him with heart and hand in his commercial labours, I had sacrificed my own inclinations. After a brief hesitation, and several questions asked and answered to his satisfaction, he broke out with—'I little thought a son of mine should have been Lord of Osbaldistone Manor, and far less that he should go to a French convent for a spouse. But so dutiful a daughter cannot but prove a good wife. You have worked at the desk to please me, Frank ; it is but fair you should wive to please yourself.'

How I sped in my wooing, Will Tresham, I need not tell you. You know, too, how long and happily I lived with Diana. You know how I lamented her. But you do not—cannot know, how much she deserved her husband's sorrow.

I have no more of romantic adventure to tell, nor, indeed, any thing to communicate farther, since the latter incidents of my life are so well known to one who has shared, with the most friendly sympathy, the joys, as well as the sorrows, by which its scenes have been chequered. I often visited Scotland, but never again saw the bold Highlander who had such an influence on the early events of my life. I learned, however, from time to time, that he continued to maintain his ground among the mountains of Loch Lomond, in despite of his powerful enemies, and that he even obtained, to a certain degree, the connivance of government to his self-elected office of Protector of the Lennox, in virtue of which he levied black-mail with as much regularity as the proprietors did their ordinary rents. It seemed impossible that his life should have concluded without a violent end. Nevertheless, he died in old age and by a peaceful death, some time about the year 1733, and is still remembered in his country as the Robin Hood of Scotland, the dread of the wealthy, but the friend of the poor, and possessed of many qualities, both of head and heart, which would have graced a less equivocal profession than that to which his fate condemned him.

Old Andrew Fairservice used to say, that 'There were many things ower bad for blessing, and ower gude for banning, like ROB ROY.'

[Here the original manuscript ends somewhat abruptly. I have reason to think that what followed related to private affairs.]

NOTES

CHAPTER XXVII

Note F, p. 149.—Mons Meg

Mons Meg was a large old-fashioned piece of ordnance, a great favourite with the Scottish common people; she was fabricated at Mons, in Flanders, in the reign of James IV. or V. of Scotland. This gun figures frequently in the public accounts of the time, where we find charges for grease to grease Meg's mouth withal, (to increase, as every schoolboy knows, the loudness of the report,) ribands to deck her carriage, and pipes to play before her when she was brought from the Castle to accompany the Scottish army on any distant expedition. After the Union, there was much popular apprehension that the Regalia of Scotland, and the subordinate Palladium, Mons Meg, would be carried to England to complete the odious surrender of national independence. The Regalia, sequestered from the sight of the public, were generally supposed to have been abstracted in this manner. As for Mons Meg, she remained in the Castle of Edinburgh, till, by order of the Board of Ordnance, she was actually removed to Woolwich about 1757. The Regalia, by his Majesty's special command, have been brought forth from their place of concealment in 1818, and exposed to the view of the people, by whom they must be looked upon with deep associations; and, in this very winter of 1828-9, Mons Meg has been restored to the country, where that, which in every other place or situation was a mere mass of rusty iron, becomes once more a curious monument of antiquity.

CHAPTER XXVIII

Note G, p. 159.—Fairy Superstition

The lakes and precipices amidst which the Avon-Dhu, or river Forth, has its birth, are still, according to popular tradition, haunted by the Elfin people, the most peculiar, but most pleasing, of the creations of Celtic superstitions. The opinions entertained about these beings, are much the same with those of the Irish, so exquisitely well narrated by Mr. Crofton Croker. An eminently beautiful little conical hill, near the eastern extremity of the valley of Aberfoil, is supposed to be one of their peculiar haunts, and is the scene which awakens, in Bailie Nicol Jarvie, the terror of their power. It is remarkable, that two successive clergymen of the parish of Aberfoil have employed themselves in writing about this fairy superstition. The eldest of these was Robert Kirke, a man of some talents, who translated the Psalms into Gaelic verse. He had formerly been minister at the neighbouring parish of Balquidder, and died at Aberfoil in 1688, at the early age of forty-two.

He was author of the Secret Commonwealth, which was printed after his death, in 1691, an edition which I have never seen, and was reprinted in Edinburgh, 1815. This is a work concerning the fairy people, in whose existence Mr. Kirke appears to have been a devout believer. He describes them with the usual powers and qualities ascribed to such beings in Highland tradition.

But what is sufficiently singular, the Rev. Robert Kirke, author of the said treatise, is believed himself to have been taken away by the fairies, in revenge, perhaps, for having let in too much light upon the secrets of their commonwealth. We learn this catastrophe from the information of his successor, the late amiable and learned Dr. Patrick Grahame, also minister at Aberfoil, who, in his Sketches of Perthshire, has not forgotten to touch upon the *Daoine Shie*, or men of peace.

The Rev. Robert Kirke was, it seems, walking upon a little eminence to the west of the present manse, which is still held a *Dun Shie*, or fairy mound, when he sunk down, in what seemed to mortals a fit, and was supposed to be dead. This, however, was not his real fate.

'Mr. Kirke was the near relation of Graham of Duchray, the ancestor of the present General Graham Stirling. Shortly after his funeral, he appeared in the dress in which he had sunk down, to a medical relation of his own, and of Duchray. "Go," said he to him, "to my cousin Duchray, and tell him that I am not dead. I fell down in a swoon, and was carried into Fairyland, where I now am. Tell him, that when he and my friends are assembled at the baptism of my child, (for he had left his wife pregnant), I will appear in the room, and that if he throws the knife which he holds in his hand over my head, I will be released, and restored to human society." The man, it seems, neglected, for some time, to deliver the message. Mr. Kirke appeared to him a second time, threatening to haunt him night and day till he executed his commission, which at length he did. The time of the baptism arrived. They were seated at table ; the figure of Mr. Kirke entered, but the Laird of Duchray, by some unaccountable fatality, neglected to perform the prescribed ceremony. Mr. Kirke retired by another door, and was seen no more. It is firmly believed that he is, at this day, in Fairyland.'—(*Sketches of Perthshire*, p. 254.)

GLOSSARY

a', *all.*
a be, let, *leave alone,* i.e. *far less,* 79.
a'body, *everybody.*
abune, *above.*
ae, *one.*
aff, *off.*
afore, *before.*
aften, *often.*
again, agane, *against.*
ahint, *behind.*
aiblins, *perhaps.*
aik, *oak.*
ail, *trouble,* 8, 88, 284.
ain, *own.*
air, *early,* 152.
airn, *iron.*
aits, *oats,* 181.
amaist, *almost.*
amang, *among.*
an, *if.*
ance, *once.*
Andra Ferrara, *broadsword made by Andrew of Ferrara,* 83. *See Waverley,* II. 412.
ane, *one.*
anent, *concerning.*
anither, *another.*
anker, *a barrel containing ten wine gallons,* 16.
answer, *suit,* 10.
apprizing, (legal), *investing a creditor with the estate of his debtor,* 114.
archilowe, *peace-offering,* 171.
a'thegither, *altogether.*

at no rate, *on no account,* 87.
atween, *between.*
aughteen, *eighteen.*
aughty, *eighty.*
auld, *old.*
auld-farran, *old-fashioned, sagacious,* 134.
auld-warld, *old-time, antiquarian,* 49.
awa, *away.*
awee ahint the hand, *a little behind with payment,* 174.
aweel, *well.*
awes, *owes* ; awing, *owing.*
awsome, *awe-inspiring, appalling.*
ay, *yes.*
aye, *always.*
ayont, *beside,* 78.

backit, *backed.*
baik, *curtsey.*
bailie, *a magistrate,* nearly syn. with *alderman.*
bairn, *child.*
baith, *both.*
band, *bond.*
banes, *bones.*
bannet, *bonnet.*
banning, *cursing, abusing,* 201.
barefit, *barefooted,* 152.
barkit, *barked.*
bauld, *bold.*
bawdron, *cat,* 325.
beild, *shelter,* 114, 131.
belanging, *belonging.*

383

bent, take the, *flee for safety*, 16.

bicker, to, *pelt*, 121; *wooden bowl*, 101, 284.

bidding, *command*, 129.

bide, *stay*, 19, 172; *endure*, 139.

biding, *awaiting*, 137.

bigging, *house, building*.

bike, *bees' or wasps' nest*, 130.

binna, *be not*.

birkie, *mettlesome fellow*, 82.

birl our bawbees, *club our money for drink*, 171.

bits, (*diminutive*), e.g. *bits o' ankers*, 16; *bits o' idols*, 30.

bittock, *a little bit*, (*applied to distance*), 8.

black-mail, *tax levied by a freebooter as insurance for protection from other freebooters*, 80. See *Waverley*, i. 150.

blaws, *blows*.

bleezing, *blazing*.

blether, *jabber*, 49.

blude, bluid, *blood*.

blue-bonnets, *highlanders*, 132.

board-end, *foot of the table*, 346.

bobbit, *bobbed*.

boddle, *a copper coin of two pennies Scots = $\frac{1}{6}$th of a penny English*, 17.

body, *person*.

bogle, *bogie, ghost*, 7; potato-bogle, *scarecrow*, 215.

bonny, *pretty, well-looking, fine*.

bountith, fee and, *see* fee.

bourocks, *dilapidated huts*, 199.

bra', braw, *fine*.

brae-side, *hill-side*.

braid, *broad*; braid claith, *broadcloth*.

breeks, *breeches*.

brent brow, *high forehead*, 326.

brigg, *bridge*.

brisket, breaskit, *breast*, 111, 261.

brither, *brother*.

brochan, (gael.), *tartan plaid*, 83.

brogues, *highland shoes*, 83.

broken man, *outlaw*, 132.

brownies, *fairy goblins*, 177.

buiths, *booths*.

bumbaized, *bamboozled, stupified*, 78.

burn, *rivulet, brook*.

by-gane, *past*, 118; by-ganging, *going past*, 300.

byre, *cow-house*, 133.

by-word, *motto*, 148.

ca' *call*; ca'd, *called*.

ca'-the-shuttle, *work-the-shuttle*, i.e. *weaver*, 140.

cadgers, *hawkers*, 120.

callant, *lad*, 50.

caller, *freshen*, 162.

calm sough, *self-possession*, 116.

cam, *came*.

camlet, *imitation camel-hair cloth*, 216.

canna, *cannot*.

canny, *cautious, shrewd, sensible*.

caption, (legal), *judicial order for apprehension for non-payment of a debt or non-fulfilment of an obligation*, 139.

carena, *care not*.

carle, *fellow, churl, old man*.

carlines, *old women, hags*, 201.

catherans, (gael.), *highland freebooters*, 246.

cauld, *cold*.

cauldrife, *cold, indifferent*, 32.

caunles, *candles*, 352.

caup, *shell*, 283.

cearments, *vestments (contemptuous)*, 80.

ceety, *city*.

chamber chiels, *chamber companions*, 76.

GLOSSARY

chapman, *pedlar, hawker,* 131.

chappin, *Scots chopin, a liquor measure of two mutchkins or eight gills Scots = about three-fourths of an imperial quart,* 185.

chapping-sticks, *weapons,* 281.

chappit, *struck,* 73.

cheatry, *deceitful,* 114.

cheat-the-wuddy, *gallows-bird,* 78.

chield, *fellow.*

chimley, *chimney,* 43.

chuckie-stanes, *pebbles,* 223.

clachan, (gael.), *hamlet,* 185.

claes, *clothes.*

clash, *gossip,* 326.

clatter, *noise, hubbub,* 43 ; *talk,* 126.

claver, *talk idly,* 49.

claymore, *two-edged highland sword,* 131.

clean, *entirely,* 91.

clean cap-out, *to the bottom,* 181.

clerkit, *wrote,* 49.

clinkum - clankum, *rhyming (contemptuous),* 49.

cloot, *hoof,* 133.

clout, *rag.*

clow, *clove,* 15.

cockits, *custom-house warrants,* 124.

cockle-headed, *whimsical,* 49.

cog, *wooden basin,* 94.

collogue, *scheme together.*

coost up, *reproach with,* 142.

corbie, *raven, crow,* 19.

couldna, *could not.*

coup, *upset.*

coup the crans, *to be overturned,* 29, 102.

coup the creels, *tumble head over heels,* 43.

cousin-red, *kinship-in-blood,* 100.

crack, *gossip.*

cracking crouse, *boasting,* 123.

craig, *rock,* 49 ; *throat,* 81.

crouse, *proud,* 30.

crowdy, *a kind of porridge,* 113.

cuitled up, *won over by wheedling,* 98.

Cumries, *islands of Cumbrae, Bute,* 203.

cuttit, *cut.*

daffin, *fun,* 72.

daft, *frolicsome,* 49, 274 ; *crazy,* 113 ; *lawless,* 134.

daft-days, *Christmas and New Year holidays,* 134.

daft-like, *crazy, venturesome,* 14 ; *odd-like,* 224.

daiker, *toil,* 86.

darn, dern, *conceal,* 364, 279.

daur, *dare* ; daurna, *dare not.*

deacon, *elected chairman of trade guild.*

Dean o' Guild, *a municipal magistrate whose court controls the erection of buildings,* 29.

dee, *die.*

deil, deevil, *devil.*

deil gae ower Jock Wabster, *the devil to pay,* 137.

deil haet, *devil a bit,* 102.

didna, *did not* ; dinna, *do not.*

ding, *beat,* 49 ; *knock,* 139.

dirk, durk, *highland dagger.*

disna, *does not.*

dooms, *minced oath equivalent to 'damned,'* 8.

douce, *sober, sedate,* 130.

doun by, *down the way,* 124.

douncome, *downfall.*

dour, *stubborn.*

dourlach, (gael.), *bundle, valise,* 129.

dow, *can, must,* 70, 172.

dow'd, *withered,* 32.

downa, *dare not,* 11 ; downa bide, *cannot endure,* 79, 139.

drab-de-berrie, *a French woollen cloth (probably ' drap de beret'),* 216.

drap, *drop.*

drave, *drove.*

dree, *endure, fulfil,* 277.

drow, *cold mist,* 75.

duinhé-wassel, (gael.), *gentleman,* 164.

dune, *done.*

dwalt, *dwelt.*

een, *eyes.*

e'en, e'ening, *evening.*

e'enow, *(even now), at this moment.*

eldern, *old,* 274.

eneuch, eneugh, *enough.*

enow, *enough,* 113.

ettled, *intended, designed,* 277.

evidents, *evidence,* 130.

fa, *who.*

fa', *fall;* fa'en, *fallen.*

fallow, *fellow.*

family chack, *dinner,* 103.

fand, *found.*

far-awa, *distantly related,* 236.

farder, *further,* 184.

fashed, *troubled,* 114.

fashion, *pretence,* 180.

fat, *what.*

faulds, *folds,* 257.

fause, *false.*

faut, *fault.*

feal, *faithful,* 175.

feared, *afraid;* feared for, *afraid of,* 155.

fearna, *fear not.*

feck, *part,* 118.

feckless, *trifling,* 326.

fee and bountith, *wages and perquisites,* 97.

fend, *defence,* 172.

ferlie, *wonder,* 152.

feught, *fought.*

files, *defiles,* 125.

fit, *foot.*

flae, *fly.*

fleech, *flatter, wheedle,* 203.

fleer, *gibe,* 286.

fleg, *fright,* 8.

fleyed, *scared,* 8.

fluf-gibs, *flashes of gunpowder,* 224.

flyte, *scold,* 201.

foist and a warming pan, *alluding to the allegation that the Chevalier de St. George, son of James* II., *was a changeling, introduced into the palace in a warming-pan,* 80.

foive, *five.*

flow-moss, *morass,* 162.

forbye, *besides.*

forfoughen, *worn out with fighting,* 171.

forgather, *meet, fall in with,* 11.

forgie, *forgive.*

founder, *fall,* 181.

frae, *from.*

freend, *friend.*

fu', *full.*

fule, *fool.*

fusionless, *weak,* 32.

gabbart, *barge,* (Fr. *gabare*), 216.

gabbling, *prating, chattering,* 153.

gae, *gave.*

gaen, gane, *gone;* gaed, *went, gone.*

gang, *go;* ganged, *gone;* ganging, *going.*

gallaglasses, *retainers,* 82.

gang-there-out, *vagrant,* 79.

gar, *make, compel.*

gash, *supercilious,* 112.

gat, *got.*

gate, *manner,* 14; *way,* 17.

gauger, *exciseman,* 16, 230.

GLOSSARY

gear, *property, money.*

gedd, *pike-fish,* 317.

ghaist, *ghost.*

gie, *give.*

gill, *see* chappin. *The modern gill is the fourth part of an imperial pint,* 172.

gillie, (gael.), *lad, servant,* 89. *See Waverley,* I. 162.

gillon-a-naillie, (gael.), *lads with the kilts,* 80.

gillravaging, *plundering,* 80.

gin, *if.*

Glasco, *Glasgow,* 171.

gleg, *quick, active.*

gliff, *little while,* 72.

gliffing, *instant,* 71.

glisk, *glimpse,* 49.

gloaming, *twilight,* 41 ; *dim,* 49.

gloom, *frown,* 257.

glowr, *gaze,* 49.

glum, *gloomy,* 288.

gowd, *gold.*

gowk, *fool* ; (lit. *cuckoo*), 161.

grat, *wept* ; greet, *weep.*

gree, *agree.*

grey mear, *masterful wife,* 139.

grew, *shudder,* 151.

grewsome, *horrible, blood-curdling,* 201.

grice, *pig,* 102.

grippit, *laid hold of,* 172 ; *arrested,* 79.

grit, gritt, *great.*

grunds, *grounds, foundations,* 286.

gude, *good,* 18 ; Gude, *God,* 90.

gudeman, *master of the house,* 77.

gudewife, *mistress of the house,* 177.

guided, *used, treated,* 100.

gutty, *pot-bellied,* 60.

hadden, *held.*

hae, *have* ; haena, *have not.*

haill, hale, *whole.*

halesome, *wholesome, healthful,* 15.

halidome, *sanctity,* 87.

hallion, *lout,* 60, 229.

hame, *home.*

hantle, *great deal of,* 42.

harried, *plundered,* 133.

harns, *brains,* 79.

harnpan, *brain-pan, skull,* 261.

harst, *harvest,* 86.

hasna, *has not.*

haud, *hold* ; hauding, *possession,* 97.

haud forth, *discourse,* 44.

havings, *behaviour, manners,* 161.

heather-cowe, *a tuft of heath,* 10.

hemp cravat, *hempen neck-cloth, hangman's rope,* 79.

hempie, *tomboy* ; (lit. *one for whom the hemp grows*), 274.

hemp to the craig, *hangman's rope for the throat,* 55.

heritor, *land-owner,* 133.

hersell, her nainsell (*in a highlander's mouth*) *himself, my own self.*

hership, *plundering,* 133, 177.

het, *hot.*

himsell, *himself.*

hinder end, *extremity,* 29.

hinderlans, *buttocks,* 79.

hing, *hang.*

hoodie-craw, *hooded crow,* 80.

horning, (legal), *a judicial order to pay a debt or to perform an act under penalty of outlawry and forfeiture for non-performance. The order was formerly preceded by the blast of a horn,* 139.

hosenet, *small fishing-net,* 274.

houghs, *thighs,* 224.

hout, hout-tout, *interjections expressive of disagreement.*

howes, *hollows,* 126.

hoyed, *called*, 192.
hunder, *hundred*.
hurdies, *buttocks*, 134.
hure, *whore*, 20.
huz, *us*.

idlers in kirk-time, *absentees from church service*, 32.
ill-fa'rd, *ill-favoured*, 16.
ill-guided, *badly used*.
ill-scraped, *rude, violent*, 148.
indifferently, *impartially*, 18.
ingle, *fireside*, 134.
Inglisher, *Englishman*, 22.
intill, *into*.
intromit, *intermeddle*, 290.
I 'se, *I shall, I would*.
isna, *is not*.
ither, *other*.
itsell, *itself*.
ivy-tod, *ivy-bush*.

jalouse, *suspect*, 304.
jaud, *jade*.
jawing, *rolling*.
Jeddart cast, *a specimen of 'Jedburgh justice,'* i.e. *being hanged first and tried afterwards*, 318.
joctaleg, *a folding-knife*, 244.
joseph, *riding-cloak*, 175.
jouk and let the jaw gae by, *stoop and let the wave go past*, i.e. *grin and bear it*, 116.
justified, *having satisfied justice*, i.e. *executed*, 86.

kail, *cabbage, broth*.
kail-pat, *broth-pot*, 171.
kail through the reek, *a severe scolding, a 'wigging,'* 203.
kaimed, *combed*, 30.
keek, *peep*, 319.
keepit, *kept*.

kelpie, *water-spirit*.
kelty aff, *to the bottom of the glass*, 175.
kemping, *striving, hustling*, 115.
ken, *know* ; kenna, *know not* ; kent, kenned, *knew*.
kernes, *sturdy beggars, louts*, 82, 287.
kilted up in a tow, *swung up on a rope*, i.e. *hanged*, 79.
kimmer, *gossip, goodwife*, 77.
kirk, *church*.
kittle, *punctilious*, 170 ; *troublesome*, 246.
kittle cast, *critical throw*, i.e. *dangerous part*, 85.
knap southron, *to speak after the manner of the English*, 225.
knockit, *knocked*.
kuineas, *guineas*, 197.
kye, *kine*, 192.
kyloes, *highland cattle*, 286.
kythes, *appears*, 289.

laird, *landlord, lord of the manor*.
laith, *loth*.
lang, *long*.
lang lug, *great deal*, (lit. *long ear*), 135.
lang syne, *long ago*, 29 ; *formerly*, 346.
lang-tongued, *loquacious*, 190, 325.
lapper, *imbrue*, 201.
lassock, *girl*.
lass-quean, lassock-quean, *a young woman*, 72, 326.
lave, *remainder*.
lawin, *tavern score*, 173.
law-wark, cauldrife, *cold law-work*, i.e. *preaching inculcating morality instead of evangelical doctrine*, 32.
leddy, *lady*.
lees, *lies*.
let a be, *leave alone*, i.e. *far less*, 79.

GLOSSARY

liesna, *lies not.*
lightlied, *disparaged, slighted,* 281.
like o', the, *such as,* 126.
likit, *liked.*
lilting, *singing gaily,* 88.
limmer, *blackguard,* 79, 246.
linking, *active, busy,* 135, 183.
listed, *enlisted,* 81.
loon, *lad, fellow, lout.*
loot, *let, permitted.*
lound, *quiet,* 186.
loup, *leap.*
lowe, *blaze,* 327.
luckie, *dame, landlady of a tavern.*
luck-penny, *money returned to a purchaser for luck or as discount,* 131.
lug, *ear.*
Lunnon, *London.*
luve, *love.*

Maiden, the, *a kind of guillotine formerly used for executions in Scotland,* 183.
mainteen, *maintain.*
mair, *more* ; maist, *most.*
mak, *make.*
malison, *curse,* 114.
maun, *must* ; maunna, *must not.*
mear, *mare.*
meddle nor mak, *interfere not and make no advances,* 154.
mends, to the, *over and above the purchase-money,* 131.
merk, 13s. 4d. *Scots* = 1s. 1⅓d. *of English money,* 175.
messan-dog, *cur,* 202.
messes, *masses.*
mettle, *spirited,* 274.
mightna, *might not.*
mint, *intend,* 237.
mirk, *dark,* 271.
misdoubt, *doubt, distrust,* 75.

misguided, *abused, maltreated,* 131.
mistaen, *mistaken.*
mistrysted, *alarmed,* 7, 112.
mither, *mother.*
mony, *many.*
morn, the, *to-morrow.*
muckle, *much.*
muir, *moor.*
mysell, *myself.*

na, nae, *no.*
naebody, *nobody.*
naig, *nag.*
nane, *none.*
nashgabs, *impertinent tongues,* 142.
natheless, *nevertheless.*
nay-say, *denial,* 154.
neb, *nose.*
needful, the, *money,* 87.
neuks, *nooks.*
nipperty-tipperty, *affectedly neat,* 49.
no, *not.*
nowte, nowte-bestial, *cattle,* 129, 287.

o', *of.*
ony, *any.*
open-steek hems, *ornamental-stitch hems ; contemptuously applied to Gothic architecture,* 29.
or, *ere, before,* 18.
ordinar, *ordinary.*
orra, *odd,* 284.
o't, *of it.*
ought, *owed,* 189.
oursells, *ourselves.*
ower, *over.*
owsen, *oxen,* 128.

paiks, *chastisement,* 192.
pailie, *bailie.*
paperie, *popery.*

ROB ROY

papishers, *papists,* 349.
parefoot, *barefoot.*
parochine, *parish,* 127.
pat, *pot, put.*
pearlins, *a species of lace,* 224.
peasweep, *lapwing,* 150.
ped, *bed.*
penny fee, *hire, wages,* 50.
penny-siller, *money,* 197.
phrasin', *palavering, boasting,* 91.
pickle, *small quantity,* 112.
pickle in your ain pock - neuk, *supply yourself from your own means,* 80.
pided, *bided, stayed,* 205.
pike, *pick,* 204.
pirn, *reel,* 82.
pit, *put.*
plack, *Scots groat* = ⅓d. *of an English penny,* 18.
plaiden, *plaid,* 324.
pleugh, *plough.*
pliskies, *pranks, riotings,* 79, 181.
ploy, *exploit, trick,* 276, 280.
pock-pudding, (lit. *pudding - bag*); *contemptuously applied to English- men as being fond of their food,* 149, 261.
poinding, *distraining,* 114.
ponnie, *bonnie.*
potato-bogle, *scarecrow,* 215.
pow, *head,* 275.
pread, *bread.*
preceesely, *precisely.*
pretty, *gallant, soldier-like, see* p. 129.
prick-eared, *crop-eared.*
provost, *chief magistrate of a Scots burgh, mayor,* 42.
public, *tavern,* 154.
pu'd, *pulled.*
puddle, *pool,* 346.
puir, *poor.*

pund, *pound*; pund Scots = 1s. 8d. *of English money,* 80.
putten, *put.*
py, *by.*

quean, *hussy, tomboy,* 49, 274.
queez-maddam, *a French pear,* (*cuise- madame*), 49.

raddling, *riddling,* 17.
rae-deer, *roe-deer.*
ram-stam, *unceremoniously,* 161.
rant, *roister,* 182.
rap and rend, *seize,* 129.
rape, *rope.*
rappit, *shot off quickly,* 322.
ready, *ready-witted,* 123.
red-shanks, *legs fitted with deerskin buskins,* hence *highlanders,* 86.
red-wud, *stark mad,* 50.
redd, *abjure,* 186.
redd out, *settle, clear up,* 75.
redd up, *pillage,* 81.
rede out, *detailed,* 223.
reek, *smoke.*
refutch, *refuge,* 184.
reik, *exploit, adventure,* 134.
reisted, *smoke-cured,* 91.
reiving, *plundering,* 78, 129.
reset of intercommuned persons, (legal), *intercourse with outlaws or proscribed persons,* 142.
riding o' the Scots Parliament, *ceremonial procession at the opening of the old Scots Parliament,* 149.
riggin', *roof,* 199.
rin, *run.*
rive, *tear.*
rock, *spindle,* 369.
roose, *praise,* 148.
roosted, *rusted.*
roup, *sell by auction,* 82.
row, *roll.*

390

GLOSSARY

rudas, *bold*, 181.
rue-bargain, *smart-money*, 145.
rug, *feed*, 300.

sackless, *innocent*, 140.
sae, *so*.
sair, *sore*.
sall, *shall*.
Sassenach, *Saxon, a lowlander as opposed to a Gael or highlander*, 69.
saul, *soul*.
sauld, *sold*.
saut, *salt*.
saw, *sow*.
scart, *cormorant*, 203.
Scots mile, =1⅛ *English mile*, 162.
screeded, *torn*, 216.
sealgh, *seal*, 296.
sea-maws, *sea-mews, gulls*, 203.
sell, *self*.
sell't, *sold*.
ser'ing, *serving, satisfaction*, 112.
set, *become*, 154.
set forms, *liturgical worship*, 80.
sett, *pattern*, 171.
shabble, *cutlass*, 131.
shank, *leg*, 73.
shased, *chased*, 184.
shaw, *wood*, 162.
shearing, *reaping*, 128.
sheeling, *hamlet*, 223.
shell-drake, *shieldrake or burrow-duck*, 244.
shelties, *ponies*, 242.
shentlemans, *gentlemen*, 62.
sherra, *sheriff*, 189.
shored, *threatened*, 186.
shouldna, *should not*.
shouther, *shoulder*.
sic, siccan, *such*.
siller, *money*, 10.
sin', *since*.

singit, *singed*.
sitten, *sat*.
skaith, *harm*, 246.
skirling, *screaming*.
skreigh, *call*, 81 ; skreigh o' day, *dawn*, 91.
skyte, *nasty person*, 153.
slabbered, *slobbered*.
slink, *worthless*, 144.
sma', *small*.
smaik, *silly fellow*, 81.
snaw-ba's, *snow-balls*, 121.
sneckit, *cut*, 112.
sneck-drawer, *sly fellow*, 347.
snell, *sharp, acute*, 101.
sodgering, *soldiering*, 19.
soger, *soldier*, 177.
soothfastly, *truthfully*, 87.
sort, *manage*, 18.
sortable, *appropriate, suitable*, 274.
soums, *sums*.
soup, *sup, draught*, 16.
souple, *supple*.
spak, *spake*.
spang, *spring, leap*, 163.
speer, *inquire*, 8.
sponsible, *sedate, reliable*, 49, 141.
sporran, (gael.), *highland goat-skin purse*, 80.
spreagh, spreagherie, (gael.), *cattle-raid, foray*, 80, 129, 135.
spune, *spoon*.
staff out o' my bicker, (lit. *a stave out of my bicker or wooden bowl*), *a heavy loss*, 101.
stane, *stone*.
steek, steekit, *shut*, 173.
steering, *molesting*, 191.
stentmaster, *assessor*, 78.
stint, *stay, hesitate*, 57.
stir, *noise*, 240.
stirrup-cup, *parting drink at the door*, 15.

391

stots, *cattle above three years old,* 131.
stoup, *flagon.*
stow, *cut,* 285, 316.
strae, *straw.*
strathspey, *a highland dance,* 74.
stude, *stood.*
suld, *should.*
sune, *soon.*
syne, *since ; late,* 10.

ta, *the.*
tae, *the one ;* tae, *toe,* 244.
taen, *taken.*
take the bent, *flee for safety,* 115.
tane, *the one.*
tass, *cup, goblet,* 15, 171.
tat, *that.*
tatty, *potato.*
tauld, *told.*
tawpie, *foolish girl,* 151.
teil, *devil,* 318.
tell't, telled, *told.*
thae, *these.*
than, *then.*
thegither, *together.*
themsells, *themselves.*
thereawa, *thereabout.*
thigging and sorning, *see* p. 129.
thir, *these.*
thrapple, *throat,.* 112.
thraw, *thwart,* 134.
thrift, *industry,* 129.
through-stanes, *flat stones,* 43.
thrums, *end threads of a weaver's web,* 130.
tig, *tug,* 146.
till, *to.*
tither, tother, *the other.*
tolbooth, *prison,* 57.
took o' drum, *beat of drum,* 29.
toom, *empty,* 57, 257.
toun, *farm buildings.*

tow, *rope,* i.e. *hangman's,* 185.
trews, *close highland pantaloons,* 164.
troking, *trafficking,* 138.
trot-cosey, *(throat-cosy), riding-hood,* 143.
tryste, trysting, *appointment, meeting,* 10, 229.
trysted, *met with,* 8.
tuik, *took.*
tuilzie, *skirmish, broil,* 121, 171.
tup, *ram,* 103.
turnpike, *winding stair,* 61.
twa, *two.*
twal, *twelve.*

unchancy, *unlucky, dangerous,* 79.
unco, *very, extraordinary.*
unfreends, *enemies,* 152.
up by, *up the way,* 346.
upsetting, *assuming,* 325.
upsides wi', *better than,* 152.
usquebaugh, *whisky.*

vera, *very.*

wa', *wall.*
wabster, *weaver,* 126.
wad, *hostage,* 276.
wad, *would ;* wadna, *would not.*
waefu', waesome, *woful.*
wally-draigle, *weakling,* (tech. *the youngest bird in the nest),* 275.
wame, *belly,* 224.
wapping, *strapping,* 88.
ware, *merchandise,* 119.
wark, *work.*
warsling, *wrestling,* 277.
wasna, *was not.*
watna, *know not.*
waur, *worse.*
weel, *well.*
weils, *whirlpools,* 322.
weird, *destiny,* 277.

GLOSSARY

weise, *drive*, 86, 261.
werena, *were not.*
we'se, *we shall, we would.*
wha, whae, *who.*
whang, *thong*, 257.
whar, whare, *where.*
what for, *why*, 126.
whaup, *curlew*, 150.
wheen, *few.*
whigmaleeries, *ornaments (contemptuous)*, 29.
whiles, *sometimes*, 16.
whilk, *which.*
whummle, *overturn*, 71.
whuppit awa, *sent off under arrest*, 18.
wi', *with.*
win, *earn*, 75 ; *get*, 287.

window-bole, *unglazed window with wooden shutter*, 113.
winna, *will not.*
winnles, *winding frames*, 78, 236.
witting, *information*, 60.
woodie, *withy*, i.e. *halter, see* p. 273.
wotna, *know not.*
wrang, *wrong.*
writer, *solicitor, law-agent*, 18.
wud, *crazy, mad*, 182.
wunna, *will not.*
wussing, *wishing.*
wyte, *blame*, 17.

yere, *your.*
yestreen, *yesterday*, 216.
yett, *gate*, 7.
yoursell, *yourself.*

This book was designed by William B. Taylor
for Heron Books, London

Printed in Switzerland